ONE MAGICAL NIGHT

She turned in his arms, the moonlight flooding her face with a mystical silver light. Beau's heart ached for her.

He captured her lips beneath his own, ravished her with a crushing, bruising kiss that demanded an end to every pain that haunted their souls. Maria groped for him, her body moving against his as if wanting to be swallowed by the fierce pleasure he brought. Arousal became like some invisible warrior that rose to slay every sorry emotion of theirs until desire became their most glorious victory. She loved him so completely, so desperately, she became utterly selfless in his storming wake, her whole being absorbed by his.

Harper Monogram

Dancing in the Dark

SUSAN P. TEKLITS

HarperPaperbacks
A Division of HarperCollins*Publishers*

If you purchased this book without a cover, you should be aware that this book is stolen property. It was reported as "unsold and destroyed" to the publisher and neither the author nor the publisher has received any payment for this "stripped book."

This is a work of fiction. The characters, incidents, and dialogues are products of the author's imagination and are not to be construed as real. Any resemblance to actual events or persons, living or dead, is entirely coincidental.

HarperPaperbacks *A Division of* HarperCollins*Publishers*
10 East 53rd Street, New York, N.Y. 10022

Cover illustration by R.A. Maguire

First printing: August 1993

Printed in the United States of America

HarperPaperbacks, HarperMonogram, and colophon are trademarks of HarperCollins*Publishers*

10 9 8 7 6 5 4 3 2 1

This book is dedicated not to any one individual, but to the collective spirit of all those who, with no vested interest of their own, supported and cared about this dream of mine, wanting to see it happen just for my sake.

This is the true spirit of love, which is, incidentally, what this very book is about. May all who read this catch a glimpse of love in its most splendid moment, when it becomes the only light that can shine through the dark.

London, England
March 31, 1674

Maria Vandenburgh sat in her father's coach, stiff and uncomfortable. The trip was already two hours long and she had yet to relax. How could anyone sit for so long on these insufferable cushions, with all these irritating buttons punched into the velvet to make them tuft. Every time she looked at the elaborately papered walls of this expensive phaeton it made her head ache. Or maybe it was the constant droning of iron hooves as the horses plodded through the outskirts of London, their pace held in check by a pair of smartly dressed liverymen. Her father made such a splashy show of his business, letting all of London know someone important was inside his crested coach this morning and being properly escorted to his home on Dabney Street.

It made her feel even more out of place.

Home was in Herefordshire County, not here. She suddenly longed for it, the Christian Convent School for Girls with its bulky stone walls and tiny slitlike windows, the musty smell of the Dark Ages forever imbedded in its narrow halls. Just sitting here in this glamorous coach made her long for the bare simplicity of it, the little spartan rooms and dusty air, the soft whisper of the sisters' robes as they passed to and fro. It was such a quiet life, tucked away in the English countryside, protected from the noisy chaos of the world.

She could have stayed there forever.

But it was not meant to be and even now she struggled to accept this contrary turn of destiny, one that had been announced so unexpectedly one morning in the headmistress's office.

"I received a post from your father today!" Sister Eustace chirped happily. Maria could still see the smile plumping the nun's round cheeks as she sat behind her ancient wooden desk, her skin scrubbed so pink and clean it shone in the sunlight. "You've come of age this year, my dear. Your father is withdrawing you from school to bring you home to London and see you properly introduced to society."

Recalling that moment made Maria's heart fall still, as if her very life hung in the crux of those fateful words.

"Father?" she remembered asking as if she'd never heard of the man before.

"Of course!" Sister Eustace had insisted. But some of the cheer dropped out of her face just then; everyone knew the notorious Arthur Vandenburgh had little to do with his only child. In fact, his years-long neglect had made Maria the brunt of many a cruel joke among the students. "Come now! Aren't you excited?"

Maria forced herself to look delighted for the nun's sake. "Of course I am, Sister! The news caught me by surprise is all." She didn't dare admit that the mere thought of living in her father's home filled her with profound dread.

"But why? You're one of the wealthiest young women in England . . . exceedingly well born! True, you've spent your entire childhood in boarding schools, but surely you must have assumed the aristocracy would one day call you home."

No, she hadn't, and her vague expression instantly gave her away.

"Maria . . ." Sister Eustace had said, leaning forward and looking at her more seriously now. "You look stricken, child. What's troubling you?"

"Nothing, Sister! I should have been more prepared for this is all."

"Oh? Tell me, what were your thoughts for the future?"

"Mine? Why . . . to take the cloth, Sister!"

"Become a nun?" Sister Eustace looked genuinely pained at this response, knowing Maria to be a woman of strong faith. Unfortunately, her birth commanded her far from a life in God's service, into a world of money and power and greed. "But my dear, you are the wealthiest debutante in London. This is your rightful place, your inherited station, and your father is entirely correct to call you home to assume your place in his home."

Place? Maria hadn't seen her father or even heard from him in over five years. She was thirteen the last time she "visited" this London home she was supposed to have a place in.

"I think the Lord has other plans for you, Maria," the headmistress whispered sadly, and Maria could still feel the weight of those words on her heart, pushing it down into some dark and lonely place of the utter unknown.

She stared through the coach window now, nervously biting her lip as she watched her life take this jagged turn. Nothing about London had ever appealed to her. The noise and confusion of the city was always disturbing, but she endured it during her rare visits out of a sense of duty to her father.

But this time was different. She'd be staying on now and couldn't imagine what it would be like to actually live in the lavish mansion where the ceilings dripped chandeliers and the floors were strewn with silk-threaded tapestries. She was always afraid to touch anything for fear she'd break something of enormous value.

The ornate iron gates of the Vandenburgh estate burst out of the fog-shrouded road ahead. Maria sank deeper into the familiar folds of her old hooded capuchin. She felt suddenly small and shrunken, powerless to prevent the hand of her heritage from claiming her.

The coach stopped to await the opening of the gates. Maria looked with pity upon the urchins that squatted on the damp, dirty cobbles of Dabney Street. They lingered at all the gates of the mansions on this particular avenue, the most prestigious address in London. They came here to beg from the rich, perhaps find a soft spot in the hearts of those who lived beyond the elaborately manicured gardens. All Maria could see of Arthur's palacelike abode were the distant stone spires of the roof as they poked into the foggy sky.

The tall humped figure of her father's butler materialized out of the misty lane ahead like a gargoyle from a child's nightmare. She shivered as a cold mist drifted into the carriage, bringing gooseflesh to her skin. Jonathan opened the gate. It squeaked loudly, and her coach lurched through suddenly to avoid the rush of beggars. They called after her, crying out for coins, bread, firewood. The butler ignored them. He glanced into the window as she flashed by and smiled at her.

Jonathan was always glad to see her even though he barely knew her.

They rambled up the drive, and the team drew to a halt alongside the winding stone stairs leading up to the front door. The last time she saw that luxurious stoop she was just a child, still clinging to the silly notion that her father's neglect was due to how important a man he was.

That was five years ago.

She'd changed since then. Grown up. She was a woman now. There were no places left to run and hide from the truth of what she was to Arthur.

Nothing.

A cold wave of dread flowed through her when the liveryman opened the door, taking her hand as if she was some kind of royal princess.

Maria alighted, smiled pleasantly, the way she'd been taught to do. She was a lady all right, more practiced than most in the shallow pleasantries of the rich. After all, she'd spent the last seven years of her life studying the fine art of ladyhood. She always knew what to say, how to act, how to appear sweet and lovely and nice, no matter what heartache she hid inside.

Maureen O'Leary, their housekeeper, swung open the front door and let Maria duck inside. Because of the damp weather, she was immediately brought before a blazing lobby fire where her wrap could be safely removed. On the wall before her hung a giant looking glass, framed in gold, which reflected the leaping flames and the face illuminated inside the drawn hood.

Maureen's green eyes gazed at her with undisguised surprise. "Saints be praised, my lady!" she murmured, sliding back Maria's hood. "You're the very image of your mother!" The capuchin was tossed aside while the maid continued to gasp in wonder at her.

It made Maria feel self-conscious. Perhaps she shouldn't have chosen this light pastel traveling gown. Its long train made her look even taller than she was. The dusty peach hue in her complexion seemed pale against such a subdued shade, her brown eyes too big and sultry, the upward slant of them a bit too exotic for such an innocent face. Or was it the figure blooming under the dress, the way the high-waisted bodice revealed just a glimpse of the swollen white flesh of her bosom. She'd put matching ribbons in the curly auburn coiffure she'd spent hours fixing this morning. Women didn't wear wigs during the day, and Maria made sure her natural hair was washed until it gleamed like a sable pelt.

"He'll pine for Loretta upon sight of her!" Jonathan exclaimed from the doorway. He issued a cackle that sounded a bit spiteful to Maria, but she couldn't be sure. He was already speeding off to announce her to Arthur.

Maureen gave her train a flap, then let it settle elegantly atop the rug. She stood up and smiled at Maria, her freckled cheeks framed by bright red hair. "You've grown a foot since I saw you last."

"I was but thirteen then," Maria said shyly, giving herself one last look in the mirror. She pinched her cheeks, thought they needed more color, the heart-shaped contours too stark and white, except for where the cold blushed them. Her chin was too pointed, but the fullness of her mouth had a way of softening it. She bit her lips to pinken them, then finally smiled at the way Maureen was clucking over her.

She was just about to pay some tribute to Maureen when Jonathan's voice announced, "M'lord awaits you, Lady Maria."

He was home.

She had hoped he might be away today, arriving home after she'd had time to settle in.

She swallowed hard. "Thank you, Jonathan," she murmured politely, nodding at the bald head that beamed at her from afar.

She passed through the door Jonathan held open, into her father's enormous private study. He was on the other side of the room, behind his long cherry table-desk, still reading whatever was in his hand.

She was immediately struck by how dramatically Arthur had aged since she had last seen him. His complexion was pasty and pale, the skin around his mouth pulled tight into weblike wrinkles that made him look pinched and sour. A white powdered wig hung like a hood over his head, two long panels of curl dangling down the front of his bony shoulders. The flamboyant chartreuse jacket he wore only added to his shriveled and ghostly appearance.

He finished the last few sentences on the parchment he held, sat back, and let it roll up in his hand. A pair of sunken gray eyes fell upon her.

"Come in . . . come closer . . . ," he bade with an impatient wave of his long thin fingers.

Maria's feet instantly moved forward across the room until nothing stood between them but the paper mountain on his desk. The glow of his lantern brought her into full illumination.

Arthur was surprised, his eyebrows leaping together above his narrow nose. The expression temporarily put some life into his otherwise blank facade. "My dear," he muttered windily, "you've grown so."

She didn't say anything, stood meekly before him and tried to appear humble. In truth, she didn't like the way he was looking at her just then. His eyes were wandering all over her, lingering too long upon places a father shouldn't notice. It unnerved her, made her feel as if something immoral was happening and she was allowing it.

"Your resemblance to your mother is uncanny," he finally said, a peculiar throatiness altering his normally brisk and impersonal voice. "Has it been so long since I saw you?" Predictably, he didn't wait for an answer. "You were just a child then . . . with only a trace of Loretta's fabulous beauty."

Maria felt uncomfortable with this conversation and decided to change it. "Your compliments flatter me too highly, sire," she demurred, bending into an elegant curtsey. "I consider it an honor to wear mother's beauty. It's all I've ever known of her."

"Yes . . . unfortunate, isn't it . . . ?"

Loretta Vandenburgh had died giving birth to Maria, a circumstance Arthur never quite forgave his daughter for. Now he waved her sharply into a chair, as if seating her would somehow make her disappear. Maria sat down, primly folding her train across her lap.

"I've been enormously preoccupied with business

these last few years, daughter. Can you forgive me?"

"Of course," she said quickly, wondering if he wasn't about to explain his behavior in some way that might make her feel better.

But he didn't; he merely rattled off a list of pressing matters, business concerns, inept partners, and the like. Maria dropped her eyes to her lap, intently studied her cuticles, and tried not to notice the sinking sensation in her chest. She should know better than to hope he might care. After all these years, it would be obvious even to a fool.

While he gave his long list of excuses, a medley of schoolgirl jibes echoed in her mind, "Maria, don't you fear for your father's fortune? Surely he's spent the lot of it on your boarding schools!" And last Christmas, when the Vandenburgh coach was once again missing from the line of carriages waiting on the convent drive to carry home London's future debutantes: "Perhaps he's just forgotten which school you're attending!" "Why don't you write him and remind him where you are!"

The small childish part of her that still clung to her only kin in the world disappeared. She felt suddenly cold and lonely here, in this chair, this house, this city full of strangers.

"You look tired, Maria. The trip must have drained you. I shan't keep you overlong." Arthur shuffled his spotted hand through a stack of crusty parchments, withdrew one, and gave it a brief glance. "Ah yes," he said, those roguish eyes of his sliding over her again. "The season opens early this year . . . on April first . . . which is tomorrow. We have precious little time for the ball."

"I've waited this long, sire, I can wait another year."

"Nonsense! My lawyer has everything arranged. The invitations are sent, the food is here, the minstrels are hired. You'll be introduced to the beau monde tomorrow night."

Maria looked up, certain she hadn't heard correctly. "Tomorrow?" He nodded. The man was serious! "But I've only just arrived!"

"Don't fret now, my dear," he said playfully. "Your gown is already made and needs just a fitting to make it perfect. You'll have plenty of time today. I've hired a dozen maids to assist you. Simmes was really quite brilliant in how he managed these arrangements."

Of course Lawyer Simmes made the plans, Maria thought dismally, not Arthur. He was entirely too important to dally in such simple affairs.

"If I might implore you, sire, I need time to rest . . . become accustomed to life here. Isn't it possible—"

"Nothing is possible except what is already planned," he snapped. "I have blessed little time as it is. If I had my way, I would have put this matter off another year but Sister Eustace insisted. Her letter was most demanding . . ."

Maria looked at him in disbelief. "But Sister Eustace claimed it was *your* letter that prompted this return, my lord."

"Mine? Whyever would she say that?" Arthur

wondered aloud, then dismissed the subject with a wave of his hand. "What does it matter . . ."

What did it matter? That Sister Eustace had a heart big enough to tell a lonely young woman a tall tale just to make her feel, for one sweet moment, that she was actually cared about by the only family she had in the world!

Maria felt every fiber in her body smart from this unexpected blow. Sister Eustace had to write for Arthur's attention, to demand a moment's notice of his own daughter! And there she had sat in the headmistress's office, frightened but feeling so important for a moment because Arthur had actually written for her.

Fool! Stupid fool!

Maria bit her lip in a desperate attempt to hold back the hot tears of shame that rushed into her eyes.

"You'll be prepared for the introduction tomorrow night, my dear, and you needn't worry for a moment. Why, Simmes has even arranged your trousseau fittings!" Arthur pretended to be delighted for her.

Maria shriveled in her chair. "Trousseau," she peeped. "What need have I for a trousseau?"

"Oh! don't be frivolous. Every girl your age needs one! After seeing you today, there's no doubt in my mind that a half-dozen notable men will ask for your hand within minutes of your introduction. Not only are you filthy rich, Lady Vandenburgh, you're also magnificently beautiful. A betrothal is imminent!"

So that's it. Marry her off to the highest bidder as soon as possible.

Maria looked at him, at the way his white brows twitched in pretended excitement. Then he noticed her stupefied expression, the water flooding into her eyes.

"Maria! Must you carry on so?"

She couldn't believe a person could be capable of such complete coldness. Couldn't he at least try to act like a loving father, perhaps have the decency to keep his frantic plans for her disposal to himself?

Her face bent as if pushed down by the weight of the intense humiliation she felt at that moment.

"Forgive me . . . I'm overtired . . ." she whispered at her hands. "Perhaps the trip was wearying after all. . . . May I retire now?"

She had to get out of here, now, before her wits totally unraveled. Under no condition would she cry in front of this man who thought so little of her. No. She had more pride than that. If she could just find one minute of privacy, she could make some sense out of all this, find a way to make it bearable.

"You may retire after remembering your good graces, my dear. Your father deserves thanks for all the trouble he's gone to on your behalf."

Trouble?

Hurt jelled into anger. He had no right to behave so abominably toward a daughter who did nothing but love him all these years.

"I'm grateful for what little time you managed to spare for me, sire, in your haste to be rid of me."

The words flew out of her mouth before she knew what she was saying.

Arthur's eyes narrowed until he was squinting at her across the desk, as if trying to see the source of that uncharacteristic remark from such a timid creature. "Just what did you expect from me, daughter? To play the role of the loving father, glad to see you home and all that?"

All that.

He scoffed, leaned a bony elbow on the desk and absently straightened a curl over his right ear.

"Tell me, Maria, what place has love in this filthy world, this decrepit city full of urchins and mites, people good for nothing but the few coins in their pockets? I've no bent for such nonsense. If you want affection, find a man who'll give it, go off and marry him if you wish, just don't plague me with such tomfoolery."

"How foolish of me," she said in a voice so small it hurt just to hear it. "Forgive me, sire."

"Of course! Be gone then!" He waved her away like some irritating insect.

Maria rushed from the room, her feet pounding up the drafty stairwell. The icy stone floors, garishly papered walls, and gilded lanterns all seemed to mock her as she wove through the upper halls, searching for a chamber she couldn't find in a house that didn't welcome her. What an ugly place this was, so glamorous and rich, yet such a dark trap for a maid with a gentle heart.

She finally found her chamber, opened the door, and stood on the threshold in startled dismay.

A dozen ladies' maids filled the room, their giggling chatter stopping upon sight of her. Maria's tear-filled eyes swept the interior, saw the bolts of flashy silk fabric propped against the cracked stone walls, baskets of gay-colored ribbons and threads seeming to decorate the drab gray floor.

She felt awkward when she stepped inside this room full of strangers, her upset plain on her face. Maureen came around the side of the lace-canopied bed, her green eyes bright with concern. "Did you have a row with him, my lady?"

"I wish to be alone," was all Maria could say. "Would you kindly dismiss the maids?"

"But the master said—"

"Kindly dismiss the maids, Maureen."

The door closed behind them. Maria could hear them whispering about her as they flocked down the hallway, gasping at this poor behavior from such a well-bred lady.

Stung with hurt, she crumpled on her bed, the perfumed coverlet dampening with a rush of angry tears. To her God she cried, her only friend, railed at Him for allowing this. How could Arthur be so cold and heartless, slap the face of a child who wanted only a shred of tenderness? Why couldn't he just pretend to care until she was properly betrothed and wed? Was she so pitiful a wench that her own father could banish her without the slightest twinge of conscience?

Through her mind paraded those happier fantasies of what her new life would be like beyond the convent walls, the spectacular beau monde balls ready to snatch her into its privileged dance. She remembered those sinful conjurings with the girls at night who whispered about the lustier side of life, the company of men, how those strange new hungers in the body could be satiated in a marriage bed. Even while they begged the Lord to forgive them, they'd lie awake and imagine their lovers, naked men with holy scepters engorged with love and want.

How quickly those images faded now. A bright future lay tainted at her feet, destroyed by her father's loveless plans to toss her abed with some wrinkled but worthy London aristocrat. She felt cheated, wasted, her life stolen from her before it even began.

"Maria!" Arthur.

She jumped up, frantically wiped at her face.

"I'm coming in!" he announced, throwing open the door so brutally it slammed against the wall and rattled all the sconces. Arthur's once ghostly complexion was now mottled with rage.

She gasped at the sight of him, suddenly terrified as she watched him stomp to the foot of her bed.

"Get up!" he hissed.

"Father?"

"I said, GET UP!"

Maria gasped as she slid off the bedtick and obediently stood alongside it, one hand still clutching the coverlet as if it might save her from collapsing. He rounded the bedside, his narrowed eyes glinting with anger. She could feel her courage drain with every step he took. A bony hand reached out, took hold of her arm and squeezed tight enough to make her flinch.

"How dare you defy me . . . sending away those maids as if your word could hold authority over mine!"

"But sire," she pleaded, "would you have me attend the ball in poor health tomorrow?"

His hand tightened. He was hurting her now. Real terror engulfed her. Dear God! What was this man capable of? Surely he would not resort to physical violence upon his own child!

"Don't try your practiced ploys on me, young lady!" he said, standing so close she could feel his hot breath on her face.

"You're hurting me . . ."

"I'll do far worse if you ever try this again!" he snapped. "You do as I say in this house. Now compose yourself and stand for your fittings as I desire!"

"But I—"

"Damn you!" he cried, and without warning, sent a palm crashing against her cheek. The blow was stunning, sent her spinning backward, tumbling across the bed.

Horrified, she groped along the coverlet, reached the headboard and clung to it with all her might. She couldn't believe this was happening, that her father could hit her so hard. Her cheek smarted from the blow, made her clench her eyes shut when she saw his hand lift to strike her again.

For the longest moment she hung coiled against

the wooden posts, waiting for a blow that never came.

Dazed and dumbstruck, she finally managed to look at him.

That roguish expression was in his eyes again and, as before, she felt completely undressed.

"You look so much like her," he said, lust mixing with anger in his voice. "It's been years since I felt the kind of desire I had for your mother. She could make my loins ache just to look at her . . ."

His sinful gaze stabbed at the heaving swell of her breasts. He looked ready to toss her on her back and make love to her.

A rush of nausea made Maria turn away from him, certain she would vomit at the sight of him.

He desired her. Coveted her.

This wasn't happening. It was just a bad dream, a terrible nightmare.

Maria felt faint, watched the room seesaw around her, until it was as strange and distorted as the truth she suddenly understood about her father.

He was mad. In his own carefully disguised manner, the man was utterly mad.

Gooseflesh crept across her skin and she shivered involuntarily.

Arthur chuckled at her fear. His eyes raked over the sight of her spread thighs, lingering between them as if he desired to tear away her skirts and plunge into her, to ease his lust upon all that was left of the flesh of his beloved Loretta.

"Learn a lesson from this, daughter," he said to her crumpled form. "There's not a person on earth who defied me more than once. You won't be any different . . ."

He turned around, walked across the room, and gave her a dangerous half-smile just before he shut the door behind him.

Port of London
The Same Day

Beau Gardiner lay across his hammock in a cabin in the belly of the *Savannah Wind,* listening to the rhythm of the old barnacled keel as it thumped into the pier and the scrape of his son's cradle against the floor beside him. It was time for the boy's nap, and young Matthew Gardiner simply would not close his eyes unless he saw his father do the same first.

It wasn't hard to lure the boy to sleep today because Beau was so exhausted himself. He hadn't slept in days. His eyes closed in spite of himself, the gentle rocking motion of the ship luring his mind away from this overcrowded Old World city until it was skimming along a less cluttered shore.

Carolina. He always went back to her the minute his eyes closed. How beautiful she was with her frontiers full of game and forests plush with life, her air moist with the tradewinds of the sea and the sweet fragrance of wild magnolias. How he longed for her wide open spaces and endless sapphire skies, majestic vistas of savannas and saltwater bays.

But a part of him didn't want to go, resisting the allure of the New World because there was horror hidden in her splendor now. He couldn't bear to remember his last moments there, a terrifying night that haunted him with its ghastly details. Those memories seemed to be carved into some dark recess in his brain that only opened in sleep, when he was the most defenseless.

It was too late now. He was already drifting into the past, walking through the back door of his Carolina home, seeing it the way it used to be when they were still alive.

Mother would be in the parlor, behind her spinning wheel, her raven hair so glossy and black in the lantern light, as dramatic as the blue eyes that would sparkle so brilliantly when she smiled. His brother Michael would look up from his books, a pout on his boyish face because Beau hadn't taken him along on his trapping expedition. His sister Louisa would ask if he liked the new way her hair was styled. It always looked the same to him, but he'd humor her the way all brothers did with their little sisters.

Julia, his bride of one year, would meet him in the back room where she worked with her collection of potted herbs. They would embrace and she would melt into him, so slender and soft and blond, always eager for his touch.

His father would usually meet him somewhere in the backyard and follow him to the kitchen to glean the details of whatever deals he had made on the trip. While Beau stuffed himself on the last meal's leftovers, he'd tell his father everything.

Pain stabbed at Beau, made him swallow a lump in his throat that he could feel even in his sleep. But sleep was in control of him now, tossing him from thought to thought, finally bringing him back to that place where he'd spent those last few hours of what seemed like another lifetime.

He was sitting around a woodland fire with four Sanchee braves on a crest of land that overlooked Sampee Bay. It was a cool night, early November, autumn just beginning to creep into the air.

They made the usual trade, Sanchee pelts for a trapper's whiskey, dispensed with their business, and went on to enjoy a pipe full of fireweed and a bit of the potent liquor. He could feel a heady intoxication coming over him, the combination of smoke and whiskey making his head swim lazily.

"Take all the whiskey and leave the pelts," Beau said to Cowachee, a Sanchee elder, in the native's tribal tongue. From across the fire, the Indian looked surprised for a moment, then gladly accepted his generous trade.

Beau's friend Langdon Miles, the only other white man in the group, turned and looked at him queerly.

"What? You're giving them all that whiskey for these few pelts?" Langdon asked in English so the Sanchee wouldn't understand.

"Why not?" Beau had shrugged. He didn't care about anything at the moment except when he'd have another turn at the pipe.

"Because they'll expect more next time, is why," Langdon said sensibly. "It should be an even exchange . . ."

"Oh, go on . . ." Beau scoffed, too giddy and witless to care. He saw the pipe coming toward him and wanted more. His other companion, Indigo, a Savannah native, looked back at Beau from his place around the fire and grinned at how avidly Beau sucked on the pipe. He drew on it hard enough to parch his throat and make him cough up huge clouds of smoke. His head swam dizzily while Indigo chortled at him, delighted by the sight of his complete intoxication.

"You waste your words on him," Indigo told Langdon. "He has no mind for trading anymore. Look at him. He's drunk and lazy . . . too lazy to carry those jugs all the way back to the village. So he'll pretend to be generous now . . . to mask his laziness."

Beau laughed, the gusty sound of it swirling around his head like the smoke from the pipe.

Cowachee nodded his thanks and watched two of his braves hustle toward another jug.

There would be many drunk Sanchee tonight.

But Beau didn't care. He was happy for them. In fact, he was happy about everything at the moment.

Life was good, never better. Especially since his first child had been born. He started thinking about little Matthew, the joy of his birth still lingering in his heart. Since then, he knew the special satisfaction felt by men who fathered a first son. Pride. Real emotional and mental pride. He felt elevated as a man.

Thoughts of Matthew made Beau anxious for home. He rose, Indigo and Langdon bouncing up at the same time. They took their leave of the Sanchee and trotted into the woods, side by side, moving along an invisible path only seen inside their minds. They knew this terrain like a husband knew the body of his wife, every curve, slope, and indentation.

With Sanchee beaver strapped to their backs, they reached the edge of the Wando River, known to Englishmen as the Cooper. They upended their canoe, slid it off the bank, and hopped aboard.

It was an indolent current with just enough draw to pull their craft into a smooth glide. They floated across the water as deftly as the wind that sweetly blended the fragrance of the nearby ocean with the spicy sap of surrounding pines.

The bow of the canoe crunched into the shell-strewn banks beside the tiny pier of Charles Towne.

Beau felt a sudden flash of anxiety. He shifted restlessly on the floor of the canoe, looking up at the tall fence that enclosed the colony. The shadow of a patrolling soldier passed behind it, interrupting the splinters of light that seeped through the split-rail wall.

Trouble brewed in his gut. It came from here, the colony, and the seven noblemen who owned it. The Proprietors. Ever since they'd pitched this settlement, a bit of the peace known to the original inhabitants was gone.

Fur. That's what it was all about. The damned fur they'd been trapping for so many years had somehow become the raiment of foreign kings. Everyone wanted it. Carolina fur. It glittered like mountains of gold in the eyes of the British, and the seven Proprietors who financed Charles Towne were determined to get it.

Beau no longer wanted to get out of the canoe. He just sat there and watched Langdon leap onto the banks, say good-bye, head toward his home in the colony. Although he was an original inhabitant of the area, his was the only family of the four trapping clans whose home happened to be within the area now claimed by the English king. The Miles family refused to move. They had, after all, been here first.

"Let us be off, brother," Indigo said, one foot still inside the canoe. He looked back at Beau, quietly waiting for him to follow.

"No. I'm not going," Beau announced.

Indigo's stare turned hard, his black eyes suddenly as stark and severe as the tension that crept across his face. In the faint light from the colony wall, his skin glowed like burnished bronze, the firelight dancing on the sweat of his bare breast.

"You must come, Beau. Follow me . . ."

Beau felt as if some invisible force slammed into his back and shoved him forward out of the canoe.

Beau snarled under his breath. He heard a distant voice whispering, "Wake up, Beau, wake up . . ."

But he and Indigo were already riding away from the colony. He could feel the warm flanks of a half-wild stallion between his thighs, the woolen blanket bunched in his groin as he thundered into the woods. Indigo was right behind him. It was so foggy. He could barely see the dirt path that lead north to the wooded homesteads of the trappers.

Out here, in the belly of the forest, lived the Gardiners, the Edinburghs, the Moores. They'd lived here for as long as Beau could remember, two generations of migration from the Saint Lawrence coming to an end here in this prime location between the Atlantic shore and the Carolina frontier. It was a trapper's paradise, hundreds of miles of unclaimed territory swarming with game alongside an endless stretch of wide-open beach. They could trap as much as they wanted, ship their harvest anywhere in the world. There were no kings to bow before, no laws to stifle them, no taxes to pay. They lived in total freedom here, like nowhere else on the globe, answering only to the land, their God, and each other.

Beau was sweating hard by the time he saw the lights of the Gardiner homestead blinking through the trees ahead. An ominous sensation prickled up his spine, whispered through his soul like the distant keen of a mourning bell.

He should have known those seven Proprietors

wouldn't let a handful of trappers stand in their way. They all should have known.

Beau jerked on the reins to stop his stallion, but it wouldn't obey. It loped across the front lawn, veered around the corner of the house, then trotted into the backyard. It knew its own way to the stable and meandered between the group of small thatched huts that housed the family's conveniences; the kitchen, the smokehouse, barns, stable. It found the hitching post and stopped.

Beau felt as though he were shoved off the horse's back, his feet slamming hard onto the ground. The weight of the pelts slid off his back, dropped into the dirt.

He noticed it then: how the normally neat bales of straw were kicked apart and scattered everywhere.

There had been a struggle here.

Dread crept through his insides, making him tremble as he fell still and stared at the ground.

Something was wrong, terribly wrong.

Beau watched the tip of his own moccasin kick aside some straw and uncover the tracks beneath it.

He squatted down, then ran his fingers through the indentations in the dirt.

The marks were deep and square.

Boot marks. Boots with heels.

What men wore boots with heels in these parts? Those who lived here clothed their feet in animal skins to allow better footing on this rough terrain. Even the soldiers abandoned their ill-suited regulation boots, opting for moccasins rather than the blisters that came from regulation-issue shoes.

Who then?

Foreigners.

A cold chill bloomed through his insides, made the hair on the back of his neck prickle.

What were foreigners doing here?

Beau shot to his feet, kicked at the straw, uncovered more tracks, and followed them up the path.

A fist of tension curled in his breast as his eyes followed the tracks clear up to the back stoop.

It struck him then, what was so terribly wrong about this. Not so much the tracks but something else. Something far stranger.

The silence.

There wasn't a blessed sound of life here. Not a single movement other than his own and Indigo's and the wind's. The atmosphere hanging over this usually bustling homestead seemed dead.

A single name sprang to mind, screaming through the inside of his skull.

Vandenburgh.

The threats. The letters this Proprietor had sent to his father over the last few months. He ran through the contents of the very last letter from that money-starved Englishman, every word recalled as if permanently imbedded in Beau's memory.

"You and your backwoods Traders are no match for the wrath of this mighty throne. Cease your manipulation of the King's people with these illicit trading practices of yours. We own your land and we'll own you. Stop on your own volition or your head will hang in my parlor like a game trophy. . . ."

Panic found him springing into the back door of the house. It exploded open, and he skidded across the plank floor. He landed against the serving table that was stacked with steaming hot plates of food.

"Father?"

No answer.

"Mother?"

Nothing, just that queer, unearthly quiet.

Now why would dinner sit waiting if no one was home? For that matter, where did they ever go on a Sabbath night? Nowhere. Not for as long as he could remember.

Beau was shaking, sweating, staring at the back of the door that lead into the main house. He felt so desperately afraid to open it, as if the dread in his veins had turned to lead and he couldn't move.

"They're gone, brother," Indigo said from behind him.

Beau whirled around, glaring at the Indian with misguided rage, but the wicked reprimand froze on his lips.

Indigo was crying.

In all the years he'd known him, Beau had never seen Indigo spill a tear.

"God help me," Beau whispered, all the fear and anger and outrage blending into a strange feeling of complete weakness.

He turned back to the door and ever so slowly put his hand on the worn wood and pushed.

It inched open, in slow motion, like the movement of his eyes across the blood-splattered walls of the dining room, across every broken dish and upended chair.

They were lying on the floor as if asleep, familiar faces upturned, sightless eyes glimmering in a candlelight they couldn't see.

Beau just stood there, paralyzed, unable to move, to turn away, to escape the terrifying realization of what he was seeing.

They were dead.

Louisa, Michael, his mother and father, and his beautiful young bride.

Beau felt his legs crumpling under him, his knees smacking hard against the planks, some queer cry rising out of his throat.

There was a huge ball of pain in his belly and it started rolling upward, into his throat, lodged there for just a moment before it burst out of his mouth like the black report of hot iron musket.

"NO! DEAR GOD NO . . ."

"Beau . . . Beau! Wake up, Beau!"

"My God . . . my God . . . why have you done this to me . . ."

"Please Beau . . . can you hear me? Wake up!"

From far away, Beau heard his own voice moaning, gasping for air, choking over the unfamiliar sensation of a throat full of sobs.

He was trying to cry but he didn't know how.

Someone was shaking him, squeezing his shoulder. "God have mercy on him!"

Langdon? What was he doing here?

Beau tried to fasten his mind upon the voice,

could feel himself trying to struggle awake, to force these horrible images out of his mind and listen to whatever Langdon was saying.

It was just a dream. None of this was happening, but he couldn't get away. He was not strong enough to push through to consciousness, too trapped in the horror of this unforgettable moment in his life.

He was reeling out the back door of the house, staggering like a drunken man. "Vandenburgh!" he cried. "Bastard! So help me God, you'll pay . . . your head will be my parlor trophy . . ."

Fury, revulsion, overwhelming grief, filled his spirit until he was walking in aimless circles around the yard. Everyone was gone, his warm and loving home completely destroyed.

His iron will melted and his clenched fists began to pound at the door of the smokehouse, faster and harder until the wood was cracking, splintering. His fingers delved into the cracks, tore at the planks, ripped the wood clear off the beams, and hurled it into the savage night.

But then a new sound shot through the air like a sudden thunderclap.

A baby's hungry howl.

Matthew!

His body shuddered with a sudden charge of energy, a wild gust of excitement that found him tearing across the backyard, leaping any object in his path.

There was life here! Matthew was alive!

Beau leapt up the narrow ladder that lead into

the sleeping loft, two rungs at a time, ran to the cradle of his infant son, and fell to his knees beside it. The half-year-old babe lay curled on his side, his headful of black hair clinging in wisps to the knitted blanket so lovingly laid across his tiny body.

"Matt . . . Matt . . . oh, thank God . . ."

He swiped up the child with a cry of joy, wondering if he had ever known true happiness before this moment. Just the feel of the boy thrilled him, that soft cheek against his own, the steady beat of his tiny heart, the warm little body clenched against his own.

The floor of the loft began to pitch from side to side. Startled, he clung to his son, looked around, watched the face of Langdon Miles slowly materialize behind him.

"It's all right, Beau. Come awake . . . give him to me . . ."

The loft was gone. He was in the cabin of the *Savannah Wind,* kneeling on the floor beside the cradle, his son clenched in his arms.

"Easy Beau. . . . Give him to me before you hurt him . . ."

"No! Get away! He stays with me. . . . He . . . he . . ." Beau blinked, saw the horrified hazel eyes of his friend and finally realized what had just happened.

The dream. It came again.

But it was gone now. He was safe. He was three thousand miles and several months away from that night. It wasn't happening again. It could never happen again.

All the strength ran out of him, and Beau slumped backward until he felt the rotted wooden wall against his spine. Matthew was squirming up the front of his chest.

Langdon could hardly look at Beau; his eyes were glazed and sightless, and his big muscled arms enveloped the tiny black-haired Matthew.

This was precisely how Beau had looked when he arrived at the Mileses' residence on the night of the murders. Langdon would never forget it, could even recall precisely what they were eating when Beau knocked on the door and let himself inside the way he always did when life was normal.

Corn pudding.

Three forkfuls halted in midair at the sight of Beau Gardiner standing in the doorway, so calm and straight, completely unaware of the splatter of blood on his leggings. It was on his face, his neck, the hands that clutched a bundled baby under the parted folds of his cloak. His normally glossy black hair was only partially tethered, a matted clump of it hanging loose on his shoulder.

"Are you all right man?" Langdon asked.

Beau was in shock, still too stunned to speak. He sat on the floor holding Matthew and staring at Langdon.

"Let me take Matt for a moment."

Langdon reached for the boy but it was a mistake. Beau jerked upright, his eyes turning the color of cold blue steel as he wordlessly warned Langdon away from his boy. Langdon backed away, put up his hands in a gesture of peace, and was thankful when Beau seemed to relax. Beau's reaction had been even more violent later on that same night, when Langdon's father had tried to take Matthew before they left for England.

"But he's just a baby," Langdon's father had argued. "You can't take him with you. He needs a woman's care. Julia had yet to wean him."

"His mother is lying in a pool of her own blood right now, Franklin!" Beau had snapped viciously. "I'd say the boy's weaned!"

Those grisly details had made Langdon's mother drop to the floor in a dead faint. When Beau realized what he'd said, he instantly regretted it and tried to apologize, but his voice had cracked and he couldn't speak.

Like now, when he turned toward the cabin wall and motioned Langdon away with his hand. "Leave us be. I need him right now."

"All right, then. I'll fetch you some whiskey."

Langdon was silent while Beau drank, held his son, and gradually began to recover. He looked so terribly alone as he sat there in the shadows, his face full of love and pain. These two were the only Gardiners left in the world, the lone survivors of one of the most beloved families in Carolina. The colony of Charles Towne would never get over the tragedy. Langdon and Beau had left that very night, embarking for England aboard the *Savannah Wind* in pursuit of the only suspect they had.

Vandenburgh. The only evidence was the threatening letters and a hunch that no one else had the gall to do something like this and expect to get away with it.

Langdon's father was left to bury the Gardiners, to break the news to the colonists, to spin the lie that Beau contrived as a mantle of life for his baby son.

"Tell them we were all killed, Franklin," Beau had instructed. "Whoever did this was after my father and probably killed the others because he could afford no witnesses. If it's discovered that any Gardiners survived they'll come back for us . . . they'll have to come back for us. Only the traders can know the truth," Beau commanded, referring to the original inhabitants of the area who were now known to the world as the Charles Towne Traders. "Trust no one else. Be sure you're the only one to go out there . . . to bury them . . ." Beau had paused then, in the doorway, his voice once again faltering as he issued the most heart-wrenching instructions of all. "Bury them on the edge of the savanna, Franklin. You know the place . . . where mother went to pray. Be gentle with them."

Langdon shook away his memories, unable to bear them. He turned to look at Beau.

"Thanks for waking me, Lang," Beau muttered, putting the flask of whiskey down on the floor beside him and running a hand through his hair. "I didn't mean to be harsh with you just then."

"Don't you think I know that?"

Beau just shrugged. He noticed the way Matthew was sucking his thumb. "He's hungry. I suppose it's time for dinner. Why don't you feed him. I want to go back to Vandenburgh's house tonight."

"Not tonight . . . you're too shaken."

Beau didn't seem to hear him. "His daughter's come home. I have an idea about her but I haven't thought it through yet. Besides, his lawyer's coming too. They might talk about something I'll want to hear."

"You need harder evidence than hearsay, Beau."

"I'll get it. I just need more time."

"You're going to get caught sneaking in there one of these times, Beau. This is dangerous, what we're doing."

"I have to do it, Lang. He killed them. We already know that. I just wish I could find something in his papers to prove it, but the man's documented nothing!" He stood up then, handed Matthew to Langdon. "You're getting too nervous about this business lately. So let me do it, eh? As soon as he goes to sleep, then follow me later."

Langdon watched Beau lean over the basin and splash a handful of water across his face. He shook himself and mopped his face.

"Soon, Lang, very soon, I'm going to bring him down . . . the richest man in England. He'll lie at the feet of this trapper and beg for mercy."

There was a ferocious determination in his eyes now, fueled by nothing other than pure malice. It frightened Langdon sometimes, how Beau looked whenever he talked about Vandenburgh. The color of his eyes became the ice blue dead of winter, hatred surrounding him.

"Be careful, Beau."

"Don't worry, I won't kill him, Lang. Death would be too merciful for that murdering pig. I'm going to do worse than that . . . tear out his soul like he did to me . . . make him know what it feels like to live like this." He swept a long black cloak off the peg beside the door and tossed it around himself. "Dead. Nothing inside. Just empty and numb where I used to be a man."

"Stop it, Beau. You're going to recover from this."

Beau's hollow laugh echoed in his wake as he left the *Savannah Wind*, his lone footsteps disappearing into the night.

Maria sat at her father's table that evening in stunned silence. She had existed through the day like a woman caught in a terrifying dream, unable to shake a sensation of numb panic. How could she have prepared for, or even imagined, the predicament she was now in? Maria was too sheltered a girl to know that men were capable of such despicable lusts, that a man could be so twisted and cruel.

He was her own father! Her only kin! She should be able to seek him for protection and security. How could he betray her like this?

And so she sat in quiet retreat behind a carefully powdered facade, feigned a proper amount of indifference to the dinner conversation Arthur was enjoying with his ever-present lawyer, Gaylord Simmes. They were too consumed in their talk to notice how little she ate, how often she had to hide her trembling hands under the table. Every time Arthur glanced her way, a ripple of revulsion danced across her skin.

She had to get out of here, but where could she go? She didn't know anyone in London except Jonathan and Maureen, and they were too loyal to her father to risk asking for help. The convent was certainly not an option. There was too much humiliation in those halls. Besides, Sister Eustace had lied to her about the letter. Maria felt particularly hurt by this because the kindly nun had been one of the few people who had pretended not to notice Arthur's neglect. Maria couldn't face her now. Perhaps some other convent would be more welcoming, but Maria could not shake the thought that if God had wanted her to be a nun, she would still be at the convent today.

No, there had to be somewhere else to go. Why did she feel so helpless and trapped, just about to step into Arthur's frantic wedding plans that would only make it harder to leave?

"I received another posting from the governor of Charles Towne today. The Gardiner affair has caused an outright riot in the colony. Governor Yeamans needs your counsel on how to suppress them," Gaylord Simmes spoke, interrupting her thoughts.

"What do those uncivilized castaways want from me, eh Simmes?"

"They're blaming the entire episode on the Proprietors," Gaylord responded. "We shouldn't have sent those threatening letters to Matthew Gardiner. They could be used as evidence against us."

Arthur looked up sharply. "I insist that Yeamans persuade the colonists away from this dangerous line of thought. I don't want Lord Ashley to hear their suspicions. You know how obsessed he is with the success of Charles Towne. Tell Yeamans to convince the settlers that we are above taking such drastic action for fur, that a few threatening letters were sent merely to frighten him off."

Gaylord nodded. Maria noticed that his hands were trembling. He poked a fork at his platter, jabbed here and there, selected not a morsel to eat.

Gaylord was aware of her attention. It only made him feel more uncomfortable, especially because Arthur was watching him at the same time. They'd see how nervous he was about this whole affair, notice the dark rings around his eyes, how stiff and awkward he felt whenever this subject came up.

He wanted to forget about it, put it out of his mind, concentrate on the budding legal career his late father had passed on to him. It was all going so well until Arthur ordered him to get rid of Matthew Gardiner. If only he'd refused.

Now that affair haunted him night and day, but he knew better than to seek sympathy from his employer. Gaylord would never forget the night he went to the Vandenburgh estate and told Arthur that the mercenaries he hired had finally returned from the colonies.

"Matt Gardiner is dead . . . along with his whole family," Gaylord had said, expecting Arthur to be shocked at the news. It was only Matt who was supposed to die, not the rest. But the rest of the family had the misfortune of being with the head of the Charles Towne Traders when his moment came to die. There could be no witnesses.

"They all had to be killed," Gaylord had said again, still groping for some human reaction from the man.

Finally, Arthur had looked up at him and said tersely, "I heard you the first time, Simmes." His thin lips twisted into an amused smile. "You look terrible. I suppose you're not used to our kind of business, eh? If your father was still alive, he'd explain it to you . . . tell you that men like me don't amass such fortunes by catering to the whims of trappers."

"I'm sure you're right, m'lord," Gaylord had acquiesced, though he hated himself for it. He found it hard to believe his father had ever participated in such murderous affairs. But there was no point in mentioning this to Arthur. No one with any wits stood in the way of Arthur Vandenburgh.

"Simmes? Are you listening to me?"

Gaylord looked up sharply and gave Arthur a brisk nod.

"I want those colonists quieted at once!"

"I'll see to it, m'lord," Gaylord said, his voice emerging as little more than a mumble. He cleared his throat and tried again. "The colonists are more audacious than we thought. To even accuse the Proprietors came as a surprise to me. I didn't figure on such gall!"

"Oh?" Arthur's glance sharpened. "What else didn't you figure on?"

"You've nothing to fear. I documented nothing about the mission. Our tracks are covered well."

Tracks? What was going on over there, Maria wondered.

"They better be," Arthur warned. Stabbing at his venison, he snarled, "and I don't want to hear another word about the Gardiners. Yeamans is to blame everything on the Westoe tribesmen, then get back to more important business. Like stopping those Charles Towne bandits from trafficking my fur all over Europe! I want the black market stopped by year's end. This should be the governor's foremost concern, not some bloody social upset!"

"As you wish, m'lord," Gaylord mumbled. "I'll send a dispatch tonight."

"Yes, well, use today's date. Knowing that fool Yeamans if we post it tomorrow, on April first, he'll think it's a joke!"

Arthur chuckled stiffly and Gaylord played along, but Maria could see that the lawyer was not amused.

Maria reached for her wine and studied Gaylord. How different he was from his father. Gaylord, Senior, had been an arrogant and powerful barrister who counseled dukes and barons and the king's ministers. But this son didn't fit such a giant role. His boyish features made his courtly wig and austere black robes look ill-fitting and overlarge. Young Gaylord seemed much more human than his father, his warm brown eyes a bit too sensitive, long thin fingers as soft as an artist's.

"What about the progress of our explorers, Simmes? How far have they penetrated Carolina?"

The change of subject brought an expression of relief to Gaylord's smooth young face. "Dr. Woodward and Sir Colleton have established themselves several hundred miles northwest of Charles Towne, on a river the Indians call the Congaree. It's in Westoe territory. Apparently, they've met the Westoe chief, Tomawausau, who gave them permission to strike a camp there."

"Permission," Arthur interrupted with a snort. "Imagine these savages, the lot of them part animal at best, fancying themselves to be in control of Crown land!"

"Preposterous, m'lord."

"Indeed."

"But this is their way."

"Their ways are about to change, Simmes."

"Undoubtedly."

"Go on."

"Colleton and Woodward will attempt to form a friendship with the chief, then convince him against trapping and trading with the Charles Towne Traders. Although the Westoe are only one of the four tribes the traders use, it's a start."

"Indeed. It's a splendid strategy!" Arthur looked genuinely pleased.

This rare praise from his employer put a whisper of confidence in Gaylord's voice. "It could work now that Matthew Gardiner's son is no longer an issue."

"What did his son have to do with this?"

"Apparently, the young Gardiner was highly revered by the Westoe. They considered him to be of divine origin . . . a god, if you will."

"A what?"

"A god, m'lord. The young man's desires were instantly obeyed by the savages."

"Oh, for the grace of God . . ." Arthur rolled his eyes at the ceiling. Both men chuckled smugly, their laughter bloated with superiority.

Jonathan's voice rose just beyond the dining room door, loud and harsh enough to make the laughter freeze on Arthur's lips. "What are you doing here, sir?"

"Waitin on the mastuh," came a man's response in a voice none of them recognized. The tone was a deep, throaty baritone.

"The master of this house is dining and shan't be disturbed."

"I wasn't gonna disturb him. I was just waitin on him."

"Well, you can't do so!" Jonathan snapped indignantly. "Kindly remove yourself from these premises!"

"M'lord said I'm to wait on the due money, suh."

"Who is your lord?"

"Eckert, the cheese merchant."

"Show me his bill of lading."

"I left it with Miss O'Leary."

"Wait here and I'll check on it."

They were sitting at the table in rapt attention, forks poised and eyes staring at the back of the door. When Arthur sprang out of his seat, Maria and Gaylord jumped, then pushed back their chairs and hurried after him.

Arthur flung open the door. The dining room candlelight flooded across the figure of a man who was unusually tall. The stranger towered in the shadows, his quiet and studying pose oddly formidable. Intrigued by his impressive figure, Maria took notice of the rags he wore, ill-fitting clothes that couldn't quite hide the magnificent physique beneath them.

A threadbare red tunic revealed tight brown flesh here and there on his arms. Loose black britches were held up by a piece of jute that was wrapped snugly around narrow hips. Beneath the shabby fabric she could see a pair of long and powerfully muscled legs that lent the man a proud, almost noble bearing. His massive shoulders were braced, his back erect, one hip cocked into the arrogant stance of a young stallion.

"State your business and be quick about it," Arthur snapped. "My dinner grows colder by the minute!"

The man came forward in a single stride, his movement smooth and agile. Arthur took a step backward. Maria didn't move, just stared at the stranger's face.

The flesh on his broadly boned face was the color of buffed bronze, as if he labored in the sun every day of his life. Even more attractive was his hair, uncovered and brilliantly glossy, as black as tar. It was well groomed and clean, combed away from his face where it could not detract from his most striking feature.

His eyes. They were the color of ice blue topaz.

"Are you the mastuh?" he asked. Was that mockery she heard in his deep voice?

"Yes, I'm the master!" Arthur barked.

The stranger stiffened. She could see his jaw set as if he was clenching his teeth for control. His eyes became pale, icy shards, his massive brown hands curling into fists at his side.

Excitement quivered up her spine. While Arthur and Gaylord seemed to shrivel beneath the intensity of the stranger's stare, Maria was strangely thrilled to see someone, anyone, react so fearlessly to the notorious Arthur Vandenburgh.

"Sorry, suh," the man growled, his tone more menacing. "I didn't recognize ya." Arthur stole a glance down the hall to see where Jonathan was. "I'm new to the job," the stranger continued, a mocking smile twisting the corners of his mouth.

The sight of it made Maria positively gleeful.

"I should have guessed," Arthur sneered. "Delivery men do not approach the master of a household for payment. Such business is conducted through the servants."

"Is that so?" the stranger asked, his cold eyes studying her father with undisguised hatred.

Maria saw that the man didn't care about the proper behavior of deliverymen, and suddenly she saw him as a complete impostor. This was no delivery boy. That station was entirely too lowly for the likes of him. This man was too confident, too sure of himself. Whatever he did for a living was meant for real men, not the pale thin boys of London.

"Sorry t'intrude, suh," he finally said.

"You are excused, now kindly get out," Arthur said without a shred of courtesy.

The man turned on his heels and started down the hall. He moved with the stalking grace of a wild animal, each foot falling exactly where he wanted it to. He threw open the front door, then abruptly spun around. To her surprise, those penetrating blue eyes stared directly at her, so bold and deliberate that her breath suddenly caught in her throat.

His cool blue eyes seemed to slide straight into her head, see her mind, read its every thought. She had the strangest feeling that he knew exactly what was going on inside her tonight.

His eyes lowered then, slowly swept down the length of her as if assessing every curve of her body. Never before had a man given her such undivided attention, such a close and thorough scrutiny. It made her feel very female of a sudden, so much so that she felt two pools of heat form on her cheeks. Even though he stood ten feet away, she felt as if he were touching her with his hands, exploring her, penetrating her. Maria was so shocked she could not look away, just stared at him in complete astonishment.

But then he turned away, abruptly, slammed the door behind him, and left her standing there feeling as if she'd just been violated.

"I didn't like the looks of that man," Arthur commented.

"Nor I. Did you see the way he looked at Maria just then?" Gaylord whispered, as if afraid the man might overhear and come back.

Maria let out her breath in one long sigh.

"How much of our conversation did he overhear?" Arthur wondered aloud.

"Surely not enough to reveal ourselves, m'lord."

"Master Vandenburgh!" Jonathan rushed up the hall, his jowled white face drawn with anxiety. "That man was an impostor! He left no bill of lading with Maureen! God only knows how long he's been in this house!"

"I'm holding you responsible, Jonathan!" Arthur fumed. "How could you allow a stranger in this house?"

"There's been so much activity today, my liege, the gates opening and closing a hundred times with deliveries—"

"Never mind your excuses! Just get out there and find him! I want him brought back here. I'll get to the bottom of this!"

"At once, sir!" Jonathan nearly leapt for the door in his haste to obey, but Arthur cursed aloud and summoned him back.

"Don't go after him unarmed, you fool! One pelt

from that man's fist will send your head rolling into the Thames!"

"Yes, sir!" Jonathan scrambled off in search of a weapon, then disappeared outside.

It was late into the night and Maria, exhausted, was still tossing on her bedtick, unable to find a comfortable position. Now and then she dozed but came awake at the slightest creak or groan from this strange house. It was so dark and forbidding and cold in her chamber. She grew frantic for rest. Maybe it would help her think more clearly. Besides, the ball was tomorrow night, the house would be filled with important people, everyone coming to see the nondescript young schoolgirl-turned-debutante. She'd fall asleep on the dance floor.

Maria heard an unfamiliar thumping noise. She sat up, listening, her eye darting toward the light that drifted under her chamber door.

It was coming from somewhere down the hall, a consistent wooden thump, as if someone were tapping the floor with a club.

The noise brought her out of bed, to the back of her chamber door where she stood and listened more intently.

Voices. Low and murmuring.

Maria eased open the door, stuck her head out into the hall. The bumping noise was louder out here, seemed to be coming from the only door in the hall that showed any light under it. Maria gathered the trailing hem of her nightdress and padded barefoot toward the door.

Maureen's voice came to her ear. The maid was groaning as if in some terrible agony.

"No . . . it's ungodly . . . you mustn't think of her like that, m'lord . . ."

What was Maureen doing in Arthur's chamber?

Maria stooped low until her eye was level with the empty keyhole. She looked inside, a shocking scene perfectly displayed within the metal hourglass frame.

Maureen was naked, her bare body sprawled across the bed, wrists and ankles tied securely to Arthur's canopy posts. Her head tossed wildly, bright red hair slashing across the stark white linens like the dance of unchecked flames. But it was the figure atop her that made Maria's feet seem to freeze to the floor.

Arthur. He was naked, his white skin like paste as it drooped from his skeletal frame. He was bucking so viciously between the maid's spread thighs it made Maureen's whole body jump and the legs of the bed leap against the floor.

"Loretta," her father gasped, "dear Loretta's come back!"

Mother? Come back?

Maria understood it then. She clenched her eyes tight as if trying not to see the thought and whirled away from the keyhole.

He was talking about her. She was the one who made him think Loretta had come back.

"Whore!" she heard Arthur cry out. "She was my whore!"

Maria ran down the hall, a fist clamped against

the scream in her throat. All the while, his words from yesterday whispered in her ear, ". . . been a long time since I felt the kind of desire I had for your mother."

Maria stumbled into her chamber, collapsed against the back of the door, both hands fisted around the dimity folds of her gown.

What was she doing in this house full of demons, everything heinous and forbidden in the world trapped within it like some private palace of hell. It was a real-life nightmare, worse than any dream could be.

By the time she found her bed again, Maria knew there was no power on earth that would make her spend another night here. Not even Arthur.

Maria moved through the following day in a state of complete exhaustion, too tired to feel anything but a bone-chilling dread. Her only comfort came from a string of rosary beads hidden in the pocket of her robe, a fervent plea for strength spoken on every bead. She kept her mind steeped in prayer while the maids bathed her, oiled her, powdered her. Maria pasted a pleasant smile on her face and kept it there all day, until her cheeks ached from the effort. But it was worth it. They were all fooled. No one had the slightest idea what she planned for this night.

The hour of the ball approached. From her bedroom window, she could hear the growing commotion on the front drive as the guests began to arrive for the gala opening of the London social season. Carriages rattled, aggravated coachmen heckled for passage, elaborately coiffed women swished up the front steps until their lilting giggles were muffled in the marbled foyer of the house.

Maria finally stood before the vanity mirror and listened to the maids sigh with pride upon their handiwork. She looked in the mirror, at the reflection of a spun-gold fairy princess on her way to a fairy-tale life. But Maria didn't recognize herself beneath the glamour of her raiment; she saw only the terrified young girl who huddled under the silk like a frightened child.

Arthur had exceptional taste in women's clothes, and Maria's gown was the latest fashion. It was pure white silk, the genuine gold thread used to stitch its sophisticated lines glittering with an expensive luster. The neckline was scooped low and daring, the rib-length bodice tufted and decorated with tiny pearls. The sleeves fit her snugly from wrist to elbow, then bloomed outward in exaggerated puffs of white lace at each shoulder. The skirt flowed to the floor in voluminous snowy folds that trailed into a chapel-length train behind her. A sash of red velvet and ermine fur was draped over one shoulder, affixed at the hip with a flawlessly cut diamond brooch.

She looked like a queen about to be crowned.

Arthur knocked at the door and sent all the maids scattering like frantic butterflies.

Maria froze as he came into the room to present her with the traditional gift given to debutantes on the night of their introduction to the world.

This was the last ritual she would have to endure, Maria told herself, purposely averting her eyes from the man who appeared in the mirror behind her.

She didn't want to look at him. He might see it, the guilt hidden beneath her mask of humility.

"You look stunning, Maria," he said softly. Out of the corner of her eye, she could see that sinful look of his. It made her remember last night, the sight of him between Maureen's legs. "I hope my gift will please you."

His wrinkled hands reached around her neck. She jumped at his touch, looked up to see him draping a necklace of meshed gold and diamond studs around her throat. Wherever his fingers brushed it, her skin crawled.

"I gave this to your mother on the eve of our wedding." His voice was as thick as the want in his eyes. "I daresay, you look as spectacular in them as she did."

Her stomach soured, and she felt a wave of nausea. Somehow she managed a smile, thanked him as graciously as her wobbling voice would allow. "I'm honored to wear them, Father."

"You look pale."

"The excitement . . ."

"Of course! But you needn't be a bit nervous, my dear. My friends are most welcoming to one of their own kind."

"I'm sure we'll get along famously."

"Indeed. Why, Lord Eddington has already filled the first two pages of your dance register!"

"How presumptuous of him!" she declared with pretended feeling.

" 'Tis an admirable trait in one of his social caliber. The ladies find him most handsome. When he asks for your hand, you'll be the envy of London!"

"Oh? Have you already discussed a betrothal with him?" Maria blurted.

Arthur's eyes instantly narrowed. "I'd suggest you get that spiteful attitude of yours under control, girl. Don't you dare embarrass me tonight!"

He meant it.

Maria felt faint. "I wouldn't think of it," she squeaked, then cleared her throat. What violence he would unleash upon her if he suspected her plans for tonight!

Don't think of it now, she commanded herself. Not now! You'll lose your nerve!

"Good." He was appeased. "I knew you were intelligent enough to learn from yesterday that I don't tolerate defiance very well at all." Yes, the bruise on her cheek was enough of a reminder. "Now then, have yourself a steadying cup of sherry until the time comes. You'll be sent for."

Arthur finally left and Maria let out such a long breath it nearly collapsed her to the floor. But there was no time for vapors. Most of the guests had arrived and she would be sent for within the hour. If she would succeed, she must act quickly.

Maria ran across the room, muttering the Lord's Prayer under her breath as she fell to her knees beside the bed. Her hand groped under it, found the pair of carefully packed satchels. She dragged them out, tugged them to the window, all the while listening for any sound from the hall. It was quiet, most of the noise coming from downstairs where the musicians were entertaining the guests with a popular minuet. Maria grabbed her old capuchin, her hands trembling so hard she could barely get her arms in the cloak. Nervous fingers fumbled to close each button until her stark white gown was completely hidden beneath the dark brown robe. She tore off her wig, yanked at the pins binding her natural hair until it fell loose and wild to her waist. The lot of it was pulled up and stuffed into her hood.

She was ready. The moment was at hand.

The window gave way with ease, letting in a gust of cold damp air. She picked up the satchels and quickly dumped them over the ledge. They crashed through the bushes and hit the ground with a dull thud. The guests arriving on the front drive couldn't hear the noise around the corner of the house even though she was no more than a hundred feet away.

Maria sat on the ledge and swung out her feet. She tried not to notice the way her drumming heartbeat was echoing inside her hood, how ragged her breathing was. Her limbs were stiff with terror, heavy and awkward as she pushed aside yards of petticoat and white silk to roll onto her stomach and feel for the trellis with the tip of her toes.

She found it, gripped the shutters tightly and tested the rickety wood to be sure it could carry her weight. It creaked loudly but held. She started down, carefully selecting each step while a strong wind swept under her garments and sent them flapping around her. Finally, her foot touched solid ground.

Maria fell against the wall, her cheek pressed into the cold stone and hung there panting for air and the nerve to go on with this. She had never done anything so daring in her entire life. For one last moment she huddled in the dark, desperately holding on to the trellis knowing what she must do.

Turn around and run.

With no destination, no one to help, Maria felt a loneliness so profound it seemed to silence all the noise of the night. In that moment, she was so utterly alone, so terribly lost, that all she could do was hang against the wall, nothing but cold stone to catch her silent tears.

"My lady?"

Maria lifted her head, certain she'd just heard a voice. She sniffed, wiped her wet eyes, and studied the darkness on either side of her. Nothing.

"Lady Vandenburgh?"

This time she jumped, letting go of the trellis and falling on the ground.

"Where are you," she breathed.

"Over here."

To her left. Maria slowly turned her head, then gasped at the figure of a man sitting not three feet away. She blinked, adjusted her eyes to the dark, and suddenly found herself staring into a face she'd never forget.

It was the stranger from last night.

"You!" She shriveled against the wall, her fingers clawing at the stone. "What are you doing here?"

He looked as startled as she was. "That's my question," he whispered. "Aren't you Arthur's daughter . . . the one they're having this ball for?"

She swallowed hard, nodded, didn't dare take her eyes off him.

"Then what are you doing out here?"

"Me?" she said, "You're the one lurking in the shrubbery!"

"At the moment, I think we both are." He moved toward her on his hands and knees, his wide-brimmed hat temporarily blocking her view of his face.

"Stay away," she warned, her bottom sliding in the dirt in her haste to be away from him.

He looked up and stopped moving when he realized it was only making her more frightened than she already was. "Don't be afraid. I'm not going to hurt you."

He was close enough now for her to see his face, to notice that there was no menace in the eyes that sparkled up at her from beneath the deep shadow of his brow. "Then what are you doing here?" she demanded.

"Spying on your father."

"Are you daft?"

He smiled at her aghast expression, his white teeth flashing for a moment before he resettled himself against the wall of the house.

Their shoulders nearly touched.

"You're in great danger," Maria insisted, hoping she could frighten him off. But she saw not a whisper of fear in the face that was suddenly close. Too close. She stared straight ahead, into the back of the thick green bushes. "My father was looking for you last night."

"I know. I saw the man he sent after me." He chuckled. "As you can see, he didn't catch me." She felt his gaze on the side of her face. "So tell me, judging from these bags you nearly killed me with, should I assume you're leaving?"

"Yes."

"Why?"

"I don't think that's any of your business . . ."

"Let me guess." The man was dauntless. "Arthur's been his usual charming self, which is enough to scare off a pack of wolves, let alone a young girl like yourself."

She caught a glimpse of the same icy hatred she'd seen in his eyes last night. "You're an enemy of his, aren't you?"

He nodded, all the hatred vanishing as his eyes swept over her upturned face. Something equally dark but much softer bloomed there now, an expression that told Maria he appreciated what he saw.

A little flicker of warmth sped through her. She couldn't decide if it was the way he was looking at her or the realization that he wasn't going to turn her in. He seemed to be an ally.

"So where are you going?" he asked.

"I haven't the faintest idea," she breathed, her

attention oddly captured by the way his mouth moved when he spoke.

"Surely you have some relative . . ."

"No, I have no one. I only came here yesterday morning, having been at school all these years."

"How many years?"

"Twelve."

She had the feeling he was only half-listening to what she was saying. They were both looking at each other more closely now. She didn't know why, at a time like this, she could possibly sit here and marvel at how strikingly handsome he was. With his dark features and his tight brown skin, Maria found him almost beautiful, for a man.

They both looked away from each other at the same time. Something awkward passed between them as they fell momentarily quiet. They sat there, listening to the wind rustle through the bushes, sweeping up bits of leaves and compost. The distant laughter of ballroom guests tinkled upon the cool breezes.

Cold, nervous, anxious to be away, Maria fumbled for the pockets of her capuchin and thrust her icy fingers into the warm woolen folds.

"We shouldn't dally here," he said as if reading her mind. "My coach waits nearby. We can talk safely in there."

He tugged at her sleeve as he started to get up.

"But I don't even know your name!"

"This is hardly the place for introductions," he said in a deep throaty voice. She was reminded of how big and strong he was, how confident and capable he had seemed last night. To have the protection of so formidable a man didn't seem like such a bad idea, especially when she considered the more dangerous elements in this sprawling city. "We'll tend to that in the coach. Then you can tell me where it is you plan to go and I'll see you safely there. God knows, I'm not so irresponsible a man to let a young maid wander the streets of this city alone. Come along . . . give me your hand."

She looked up at him, unable to find an argument. Besides, what difference was there between one stranger or another?

They bolted through the darkness, across the lawn until they reached the hedgerow at the curb. The man at her side issued a strange, birdlike whistle that instantly brought a coach to halt in the street not five feet from where they were hiding. The stranger went first, pushing through the hedge to the place where several spokes in the gate were missing. They passed easily through the opening, jumped directly into the coach, and shut the door.

Maria slid across the seat, and the stranger took a seat across from her. Within the soft light of the interior coach lantern, she watched him snap the window shut so no one could see inside. He turned to look at her then.

Lord, but he was a magnificent man. No longer clothed as a beggar, he was smartly dressed in a conservative black broadcloth suit that was only half-hidden beneath a cloak of the same color. His dark hat was wide brimmed, tilted low over his disarming eyes, a dashing cap to the mahogany locks that escaped from the tether at the back of his neck. Except for the bright color of his eyes, he had a dark, mysterious look to him. Yet he was so masculine and strong. She could almost feel the physical power lurking beneath his stark black robes.

"Now that we're safe," he began, and Maria saw the flicker of a smile cross his ruddy face, as if he enjoyed the way she was perusing him, "my name is Gardiner . . . Beau Gardiner."

"Gardiner!" she gasped, instantly recognizing the name. "Of Carolina?"

He nodded.

"Why, I heard my father talking about the Gardiners just last night!"

"I know. I was listening from the other side of the door, remember?"

"Have you no mind for danger?" she said.

"I suppose that depends on the danger," he replied. For the first time, Maria noticed his accent. It was strange. Not British, Irish, German. In fact, she'd never heard one like it. Articulate but plain, the barest drawl over each consonant. "Your father and my late father had many conflicts. They concern the business of selling Carolina fur. I'm afraid the details would bore you."

"Of course," she acknowledged, pushing back her hood and setting loose a flood of unbound hair. Auburn curls fell around her waist in lustrous disarray, a few pins still dropping out.

She was too busy trying to straighten herself to notice how struck he was by her unveiled beauty. The woman was magnificent, her cheeks high and carved and subtly colored in a healthy shade of peach. The color melted into her temples in a way that accented the exotic upward curve of her dark, sultry eyes. They were as expressive as her mouth, full and sensual and inviting. She was a bit too much of a woman for such a young girl.

"How ignorant of me to act so suspiciously of you, Mr. Gardiner. Please accept my apologies."

"My given name is Beau."

This brought her attention back. It was not proper to address a man so familiarly. She blushed at the invitation, dropped her eyes once again, and murmured demurely, "You may call me Maria if you wish."

"I do," he said softly, his voice sounding a bit deeper in his throat. Without looking up, she could feel the intensity of his gaze upon her. As if he was touching her.

The sensation was disarming. She had never felt anything like it before even though it was not entirely unpleasant.

"You are the most fetching woman I've ever had the pleasure of looking upon. The idea of you wandering these streets alone is becoming less appealing by the minute."

The blushing luster dropped out of her face. She looked at the window, worried again. "I should think of something . . ."

"I can't imagine what he's done to make you do this . . . run off with nowhere to go . . ."

He let the sentence trail, waiting for her response. Maria couldn't give one. Through her mind raced such a flood of evil recollections that her cheeks flamed with shame and horror. The best she could do was to murmur, "I can't stay here . . . have got to find a place as far from his reach as I can manage."

"Did he hurt you?" Beau asked, his voice gentle but still intrusive.

"Not yet . . . but he will."

The mere sight of her, sitting there so alone and afraid, filled Beau with anger. Who could do this to such a gentle creature?

The same man who could slit his mother's throat.

"Let me help you, Maria."

"How?"

"Come with me . . . to Carolina."

Carolina?

The New World! Why hadn't she thought of this before? Arthur would never find her there. He'd never even think to look for her there!

"Yes . . . the New World . . ." she said, staring at Beau Gardiner as if she could see a picture of Carolina on his face. "Father would never find me there, would he? I could use these to come up with the coin for passage." She untied her cloak and presented him with a chest full of glittering diamonds and plump round breasts that sent an involuntary flutter of warmth through his loins.

He looked away sharply. "Never mind that. I've plenty of money for your passage."

"But I wouldn't think of burdening you . . ."

"No, but you should give some thought to where

you intend to wander, my lady. The New World is no place for unescorted women."

This sobered her. He was right, of course. "Oh, how foolish of me."

"However, I recently lost my wife, who died shortly after giving birth to my son. It's been quite difficult to tend him without a woman's aid. I suppose a maid of your background is hardly suited to caring for infants."

"I'm very well educated," she quickly defended. "I learn very quickly." She looked at him pleadingly.

He could barely believe his good fortune, this miracle that was dropping into his hands.

"Is that so?" He studied her carefully to be sure she was as interested in the job as he thought she was. "What about America? Have you any idea how primitive life is over there?"

She answered with a burst of enthusiasm that made her whole face light up. "Oh, yes! I've read all about it! Why, I hear the ladies dress their hair every day and are forever importing fine laces and ribbons from Europe. They can't be so doltish then, can they?"

Beau laughed, genuinely amused by her naiveté. "We're quite civilized, despite what the Old World likes to advertise." He leaned forward, more serious now. "But I don't live in the settlement of Charles Towne. When I return home, I intend to reside in my father's trapping lodge on the Savannah River . . . a considerable distance from Charles Towne."

She didn't seem at all distressed. But why would

she? Maria hadn't the slightest idea what he was talking about.

"Would you like the job?"

"Oh, yes! If you would have me, I'd be most grateful!"

"Very well. Let's be off then." Beau turned around to rap once on the panel above his head. It slid open. "Let's get back to the docks, Lang."

"Who's the girl?" the driver asked.

"Maria Vandenburgh."

"What?"

Beau started to shut the panel but a gloved hand slid inside and held it open.

"You said you were just thinking about it." the voice accused.

"Well, I've made up my mind, haven't I? Come on. Drive!"

The panel slammed shut.

She looked at Beau in concern. "Perhaps I'm in the way after all."

"Nonsense. He's not angry about you. Something else is eating at him." Beau brushed off her worries with a wave of his hand.

The coach made an unexpected lurch forward. Beau banged his head against the wall, his hat tumbling into his lap.

"Why you . . ." A big brown fist slammed into the panel. "Langdon!"

The panel slid open. "What?" snapped the voice outside.

"Mind your temper! There's a lady in here!"

"I want an explanation, Beau."

"You'll get one at the docks. Now hurry! Vandenburgh doesn't know she's gone yet and I'd like to get out of here before he does."

Maria nodded in complete agreement.

"Very well," the driver conceded reluctantly. Then he murmured through the panel, "My apologies, Lady Vandenburgh."

It seemed like hours before they were able to pick their way through the congestion on Dabney Street and find a quieter avenue of travel. The rawness of her nerves didn't ease until they were finally away and traveling briskly toward the sea.

Maria settled into the worn leather cushions and opened the window a crack to let in some fresh air. It felt good on her tear-stained cheeks, refreshing enough to steal the stiffness from her posture. She sighed, finally relaxed, watched the gaily lit city of London rush by in a whirl of lights and glassy cobbles and streets full of strangers out enjoying the night. The scenery changed as they neared the docks, brick-faced buildings giving way to the rope-twisted towers of tall masted ships. She looked at the lofty configurations of jute and sheet that seemed to reach clear into the night sky, the earthy smells of fish and tar clinging heavily to the damp air.

The coach stopped. "Wait here just a moment," Beau said as he climbed out of the coach and shut the door behind him.

A brief shuffle in front of the coach brought the driver to the ground a few feet from the window. This man looked about the same age as Beau, equally as fit, although he was fair-haired and a few inches shorter. They didn't seem angry as they walked toward the waterfront, their heads bent together in deep conversation. They reached the pier and turned toward each other, a pair of tall silhouettes surrounded by the shimmering glass surface of a lazy sea at low ebb. Now and again she saw Beau motioning toward the coach with his hand, obviously referring to her. They spoke for several minutes before Beau returned to the coach.

He climbed back inside and shut the door. He retook his former seat and said, "My friend Langdon will see you aboard." With his hand he motioned to the man who was still standing on the pier. "I'll need to take care of a few items of business with the captain, then I'll rejoin you below. I suspect Matthew will still be asleep."

"Matthew?"

"My son."

"He's here?"

"Of course. I couldn't very well leave him on the frontier, could I?"

"Surely you have some relatives . . ."

"No. I'm quite alone."

"I see." Her face dropped, a timid smile awarded to the back of her primly folded hands. "That makes two of us then, doesn't it?"

"Indeed it does, my lady."

She looked up, watched his eyes fill with a genuine understanding that instantly comforted her. He leaned forward so he could slide his hand over the fists in her lap. It wasn't the strength of his hand or the gentleness of his touch that struck her. No. It was how warm his skin felt against her own. She liked the feel of him and let him untwine her fingers and slide them between his own. Maria wondered if he was as aware of her as she was of him, if their touch was what brought that sudden stillness to his face.

"I know how dangerous he is, Maria," he said, "probably better than anyone on earth."

"If he finds me—"

"He won't . . . not so long as I'm alive."

"But he's mad," she whispered, not really sure why she was telling him this, just that he was the most compelling man she'd ever encountered. The way he looked at her with those pale but piercing eyes, his gaze so level and concentrated, made her feel like the most important person in the world.

"I know," he said, and she was only half-hearing him now, distracted by the seemingly absent way he toyed with her fingers caught in his hand. "And you were wise to fly from him. Matthew and I are most fortunate to have found you."

His head bent, the felt brim of his hat grazing her arm as he brushed his lips across the back of her hand in a most chivalrous kiss. Her eyes widened as a wicked little shiver coursed clean through her womanhood.

But then he was gone, hopping out of the coach and disappearing into the shadowy pier.

Langdon Miles was the exact opposite of her new employer. Where Beau was dark and masculine, Langdon was fair and boyish. His clean-shaven face sported two round pools of windburn that made his skin look a bit too red when matched with such white-blond hair. Yet it was a clean mane, bluntly cut to his shoulders with a thick and glossy bang covering his forehead. A pair of close-set hazel eyes twinkled with what she was sure could be a hearty mirth if not for his nervous disposition. This man had a stiff carriage that made him seem abrupt despite his gentlemanly manners.

They boarded a small merchant ship called the *Savannah Wind* and crossed the deck without much notice from the crew. With her head down and her hood pulled low, she was aware of men working in the masts overhead, changing the rigging from standing to running in preparation to depart. She glanced about in search of Beau but she didn't see him before Langdon led her below.

The companionway was musty and narrow. The sleeping berths looked like stables on one side of the corridor but were enclosed on the side Langdon chose. A small door was pushed open and she stepped into a cabin of such scant proportions it was hardly bigger than her wardrobe in the Vandenburgh mansion. A pair of hammocks was strung across each wall, a small washstand and commode just inside the door. Under the lone porthole sat a crudely built cradle with rocking legs and a big thatched bonnet.

"Let me help you with your wrap, my lady," Langdon offered, then issued a low whistle upon sight of her glittering ball gown. "Beau should be ashamed to bring such a beauty aboard this rotting rig."

"Nonsense," she chided sweetly, unable to utter a complaint about the spartan living conditions. "He's been very kind to me."

"Hmmm," Langdon said as he hung her cloak on a peg beside the hatch. He took off his hat, ran his hands through his hair, and looked at her for a moment as if wondering what to do with her. "Well then, you must be exhausted after such a frightful experience."

She nodded, weary but unable to relax. She went to the cradle instead, leaned over, and looked inside.

An infant of less than a year lay sleeping inside, snuggled beneath a plush sable pelt that kept away the damp cold. No one could mistake who had fathered him. The babe sported the same thick shock of black hair as his sire, and his closed eyes, heavily feathered with sooty lashes, lay upon his cheeks and curled upward.

"He was only six months old when his mother died," Langdon explained. "Beau and I do our best to care for him, but a woman is sorely needed with a child so young. When we landed in England five months ago, Matthew's health was dreadfully weak. He needed milk. I thought Beau would go out of his mind with worry until he found a doctor for the boy. He advised us to use goat's milk to nourish him and he improved almost at once."

Maria thought the boy looked quite healthy. His skin was pink and plump, a chubby little fist thrust against a pair of rounded lips. Occasionally, he sucked on his hand as if his dreams made him hungry.

"He's adorable." She couldn't resist reaching down to smooth his tiny head. He was so warm and soft, his hair like jet velvet against her fingertips. Something about this helpless little creature who was surviving so well in Beau's care brought her a powerful feeling of security. For the first time in two days, Maria began to feel safe. She stood up, her smile full of gratitude as she turned to Langdon. "I can only hope I'll tend him as well as Beau."

"I'm sure you will!" Langdon beamed at her. He stuck his hands in his pockets. "But I must warn you about Beau and his son. They are absolutely infatuated with each other. Look how Beau is spoiling him . . ." He motioned at a pile of toys under the cradle. There were enough objects there to keep a roomful of children occupied.

Maria was touched. She bent down to pick up one of the wooden toys that was so lovingly created to amuse the baby. She rolled it in her fingers as if trying to glean a bit of paternal affection from the toy, the kind she had never known. It made her feel sad, cheated. But at the same time she could feel her admiration for Beau rising to a new level as she noticed the fine craftsmanship of the figurine.

"How sweet," she murmured, not wanting Langdon to read her emotions. "Wherever did he learn to carve so well?"

"In the New World, a man must be resourceful in order to survive."

She put the toy back and stood up then. "Is it so crude over there?" She sat down on a hammock and looked at Langdon entreatingly. He saw her interest, took off his hat, and sat in the opposite hammock.

"I suppose it is for newcomers but not for the likes of us, men born in the New World. It's all we know. Life in London seems so crowded and dirty and . . . well . . . foul-smelling, if you will. What I mean is, Carolina is so vast and untouched by man . . . so unspoiled. Especially on the frontier where we spend most of our time, being trappers by trade. As you'll soon realize, life in the wild can be quite comfortable if you're with someone who knows how to do it. Like Beau. He's better at it than I, really, but then he's had so much more experience with the natives."

The mere mention of natives made her eyes shine with a kind of horrified wonder.

"Don't be alarmed, my lady. The tribes are really quite civilized in their own way. You'll see. Beau will show you. He's a linguist, you know, speaks seven tribal languages as well as French and Spanish. That's what enabled him to become so familiar with the tribes. He can talk to them . . . communicate with them. All I know is a bit of Savannah and some Sanchee."

He took a moment to demonstrate the language to her. Maria found the sound of it choppy and inconsistent. More like grunts than words.

"You could not have found a better guide into the New World than Beau Gardiner. He is highly revered over there . . . is perhaps the most respected man in Carolina. He knows the land like a man knows the feel of his boots. He'll teach you so much if you let him, show you a country full of vistas so beautiful it'll steal your breath away. Believe me, once you get over the strangeness of it, you'll love it the way we do. And rest assured, Beau will take good care of you. He's a good man despite the bitterness he's given to since the—"

Langdon abruptly stopped himself, looked away from the confusion on her face. He sighed, muttered something under his breath that sounded like, "This will never work . . ."

"I beg your pardon, Mr. Miles."

"Oh, call me Langdon, miss," he said, flinging himself into a different subject. "I know it's not considered proper in Europe but we're not nearly as formal in Carolina."

Maria could confirm this by everything she'd read about New World men. English explorers described this new breed of white man as being quite arrogant in nature, indefatigable in work and play, exceptionally dependent upon weapons, and given to debauchery of all kinds. They consumed alcohol in enormous quantities, which was supplied by an infinite number of dramshops. It was said that for every church erected in the New World the men built three taverns. Their excuse was the unavailability of fresh milk and of water that was too laden with minerals. In six weeks time, Maria realized, the New World was going to be her world.

"Of course," she said to Langdon, smiling graciously, "if this is your custom, then please do address me as Maria."

"I'm honored to do so." He stood up, nervous again, put his hat back on and went to the door. "Why don't you try to get some rest. I'll see what's keeping Beau."

Maria tried to keep her thoughts still and busied herself by preparing for bed. She wasn't sure if it was proper to wear a nightdress around two strange men, so she donned an old shift instead. She tested the hammock by lying in it to see how easily it swung from side to side. Any movement too far in either direction would send her tumbling to the floor, so she collected herself in the center of the canvas sling and lay there as stiff as a block of wood.

She closed her eyes and the worries came at once. By now, her father knew she was missing. How would he explain this to a ballroom full of royal guests? He would be livid at the embarrassment she had caused him in front of his blueblood friends. The idea of his rage scared the wits from her. If he found her, the consequences would likely leave her maimed for life.

Maria started praying again, losing herself in fervent words. Before long, the gentle pitching of the ship, the tender breathing of the nearby babe, began to calm her. Once or twice Matthew stirred in his cradle, sucked his hand, cooed to himself, then yawned himself back to sleep. Maria had had little exposure to infants and found his little noises to be oddly comforting, like a tender lullaby. Slowly, her exhausted spirits began to drift into the same innocent rest.

Beau leaned over the rail, beyond the glow of the deck lanterns. Clothed entirely in black, only his face was visible in the darkness. "I tell you, she dropped to the ground not five feet from where I was hiding. What would you have me do, Lang, let her run off?"

"But what you're doing is so dangerous! Vandenburgh is a powerful man. He won't be so easily blackmailed. Besides, what if he finds us—"

"He won't," Beau interrupted quietly. "He has a houseful of notable guests tonight. He's not about to tell them his daughter ran away. He'll lie, contrive some kind of excuse to spare any scandal. He won't get the ransom note until the morning, and by then we'll be safely at sea."

Captain Zachariah Deane propped his short frame against the rail beside Beau, his leathery skin wrinkling around a quick and easy grin. His narrow eyes shone like a pair of shiny black beads. "I'm ready to shove off just as soon as my man gets back. We sent him to return the coach and hire a messenger for the note. He's got plenty of coin with him. Gonna make some young lad real happy tonight, he is, thinking he just landed himself a fortune!"

"What do you think he'll do when he gets the note?" Langdon persisted.

"Nothing," Beau said, and Langdon looked startled. Beau gave him a sidelong glance, then returned his gaze to the black tide. "If I judge him correctly, he won't do anything . . . at least not at first."

"But this is his daughter, Beau! His only child! Surely he'll—"

"Not Vandenburgh," Zachariah scoffed. "I know the likes of men like him. His kind keep quiet about affairs like this. They don't want no one to know. Humph! If I figure him right, he's gonna lie about it tonight, then get caught when we deliver the next note—"

He waited for a sailor to collect a pile of rope from the bow before continuing. No one aboard knew who the woman was but the three of them. To everyone else, she was Matthew's governess and perhaps, as many of them seemed to think, a woman for Beau. They could think what they wanted. If anything, it would ensure Maria complete safety while aboard. There wasn't a man alive who would cross Beau Gardiner.

The sailor left. Zachariah looked at Langdon and smiled craftily. "You see, we're gonna deliver the second note a little different from this one. The next one gets published in the London *Chronicle*."

"The press? How are you going to arrange that?"

"Money," Beau said simply. "There's one thing you can count on with the aristocracy, Lang. Greed. It works every time."

Langdon paused, searched for some new argument. "What about bringing her so close to Charles Towne? You can get away with hiding her identity here, but sooner or later she'll be found out if you—"

"I won't be anywhere near Charles Towne," Beau interrupted. "I'm not ready to let anyone know I'm alive, not for a long while. Zachariah will land us off Cape Fear, fifty miles downwind of the settlement. From there, I'll take her to father's camp on the Savannah."

"But the camp is only a few miles from Cussitah. Every man on the frontier comes there to trade for supplies from the Creek. Eventually, word will spread, filter into Charles Towne . . ."

"If I ask them, the Creek will make sure no one passes through my land."

"You've thought of everything, haven't you?" Langdon was not yet willing to resign himself to what they were doing. "What about Maria, eh? Have you thought of her? You see how innocent she is. Don't you feel even a bit guilty about deceiving her like this?"

This made Beau turn around. Beneath the brim of his hat, his shaded eyes turned hard, cold. "Is she any more innocent than my mother . . . Julia . . . Louisa?"

Zachariah looked up sharply. Beau never spoke about what happened to his family, rarely even mentioned their names.

"Don't ask me to feel guilt right now because I can't." He turned away, scowling at the dark water. When he spoke again, the harshness had left his voice. "But you know me better than to think I would direct any cruelty at a maid as tender as Maria. She won't tell me what he did to make her leave like this but it's obvious the woman is profoundly terrified of the man. God knows I'd tell her the truth if I could but she's so bewildered and hurt and frightened right now. If I thought she hated him enough, I'd ask her to help us but she doesn't, Lang. Like you said, the maid is too tender for such foul sentiment."

"Yes." Langdon sighed, finally joined his friend at the rails, and studied the water lapping against the hull. "I suppose you're right. The truth will only terrify her more."

"Precisely. If she ran from Vandenburgh, she could run from me so let's just leave it the way it is, eh? Think of tonight's uncanny coincidence in the shrubbery as a stroke of enormous luck and use it accordingly. For tonight, Arthur thinks she ran away. It's a perfect cover . . . let's us get away under a cloak of temporary obscurity."

Langdon didn't say anything for a long time. "Where do I fit into this?"

"You're my link between the frontier and Charles Towne. I'll send messages to the traders and Zach through you, then bring me the results of each step of the scheme."

"I'd rather be with you on the Savannah."

"You'll be more help to me in Charles Towne." Beau looked at him then, and patiently waited for his nod of agreement. "Good man." He rewarded Langdon with a friendly clap on the back. "You'll have plenty of time to sport your bow on the frontier, Lang, days full of good hunting!"

Langdon tried to be cheered by the prospect of months-long gaming. "I'm just worried about you being alone so much out there . . . where there are so many memories of you and Matt and Michael."

Beau looked away with the usual quiet pain carving itself into the stark bones of his face. "It's better than going back to that house." His head dropped as if it was suddenly too heavy. "I don't know if I can ever go in there again."

Neither of his companions responded. Zachariah didn't look so smug anymore as he awkwardly shifted in his boots. No one ever knew what to say to Beau about the murder of his family. It was a tragedy of such enormous proportions it left everyone feeling uncomfortable.

Beau could sense it now, the anxiety, a kind of smothering tension. They were frustrated, he knew, always trying to say something comforting but never quite finding the right words. No one dared tamper with this tragedy for fear of making things worse. Their reaction only enhanced Beau's loneliness. At times, it made him feel like some kind of two-headed monster.

"Very well," Langdon conceded. "Just be easy on the girl, eh? The New World and the way we live will be very strange to her."

"Don't worry. I have no intention of punishing her the way Arthur punished my family for the traders' deeds. I'll never stoop to such despicable levels."

"I didn't think so."

"There he is now!" Zachariah pointed to the

messenger skipping up the gangplank. With just a nod at the captain from across the deck, they knew the ransom note had been delivered.

They launched within minutes. Langdon and Beau stood in the bow and watched the lights of London slowly melt away until the city was just a tiny yellow pinpoint in the night.

They were committed now. There was no turning back.

"God help us," Langdon breathed at the last sight of Europe.

"We're not the ones who need the help, Lang. It's him who needs help right now," Beau said.

Langdon looked at his life-long companion, who stared at the distant shore as if seeing Arthur's face out there in the night. How could he be so blasted confident?

But then he saw it, the hatred, the raw malice that Beau usually kept so well concealed.

"I'm going to crush him," Beau whispered in a voice so soft Langdon had to lean forward to hear it. "Break him . . . like he broke me."

"Don't say that, Beau. You're not broken."

Beau pulled down his hat and turned away. "You're right. I suppose dead men can't be broken, eh?" he said over his shoulder. His tall figure was slowly engulfed in the whirling folds of his pitch black cape as he disappeared belowdeck.

The *Savannah Wind*
April 2, 1674

"Paw-paw. Tokee."

"I see the turkey, son. Is he a big bird?"

"Big!"

"Shh! Uncle Langdon's sleeping."

"Wangon."

"Open up now. If you want to be a big bird, you have to eat."

"Shhhhh."

"Smart alek."

"Ha!"

Dawn's first light floated through the porthole like a pale pink streamer, a thin band of illumination that seemed to fill the squat little cabin with a layer of rose-colored fairy dust.

"Gobba . . . gobba . . . gobba . . ."

"Swallow, keeta. That's right. You're Papa's keeta."

Maria looked across the room, in the direction of the barely audible whispers.

Beau was sitting in the inside corner of the cabin, away from the drafty porthole. His figure seemed broad and hulking in the deep shadows; or perhaps he just seemed gigantic in comparison to the smaller figure perched on his lap. Beau was sitting cross-legged on the floor atop a woven straw mat. His hair was untethered and hung to his shoulders in dense mahogany waves that partially obscured his face. He'd changed his clothes, and the only place she'd ever seen the kind of attire he wore now was in sketches of American natives. Animal skin, soft and fawn colored, draped him in a thigh-length tunic that was plain and undecorated except for the leather ties that cinched it at the wrist. His leggings were of the same make, hugging the powerfully muscled contours of his long legs and disappearing into a pair of soft-soled boots that were laced to his knees.

His baby son was similarly garbed in a bunting of the same material. She could see the sack was meant to be tied shut at the hem, but now it was open. Matthew's tiny feet pumped and kicked at the air between his father's thighs with great energy and enthusiasm, one of his booties undone and flapping off the tip of his toes.

She wondered now whether these people weren't

part savage. But Langdon had specifically told her they were French by origin. Concern made her look closer, to see that their features lacked the severe contours of the natives she'd seen pictured in pamphlets. No, their faces had the finer bone structure of Europeans and neither father nor son had even the vaguest hint of red in his skin. They were white men all right, just a brand new breed of them. New World people.

Suddenly she realized why the ship was rolling and pitching the way it was. They were in sail. They had already left England. She'd slept straight through the launch.

"You have the fiercest turkey in the land, son."

Matthew waved the wooden turkey figurine at his father, then poked it into the place where Beau's V-necked tunic exposed his chest hair. "Ow!" the boy gasped, clapped his hands, and did it again when he saw how he was amusing his sire.

Beau beamed at his boy's antics, hiding none of his pride. "Silly bird," he murmured in a deep, throaty whisper that somehow managed to convey tenderness when directed at Matthew. "Papa is going to kill the turkey and eat him for dinner."

"Oohh," Matthew said, laying his head back on Beau's arm and seeming content to just stare at his father.

Beau seized the opportunity to get more food in him, quickly delivering three more mouthfuls from a plate on the mat next to him. She noticed that every time Beau looked away from Matthew, the child reached up and touched his face to bring his attention back.

It was moving, the way they were with each other, their love so open and unguarded and natural. She almost felt guilty watching them, as if she was invading something private and precious meant only for a father and his son. But she couldn't look away.

Beau took a cloth from a dish of water and wiped the food from Matthew's chin. His hand looked so big and clumsy on the baby's face, yet somewhere in his masculine awkwardness there was a touch just gentle enough for an infant's delicate skin. Suddenly Beau looked wildly attractive to Maria, more compelling at this moment than any man had ever been. She didn't know love could look so pure and natural on a man's face, that it could fill up his eyes with a soft, warm radiance.

The sight of it brought a surge of emotion into her throat. It tasted sweet but at the same time, so very bitter.

Longing. It bloomed out of her like a crocus through winter snow. Maria had an overwhelming need to know what a parent's love felt like. She lay there watching it unfold, yet she knew she was too far away ever to be touched by it.

After all these sorry years, Maria could not remember a time when she wanted her father's love as much as she did now. It made her smart with pain, sharp enough to bring tears to her eyes as pitiful memories came to her. *"Surely you don't expect me to play the role of the loving father, do you?"* *"If it's love you want, find a man who'll give it but don't plague me with such tomfoolery . . ."*

Father, why have you done this to me?

She wanted to cry for that stranded little girl in her who was still standing on the convent steps, waiting for a coach that would never come.

Maria rolled over, buried her face in the hammock and, ever so quietly, she wept.

London, England
The Same Day

"It should be known that the Lady Vandenburgh has been taken against her will and is being held until the following terms for her release are met: first, the total of all Vandenburgh assets, both here and abroad, shall be liquidated and the cash value rendered into my hands; second, a public confession must be made to all Crown subjects in order that they may know Arthur Vandenburgh brought this cruel fate upon his own flesh and blood by no other hand save his own. He is to confess all criminal activities he initiated, particularly those deeds heinous enough to cause an enemy to resort to such extreme measures in pursuit of justice.

"When he has spoken the truth to the people and delivered to me the fruits of his sins, Lady Vandenburgh shall be speedily returned to her estate.

"Until then, she lives ever closer to death,

and every day you delay will bring her nearer
to a punishment she cannot possibly deserve.
The April Fool

Gaylord finished reading the note and turned to Vandenburgh, who was pacing furiously. "Methinks the lady has been kidnapped, m'lord."

Arthur threw him a withering glance. "Blast that girl! She's been nothing but trouble since the day she arrived!"

"Not meaning you any disrespect, sir, may I question why you vent your anger upon the girl instead of this man who labels himself a fool."

Arthur whirled away from the fireplace and leveled the full force of his outrage at Gaylord. "Because she embarrassed me in front of everyone last night!" he thundered. "You saw me standing up there in front of everyone like a dribbling fool . . . trying to fabricate some story about her suddenly taking ill . . ."

"No one questioned you, m'lord. They all believed it!"

"I don't care where the devil she is, Gaylord, but I can tell you this: she better stay there because if I get my hands on her, I'll kill her myself!"

The man was senseless with rage. Gaylord could see he was temporarily incapable of addressing the much more serious matter of the ransom note. While he waited for Arthur to calm down, Gaylord read the note again, studied the handwriting, tried to think of who had been slighted by Arthur to this degree.

Lord! It could be anyone. Arthur had enemies everywhere. He hadn't made a single business transaction without resorting to some illegal method. He'd cheated half the world.

Gaylord put the note in his pocket and fetched himself another drink. What bothered him the most was how cleverly this incident was handled, while they all thought Maria had run off. It was the first thing Arthur had said when he discovered her missing, that she did this to spite him because she disagreed with his plans for her. He'd cursed her so wickedly that Maureen had burst into tears and run out of the room. Even Jonathan was horrified by the way Arthur spoke about his own daughter. Worse, he refused to authorize a search for her. Gaylord was secretly relieved because had Arthur found her last night, he might well have killed her.

And now this.

"We must address this note, m'lord. It puts you in a very bad situation."

"Oh, to hell with it! The man is indeed a fool if he thinks I'll give in to his terms!"

"But how are we going to explain Maria's continued absence? People will get suspicious if they never see her attending any social functions."

"Tell them her health took a turn for the worse and she's been sent away to a drier climate."

"And if she turns up dead?"

"Then I'll don my mourning suit and give her a funeral fit for a queen. And all the while, I'll keep London humming with news of the most intensive manhunt ever conducted for my daughter's killer!"

Arthur was beginning to like his own ideas. For a moment, his eyes sparkled with zest. But then he sat down at his desk, put a pinch of snuff under his nostrils and inhaled deeply. "And while they sit buzzing like a swarm of bees I'll be getting on with my own affairs, which is precisely what I intend to do now." He picked up his quill and started writing.

"M'lord?"

Arthur looked up. "What is it?"

"The note, sir."

"Forget the note, Gaylord. We've more important business to tend to."

Gaylord stared at him in complete astonishment. "But, sir, your daughter's life could be at stake."

"For her sake, I hope it isn't." He went back to writing.

"Then you don't intend to do anything about this?"

"No, Gaylord, I do not. And stop looking so fretful. The best way to handle this ransom note is to do nothing. To run around like frantic cuckolds is precisely what her captor wants. When he's ready to get reasonable, perhaps I'll discuss his . . . er . . . problems. Now then, this is a list of matters you should tend while I'm in Paris next month . . ."

Gaylord climbed into his coach and eagerly shut the door against the sight of the Vandenburgh mansion.

He was starting to hate the place. It was evil. His entire relationship with Arthur was wrong, as it forced him to do things he would never have even considered for another client.

Like murder.

He looked out the window, scanning the quiet Sunday sidewalks of London. He thought of the lovely lady who had sat across from him at dinner only two nights ago and wondered where she was now, if she was suffering at this very moment.

He wondered if anyone else really cared.

The *Savannah Wind*

Beau stood beside Maria's hammock, listened to the tiny noises she made beneath her fur cover, and realized she wasn't having a bad dream.

She was crying.

He felt suddenly inept and clumsy, the way he always did around weeping women. They were such delicate creatures, much too sensitive for a man like him, especially when they were distraught. He was always afraid he'd say the wrong thing and accidentally shatter them.

He looked at Langdon for help, saw that the man was awake and aware of Maria's whimpers. But he didn't offer any suggestions, just looked at Beau in a way that reminded him who was responsible for Maria Vandenburgh.

He was. Bringing her here had been his idea.

Langdon got up and padded barefoot to the

hatch, grabbed his moccasins on the way out and shut the door behind him.

Maria stirred under the pelt, sniffled and burrowed her face deeper into the hammock. She looked so tiny under there, curled in a ball, hugging herself in despair. Whatever private torment she suffered made her pretty auburn curls shiver as they draped over the edge of the hammock. It wrenched his heart to see her suffer like this, the way it had last night when he'd watched her huddle against the wall of the house.

Beau tucked Matthew around his hip and sat down on the edge of her hammock.

She stopped crying immediately, her body tensing beneath the coverlet.

Matthew took his finger out of his mouth and pointed at her, his eyes full of wonder as if gazing upon a creature from another planet. His lips formed a silent "oh!" as he watched her head lift, her hands hurriedly wipe her eyes just before she turned over and sat up.

A perfectly matched set of pale blue eyes settled full upon her, wide and wondering.

"Forgive me," she murmured, "I was thinking of Father." Just before her head bent, Beau saw her face fill with hurt and anguish, could almost feel the pain she tried desperately to blink away.

Arthur. What a despicable mess he made out of every life he touched.

No wonder she looked so dejected, cowering in a place too dark to find a way out. He was genuinely sorry for her, but what right had he to comfort this innocent young girl who would one day be wounded by his own hand? She had already been betrayed in the worst possible way, by her own parent. She didn't deserve this, to be led unsuspecting into yet another cruel betrayal.

He should tell her the truth, that he wasn't the kind and helpful friend he appeared to be, that he was using her to exact his own revenge.

But then the memory of the murders flashed across his brain. Blood dribbling down the walls, dark red pools of it oozing out from under crumpled bodies.

He shot off the hammock, his insides shaken and shuddering, his hands cold as ice. With his back to Maria, he fought off the images, shoved them into that dark place he kept sealed in the back of his mind.

"He's a monster, Maria," he said from across the room, his voice low and harsh, "a damned monster."

She didn't say anything. When he regained his composure, he glanced back at her, saw how her wet eyes begged him to convince her of Arthur's worthlessness.

He wanted to, especially when he came to the galling realization that he wasn't the only person Arthur had left reeling in an empty void that used to be a life. He had done that to Maria, too, his own daughter. What a morbid connection Beau felt with her, as though a thick black cord of pain linked their broken hearts. They would never fully recover from what Arthur had done to them.

"I don't mean to act so undistinguished," Maria said.

"Don't apologize for being human, Maria." He reached out his hand, caught the edge of her chin on his fingertips and gently lifted her face. "Look at me," he demanded quietly. "Any man who could forsake his own child is not a man. That is the way of animals, not humans."

"But he could be a good man if not for his greed. It consumes him, ruins him . . ."

"You're making excuses for him. Not even greed can cut the heart out of a man who is truly good. You waste your tears on him. Forget him."

"He's my father!"

"Since when?"

She pushed his hand away, averted her eyes.

"I didn't mean that as an insult. Why do you take it as such?"

She didn't answer, merely bit her bottom lip in response.

"You're embarrassed by his treatment, aren't you?"

She thought for a moment, then nodded her head, causing a flood of auburn curls to topple forward, temporarily veiling her face. He wanted to see her when he made his point, and once again reached for her until his palm found the side of her face.

Her skin felt like wet velvet in his hand. It disconcerted him for a moment, how fragile she was, how silky and luxurious her hair felt as it slid between his callused fingers. He should feel awkward when touching such an exquisite creature. His hands were accustomed to coarser maids from a different world than hers.

But he didn't.

No, he liked it, the warm sensuality of her. Touching her made him feel something deep inside, in a private place of his that had been dead for a long time.

Once again her eyes lifted, so shy but somehow managing to look sultry and inviting to him. It made him wonder if she was as aware of him as he was of her at this moment.

"You needn't blame yourself for his neglect, Maria."

"No, but he did," she said, her plush pink mouth looking far too sweet. "You don't understand . . . my mother died when I was born and she was the only woman he ever loved. He never got over it. That's why he sent me away. I don't think he could bear to look at me because of it. If she'd lived, he might have been a different man."

"You don't really believe that, do you?"

She raised her eyebrows in question.

"If he were a decent man in his heart, he would have cherished you for the part of your mother that lives in you . . . the way I cherish the part of Julia that lives in our son. Your father was wrong to treat you as he did, dead wrong. But you only further the wrong by believing his treatment is a reflection of yourself."

She was hardly even aware of the way she

winced. But Beau saw it, knew he had grazed a sensitive area.

"The man's a fool," he muttered bitterly. "Forsaking this beautiful creature he created with his ugly loins when you are surely the only aspect of his life that bears mention. Any father who would trade his own lamb for a pile of paper and metal is certainly incapable of sound judgment, don't you think?" He saw the barest semblance of a smile flicker across her mouth. "There now, we've more important things to do with our lives than waste them on the likes of him."

He realized he was still touching her and quickly withdrew his hand, causing a sudden awkwardness between them. This conversation had become a bit too personal for strangers.

"Well, I suppose you're hungry."

She nodded, studying him with a kind of bewildered curiosity.

"Mind him for me and I'll fetch you a tray."

He plopped Matthew on her hammock and made a hasty retreat through the hatch.

"Matthew! No! No!" Maria reached him just before he stuffed a fistful of soap in his mouth. "Heavens! But your belly will ache for days." She uncurled his fist and wiped the soap from his hand. He just sat there gurgling and grinning and sinking himself ever deeper into her heart.

She adored him too much to scold him.

"Off with you! Go play with your toys." He crawled under his cradle and let out a shriek of delight before making his selection.

Of course, he picked the turkey. It was his favorite.

"Tokee!" he squealed excitedly.

Maria sighed, resettled in the hammock, and resumed folding a pile of diapers.

She was busy these days. Caring for a healthy baby was more work than she'd ever imagined. There was a daily bath, three feedings, two snacks, countless changes of diapers and an endless supply of soiled ones to launder.

She should have taken Beau's advice about the diapers. She could still see the distaste on his face when he said, "Just do what I do and toss the worst of them out the porthole." Maria giggled at the thought of Matthew's diapers washing ashore all over Europe. Men! How could they be so tough and squeamish at the same time?

She looked up just as Matthew crawled out the hatch to gallop his turkey up the companionway. "Oh, no, you don't!" She ran after him, retrieved him back into the safety of the cabin for the hundredth time that day. She should know better than to take her eyes off him for even a moment while he was awake. Attending him this last month had taught her many things, but the most important was how quickly he could move—just like a jackrabbit.

Especially in the morning.

Matthew awoke like a sudden explosion of energy. He couldn't get anywhere fast enough. She often had to crawl after him on the floor to spoon enough breakfast into him before he'd refuse to open his mouth. He was teething, so every object in his path was stuffed into his mouth. She once caught him gagging on her rosary beads, and another time reached him just before he swallowed a mouthful of lamp oil. If he wasn't searching for things to chew, he was busy exploring his surroundings. She never knew a child could be so fast on his knees. He could crawl almost as fast as she could walk. Until his midday nap, Maria was constantly on the run, chasing him, playing his favorite games, washing him, changing him.

Beau thought she should be sterner with him, at least raise her voice a little when telling him no, but the child was just too lovable for discipline. He was such a happy little soul, laughing at the slightest provocation, conducting long and ebullient dialogues of complete gibberish. He loved being cuddled, kissed, and he openly sought her affections more and more as they grew accustomed to each other.

Those were her favorite times, when Matthew's energy would wane and he'd climb into her lap, rub his face on her breast, and snuggle close to her warmth. No one had ever done that to her before. Her life had been totally devoid of human touch until she met this loving little boy. And even more wonderful was when he fell asleep in her arms, hanging limp and trusting and completely at the mercy of her care.

For the first time in her life, someone needed her.

Thoughts of Dabney Street fell away until those black days seemed to belong to someone else's past. Not hers. Her life was so full and purposeful now.

Another day's light began to wane. Maria put away her mending and began straightening the cabin for the night. With Matthew contentedly napping in the cradle, she tended to herself the way she always did in anticipation of the mens' return. For the hundredth time she longed for a looking glass. Without one, she couldn't dress her hair, only braid it or leave it loose and hope it looked tidy.

Langdon brought her meal, which she always tried to eat before Matthew woke from his nap. Maria was secretly disappointed it wasn't Beau. Only once or twice had Beau brought her meal, sharing it with her during one of the few moments of the day when she could be found alone. In fact, she had rarely been alone with Beau since her first morning aboard, and never again did they share such an intimate conversation. It had left a closeness between them that was evident only in the way they felt around each other, the way he looked at her when he thought she wasn't aware.

Excitement.

Maria felt it the minute he walked into the room, a vague kind of tension that always left her wondering whether it was a good or bad feeling.

"If these winds hold, Zach thinks we'll reach Cape Fear in a fortnight."

Maria looked up from her tasteless pork, startled by the news. "But I thought it would be another month yet."

Langdon swiped at his wind-blown hair and heaped a pile of rice on a wooden spoon. "We tacked southwest this morning, which means we've reached the other side of the Atlantic." He grinned with genuine pleasure. "Our side!"

She was careful not to let Langdon see her apprehension. She knew he longed for his home. It was evident in the way he spun tales about the New World, as though he were describing the garden of paradise. He was utterly smitten with the place.

"I should start paying more attention to all those stories you tell me about the New World."

"Whatever for? You'll be with Beau."

"But what about you? Won't you be there?"

"No. I'm going to Charles Towne." He winked at her appalled expression. "I'm flattered that you'll miss me."

"Don't be such a tease."

"How she wounds me with her indifference!"

"Langdon!"

"But I'll hasten to rejoin you at the camp just as soon as I can get there."

"Why can't you come with us?"

"Because I haven't seen my family in months, Maria."

"Of course," she murmured sheepishly, "how selfish of me."

"You're forgiven." Again he winked, swallowed another hearty mouthful. "Beau was busy all day with the preparations. It's the most life I've seen in him for weeks."

Genuine worry crept into her voice. "Has he slept at all?"

Langdon shook his head dismally. "I keep hoping Carolina will snap him out of this . . . bring some whit of peace to his soul. God knows, he could use some."

A heavy silence enveloped the cabin as Maria

waited, hoping Langdon might elaborate on the subject of Beau's poor condition. After a few minutes, she realized he wouldn't; he never did. The source of Beau's suffering was some evil secret the two guarded between them. All she was ever told was that Beau was mourning the loss of loved ones. They never said how many, what happened, why he had those terrible dreams sometimes that made him avoid sleep for days afterward.

The time was fast approaching when someone would have to explain Beau's unusual behavior, the dark side of this soft-spoken New World man. Although he was always kind and well mannered with Maria, Beau was profoundly grief-stricken, given to periods of the most silent and bitter brooding she'd ever encountered. Nothing could penetrate the black shell he wrapped himself in after one of his nightmares. Not even Langdon knew exactly what those dreams were about. Beau never said. He didn't have to. Maria could sense the enormous tragedy that haunted him, could see how it tore at Langdon to watch his friend suffer alone, unable to comfort him.

"He's exhausted, Maria. Why don't we try to sneak some sleeping powders in his ale tonight, eh?"

"You know what happened the last time."

Beau had caught them, tossed the mug out the porthole, and had gone topside where he could be awake in peace. He didn't get angry with them or even look at them as he quietly took up his cloak and left the cabin. They didn't see him again until the following night, when his need for time with Matthew brought him below. Not a word was mentioned about the episode as Matthew spun his wondrous magic over Beau, enchanting him away from everything until they were the only two people in the world.

Matthew was just beginning to coo himself awake when Beau popped open the hatch and came into the cabin. Langdon was right. He looked weary, his eyelids heavy, his movements slow and leaden as he passed between the hammocks.

"Princess," he said in greeting, his voice gruff.

She liked when he called her princess. It was a term of endearment, and although he never said so, she guessed it was Beau's way of reminding her that she was important no matter what her father thought.

"He's just waking up now," she said, quickly straightening her plait and smoothing a few wrinkles out of her lap. She stole a glance around the room to be sure it was in order, not that Beau would ever chide her. He had never demonstrated even a hint of displeasure about her services.

"Paw!" Matthew called sleepily.

Beau bent over the cradle, the tired lines of his face easing somewhat as he gazed at his son. "Were you a good bird today?"

"He was perfectly behaved," Maria said. She took one last mouthful of rice and put her tray aside.

"You always say that," Beau murmured over his shoulder. "The truth is, he's spoiled."

As if in proof, Matthew's chubby hands rose into the air and waved impatiently at Beau.

"In a minute. Let me wash first."

"Paw!" Matthew was indignant, pushed himself up and peered at his father over the edge of the cradle. "Mafooo!"

Maria caught a whiff of fresh salt air when Beau passed by. The topside winds had left his mahogany mane tousled around his face despite the tether that cinched the bulk of it in place. He bent wearily over the water basin, his eyes lazy and vague until a splash of water made them pop open. He blinked, shook himself hard, and sent a spray of water into the air around his head. Then he sighed, leaned heavily against the wall, and mopped his face and hair.

"Paw-Paw!" Matthew was standing up now, holding on to the cradle edge and bouncing up and down with great eagerness. His huge, saucerlike eyes followed Beau's every move.

Beau winked at him.

Matthew let out a piercing squeal and bounced until the cradle shook.

"Is it true we're going to land soon?"

Beau turned to Maria, and his eyes swept over her in a way that made her feel as though he saw every thread in her seams. "Two weeks perhaps, not much longer."

"And Langdon isn't going with us?"

Langdon couldn't resist teasing Maria. "She was absolutely devastated when I told her that . . . heartbroken actually."

"Oh, go on!" She giggled, putting her hand out to keep the cradle from teetering.

Something close to a smile whispered at Beau's lips as he enjoyed their banter. "He misses his mama." Langdon hurled a spoon at him. Beau ducked, chuckling under his breath when it hit the wall just behind him. "Good shot man. You've not lost your aim." He reached for the heavy leather belt around his hips, snapped it open, and let it drop to the floor. "But you mustn't be offended if he fails to rejoin us in good time. No maid makes him hurry from his mother."

"That's not true! I thoroughly enjoyed Malinda's company for a long while . . . nearly a year!"

"Yes, but you didn't marry her after all. She was comely, Lang. You let her get away too easily. I might have fought a bit harder for that one."

"Bah! The tax collector charmed her with his power and position."

"Humph! Position perhaps, but definitely not power. If I recall correctly, you got barely a sour word from him when you resisted your fines for another year."

"He knew better than to press the point. He stole the woman I might have married in order to escape the fines!"

Beau turned to Matthew again, hoisted him out of the cradle and lifted him in the air until his back touched the ceiling. A broad grin finally bloomed through the quiet exhaustion on Beau's face as he watched his son flail in complete pleasure. "You weren't going to marry Malinda any more than you were going to pay those bachelor fines."

"Bachelor fines? Do you mean they punish you for not being married in Carolina?"

"Every year," Beau said, taking the hammock Langdon had abandoned and stretching out on it. He propped Matthew on his stomach. "Settlers are supposed to proliferate themselves, Maria, not sap the resources of the community without returning something of benefit. The privilege of reaping what one doesn't sow is the exclusive right of His Majesty, King Charles." He glanced over at her, his expression becoming mischievous as he drawled, "But of course, we're not settlers, so what do we care about their bloody taxes, eh?"

"Humph!" Langdon scoffed. "They should pay us for saving their poor starving colonists."

"But didn't England send them food . . . supplies?"

"Of course, but the first three ships ran afoul on the shoals and were wrecked at sea," Langdon said. "It was almost eighteen months before a ship managed to navigate itself through the mouth of the bay. By then, they had already turned to us for help and we gave it, of course. What else could we do . . . let the poor people starve to death? So we gave them food, helped them clear the land, plant, and then, eventually, how to make a very fine living in the trapping and trading of fur."

Maria put her tray down. "Which is what started all the trouble between England and Charles Towne, eh?"

"Precisely. They intended to mine the fur themselves and had no idea we were already there, already mining it and exporting it through the Spanish port of Saint Ellens, which is a mere hundred miles south of the settlement. In other words, it was relatively easy to access the world market. We'd been doing it for years!"

Langdon looked at Beau for a comment, but none came.

The man was sound asleep.

Maria and Langdon grinned in triumph, hurriedly took Matthew away and spent the rest of the evening barely whispering for fear they'd disturb Beau's desperately needed rest.

Langdon continued his explanation of how the Charles Towne Traders came to be so notorious in the world of fur marketing. She sat enthralled with his story of how four inconspicuous wilderness families managed to hold the most powerful king on earth in a vise. They were in complete control of what the Crown wanted. Carolina fur. The richest pelts in the world. The raiment of kings. And King Charles couldn't touch a bale of it without the four original white trappers who just happened to be the men responsible for mining it and selling it.

None of this might have happened if not for those three hapless ships running afoul with such desperately needed provisions. The colonists, panic-stricken and nearly starved, were ripe to be redeemed by the only other white men in the area. The Charles Towne Traders were stout descendants of the French who had come to trap the Saint Lawrence two generations before, and being Christian besides, they didn't hesitate to lend their assistance to the three hundred stranded colonists. It was in those earliest days that the settlers allegiance was fused to the traders, a bond that to this day seemed impossible to break.

The traders had not only saved their lives but taught the colonists how to trap and trade in what was already a thriving avenue of export between the natives of the interior, the four white families, and the Spanish of Saint Ellens.

Not only did they survive, they started to make money.

Lots of money.

More than anyone dreamed.

By the time those three gale-battered English vessels arrived with provisions nearly eighteen months later, the settlers didn't need them anymore. They'd made their own way, and it was far grander than what England had planned.

The Crown intended to have its settlers mine the fur and ship it to England, where the seven powerful proprietors of the colony could sell it at an enormous profit. In exchange, they'd give the settlers barrels of salt-pork and other necessary provisions.

Maria thought such a lopsided deal had probably been arranged by her father, who was the chancellor proprietor of Carolina. She was thrilled to hear that the settlers had refused the puny deal, unwilling to give up Spanish doubloons and Persian gold in exchange for pork.

Furious at their impertinence, the proprietors

started creating regulations meant to hinder the settlers' activity with the traders. Any settler who sold his fur through the traders' channels was considered a traitor to the king. Soldiers were sent to police the port of Charles Towne. Navigation Acts were levied, so that any ship caught sailing within a fifty mile radius of the shore was subject to search and seizure. There were bachelor fines, stipends and taxes galore that did little more than enrage the colonists.

The four original white trappers had become a global phenomenon. These inconspicuous trappers were now known throughout Europe as the Charles Towne Traders. The names of Gardiner, Miles, Edinburgh, and Moore had become notorious, and to this day, the Charles Towne Traders remained unstoppable. They were not Crown subjects. They could not be arrested, hung as traitors, fined, or taxed. Against them, England was completely powerless.

Langdon's tale delighted Maria. Anyone who stood up to her father was a champion in her eyes, especially the man who was sleeping so soundly in the hammock across from her own.

Beau hadn't stirred an inch by the time she climbed into bed. He was still in the exact same position, on his back, a pair of long legs open and sprawled, one arm dangling over the edge of the hammock. His sleep was so deep and sound she barely heard him breathe. How serene he looked just then, the expression on his face relaxed and unguarded.

She fell asleep, and wasn't sure how many hours had passed before a strange sound in the cabin brought her awake. She lay listening in the darkness for the noise to come again, wondered if it had been real or a dream or just a new creak in the old wooden seams of the *Savannah Wind*.

There. It came again, a low guttural moan, so hoarse and anguished it sent a shiver through her body. Then the sound faded, the cabin was quiet again except for the tread of Matthew's cradle legs rolling against the floor.

There was a flash of motion from the hammock across from her. Maria jumped, startled by the sight of Beau sitting upright in his sleep. His head pierced the narrow band of moonlight coming from the porthole, a splash of silver suddenly illuminating his upturned face.

He was soaked in sweat, his hair, his tunic, his skin. There was no expression on his face. Just shock. His eyes were open, glazed and blind, as if he was locked in some kind of horrified rapture. He was trembling so hard that sweat trickled down the sides of his face.

He frightened her, the way he looked, how hard and fast he was breathing, the relentless stare of his glassy eyes. Why didn't he move? She should help him, make it stop.

But then a shadow moved across him, temporarily blocking him from her view.

Langdon.

"Beau . . . come on . . . come around, man . . ."

He slung an arm behind Beau's neck, ever so slowly tilted his head backward and rapped on his temple.

Beau blinked once, twice, his dazed eyes finally settling on Langdon's face. A long rattling sigh flowed out of him. He didn't fight Langdon, who eased him back down into the hammock.

"You want a drink?"

Beau's response was slow in coming, but finally he shook his head and whispered, "Sorry . . . I woke you again . . ."

"Oh, for God's sake, you think I care about some lost sleep?" Langdon's whisper was harsh in the quiet. "If I could spare you just one of these godawful nights you have, it would make me feel enormously better. I can't stand this anymore."

Langdon retreated into the shadows near the hatch to collect a basin of water for his friend. She heard him sigh just before he returned to Beau.

Maria felt a wave of pity for Langdon. So many times he tried to make his friend talk about his deep emotional pain but to no avail. Beau just wasn't the kind of man who opened his heart easily.

But Langdon never gave up. Maria watched him put a basin of water on the floor and kneel beside the hammock.

"You're drenched, Beau."

"Give it to me." Beau took the rag and wiped his brow and face. His hand was still trembling noticeably. The face that turned toward Langdon was drawn and haggard now, his beautiful eyes seemed drained. "Thanks." He handed the rag back.

Langdon slapped it in the basin.

Beau sighed, turned away, and closed his eyes. For a long time, he didn't say anything. But then he spoke in a whisper so lifeless she almost couldn't hear it. "Who but a true friend would want to know this hell of mine?"

Langdon looked up. "I do," he said without hesitation.

Beau whispered with real feeling, "I know . . . and that's enough for me, Lang."

Maria felt a lump in her throat.

"These last months have been the worst of my life, Beau. I feel so helpless, so utterly inept . . . to help you . . . a man who could be my brother for all the years we've walked side by side on the same paths . . . yet you've gotten too far ahead and I can't seem to reach you . . ." Langdon stopped, his shoulders drooping a moment before he muttered dismally, "I grieve for them too, think of them everyday . . . but my soul aches not so much for them as it does for the one they left behind."

Them? Just how many people had died in Beau's past?

Maria felt a tear escape but she refused to move, to do anything that might interrupt them.

"We're with the Sanchee in the dream," Beau said, his voice harsh and rough yet so strangely quiet, as if some inner wall of resistance had broken and he no longer cared to save it. Langdon fell still, like a kneeling sculpture, completely spellbound by the sudden release of these long-awaited words.

"It's always the same. Night falls and we're in

the woods and I see the Sanchee faces across the fire . . . exactly as it was that night. We're all laughing and drinking and smoking fire weed . . . and then I hear it . . . from far away at first . . . their voices calling to me. I pretend I can't hear them, try to laugh harder, louder, to cover it, but their voices just keep getting closer . . . until they're beyond the firelight . . . right there in the woods . . . screaming at me . . . begging me to help."

"Oh, God!" Langdon groaned, covered his face.

"That's what I dream about, Lang, over and over again . . . the same thing . . . sitting out there laughing—" his voice cracked, choked off. He turned his face away but she could see he was clenching his teeth, his whole body coiled against the agony, "while they scream . . . and die . . ."

Maria was too stricken to move. Dear God, was she hearing right? She knew his kin were dead but never suspected they might have all died at the same time!

"That's it, isn't it, Beau . . . what tears you apart inside . . . what we were doing that night." Langdon cinched his friend's shoulders in a desperate grip. "You blame yourself for not being there to help them."

Beau winced. "Yes, that's what rips my guts out," he snarled, "what I was doing up there in the woods while they were dying such horrible deaths . . . oh, God . . . the mere thought unmans me . . ."

He shoved Langdon away and got off the bed, his tall form flashing in and out of the moonlight as he grabbed the flask of rum off the wall beside the hatch. She couldn't see him, could only hear a gulping sound. He drank until he staggered and his breath ran out in one long, ragged wind.

"Can you think of a worse hell than that?" he asked. "For a man like me to sit powerless while my kin die."

"No, Beau, dear God, no."

"Sorry you asked?"

Langdon looked over at him, his face marred by two glistening tracks of tears.

Maria lay there in the stifling silence, as the two friends met on a dark road they had never traveled together before. For a long moment, she could hear nothing but Beau's labored breathing.

"No," Langdon finally said. "I'm not sorry I asked."

Beau came back to the hammock and sat down. He looked lifeless in body and spirit. "So now you have it . . . the worst of it . . . this plague of a dream." He looked up at Langdon as creases of pain formed around his eyes and mouth. "Maybe your father was right: We shouldn't have left Carolina right away, but remained long enough to bury them. As it is, it seems as if I had a bad dream the night before leaving on a journey."

"Yes, it does seem like that sometimes, doesn't it?"

"But it wasn't a dream. They're not going to be there when we get back."

Beau looked toward where Maria lay in the shadows. "Remember that old adage Father used to chant at us every day . . . how a man's thoughts should be his own?"

Langdon chuckled under his breath, finishing the maxim, "If you say too much boys, it'll tell a man how to trip you."

Beau didn't smile. "He was wrong."

"Why?"

"Now that I'll never talk to them again there's so much I would have said. Some days my head is full of talk . . . words . . . useless now except to make me regret it."

"What would you say . . . if you could?"

"I loved them, Langdon."

Silence.

"They were in my soul."

Langdon slumped back on his heels.

Beau didn't notice. "Julia bothers me the most . . . I spared too many words with her."

Langdon looked up. "Why do you say that? You were devoted to her, Beau."

"Yes, but I wasn't in love with her and Julia knew it. She never said as much, but she knew."

"You did love her."

"As a companion, the mother of my child, but not in a romantic way. You know, all that poetic nonsense women fill their heads with. Julia wanted it but I never felt that way about her . . . or any other woman for that matter."

"Beau, your feelings for your wife were honest and good. You made her the happiest woman in Carolina. You know that. Everyone knew how deeply she was in love with you."

"She deserved more. I could have tried harder."

"How?"

"I could have at least told her that it didn't matter to me . . . she pleased me anyway. God, I hope she knew that. I was satisfied with her, Lang, she was a good woman to me."

Maria was touched and surprised by these sentiments.

But Beau lost his taste for talk then, got on his feet and gave Langdon a cuff on the back. "I need some air."

Maria sat up when the door shut behind him, not realizing until then how hard she had been crying. The ruffled collar of her nightdress was wet where the tears had collected.

"You're a good friend to him, Lang," she whispered.

Langdon turned around on the floor between the hammocks. "Why didn't you announce yourself?"

"He would not have said as much in my presence."

She was right and Langdon knew it, but he was too worried about what had been said while she was listening. Nothing about Arthur. He was certain of it.

He wasn't prepared for her next question.

"How many died, Langdon?"

He looked away quickly, nervously straightening his blanket on the floor. "I'd rather let Beau answer that. It's his personal business, not mine."

"Very well." She got up, went to the footlocker and mixed a cup of ale laced with sleeping powders.

"What are you doing?"

"First, I'm going to coax this brew into him so he'll get some rest. Then I'm going to ask him a few questions." She drew her capuchin over her night-dress.

Langdon sat on the floor, only his eyes questioning her.

Maria felt sorry for Langdon. He had become such a good friend to her these last four weeks. He deserved an explanation even though she knew he was too much of a gentleman to ask outright.

Maria stood over him and whispered, "I can't help him if I don't know the truth, Langdon. Once and for all, I'm going to tend him as he hired me to do."

The door shut behind her.

Beau heard the commotion amidship, men whistling, catcalling, darting around the lone figure that moved so doggedly forward.

Maria.

He couldn't believe his eyes.

What the devil was she doing topside? He forbad her to come up here unescorted. This was a pirate rig, full of hungry men who didn't need much to tempt their male urges. And this sultry young captive of his was more than enough woman to make a man restless.

He sat up, watching her move toward him with her head bent against the men who darted into her path. They teased her, tried to waylay her by posing in her path, but he noticed that none dared to touch her. They wouldn't. They had been told Maria belonged to Beau and there wasn't a man aboard with the gall to cross him.

So he sat back and watched her pick her way across the deck, her scantily clad body not entirely hidden by that ragged old cloak of hers. The wind flung it open, revealing the curves of her slim body, the sway of her hips, the subtle bounce of her unbound breasts. Her legs moved with the hallmark grace of a dancer, long and slender and well formed beneath the molded veil of her delicate white cotton sheath. With her hood blown back, her unbound hair whipped wildly in the wind like dark red streaks of satin slashing at the night.

Lord! but she was a beautiful woman, the daughter of Satan himself, as pure and sweet as Arthur was evil and cruel.

Arousal surged through his loins, made him look away, take a deep breath, fight it off. He didn't want to feel this for her. It was wrong. Why couldn't he stop himself?

Her feet were bare. He could hear them pad to a halt in front of where he sat in the bow. His eyes took in the pure white skin of her feet, then slowly moved upward, raking over the gentle curve of her belly, the pointed tips of her breasts, and settled hard into the sweet darkness of her downcast eyes.

"What the devil are you doing here?" He tried to sound firm, reprimanding.

"Looking for you," she said breathlessly. "I

brought you this." She thrust out a mug of ale. "Drink it, Beau. It will ease you."

He reached, took the mug, his fingers and hers just glancing. The spicy scent of sleeping powders wafted up his nostrils, making him look away and scowl at the night.

"Did Langdon send you up with this?"

"No. It was my idea."

"I see." She didn't have to say where the idea came from. Maria had been awake down there. He looked away, reviewing everything he had said, but couldn't think of what might have betrayed his scheme. No. It was just an intimate moment that she had stolen from him. "You overheard us."

"Yes."

He sighed, exasperated. "Can a man have no privacy?"

This brought her to the deck before him, just inside the space between his upstretched knees. His head bent, the brim of his hat shielding his face except for the lower portion. All she could see of him was his jaw, his mouth. She feared he was angry with her, and she couldn't blame him. Pity welled in her heart, but she knew she had to swallow it and didn't let him see it. Her voice was light, careful, her eyes pinned to the contours of his mouth for some sign of his feelings. "Privacy is sorely lacking for us all. Thank God we're among friends."

He didn't look up but she saw nothing stern about his lips. They were relaxed, parted slightly, just enough for her to see the tips of his teeth. "I suppose the time has come to explain a few things to you, eh?"

It was a handsome mouth, she thought, wondering for a moment what it tasted like.

"Only what will guide me to help you, Beau. That's all I want. Not to pry where I don't belong. But you ache so miserably, with some great tragedy that I know nothing about."

"You're too tender for the whole of it, Maria."

"Perhaps, but there's a part of me left hardened by my own personal losses. You know that, Beau, I've told you as much." Her voice was so sweet, like a lilting melody except for the dismal chord struck with her words. A chord that sounded strangely familiar to him.

He looked at her then, square in the face. It was there, hiding under the virginal humility, the uncertain boldness of a woman trying to probe a man in places she knew little about. But she did it anyway, beseeched him with her eyes, so eager to use her own pain as a bridge into his own. No matter how embarrassed she was by Arthur's rejection, Maria looked beyond it now, just for his sake.

It touched him, deeply, made him feel suddenly tender. Unwittingly, he reached for her, cupped a smooth cheek in his hand and let the goodness of her flow into his flesh.

"You are remarkable, Maria. However do you manage to stay so blasted sweet while the blood of an infidel seeps through your veins?"

"Don't talk about Father now. I don't want to—"

Her eyes flew away from him, smarting with sadness.

He fingered her cheek until she forgot her dark thoughts and became aware of the way he was touching her. "All right, princess, I won't mention him anymore because I know it upsets you."

Her gaze returned, searched his face for a fleeting moment as if in final judgment of his mood. "Tell me who dies in your dreams, Beau."

He blinked, thought hard about a way to tell her without saying too much. "They all do . . ."

"All?"

"My family."

Pain clouded his eyes. She was surprised that he let her see even this tiny glimpse of his tormented soul.

"It happened last November. I came home to find them all dead . . . my parents, a brother and sister . . . my wife . . . they all died without warning . . . not a hint—"

Her eyes widened in shock. "How?"

"A poison," he explained and felt his grief tugging at him again. "a rotten stinking poison that came straight from hell and killed every last one of them . . . except Matthew. And me. I wasn't there . . . didn't eat the meal . . . but believe me, I wish I had."

"Dear God!" she breathed in horror, her hand suddenly fisting around his sleeve.

"I shouldn't have told you . . . your spirit is too innocent for such ghastly details."

She wanted to say something but shock stole her

wits. Dear God! she prayed to the heavens. Take away the horrible pain this man must be feeling inside.

"Look now, I've made you cry."

His fingers caught a tear, brushed it away. Maria leaned toward him. Beau let her come closer, until he could feel the sleek contours of her torso lean against the inside of his thigh. He couldn't move away from her, from the genuine compassion that seemed to radiate from her, bringing him into the place where she lay as crushed and broken as he. Arthur. What a despicable bond he fused between them, which made him want her pain because it so perfectly matched his own.

Yes, that was what made Maria so attractive to him, so strangely compelling. Her enticement comprised more than just physical desire, the way any man would want a woman so young and ripe. No. It was her spirit that tugged at him. Maria was so tender, so exquisitely gentle in nature, she made a hurting man like him want to leap inside her and never come out.

He drew her toward him, his brown hands framing her delicate white skin, pulled her between the spread of his thighs until her breasts grazed his chest. The contact was far too subtle for the fierce reaction it caused in their bodies, a pulsing jolt of heat. Her breath and his drew in at the same time, just before the brim of his hat blocked all the moonlight from her upturned face.

He held her there, spellbound in the shadows. Desire. They wanted each other. It was suddenly obvious and for a long moment they just sat staring in utter fascination. Her lips were poised only inches beneath his own, parted and breathless and enchanted by the way his mouth opened in want of her, to taste her, sip her sweet nectar.

But he didn't.

No.

She was forbidden, a fruit he must never taste.

They pulled away at the same time.

"I'm sorry . . ." he muttered. "Forgive me that, will you?"

"Of course."

He snatched up the mug from the deck, put it to his lips and guzzled its entire contents. "There now . . . you got your way."

A shaky grin touched the corners of her lips. "You drank it!"

"I did." He stood up, reached down to help her off the deck. Her hand shivered in his palm. "The angel of mercy has won the day."

Maria stood in the center of the cabin and wrung her hands in despair. She couldn't decide what to pack and what to leave behind. She felt like a mother trying to choose which child to give up and the further the sun retreated from this last day aboard, the more distraught she became.

These belongings were her only possessions in the world. How could Beau expect her to pack a mere quarter of them for the trip? The rest were to be dropped off in Charles Towne by Captain Deane, for how long she didn't know. She might never see them again.

Mens' voices drifted down the corridor. Maria

panicked, grabbed a few dresses, and hurriedly stuffed them into Beau's pack.

The men walked by her cabin door without stopping—it wasn't Beau or Langdon.

She ripped the dresses back out of the pack and left them in a heap on the floor. The first anxious tears began to collect in her eyes.

Maria was scared. All the colorful stories Langdon had told her about Carolina now seemed frightening and savage. There were Indians in the New World, wild beasts, dense forests. She wasn't rugged enough for such a primitive life.

For the first time since she had left England, Maria regretted leaving. London, at least, was predictable.

The air in the cabin was hot and insufferably humid. She fanned herself with Langdon's hat and opened the porthole. The cool sea breezes felt warm and balmy on her skin. They had left England when spring was still cool and youthful, they would arrive in the New World in the heat of June.

She began to feel flushed, feverish. Matthew crawled over a pile of her toiletries and selected a fine lilac talcum to eat. She caught him just before he dumped the lot of it down his throat.

Maria threw up her hands and let out a cry of dismay that didn't quite mask the sound of the hatch popping open.

Beau stood in the doorway. Beneath the dipped brim of his hat, those disarming eyes of his swept through the cabin and saw every messy detail. He looked at her in surprise.

"What in God's name is happening in here?"

She cringed and felt hot tears sting her eyes. The last of her usual poise disintegrated. She threw the talcum powder to the floor, flung herself on the hammock and burst into tears.

Beau stared at her in complete astonishment. Maria had never acted like this before.

"Wee . . . Wee . . ." Matthew mimicked as he crawled over to her and tugged at her hem.

Beau fumbled in his sleeve for a rag. It was tar-stained, smelling of fish oil. He looked around for something better but nothing presented itself. Stepping between piles of feminine paraphernalia, he came to the hammock and dangled the kerchief near her hand.

She snatched it, buried her face in it and wailed, "I just can't decide!"

"Decide what?"

"What to pack!" she choked.

"Oh. Is that all? Well then . . ." He squatted on the floor, his son between his legs, the child still pointing at Maria in consternation. "Do you want me to help you decide? Will that make you feel better?"

"No," she said, sniffling into the cloth. His smell was imbedded in the fibers, musky and delicious. It only made her feel worse. She suddenly wished for Langdon. Why couldn't Beau be just a friend, instead of inspiring these strange sensations? "I just can't part with my things, Beau! I don't have anything else in the world but these few possessions—"

"Here now! You act as though I'm going to

dump them in the sea! Captain Deane will see them safely stored in Charles Towne. If you want, I'll have Langdon or Indigo bring them out to the Savannah."

"Who's Indigo?"

"My friend."

"Why does he have such a strange name?"

"Because he's a Savannah Indian."

"Oh!" she wailed anew. "How will I get along with such people? They frighten me!"

"So that's your trouble, eh?"

She peeked at him over the edge of the kerchief.

"It's more than just the packing, isn't it, Maria? You're afraid to land tomorrow."

She turned and looked up at him with pleading eyes. His face was filled with concern, his windswept hair framing his rugged features. He met her gaze and caused a quiver of pleasure to bloom within her. A brush of his fingers pulled away the wisps of hair that clung to her damp temples. His touch made the quiver become a pulse. She wanted to move away, stop looking at him, refuse what he made her feel.

But she didn't. She'd lost too much of her courage already. "Yes," she admitted, knowing it was useless to hide. When he looked at her like this, he could see everything. She might as well be lying there naked.

"Tell me what frightens you and let me ease your fears. Come on now, don't be embarrassed. If I were you, I'd be a bit scared myself."

She doubted this champion of a man had ever

known real fear. Why should he? He was so strong and powerfully built.

"You would not. You'd be braver than me."

"That's a lie." He liked the way she pouted, how her tears made her dark eyes shine. Tiny droplets of water clung to her lashes, glistening in the light from the porthole like diamonds.

"I didn't think I would be so afraid . . . but I am."

"I can see that," he murmured, watching her lips move as she spoke. Although he tried to concentrate on what she was saying, he thought of how that plush, full mouth of hers would feel beneath his own.

"Is it true the Indians hatchet white settlers in their beds?"

"No. At least not in Carolina. There are seven major tribes in the territory and none of them are warring. They're farmers, devoted to the land, a very quiet and peaceful people. They keep to themselves mostly . . ."

"But they're still strange . . . pagan. Gaylord told father they think you're divine . . . a god . . ." He was surprised she remembered this from the conversation he had also overheard in the Vandenburgh dining room. The woman had a mind for detail, he warned himself. "Why would they think that?"

"Some behavior of mine was interpreted as divine but—"

"What behavior?"

"Being impervious to pain." She looked shocked.

"Never mind that, it's not a tale for the ears of maids. Just remember, their religion is as sacred to them as yours is to you. They are very moral and upright, really. If you resist condemning them, you will learn many things from the natives of the continent."

"What will I learn?"

"The way of the land . . . of nature . . ." he said and wondered how much of nature she'd learn from him. As his eyes roamed her winsome face, he realized how easily she awakened his long dormant body. Even now there was a subtle tugging in his loins, a feeling that had been absent since the death of his wife.

"What about the wild beasts?"

"Rest assured, none will ever get close enough to threaten either you or Matthew. That's why you'll stay behind me on the trail, with Matthew in your harness, so I can flush the game away from you."

"Oh . . . that's quite gallant of you."

"I'll always be gallant with you, princess," he said. But he wondered how long he could keep that promise. He was too familiar with the ways of nature to deny that he wanted her. And despite her outward innocence, she was aware of it, too. They both were, ever since that night on deck. It wouldn't be entirely safe to be alone with her in the woods, but he dared not mention this at such a delicate time.

"What about the trouble between your people and the Crown? What if Charles Towne erupts in war?"

"It won't. The trouble concerns the traders more than the settlers."

"But you're one of them, aren't you? You're a Charles Towne Trader."

"I am the son of the man who headed them, yes. My father groomed me to trap amongst them, to one day lead a new generation, but his early death has thrust me into his boots. Maybe he knew he would die young. Maybe that's why he taught me so urgently and strictly. He had me trapping alongside him from the time I could walk and drag the links behind me in the dirt. It'll be lonely without him but not for long, eh? Soon I'll teach Matthew my trade."

"Will we ever live in Charles Towne?"

"Perhaps one day I'll return there." A vision of blood and bodies and half-eaten food flashed through his mind. Beau stiffened. The spell was broken. He rose. "I'm not ready to go back there yet . . . see the house again . . . where I lived with them. No, I can't, Maria . . . not yet."

"Of course you can't!" she said at once, alarmed at having upset him. "Forgive me for pressing you. I have no right to complain like this."

She got to her feet and within ten minutes had packed a satchel of necessities and folded the rest away.

Beau stood at the rails and thrilled at this first sight of his homeland, watching it loom out of the ocean like some great hulking beast. Carolina! How he longed to be with her again. Even from a distance, he knew the forests were laden with the fruits of June, foliage budding new and fragrant limbs, streams frothing with the rush of recent thaws. He could almost feel the balmy caress of the faithful tradewinds, smell the scents of nature in bloom. A rush of good feeling coursed through his ragged spirits. For the first time in months, he realized how homesick he was.

"Sure you want to go through with this, Beau?" Captain Deane interrupted his thoughts. "It's not too late to take her back. I'll do it if you ask."

"I'm not changing my mind, Zach," Beau said.

Beau was determined; Zachariah could see the glint of it in his eyes, and it brought a fresh worry to his mind. He loved this man as all Carolina did. The Gardiners were the best, the most devoted to the wild paradise of the New World. Could he forgive himself if anything happened to the surviving sons of that beloved clan?

"You're sure the other proprietors didn't have a hand in it?"

Beau leaned into the wind, struggled to light a pipe of tobacco. "I'm not sure, Zach, it's just a hunch that Vandenburgh acted alone. From what I read in his papers, the chief proprietor, Lord Ashley, is very respected. Charles Towne is more than a settlement to him. It's an experiment."

Briefly, Beau described the theories being tested in Carolina that made it unique. Charles Towne was the only colony to have a fundamental constitution, an elected legislature, and judicial rights such as trial by jury and freedom from double jeopardy. Although Englishmen were sent to rule it and enforce Crown policies, Charles Towne was nonetheless an experiment in personal liberty.

"So why don't we just take the girl back and lay the facts before Lord Ashley?"

Beau shook his head. "Because Arthur is too powerful. He can buy whatever verdict he wants. No. The key to succeeding with this scheme is to expose Arthur to everyone . . . the other proprietors, the king's ministers, the people of England. I don't want Arthur's fate to hang in any one hand, but in many hands."

Zachariah whistled through his rotted teeth. "Wouldn't it be grand if it worked? Tell me what I'm to do next, Beau."

"Deliver the next ransom note and wait long enough to see how Arthur reacts to it. Then get back here fast. Go straight to Langdon with the information. He'll keep the traders abreast and bring word to me on the Savannah." Beau drew imaginary lines in the air with the tip of his pipe. "Langdon is the link between you and the traders and me and the woman. From here on, you'll get your instructions from him. In the meantime, don't dally in Charles Towne. I don't want any of your crew to get loose-lipped in Mierda's Taverne one night . . . start a rumor that I'm still alive."

"They'd cut their tongues out first, Beau." Zachariah thought for a moment, then threw back his head and laughed. "Or I'll do it for them! Ain't a man in Carolina that would do anything to wreck a plan to smash the proprietors. There's too much at stake for all of us."

"Don't take any chances, Zach."

"Not a one. I want this to work, Beau, for your sake more than anyone's. Revenge'll taste sweet after what he did to you, eh? Maybe then you'll have your peace. You and Matthew can start all over again."

"Perhaps." Beau managed a smile. They both knew his pain was as deep as his soul.

Beau reached into his pocket and withdrew a sealed note. "This is the second ransom letter. Deliver it to a man named Jacques Moineau. His politics are radical and he operates an underground press in the basement of his office on Bleeker Street. He is known to have no great love of anyone in power in England. His publications are controversial but widely read in the city. He'll publish this note in a pamphlet, but his price will be very high."

He pulled a leather sack from his belt and dropped it into Deane's hand. The sailor opened it, his eyes widening at the glittering contents. Gold. Deane reached inside to finger a nugget.

"Moineau could live the rest of his life in comfort with what's in that sack. I'm sure his price will be met."

Deane looked awestruck, the way he always did when he caught a glimpse of the Gardiner wealth. It was usually measured in wampum or fur. Seeing it in gold was far more dramatic.

"Give the note and the money to Moineau and be sure to disguise yourself. Wear street clothes.

Don't be seen in buckskins and moccasins. That will mark you as a New World man. Remain in London long enough to gauge Arthur's reaction, then return to Charles Towne and report it to Miles.

"Be careful, Zach. Not even your crew can know what you're doing in London. If you serve me well, you'll have enough of those nuggets to turn this rig to firewood and live like a king for the rest of your days."

Deane's eyes lit up. No one could wage a deal better than Beau Gardiner. His tactics were infamous in the New World; legend had it that if Beau wanted the throne of England, Charles would sell it and live his remaining days grinning over the deal.

"Godspeed to us both," Zachariah said and walked off, caressing the sack and imagining it was his own.

It was still dark when she felt the gentle nudge on her shoulder. "Come awake, Maria. It's time." She had slept fitfully, but the surge of adrenaline made her instantly alert. She lifted her face out of the old canvas pillow and listened to Beau's instructions. "Make yourself ready. I left a tray for you and Matthew to eat. I'll come for you in about an hour." She nodded, mumbled a greeting, and listened to the quiet tread of his feet as he left the cabin.

Her body was stiff, her fingers trembling so hard she could barely work the buttons on her bodice. While she bathed and dressed Matthew, she listened to the commotion on the deck above, the thump of running feet, halyards clanking, chains rattling. Tension tightened her throat, making it hard to swallow the breakfast Beau had left for them.

Their belongings were already stripped from the room, her satchels gone, the pelts rolled up, nothing dangling from the pegs beside the hatch. Matthew's harness was propped against the wall beside his cradle, its interior lovingly lined with a strip of fur.

She gathered Matthew on her lap and sat on the hammock to await Beau. She tried to concentrate on the child instead of her own fear. Beau would surely release her from his service if she permitted another outburst like the one yesterday. She must be strong and brave and helpful, even if his homeland scared the wits from her.

Beau had taken her topside with Matthew to see it last night, the land mass that loomed out of the sea on the distant horizon. The New World looked like a long strip of green velvet ribbon, curled lazily along the far edge of the ocean. Maria watched the sun set behind it, a huge swollen ball of orange light swallowed in the dark mass as if gulped into the belly of some savage beast. While she favored Beau with sweet remarks, Maria searched for some sign of civilization there, a house or a pier or even another ship anchored nearby. But there was none.

Now Matthew pumped his feet and plucked at the string on the hem of his bunting, not the least bit concerned about where they were going today. It was his homeland, his birthplace. She wondered how something so untamed could produce something so innocent. Matthew presented a bootie for her inspection. He bent his head back to look up at her, his enormous blue eyes fluttering plush black lashes at her while he babbled. She smiled at the little shoe and gave him a sudden, tight hug.

He was a blessing. If not for Matthew, she would have gone to pieces a long time ago.

The hatch pushed open. Beau bent through the door with his usual stealth and came into the dim light of the cabin.

She almost didn't look up for fear he'd see how unnerved she was, but a brief glance in his direction presented a sight that stole her attention completely.

Beau was no longer dressed in the baggy tunics he wore around the ship with just a loose belt to hint at the sleekness of his body. Oh, no. He wasn't protecting himself from the elements of the sea any more and stood before her now, a man transformed into his former self. A son of the New World, virile and strong, Beau was dressed for the frontier of America.

He wore a short sleeveless vest of rawhide meant to protect his back beneath the weight of their heavy gear. The tan flesh of his upper body bulged into view, his chest and shoulders and arms thickly muscled. He was beautiful, perfectly formed beneath snug fawn britches that fit him like another layer of skin. His body tapered sleekly at the waist, his hips were slender and tight, his belly as flat and hard as a board. Her eyes traveled down the length of his long legs to the meaty power of his thighs, the way they cradled the heavy loins that strained against the seams of his buckskins.

She blushed from her scalp to her toes but still couldn't look away. He was spectacular. Maria was certain that when God created man in His likeness, He had Beau Gardiner in mind.

Maria remembered the last time she had stared so blatantly at the body of a man. The girls at school were invited to a nearby church where they found stained glass windows depicting nude male angels. So awed were they by the sight, this first glimpse of male genitalia, that none of them paid a whit of attention to their prayers. Instead, they studied the angels with great diligence. The sisters did not appreciate their gawking, cut short the prayer session, and herded them back to the convent. They never prayed at that church again.

". . . ready to leave. Maria? Are you all right?"

She looked at Beau just in time to see the grin on his face.

"Of course," she said, affecting her most demure voice. "Why?"

"Because you looked at me just then as if you'd never seen a man before."

Mortified, she looked down at her hands and wished a sea serpent would rise out of the ocean and choose her for breakfast.

"You have much of the world to see, Maria." Beau chuckled. "You mustn't be afraid to look." His finger slid under her chin, gently urging up her flaming face until she could see the amused luster in his eyes. "Be it a man or a beast or a breathtaking landscape, you'll see the best of nature in Carolina. I want you to look . . . to enjoy . . . to make my land your home. Can you do that?"

"I'll try."

"Good, then come along quickly. I'm anxious to get home."

Langdon was dressed exactly like Beau but Maria dared not inspect him as thoroughly as her employer. Instead she tried to hurry, helping to store Matthew and their gear in the dilapidated skiff Captain Deane had so generously donated. She listened to him tell Beau to pitch the "rotting ole tub" on the beach or cut it up for firewood. One look at the dark and angry sea below made her insides flutter at the thought of rowing ashore in such a rickety craft.

She started plying the rosary beads in her pocket, praying, imploring, then begging the Lord to award them safe passage to this great continent of a thousand more perils.

Beau spread a tarp on the bottom of the boat where Maria could sit with the baby. He faced her in the bow, Langdon at her back. The ropes were loosened, the little craft tipping and shifting in the predawn wind as they were lowered into the sea.

The tide was rough and dangerous. It snatched the boat and yanked it four feet off the *Savannah*'s keel just seconds after it touched the surface.

Cape Fear. She'd read about these wicked waters, known to mariners everywhere as the graveyard of the Atlantic. It was the most treacherous coast in the New World, the primary reason why earlier colonies had failed as ships were unable to navigate the deadly shoals. It was easy to believe that now, as she clung to the sides of the craft and felt the anger in the water beneath them. It picked up the boat, slammed it down, yawed it right, then left. Sprays of saltwater hit their faces, snarling waves curled over the boat's edge, and splashed into puddles around her. It was a wild, frenzied dance that found Beau and Langdon rowing for control with all their combined might.

They righted the rig after a furious struggle, shouting at each other. Maria clung to Matthew, watching every stroke of the oars become a grueling labor as they headed toward shore.

The morning sun began to rise and she tried to concentrate on its beauty instead of the way her heart was slamming against her ribs. She watched the brilliant purple rays of dawn sear through the black sky overhead until the stars melted away. A big golden ball of heat rose out of the dim horizon and made the rampaging clouds glow. It was an exquisite sky.

Langdon let out a groan of despair. She turned, saw him level his oars and lean forward until his head hung between his legs. He was drenched, his skin bright red with exertion.

She saw the strain on Beau's face as he plied his oars. With his head back and his eyes closed, he seemed to be in some other world where his hands weren't blistering, where his shoulders weren't cramping in pain. The oars rose and fell steadily, powerfully, with an almost brutal determination.

His skin gleamed with sweat and saltwater, the muscles in his arms trembled.

"Let me help," she cried, genuinely worried that his strength would fail and they'd perish out here in this evil water. "Please . . . I can work an oar."

His eyes popped open, his head slowly bending until his eyes found hers. He blinked once, as if remembering she was there. The ragged sound of his breathing frightened her. "What?"

"I want to help row! Look! Langdon's stopped . . . you can't do it alone."

She pointed at Langdon. Something about her pose struck him funny, how pretty and prim she looked in her soft yellow dress, her whole face aghast in panic. Like a princess being borne to a coronation gone suddenly awry.

A laugh shot out of his throat before he could stop it. "Lord! this is no parlor game. This surf would rip your arms off!"

Now her eyes really widened but there was a definite pout to her lips. "I'm sure I could at least try," she said in her sing-song, demure British voice. "And I could give you a spell!" she suggested brilliantly, then snatched at a loose ribbon end that was flailing around her carefully wrapped and braided coiffure.

He rested his oars on his lap for a moment, leaned over and said, "I think your spirit is a might stronger than your body, princess."

"You do?"

"Most certainly." He grinned in amusement, sat

up, and started rowing again. "But I'd rather you keep your strength for the day's walk, eh?"

"I suppose you're right." She resettled herself, sitting on her haunches with her back straight and her hands folded between her thighs.

Matthew was sitting in a puddle before her, playing with her rosary beads, splashing in the water and squealing with glee. When she looked at the boy, Beau saw the soft love in her smile, how gentle was the hand that stroked through his son's raven hair. Matthew clapped his hands and beamed up at her like any child would bask in the special light of a woman's love. And how freely she gave it, this woman whose own life barely knew the joys of receiving love, only giving it.

He admired her, the dark eyes that expressed so much, the high sculpted cheeks that so easily blushed at his notice, the sensual mouth that always whispered a smile. The more he knew her, the more fascinated he became. Ever since the first time he saw her, standing in the shadows of Arthur's Dabney Street home, this melancholy lady never ceased to intrigue him. She was fabulously rich yet so completely unaware of it, so startlingly beautiful yet so thoroughly chaste, so warmly affectionate yet so sadly alone. It was all these characteristics that titillated him, always left him wondering, musing, thinking about her.

His oar struck shoals.

Beau snapped out of his trance, threw down his oar, and leaned forward with a fierce groan of pain. He had tested himself to the limits of physical strength and Maria was impressed. For the last twenty minutes, Langdon had barely been helping at all.

"Hallelujah!" Beau cried, taking off his hat and shaking the sweat from it. He flashed a brilliant smile at Langdon in the stern. "We're home."

"Praise God!" Langdon panted. "I thought we'd never get back to civilization!"

Maria looked at them in perplexion. How could anyone describe this untamed continent as civilized? How different their worlds were!

Beau winked at her, grinned playfully, and promptly rolled off the back of the boat. He hit the water with a splash. Langdon let out a whoop of joy and dove overboard.

They swam like dolphins just freed of a fisherman's net, swooping in and out of the surf amidst sprays of foam. She smiled with relief, until she realized the boat was drifting.

"Beau! Langdon!" she called. "Gentlemen!" A pair of wet heads turned around, eyed her from the distance. "The boat is drifting!"

Beau nodded, and both men instantly disappeared underwater. She assumed they were coming for her and waited for them to emerge nearby. Neither man surfaced. Minutes went by. She began to worry, peered over the edge of the boat, and searched the water for some sign of them.

"Looking for someone?"

She whirled around to find them looking up at her from the other side of the boat. They grinned when her scolding eyes fell upon them.

"You frightened me!" Beau widened his eyes as if dreading her wrath. With his hair flattened around his face, his eyes looked like a pair of giant blue saucers. Langdon chortled merrily. "I've never seen either of you act like this before!"

"We're just having some fun, is all," Beau replied. He submerged himself again, then came up whipping his hair out of his eyes. A pair of big brown hands curled around the edge of the boat. "Why don't you join us, eh?"

"Good heavens, no! I can't swim!"

"She can't swim!" Langdon gasped, feigning surprise.

"Oh, go on!" She waved them away. "I'll row us myself, won't I, Matthew?"

She never reached the oar. There was a splash behind her, two hands cinching around her waist, a glimpse of bleached white petticoat flashing through the air above her as she went spinning into the sea.

A second later, she popped through the surface, flailing her arms.

"Beau Gardiner! How could you!" Beau and Langdon roared with delight. "I don't know how to swim! Oh! Something's nipping at my foot . . ."

"It's probably just a crab," Beau said.

"A *crab?*"

Langdon chortled.

Beau swam behind her, ready to intervene if necessary. "Just keep paddling, princess. You're doing fine," he coached while Langdon began tugging the boat ashore.

Her hair was unwinding, the ribbons floating loose. "Oh, Lord, deliver me!" she gasped on the verge of tears, turning toward shore and beginning to paddle with an almost desperate fury.

Beau saw the wave before she did, watched it swell forward, catch Maria in its grip, and send her hurtling forward.

Caught by surprise, her mouth open as wide as her eyes, she was swept underwater and spun against the sandy floor.

She tumbled and twirled once, twice, then realized she was too disoriented to find the surface. A blinding flash of panic snatched her at precisely the same moment Beau did. He caught her firmly around the waist as his legs pumped once with enough power to shoot them clean through the surface.

"Oh!" she choked, spluttered, clung to his neck until her fingernails nearly penetrated his skin. "Don't let go . . . I'll surely drown."

The concern left his face and found him launching forward with Maria safely tucked under him. He swam with her face looking up at the sky over his shoulder. He let her relax, catch her breath, then he slowly rolled onto his back.

"Easy . . . just relax . . . float over me . . . I'll swim for us."

He pushed into a strong backstroke, his body free to move under her.

Maria obeyed his directions, letting herself float above him while his strokes compelled them toward the beach. It was a smooth, easy motion, her body gliding along, her face tilted above his own.

He was watching her. Closely. Very closely.

She looked at him and suddenly noticed how bold and direct and completely focused was his attention. She didn't need to ask what had him so suddenly arrested.

The way they were swimming.

Maria became instantly aware of it, shocked by the unexpected intimacy between their swimming forms. His body moved close under her, his hips pulsing against hers every time he kicked his legs. Her breasts swayed across his chest, touching him, discovering him, suddenly knowing how hard and solid those muscles felt against the soft curves of her body.

A flash of heat started between her legs, radiating upward until it flushed through her cheeks.

He seemed to feel it, her arousal. She could see it in the way his eyes darkened as he studied the fire on her face. Her breath came faster, harder, his own matching its rhythm. Their faces were so close they could taste each other every time they breathed.

And all the while, beneath the churning sea, their wet bodies moved in a slippery caress, a delicious dance of private touching. Unknown parts of her body and spirit awakened to every pulse in the male muscle beneath her, the teasing entwining of their thighs, the way their hips writhed and hugged and knew the other as man, as woman.

Sand and broken shells scraped against his back. Frothy breakwater poured over them and pushed them partially out of the sea and onto the slick wet surface of the beach. His arms relaxed down her back, holding her atop him while the waves crashed around their legs. She was too spellbound to move, to get off him, to stop lying on top of his body and thrilling at these heady, sensual feelings.

There was nothing hidden now, this compelling attraction of theirs was finally unveiled in the bright morning light. Neither of them fought it or tried to hide it. Now that it was acknowledged, it became even more real.

One of his hands slid into her drenched sable locks to pull her closer. How directly he looked at her then, his passion seeing hers, all of it taught during this simple swim.

"We should speak of this now, Maria," he whispered, his voice deep, husky. "What is between us."

The breath caught in her throat. "I don't know what's happening."

"Of course you don't. You're a maid, not a woman yet." His expression softened with understanding. "I think I felt this way when I hired you."

"What way?"

The hand in her hair came around to capture her cheek, hold her still so he could see straight into her eyes, her mind, her soul. "I want you, Maria, for myself . . . not just for my son. Do you understand that?" She nodded as if in a trance, her face cocking into his hand, her eyes closing for a moment to savor the feel of it. "And you?"

"It is the same with me," she admitted and tried to push away the bashfulness. It was too girlish for the way he made her feel, for the kind of man he was. She reached down, wiped the wetness from his brow with the tips of her fingers. It felt so good to touch him, to admit the satisfaction he brought with his words, his private gazes, his body. Especially from a man who was usually so silent and unapproachable, except for the part of him that opened up when he loved his little boy. This was the hidden side of the man lying under her now, the part that made him so strangely irresistible to her.

He was a special man. Devoted to his child. Wealthy but without pretense. Arrogant but never cruel. Tender but hardly weak. And most of all, she knew he could love enough to nurture a motherless baby, to spare a frightened girl one night in London, to lie awake at night with pieces of his heart lying broken in his hands.

Langdon's boots crunched to a halt beside them. Startled, Maria rolled off of Beau, too ashamed to look Langdon in the eye as she fled to the boat and Matthew.

Beau thought Langdon should look more surprised at what he had just caught them doing. But he didn't. He flopped down in the sand as Beau curled his arms under his head and stared at the sky.

"I knew there was something between you two," he muttered. "I've wanted to ask you about it for a while now."

"Is it so obvious?"

"Sometimes." Langdon glanced down at him, a new emotion clouding his expression. Anger. "Why are you letting this happen, Beau? You needn't go so far to insure her cooperation. Why drag her heart into this?"

"You know me better than to accuse me of such heartlessness . . ."

"Then why, Beau?"

It was too difficult to explain, how the scheme against Arthur did not seem to be enough to drive a wedge between himself and Maria. Somewhere within the wreckage her father caused in both their lives, a bond had been fused between the lonely captive and her aching captor. As impossible as it should be, Beau needed the part of her who could understand his pain.

"Tell me," Langdon persisted, "tell me how you can ignore the circumstances that surround her."

"Maybe these 'circumstances' are a part of it for me, Langdon. She bleeds from the same hand as I."

"Then you should tell her the truth . . . let her judge you by what her father's done."

"No. She's not recovered from what Arthur's done to her yet, let alone confront what he did to me. To tell Maria her father had my family murdered would be so shocking and heinous to her, it would leave her stricken for good. No. I'll spare her those gruesome details for as long as I can."

"But why promote feelings that have no future, Beau?"

"Dammit, Langdon, we're still human beings! Just because we're linked to that murdering pig is no reason to deny us our human nature."

"True, but what happens when the time comes to

send her back to England? A year from now, if our scheme works, she'll be returned to her world and you'll be left without her in yours."

"Her world?" He rose on his elbows to look at his friend squarely. "Her world is a convent, Lang; it was never Arthur's house . . . or London. That part of her life betrayed her. She may have to go back but do you really think she'll stay? I doubt it. Haven't you ever wondered about this prim and proper debutante whose delicate hands never flinched from scrubbing cabin floors and soiled diapers?"

Langdon said nothing, but looked at Beau and then Maria, scratching his head in confusion.

Beau chuckled and gave Langdon's shoulder a hearty pat. "She's a maid of simpler wants than those of the highly bred. Perhaps Carolina will set her free . . . give her a taste of happiness for the first time in her life. Let it be. Mother nature commands this place and she'll press her will upon us both in time."

Langdon found Maria beside the boat, sitting with Matthew, letting the child fill the lap of her gown with fistfuls of sand. He felt a rush of pity when she blushed and stared at the sand.

"Don't be ashamed, princess," he said, squatting down as he tried not to let her see how worried he was. How badly this scheme would hurt her! She didn't deserve it. "I'm not here to judge the will of your heart."

She nodded, stole a shy glance at him when he took her hand, and gave it an affectionate kiss.

"I'll come to the Savannah in midsummer. Until then, I'll carry you fondly in my thoughts."

She looked up at him then, her dark eyes full of intensity. "I'll miss you very much. You've been a good friend to me."

He smiled, unable to hide his admiration at her refined beauty. If he wasn't so sure her favor was with Beau, he would have spoken for her a long time ago.

Beau joined them and they clasped hands in farewell. "Godspeed to you, Lang. Give a brave word from me to the traders, won't you?"

"I will. They'll be anxious to hear from us. In the meantime, take your usual pleasure from the frontier. I know it brings you peace."

"Indeed." Beau looked at the woods as if he couldn't wait to throw himself into them.

Maria watched Langdon trot down the beach, his solitary figure moving with a sure and practiced speed. He became just a distant speck, another part of the scenery, wild and free and uninhibited. Carolina surrounded her native son, took him back in her arms until he disappeared inside her.

It was just the three of them now.

They were acutely aware of their diminished numbers as they prepared themselves on the beach. Maria stood before Beau and let him aid her arms through the leather straps of Matthew's harness. He made adjustments to the strap around her waist and shoulders, lifted the yawning Matthew from the sand and carefully eased him inside. Maria walked a few steps to test the device. The wooden frame assumed most of the stress and she didn't feel burdened by the baby's weight.

Beau had to squat into his own pack, then bend forward to shift the heavy weight into a comfortable position on his back. The huge canvas sack was framed more rigidly than hers, their provisions bulging inside. There were two changes of clothes for each, two pounds of beef jerky, a sack of oats, three flasks of whiskey, four pelts of fur, a casket of wampum, some cooking utensils, and a large chunk of soap. Beau assured her they had everything they needed, but a single glance at her surroundings made Maria suddenly skeptical.

Beau picked up a thick mahogany crossbow and rested the ironworks against the leather band around his wrist. There was a quiver tied to the side of the pack, the feathered tips of a dozen arrows rising just behind his left shoulder.

Maria presumed this was their sole source of protection and food. She hoped Beau's skills as an archer were as good as his renowned abilities as a trapper.

Just beyond the sands, the forest loomed, trees and foliage so thick you could barely see a few yards ahead. Exotic birds screeched through the air and strange insects buzzed around them. Maria swallowed hard, tried not to notice how dry her mouth was as she followed Beau through the thorny woods' edge, and stepped into the new continent.

The world suddenly turned vibrant green. It enveloped her, an exotic labyrinth of life that bloomed through the sloping forest floor and twisted up the gnarled trunks of a thousand trees as if reaching for the bright white shafts of sunlight that streamed down from the blue sky above. Inside the belly of this alien land the atmosphere was moist, the air misty and ripe with the musk of nature. And the deeper they penetrated, the more breathtaking it became.

The soft brown earth was strewn with a gay carpet of wildflowers in dazzling shades of red and pink and purple. The trees were wrapped in creeping vines that disappeared beneath branches weighted with an assortment of berries and buds. Maria was stunned by it all, as though caught in a wonderful dream. The beauty of this place was so pure and natural it didn't warrant her fear. Instead, her fright was transformed into a heightened sense of excitement.

She lost track of time, as if it didn't really matter here. Even Matthew noticed the spectacular surroundings. Now and again he'd let out a wild squeal that would make Beau turn around and smile at the boy.

But he said nothing, remaining a short distance ahead of them, occasionally munching on a strip of jerky and following some invisible path as if he knew exactly where he was going.

How a person could keep a sense of direction in this cluttered place was beyond her. Now and again Maria saw him glance at the sun, then shift direction. But she didn't question him, could do nothing but place her complete trust in him.

Their pace was slow but relentless; they paused only for a drink at a stream or a snack at a bush full of berries. Beau made sure she rested just long enough to be revitalized, then he would once again trail off into the woods with Maria and Matthew dutifully following.

Maria was astounded that the sun was already setting when Beau brought them to the bank of a swollen creek. She couldn't believe they had walked for so many hours. At least not until she sat down on a cool carpet of plush moss and realized that her limbs ached, and the balls of her feet stung with blisters. Her back turned sore the minute she leaned it against the sturdy bark of a tree. She closed her eyes, trying to ignore the swarm of gnats buzzing around her head.

Beau took off his pack and sat on the banks of the creek, his legs dangling over the edge. Matthew sat between his thighs, wide-eyed with curiosity. He inspected the moss under his diapered rump, then poked a finger into it. The movement of the water caught his eye and he studied it intently. A bird swooped low, then flew high into the dancing greenery. And all the while, his father beamed at the top of his shiny black head.

"I think he likes it," Beau said, glancing at Maria and deciding she had fared quite well.

She opened one eye and looked at them, a dreamy smile curling her lips. There was relief in her sigh when she closed the eye and went back to resting. Beau admired her, the London debutante turned wilderness wife. Her unbound hair tumbled around her in a curly mass, the thick locks sundried into a satin luster, as smooth and rich as her skin. The serenity of her pose contrasted sharply with her disheveled appearance, lent her pristine beauty a primitive air. The sight of her was subtly arousing, reminding him of how alone they were.

"He missed his nap today," she murmured, always the dedicated governess.

"It's a special occasion. He's come home."

She opened her eyes again and watched the way Beau bent and gave his son's crown a quick nuzzle. "This is his first sight of it, isn't it?"

"Indeed. The night I left Charles Towne, he was sleeping under my cloak . . . so small his whole body fit between my palm and my elbow." Beau chuckled at the thought. "He's grown well, eh? You've taken good care of him, Maria. I meant to tell you that—should have—but I suppose I wasn't such good company most of the trip."

She sat up, wanting to tell him there was no need to apologize, but she'd lost his attention to something in the creek. He removed Matthew from his lap, his fingers fast and deft as he drew an arrow out of his quiver, and slid down the banks.

Beau straddled the water, his feet sinking in the muddy banks as he watched the plump young trout wriggling up the creek. Instinctively, he laid the arrow over his shoulder, used the tip to focus on the movement of the fish. It stopped, nibbled from the streambed. He seized the moment, launched the arrow with swift precision, impaled the creature, and pinned it to the bottom of the stream. He grabbed the arrow, flung the flapping trout on the banks, and waited for another unlucky wanderer. For ten minutes, he crept along the banks and fished, tossing his catch ashore, his whole spirit engrossed in the hunt. He was lost in it, the simple pleasure of it, this first moment of genuine gladness after so many bitter and lonely months. By the time he returned with dinner, he felt cleansed of the murderous stench of London.

Maria awarded his skill with a lazy smile, watched him build a fire and smoke the gutted carcasses into a hearty feast. The three of them ate until they were full.

She drew water out of the stream to wash Matthew, spread a tarp, and tended him. Although he was not aware of her attention, Maria watched Beau fashion a cup out of a few leaves and fill it with every scrap of debris from their meal. Every bone, scale, innard. When he was satisfied that nothing remained, he carried the cup downstream where it was laid in the water, secured to the bank with a handful of stones.

"Why did you do that?" she asked when he returned.

"What?"

"Set the garbage in the stream."

"It's not garbage; someone will find it and eat it. The cold water will keep it fresh."

"Who?"

"A Stono native perhaps, or an animal."

"Indians?" The breath caught in her throat. The mere thought of natives lurking nearby brought a look of danger to the darkening scenery.

Beau used a reed to stir the tobacco in his pipe, sat down, and propped himself against a tree to light it. The bright flare of his flint made her aware of how dark it was getting.

"Yes, Maria, Indians. You know them as the people Europeans call pagan." He laughed dryly. "Let me tell you how savage they are and use the cup of 'garbage' as an example.

"In the New World, hunting is not a sport. Nothing is killed just for the sake of killing. To destroy an animal without cause is considered a sacrilege among the native inhabitants. One kills for the sake of survival, and every bit of the slain creature is used. Nothing is wasted. It is unthinkable to kill an animal just for the sake of mounting its head on a parlor wall. Animals are sacred here. So sacred, in fact, the Savannah always pray before a hunt and beg forgiveness of the creatures they will slay. When its life is taken, the whole body is used and they leave a pile of stones on the place where it perished —as a kind of altar—giving homage to the life it gave in exchange for their own."

"But you're a trapper by trade!"

"Which doesn't mean skinned carcasses are left to rot in the sun. If I can't use the meat, it is given to someone who can, such as the 'garbage' I've left in the stream tonight. Nor do I set my traps and wander off for a week, leaving the animals to suffer. Over here, we stay with the links until the harvest is done. There is no unnecessary suffering."

Maria listened to his words very carefully, knowing Beau was well respected for his knowledge of the land. She was still considering all that he had said when Matthew climbed into her lap, snuggled his face in her belly, and yawned sleepily. She hugged him close as if to protect him from the falling blackness of night.

How different the scenery looked at night, when the twisted menagerie of forest growth turned into eerie silhouettes. Beyond the glow of the campfire, weird orange shadows flickered across the trees like spirits performing a macabre dance. A nearby owl hooted, making her skin crawl. Insects chattered until the noise was deafening. Each time the fire hissed, she jumped.

"Are the ants nibbling at you?" Beau asked, careful to hide his amusement. A first night in the New World frontier was an experience never forgotten by newcomers.

The whites of her eyes shone prominently as she stared at him across the fire. "English nights are not so dark . . . noisy . . ."

He barely noticed the racket of crickets and locusts; his ears were too accustomed to it. "It's just the animals. Many of them sleep during the day and forage by night."

She wasn't the least bit comforted by that explanation. She shivered. Beau came around the fire to drape a pelt across her shoulders. With only her eyes, she begged him to stay close.

He sat down beside her, emptied his pipe in the fire, and refilled it. "You have nothing to fear, Maria."

"You can't be serious," she breathed. "Any kind of beast could invade our camp!"

"I hope so. It will make fetching breakfast much more convenient."

She looked at him in disgust. "What if you're asleep when it comes."

"I'll hear it," he replied confidently. He leaned back on his elbows, stretched out his legs and let the fire warm the soles of his moccasins. "Danger has a smell. If it comes near enough, I'll know it." Beau sighed, beginning to feel tired, and nodded his head at the trees overhead. "There are night birds singing just over there. Can you hear them?" She strained to distinguish the sound among so many others. "The Indians call them nightingales. Legend claims they only sing in peaceful places. If they are here, danger is not."

She tried to look convinced but the effort failed. Beau knew nothing would calm her short of an armed gauntlet of soldiers. He lay down, draped an arm over his eyes, and sighed. "Lie back with me . . . it will relax you."

She inched downward, her body stiff and unyielding as she settled her head against the ball of his shoulder. His nearness distracted her.

Maria concentrated on the warm strength in Beau's body, how soothing it felt. "It was so beautiful today. I was struck by it . . ."

"I know. I could see it on your face."

"I don't want to be afraid of it."

"Don't then."

"I want to belong here, Beau."

He opened his eyes and glanced at the face beside his own. "Why is that so important?"

"Because I never belonged anywhere before." She closed her eyes. Why she was telling him this? "Certainly never with Father."

"Give yourself time," he said. "You attempt a

mighty transition, from the most civilized country in the world to the least civilized. Trust me and lose your fear. Then you'll learn enough to feel like you were born here."

"I hope so. I want nothing more than to forget England . . . that whole part of my life."

"Won't you miss his wealth? Your status there?"

"Humph! His wealth is only money. I would gladly exchange his precious coins for the riches of a real home . . . a loving family."

She smiled with imagined contentment as her head dropped an inch lower on his chest. Beau felt affection for her just then, and slid his hand through her silky hair, letting the sweet rosy scent of her drift up his nostrils.

"I hope you find that happy home one day, Maria. You deserve it."

She didn't respond. Her breathing was deep and rhythmic as she slowly fell asleep. Beau finished his pipe, drew Matthew against his side, and momentarily watched her sleep.

Sleep seemed to emphasize the vulnerability in her youthful beauty. She looked so young and fragile, so unable to protect herself against the hurt in her cold and lonely life.

It pained him to realize how badly he was deceiving her, how much it would hurt her when she learned the truth. Perhaps he should tell her about the scheme, the kidnap, everything.

Disconcerted, he moved away from her and tried to settle into sleep. The minute he withdrew his arm, Maria's eyes popped open. She tried to sit up but he held her back. "Sleep. We have a rigorous walk ahead of us tomorrow."

She frowned as if he'd just asked her to perform some kind of magical feat. She clenched her eyes and made a poor attempt at sleep as she kept plucking at her legs and arms, tossing off imaginary insects. He could hardly sleep with her twitching and resisted the irritation rising in him because he knew how desperate she was for rest. Her eyes already showed rings of fatigue from the night before.

Finally, she withdrew her rosary beads to seek her peace in prayer. She rolled onto her stomach, kissed the crucifix, and bowed her head to recite the Creed.

Maybe she'd pray herself to sleep. He sighed, listening to the familiar lullaby of the windswept forest, the scampering wildlife, the calm continuity of the gurgling creek. Sleep slowly drew him into its embrace. Just as he succumbed, a hand gripped his arm and gave it a frantic jerk.

"Over there!" she cried. "I heard it over there!"

"Heard what?" he growled.

"A beast of some sort!"

He grit his teeth. "For the love of God, will you *please* go to sleep!"

"Oh, please don't be cross with me, Beau! I'm afraid to be awake when you're asleep. Forgive me! I've never slept outside before."

He groaned, knowing it was useless to hope for rest. She was bound to pester him all night long. He rolled over, snatched her into his arms and buried her face in his rawhide vest. "If it's the only way, then I'll hold you and stay awake until you fall asleep. Will that make it easier?"

Maria nodded at once. The voice rumbling inside his chest was deep and stern. She closed her eyes, intent on obedience, listened to the sound of his heart. She felt enveloped in him and let herself be enclosed, reveling in this rare treat of being held by another human being. The warmth was as soothing as the slow massaging motion of his hand on her sore spine. She sank into the nearness of him, the musky scent of him, the way his chest rose and fell with each breath, until she lost sight of everything but him.

Her first thought the following morning was what a terrible night it had been. She sat up, looked for the man who had held her through the night.

Beau was standing over the fire, enjoying a long and languid stretch that made all the muscles on his back ripple. She appreciated the view, how tall and magnificent he looked against the backdrop of virgin forest. His jet black hair was sleep-tossed, spilling to his shoulders where glossy black waves danced and shivered in the morning sunlight. His fawn-colored buckskins blended naturally into the surroundings, hugging his sleek masculine curves. She could see every bulging inch of him, from his powerfully proportioned back to the athletic arch in the base of his spine, from the tightly sculpted curves of his buttocks to the sinewy strings of muscle that trailed down the backs of his legs. Just to look at him made the woman in her stir to life, a ripple of warmth fluttering inside some deep and secret place in her body. She didn't fight it, but let the feeling wash over her the way it had yesterday morning after that heady swim of theirs.

Maria was beginning to enjoy the sensations Beau caused in her body. He made her feel so alive and energized, so wanted and adored, so completely aware of the physical magic between a man and woman who desired each other. In England such an earthy attitude would be called improper, but not here. Something about the wildness of this man and his land made those English notions seem ridiculously out of place.

Matthew stopped gnawing on his toy turkey and pointed at the birds flitting among the trees overhead.

"Dat?" he asked.

"Birds."

He bent his head back and watched Beau's mouth as he repeated the word.

"Burr."

"Good! Smart boy!"

Matthew giggled, hugged himself in delight at his father's praise. Maria finally got up. The muscles in her legs still ached; the blisters on the soles of her feet smarted so painfully they made her eyes tear.

Maria doubted that she could spend another day traveling at yesterday's pace. Of course, she wouldn't dare say anything to Beau. Not after how she had irritated him last night. With an airy smile held firmly on her face, she helped him stoke a new fire in last night's pit and boiled a breakfast of oats. They refreshed themselves in the stream and Maria let her ragged feet linger in the cold water as long as she could, then obediently followed Beau out of camp.

His pace was the same as yesterday's but now it seemed too fast. They had walked less than an hour when her exhausted body pined for rest. She said nothing, doggedly trailing Beau even though her every step was a labor.

The hours wore heavily upon her, testing her physical endurance as never before. The higher the sun rose, the hotter it got. A recent rain left the forest air muggy and stifling. By midday, the linen bodice of her gown was saturated with sweat, her skin chafing wherever the cloth rubbed. She had a nagging stitch in her side that was sometimes so sharp it stole her breath away. But still, she followed Beau relentlessly, tried to be grateful each time he stopped at a water source. It just wasn't frequent enough but she refused to hamper his progress by asking for a longer spell.

It was at the height of the afternoon when they came upon a sudden change in the landscape. The forest opened into a broad expanse of cleared land, a natural meadow that Beau called a savanna. He explained that it was a favorite feasting ground for animals and fowl. Lush green grasses stood four feet high in some places, providing a roof of swaying reeds above an abundance of wild rye and wheat, bluegrass, and clover.

"Why don't you stay here in the shade for a few minutes," Beau said, and Maria wanted to fall at his feet with gratitude. "We need something to eat."

He shirked off his gear and his vest, unlashed the quiver, and slid it onto his bare back. "I'll keep you in sight."

The minute he turned his back, Maria unstrapped the harness and slumped weakly to the ground. She pressed her fingers into the stitch in her side and took several deep breaths until the pain finally eased.

"Paw-Paw!" Matthew whined from inside his harness, pointed at the figure of his father.

"He'll be right back," she said soothingly, took him out of the device, and sat with him against a tree where he could watch Beau. "He's gone to fetch some dinner."

"Yum!"

She used her hand to fan them, wishing the shade felt cooler than it did. Sitting still made her too aware of how fast her heart was racing, and how winded and shallow her breathing was. A vague feeling of nausea rose up but she fought it off, made herself concentrate on the lone figure moving through the distant meadow.

Beau hunched low in the grass, sometimes disappearing from view completely. He moved with such stealth that the reeds barely rustled when he passed. She would lose sight of him, then marvel at how far away he was when he reappeared. The man was fleet-footed and sneaky, like a cat, as he wove through the center of the savanna until he finally squatted out of sight.

He remained hidden for several minutes, buried in a sea of waving reeds.

She watched, waited, about to look elsewhere for him when a huge flock of wild turkey exploded out of the savanna not ten feet from where Beau was hiding. Maria jumped, watched the birds spook into the sky, wings slapping with a horrendous noise as they rushed into the sky.

Beau sprang upright, his figure poised as he followed their frantic flight with the tip of his bow. An arrow aimed with faultless control, the string pulling taut and rigid.

He fired.

The arrow shot across the sky, thudded straight through the airborne body of a bird. It dropped into the grass a hundred yards away.

Another arrow flashed from the quiver, his body turned toward them now as the birds swooped and dove toward the woods. She could see the perfect line between the arrow and the eye just before he fired again. A second bird somersaulted to the ground.

He lowered the crossbow as the flock sped beyond its range. Beau slung it over his shoulder and trotted after his catch.

Maria gazed at him in complete astonishment, unable to believe what she had just seen. How quickly she recalled those pamphlets about the New World, what the English explorers described as the legend of American frontiersmen. No casual skill was this. To fell a bird in midflight with a single arrow was more than just commendable.

It was incredible.

From afar, she admired his prowess, the way he

picked up the birds and started back toward them, tucking the legs in his belt as if there was nothing unusual at all about what he had done. He leapt and twisted through the grass, breaching the distance in a few short minutes.

He was only slightly breathless when he came upon them, his eyes only for Matthew as he laid the enormous feathered bird on the ground before him.

"Look," he said, pointing to the bird. "Turkey."

Matthew ogled it in wide-eyed wonder, watched Beau take the figurine out of his hand and lay it beside the turkey.

He pointed at the figurine, and then the real bird. "Turkey."

"Tokee," Matthew repeated in a solemn whisper, his eyes round with interest. But the difference between the tiny toy and the huge feathered fowl was too much for his young mind to comprehend. He finally looked up at Beau, thoroughly perplexed.

Beau grinned broadly, his white teeth flashing against the dark tan of his skin as he tousled his son's hair affectionately. He winked at Maria and muttered, "He'll learn, and this will keep him amused while we walk." The legs of the turkey were tied to the back of Matthew's harness where the child could see it.

Beau was anxious to move on and reach the other side of the savanna before nightfall. He turned his attention to Maria then, frowned, and asked, "Are you all right? You look spent."

"Heavens no!" she quickly lied, flashing him a bright smile. "The rest restored me."

They weren't a hundred yards into the meadow when she was wincing again. Worse, there was no longer a canopy of trees to shade her from the sun. It streaked down on her like a bath of fire.

The stitch returned. The pain bolted up her side, shot so deeply into her rib cage she gasped and clenched the spot. An enormous pressure was building in her skull as if a band of iron was wrapped around her brow, squeezing tighter and tighter. Her vision blurred, making the clover look like fuzzy green tufts. A moan escaped her throat but Beau was too far ahead to hear. She had to stop him. It was only common sense. But not here. Not in this brutal sun.

Maria tried to keep going although she could feel herself beginning to panic. It made her legs shake as her gait began to weave from side to side. The muscles in her thighs trembled and couldn't support her weight anymore. She could feel them collapsing under her, heard her own voice cry out in dismay as if it was coming from far away.

The grass was suddenly in her face, the earth scraping at her sunburnt skin. Through the ringing in her ears, she could hear Beau's voice.

"Maria . . . hear me, Maria?"

She could feel herself being swept out of the grass, the whole world bouncing in front of her, a whir of blue sky and green grass and a black felt hat brim.

"Why didn't you tell me . . . ? You and your godforsaken humility . . ."

She couldn't seem to make her mind attach to

anything coherent. She opened her eyes to see why Beau was running so fast, so hard she could hear him grunting with exertion.

"Oh, God . . . Beau . . . where . . ."

". . . pool around here . . . spring water . . ."

"Help me . . . oh, God . . ."

She thought her head was going to explode. There was a loud splash and her body was surrounded by something so cold and wet that she gasped in shock.

". . . I have you . . . please be still!"

Beau. He was holding her in water, gripping her tightly to stop her thrashing limbs.

She must have fainted because when she woke again, she found herself steeped in water, floating flat on her back. Her vision swam for a moment, then settled on the face hovering above her.

Beau.

He was in the water with her, one arm around her back and the other under her knees. There was water dripping from the brim of his hat, as he peered down at her. She had never seen alarm on his face before. The sight of it frightened her.

"What . . . where . . . ?"

"Just let the water cool you." He moved her through it, slowly, languidly, until she turned her face into it and started to drink. "Easy . . . drink slow . . ."

Her belly filled with the cold draft, and she moaned at how glorious it felt, how the sound of her frantic heart was finally slowing.

Relief flowed through her and she let her body go slack, floated on his strong arms while the water lapped at her cheeks and licked away the heat in her skin. She finally opened her eyes, looked up at Beau, and saw that he was as relieved as she felt.

"What happened?"

"You just collapsed from heat stroke."

"What?"

"Ssh! The danger is passed. Just lie here and enjoy it."

She obeyed, lying there in the titillating bliss of Beau's attention.

It was on her. She could feel it raking over her, knew she was drenched to the point of near nakedness, but didn't care. Maria wanted him to look at her, see her. But only him, never anyone but him. He was her savior, her provider, her only family now.

She opened her eyes, looked down at herself, saw that she was soaked to the skin. Her breasts rose high and swollen from the water, the pale yellow of her dress revealing the round pink shape of her aureoles. They looked taut and impertinent, as if goading Beau to touch them. He wanted to. His eyes were bold and hungry as they drifted over her, across her slim waist, the soft roundness of her belly, the long curves of her nestled thighs.

He moved slowly to the edge of the pool, until his back brushed the muddy banks. The arm under her knees withdrew. His hand glided along the outside curve of her legs as they dropped downward, lightly grazing his thighs until the tips of her toes sunk into the muddy bottom of the pool.

Their eyes met, full of storms too hot and raging for the sweetness of this moment. Excitement passed between them, made her turn in his arms until their bodies molded together beneath the water. The contact jolted them, sudden and savage, made her realize that he wasn't fighting this desire of theirs any longer, nor was she.

Maria's long-suppressed womanhood awakened with an irresistible urge to tempt a man. Her arms snaked around his neck, pulled him down until their faces were shaded by the brim of his hat. The intense desire he radiated seemed enough to consume her yet she had no will to resist it, only a daring and reckless need to finally know it.

His arm tightened around her waist, ever so gently drawing her against him, as if to tell her, without shocking her, just what he wanted. It took her breath away, the feel of his manhood nestling against her belly, so stiff and full. His name breathed out of her lips, her eyes wide with wonder as she watched his face lower.

She wanted his kiss, to know the taste of him, feel the warmth of his mouth blend with her own.

His lips brushed hers, light and glancing at first, then pressed closer as he began to explore every curve of her mouth. She just hung there for a long moment, her every sense keen to the feel of his lips, the careful way he searched her, urged her, showed her how to respond to a man's kiss.

She learned quickly, eagerly, felt a new kind of

aggression well from somewhere deep in the center of her being, from the exact place where he aroused her. She reached up, her fingers trembling as they slid into his dense black hair, her mouth adhering to his, pressing and demanding, wanting more of whatever peculiar magic this was. It seemed to thrill him, the feel of her fresh hunger, as a shudder coursed through his body just before he gave her what she wanted.

Passion spilled from him like a blast of pent-up heat, made him clench her in his arms, his kiss turning hard and hungry and savage. She moaned at the fierceness of it, her fists clenching his hair, her body writhing. She was aware of nothing but his fury, how much he wanted her, how a man's body responded to the touch of the woman he desired. They melted against the wall of the pool, their bodies locked in the unexpected turbulence of this first sensual contact. They rolled out of the pond, free-falling across the mossy bank, entwined in rapture, burning in the fever of it, drinking from each other with a wild and frantic thirst.

Matthew let out a howl of displeasure.

The sound of it snapped them apart like two people rudely awakened from the most compelling dream of their lives.

Dazed, panting, they lay there staring at each other in complete amazement, as if they didn't recognize each other.

Matthew cried out again.

They both whirled around to see him dangling half in and half out of his harness, looking at them with big wounded eyes. How dare they leave him out of their embrace! He finally got out, toppled to the ground, and burst into angry tears.

"Dammit!" Beau cursed and the spell was broken. "I'm going to teach him how to mind his own business."

Beau snatched him up, flipped him in the air once, then plunged into the pool with him.

Matthew's cries turned to sniffles, then a whimper, finally a delighted laugh.

Beau growled something inaudible. He looked at Maria over his shoulder and shrugged in a combination of longing and apology.

She sank to the ground, her body still throbbing with pleasure, pressed her cheek against the soft grass, and took a long, steadying breath. She closed her eyes, saw him there behind her lids with his burning eyes and hungry mouth and that steely swollen body she could still feel in her arms. It was magical, recalling that long moment until nothing in the world mattered but what had just happened beside the pool.

She didn't know how much time had passed before her eyes opened again. She looked around, half expecting to see Beau and Matthew still swimming in the pond.

But it was dark now. Both the pond and the savanna were gone and they were back in the forest again. A healthy fire was glowing, the delectable aroma of cooking meat filtering up to her nostrils.

"Tokee pay," Matthew was saying.

"It can't play, son, it's dead. Now put it down and eat."

"No! Mine!" the boy snapped. He must have missed his nap.

Maria lifted her head from her furry pallet and looked over her shoulder. Sleepily, she assessed the camp, the figures silhouetted against the bright yellow light of the fire. They were sitting side by side, their backs to her.

Beau plucked a somewhat mauled turkey away from Matthew and tossed it aside. He gave his son a stern look, but his voice was mild and patient as he said, "Never mind the sad looks, boy. If you don't eat you can go to sleep. Which do you want?"

Matthew turned to his father. The firelight sparkled in his big eyes. She could see them fill with hurt and tears. He lifted his arms but Beau remained firm.

"Sleep or eat?"

Matthew burst into tears.

"To bed then," Beau sighed, scooped up the child, and took him to a nearby pelt. Matthew clung to his neck, wailing miserably, but Beau was practiced. He knew how Matthew behaved without a nap, that he would weep inconsolably for about two minutes before dropping into a dead sleep.

A few minutes later, Matthew was sniffling and sucking his thumb as Beau sauntered back to the fire. She watched him sit cross-legged on the ground. He lit his pipe, dragged on it, and blew the smoke up into the night. Now and again she noticed him flexing his back, arching and rubbing at a spot low on his spine, as if it ached him.

Maria was concerned, realizing that his back undoubtedly ached because he had carried her here. Along with Matthew, the gear, the harness. How far?

She started to get up, but Beau heard her, instantly turned around, and said, "No, don't get up. Tell me what you want and I'll bring it."

"How did I get here? Say you didn't carry me."

"All right then, I won't." He shrugged and turned back to the fire, to the roasting turkey carcass, and started shaving pieces of it into Matthew's mug. "Just stay off your feet until the dressing has time to do some good."

Maria looked down at her feet, startled to see that they were wrapped in what appeared to be one of Matthew's diapers. There was a greasy sensation between her toes, a faint odor of mint oozing from them.

Beau crossed the camp in two long strides, came down on one knee before her. The instant their eyes met there was intimacy, a flash of memory of how they had touched each other in the pond today.

"How do you feel?" His voice was low and husky. The sound of it, the way they were looking at each other, made her body stir.

"You astound me," she whispered.

Surprise lit his eyes. "What?"

She could see he had no idea what she was talking about. How could she explain that at this moment, in her eyes, he loomed like a multifaceted diamond, every angle cut with the same brilliantly perfect edge. European men seemed so shriveled and small compared to him. "Oh, nothing." She took a deep breath and reached for the cup, enjoying the way their fingers brushed, lingered. "I was concerned about your back if you did indeed carry me. I saw you rubbing it . . ."

"Did you, now?" He made a scoffing sound under his breath, sat down, and folded his legs in that peculiar fashion of his. "Your attention is better honed than mine then."

She looked at him queerly.

"Just eat."

She daintily plucked a piece of meat from the cup and tasted it. Her eyes widened at the delicious flavor. A moment later, she had greedily devoured the contents and started up to refill the mug.

"Sit."

"But I—"

"Maria!" There was no mistaking the firm command in his voice. He rose, staring down at her, his eyes hard with disapproval. "I'm appalled at the condition of your feet, madam." He reached into his pocket and withdrew her slippers. They landed on her pelt, two balled up scraps of cloth. "Not only are your feet blistered, but by the time I discovered them, the sores were torn open and bleeding. Tell me how you managed to walk so far on them, Maria. I would like to know how you did that."

He wasn't playing with her. The man was dead serious. She couldn't think of an explanation and felt suddenly stupid and embarrassed.

"Don't look away. I'm not trying to shame you."

She didn't move, just sat there feeling terrible for upsetting him.

Beau bent over her, his hand gentle but firm as he lifted her face and made her look at his sad concern. "Why didn't you tell me how bad you felt? Please explain it to me, so next time I'll know how to take better care of you."

"I just didn't want to bother you," she blurted.

"Bother me? Have you any idea how much it *bothered* me to see you collapse in the grass?"

"Please don't be angry with me."

He sighed, exasperated with her. "I'm not angry at you . . . I'm angry at *him* . . . that bloody bastard who sired you. He's the one who taught you how to do this kind of thing . . . bend to the will of others no matter how much pain it causes you." He snapped upright, whirled away, as if stung by his own words.

She watched him stalk the fire, back and forth, like a prowling beast. It frightened her to see him like this, struggling for composure, his hand running through his hair, the tip of his foot kicking stones in and out of place around the firepit.

"Beau—" she began but he silenced her with a brisk wave of his hand. He growled something under his breath, squatted beside the fire, and unsheathed his hunting blade so viciously it made a sharp metallic whine. His grip was tight as he stroked it through the roasting carcass. Slivers of meat dropped into the cup. Its juices dribbled into the fire, making the flames hiss and spit.

"I've upset you, haven't I?" he asked, his voice calm and quiet again.

She was about to say no, then thought better of it. "The truth upsets me, not you."

"And what is the truth, Maria? That he's made you believe you're unworthy of anyone's care?" He waited for an answer, but she could only stare at his back in speechless indecision. "It's the only conclusion I could reach for why you would behave like this . . . punish yourself to the point of heat exhaustion before uttering a word of complaint to me. That's what I did while you were sleeping . . . sat here and thought about it." He picked up a pair of rawhide boots and tossed them toward her. "Oh, and I made you some new shoes. They're not so pretty but they're far more practical than those dainty things you were wearing."

Maria picked one up. It was round and bulky with a leather tie around the ankle. She slid it over her bandaged foot. It fit. He'd used one of her slippers to measure.

But then she realized why the skin was so familiar.

It was his vest.

He'd cut up his vest to make shoes for her and the leather ties were fashioned from the tethers he used for his hair.

She looked at him then, so profoundly touched by the gesture it brought a rush of tears to her eyes. Oh, God, how she loved him at that moment, in all of his rough but tender ways, in his brutal strength and the hidden grief that made him tremble in the night.

She crawled off her pelt, aware of nothing but how much she loved the warm feel of his skin on her cheek, the subtle start in him when he felt her press close against his back. Her hands smoothed him, caressed every curve and indentation of his broad shoulders while her tears coursed down his back in trembling rivers of sorry love.

"Don't cry," he whispered at the black sky overhead. "You've had enough upset for one day. I shouldn't have said any of this. . . . A man's thoughts should be his own."

She let him reach around, snatch her, cradle her in his lap. While she wept on his breast he soothed her, his strong hand in her hair, his warm lips on her temple, his voice whispering words of tender solace.

She lay in his arms for a long time, choked with love, the bliss of his touch, unable to find any words as powerful as the message she gave in her caress. They clung to each other, let their lips find their way together until they were kissing one another again. But not like in the pond. These caresses were soft and leisured, lacking the hungry demands of passion. He didn't let it get that far now. There was something else in his mood that kept the fires low. When they finally emerged from this suspended moment, their bodies were warm and throbbing, physical arousal blending with heady emotions to make a delicious new closeness bloom between them.

Beau laid her down, on her back, his long, hard

body falling partially over her own. He held her face in his hands, kissed her brow, and whispered, "What a wreck he's made of us. Why do we allow it?"

"How can we stop him? He's too powerful, Beau . . . and so . . . so wicked." A memory breezed across her mind, Arthur with Maureen, pretending she was his daughter, the reincarnation of his long dead wife. Maria winced, shuddered in Beau's embrace.

Beau felt it, his eyes washing over her face in close scrutiny. "What happened those last few nights of yours in London? Why were you running away?"

She blinked, startled by the question. "Because he—he frightened me!"

"Why?" he asked quietly, drawing her an inch closer as if to make her feel more secure. She sighed, adored the way their bodies nestled, their thighs entwined, her heart and his thumping close and fast. "Tell me . . . tell me what happened to make you run away."

Maria had never told anyone what she told Beau then, the whole story, every bit of it. The more she revealed the easier it became to spill a little more until she was emptying it all, releasing the anguish she had secreted for so long.

The forgotten daughter of Arthur Vandenburgh. A little girl so full of love for a father who cast her from school to school, who never visited or wrote or lent her more than a few minutes of his time. But he was such a busy man and so very important! She adored him, made excuses for him, tried never to stop believing he loved her just the same.

The little girl became a woman. Maturity was sobering. There was no point in standing on the steps of the convent anymore. The coach wasn't coming. She'd spend another holiday alone in the empty convent, praying with the nuns, rejoicing at the birth of the Christ Child because this was what Christmas meant to her. Not yuletide balls, pretty new dresses, new dance steps to learn. There were no presents to open. Not a single gift from the richest man in the British kingdom.

How foolish she had been to expect an open-armed welcome when she came to London that morning.

This part of her tale was the hardest to tell. She stopped then, in a vain attempt to escape telling it, but Beau wanted it all. He wrapped his fingers in her hair and made her look at him.

"What then? Tell me. You know my worst, now tell me yours."

She did so, her voice halting as she told him about the letter, Sister Eustace, the conversation with Arthur that morning. "The ball was the very next night, Beau. He had it all arranged—the music . . . the food . . . the guests . . . even my dress! And when I wasn't enormously pleased about it, he acted as though I'd lost my mind. I couldn't believe what I was hearing, the way he made me sit there until I showed him 'some small bit of gratitude for all the trouble' he'd gone to. . . . I was so angry but I didn't say anything . . . like you said tonight

. . . just sat there like a stupid fool and murmured something about being tired from the trip."

Beau saw the wounded pride on her face.

"I refused to go along with him . . . with the maids I found in my chamber. I ordered them out . . . all of them." She looked away then, up at the sky, a new expression tightening her face. Fear.

"He came to my chamber and he was livid . . . furious at me for banishing the maids . . . resisting him. The way he slapped me . . . it was so hard! I couldn't believe it! But then that look came in his eyes again . . . that awful . . . that—"

She stopped, clenching her eyes tight.

"What look?"

"No." She hardened with a stubborn defiance. "I won't speak of it. Not that—"

"Maria . . ."

She jerked away from him with a strength that surprised him, and made him stare after her as she fled back to her pelt. "Enough now, I'm tired." She flopped back down on the fur, stiff as a wooden board.

"Can it be so bad?"

"Yes!" she snapped. "It's vile and despicable and I won't speak of it!"

He was completely astonished. He'd never seen her angry before. "All right then, I won't press you."

"It's too shameful."

His curiosity got the better of him. "What the devil did he do? Did he beat you? Is that it?"

"No, he didn't beat me. It was . . . well . . .

worse than that." She muttered something under her breath, flipped over, and lay on her stomach, glaring at the woods.

My, but she was fetching in a passion! He had a fleeting urge to go over there and sample some of it.

"It must have been quite awful to make you run out on your own announcement ball."

"I had to do it . . . get out of there before he did to me what he did to her . . . oh!" she gasped, putting a hand to her mouth and feeling the shame blushing up her neck and across her face. "Maybe it wasn't the way it appeared, maybe he always played those games with her . . ."

"With who?"

"Maureen . . . the housemaid . . . she was his concubine." She blushed scarlet.

A thick silence fell over them. At last Beau spoke. "These games he played with her, did they have anything to do with the way he looked at you?"

She didn't answer, just bent her head. This was her final shame. She was so humiliated she couldn't even look at him when he came to a halt beside her pelt.

"He coveted you, didn't he?" Gone was the softness in his voice. Now it was low, ragged with fury. "Did he touch you?" The question came in a rush of pure black rage. "Tell me the truth."

"No, he didn't, but had I stayed another day, he might have. That's why I ran, because I knew my resemblance to mother was more than he could resist."

Beau couldn't comfort her, touch her, go near

her. His hatred was reeling out of control, the mere sight of her making the blood in his veins swell with outrage. He should have killed Arthur the night he was caught in the house. How he had wanted to do that while Vandenburgh was reprimanding him in the hall, wanted to sink his hands into his scrawny neck and rip his throat out.

Just as Arthur had done to his family, only Beau wouldn't use a knife. No. That was too fast and clean and merciful. He'd do it without a shred of mercy in his heart, with a soul full of a malice so ripe and black Arthur would die in absolute horror. As his family had, caught in that tiny room full of men with slashing blades, watching each other get cut to death until their own turn came.

"Dammit!" Beau's arm slashed like a whip as he hurled her empty mug into the woods. It careened through the foliage, smacked against a tree, shattered into a hundred pieces.

Maria jumped, moved away from him. Beau was not prone to violence and she had no idea how to address him when he was in such a state. So she sat very still, waiting for the blackness to leave his mood.

Beau grabbed his pelt and dragged it across the camp. He was shaking inside from the cold hatred in his soul. Damn that godless, unconscionable man!

"Beau . . ."

He didn't answer her. He didn't dare, just lay down next to his son and tried to let the boy's sleeping face bring him some semblance of sanity. The way it had that night, when he'd heard Matthew cry out from a house full of death.

It took every ounce of his control to keep his voice steady as he finally said to his stricken captive, "One day I'm going to kill your father, Maria." She gasped, shocked at what he'd just said. He didn't care. All that mattered was preparing her. "Remember that. Now go to sleep."

Neither of them slept for a long time, just lay there listening to each other toss and turn on their pallets. Beau watched the embers die in the firepit while his weary mind drifted in and out of the sleep it craved.

He thought of Langdon, wondered how close he was to Charles Towne tonight. In a different time he would be with him now, traveling alongside his friend with Indigo in tow.

How long ago those days seemed now. Like some other lifetime.

It was only months ago.

As much as he enjoyed the frontier, he was always anxious for home after a long trip, for a soft feathertick mattress, the bustling activity of the family parlor.

But he had no home anymore. No mother busy spinning in the parlor or sister primping at the looking glass or brother frowning over a book. Never again would he hear the hearty laugh of his father or the sweet sigh of his bride as she nestled near him in sleep.

Pain stabbed at him. He swallowed the lump in his throat the way he had a thousand times before.

His mood sank. Lord! but this life was insufferable. He looked up at the black sky and wondered how they could do this to him, die without him, leave him behind and so desperately alone.

Sleep came warily, as his restless mind tossed from thought to thought. Visions of the Sanchee around a fire in Sampee Bay kept flashing in and out of his mind, trying to lure him back to that ugly night where life as he knew it came to an end.

But he refused them, wouldn't let the visions stick. He was tired of the dream, tired of reliving their deaths over and over in his mind. They were gone. He was alone. Somehow he had to learn to accept that.

Half-asleep, he didn't realize how fretfully he was tossing on his pallet, how that strange moaning noise from the woods was really coming from his own throat.

But then a new sound came. Maria's voice. "Beau, come awake. . . . Drink this." His eyes opened to a flask of whiskey hovering in front of his face. She was behind it, her gaze as genuine as the sweet solace in her voice. "Are you all right? Was it the dream?"

"No." He suddenly didn't want the flask, pushed it away and reached for her instead. "Come here . . . sleep near me . . ."

She responded instinctively. Maria Loretta Vandenburgh had the most giving heart of anyone he'd ever known.

Her arms floated around him, her soft hair falling like silk across his cheeks. The scent of roses flooded over him. She was holding him in her arms, her fingers stroking through his hair, along his face, the heaving expanse of his chest.

He didn't say anything, just closed his eyes and lay there in her arms. He should push her away, be strong like a man was supposed to be, but he didn't want his strength right now. No, he tossed it away like an old blanket and let her love wash over him like a warm bath on a cold winter night.

She was alone too, just as he was.

His arms snaked around her, pulled her close until he could feel her heart beating beside his own. Somewhere inside that moment, he found her spirit, a slow and gentle river that lay buried beneath mountains of pain.

His torn soul found solace there. And then, finally, he found sleep, in her arms, in the shade of her gentle heart.

They awoke on the same pallet but with their backs to each other. Last night's exposed secrets made them feel undressed in the morning light. They went in different directions to tend their morning rituals, breakfasted in preoccupied silence.

Maria's feet were sore but the mint dressing took away the sting, and her new shoes were surprisingly comfortable. Soft and smooth against her bruised skin, they cushioned her every step. Beau kept their pace leisured, seeming content to meander through the woods. He stayed close to Maria and Matthew, but remained distant in his brooding mood. The only crack in his facade was when he took Matthew out of the harness and explained the wonders of the frontier to his wide-eyed boy. She could see that Beau enjoyed exploring the New World again through the eyes of his son, and for the hundredth time she thanked God for the blessing of Matthew, for what comfort this innocent babe brought his lonely father.

They would always be special to each other, she knew, tragedy linking this father and son in ways that time couldn't sever. How lucky for Matthew!

Matthew slept with Beau that night, a little lump of fur snuggled inside the sprawled curl of his father's body. She was still watching them when sleep came to claim her, still aching to be a part of what they had.

A good sleep brought her awake with renewed energy and strength. As they traveled ever deeper into the Carolina woods, Maria grew more and more determined to belong here. Beau seemed pleased with her eagerness, his silent mood slowly dispersing as he began to teach her the ways of the land.

Before long, they were talking freely, their somberness brightening in shared enthusiasm for what soon became her favorite subject. The New World. She began to feel like an explorer, privileged to be learning firsthand what Englishmen could only read about in pamphlets. It made her feel especially smug when she thought of her father's hired explorers, Dr. Woodward and Sir Colleton. They were out here somewhere in a desperate attempt to undermine the Charles Towne Traders while she walked in the exclusive company of Beau Gardiner himself.

And what a thrill it became to be with him, to realize what made him such a champion among New World men. Watching Beau perform the rituals of survival in his wild land was a source of endless delight. He was swift and cunning as a hunter, exceptionally skilled even though he made it look so easy. The crossbow in his hands was always lethal, rarely missed a target whether it was on the ground or in the air or in a creek. There was meat for them everyday, sometimes twice a day. And he was always alert for game, would sometimes string an arrow in midstride and pause on the path ahead just long enough to line his sights. As the days passed and she grew accustomed to his habits, Maria knew to stop walking and be still for a moment. Just a moment. It never took long to bring in dinner. The man was a crack shot.

She no longer wondered why Beau and Langdon and the New World sailors she met were such thickly muscled men. Beau used his body like one would use an iron tool. Especially in the pursuit of game, he could run and leap with the titanic agility of a tiger, twist and pivot through the timber with the precision of a jackrabbit. Felled timber blocking a trail was hurled aside like a twig. Giant rocks yanked from streambeds and hauled to the night's firepit barely produced a sweat. He was a man of brute strength and she knew how and why he came to be that way. Necessity.

Langdon was right when he said Beau could make outdoor living surprisingly comfortable. He had a knack for finding campsites. They were always nestled near water where the ground was covered in carpets of moss or clover. Leaf-laden trees provided shelter from rain and wind. Broken stumps and fallen trees became tables and chairs. He could carve anything out of a hunk of wood, a toy for Matthew, a wooden spoon for Maria, deadly pointed arrows for his quiver.

He began to teach her everything; how to create feasts of roasted game, gruels, cakes, fruit puddings, even how to spice them with wild herbs she could gather from the forest floor. Beau amused her by showing how the Indian women used the waxy leaves to fashion baskets for collecting food and wide-brimmed hats to keep the sun off their faces. Maria was proud of the first basket she made and used it every day to collect snacks for their ready refreshment. She learned to identify wild figs and plums, raspberries and juicy maycock apples. Natural orchards were plentiful, the balmy climate nurturing limbs full of succulent peaches and apricots. She could nibble all day long on plump strawberries, mulberries and barberries.

She started dressing her hair every day with wildflowers. Violets, princess feathers, wild roses, clove, july flowers. They grew everywhere, bursting out of the ground in vivid explosions of color.

Across forest land, savannas, marshes, and rivers they traveled for an endless succession of days. She was lost in the awe and wonder of it all. The Old World began to seem like life on another planet. Her heart was slowly purging itself of its bitter troubles, refilling on a nectar far sweeter than any Maria had known before.

And she knew why. It was more evident as each day passed and her attachment to Beau grew stronger and stronger.

She was in love with him. Sometimes gently, sometimes madly. It was a powerful, compelling feeling, one that seemed to wash through her heart like a river of healing. Although neither of them said as much aloud, it was there between them, growing more pronounced as their days together grew longer.

She craved any touch of his: when he took her hand to lead her across a creek, played with her hair while they talked, brushed her cheek with his fingertips. Their eyes never met without lingering, without a telltale shock of contact between two people who desired what they saw. But he seemed content to keep it at bay, give their developing friendship room to grow while he watched Maria bloom like a ripe young flower. His admiring attention only added to this new lightness in her heart, to the goodness this man brought to her body and spirit. She couldn't consider any aspect of their closeness to be sinful. After such a long and lonely childhood, the fullness of life with a man became so precious she praised God for it with an ever deepening gratitude.

Within a fortnight of travel, Maria added another sport to her life.

Flirting.

His desire for her quelled her timidity. Nothing

pleased her more than to bring that hungry look into his eyes. It made her feel beautiful, adored, and so very womanly. She employed her best devices, discovering some she never knew she had. A dazzling smile, a lilting laugh, a deep warm gaze from across the trail. She loved to lure him from the path, to let his strong body pin her against the gnarled trunk of an old willow and ravish her with a long and succulent kiss behind the wispy green net of weeping branches. Matthew always pouted until they drew apart, but not before they had filled each other with a greedy drink of pleasure.

It would linger in them for the rest of the day, a kind of heightened awareness, a subtle throbbing excitement that seemed to enliven them both. Beau's dark, mysterious moods began to dwindle in the distraction of her company. She discovered his good-hearted and husky laugh, how quickly he could grin at her antics, how his eyes shone with a vivid interest when he taught her about his birthplace. Maria noticed the easiness of his nature, how the cessation of his nightmares left him more vital and refreshed. Even his tone of voice changed, still deep and resonant but with a much lazier drawl. She loved to listen to him, marveled at how articulate he was despite his primitive upbringing. He understood all aspects of life, from the secret details of a forest floor to the twisted corruption of world politics.

"No, it was Clarendon's idea to pitch a settlement here."

"How can you be so sure, Beau?"

"I read it in your father's papers."

He chuckled at her aghast expression. He sat high above her on the banks of a stream, watching her bathe his son.

She cocked her head up at him. "Just how often did you steal into his house while you were there?"

"Whenever I pleased," he said. "According to Arthur's notes, Clarendon became a giddy fool the minute he discovered where Carolina pelts were being harvested. Most thought they came from Saint Ellens, a Spanish port fifty miles south of Cape Fear. We used to ship from there, years ago. I can remember dragging skids of fur down the coast when I was just a boy, but the harvest always came from the Carolina frontier.

"So Clarendon rushed to start a settlement here. It was unclaimed land. Lord Ashley had the dreams for a model colony; your father had the money to finance it. Lord Carteret and Lord Craven were popular with tradesmen and could convince skilled laborers to resettle in the New World. Sir Colleton is no more than an avid explorer. He leapt at the chance to become a part of the proprietorship. Then there was Lord Berkeley, who had the ships to establish supply lines. And last, Lord Albemarle, the chief of the proprietors, sitting atop them all merely because he's distantly related to King Charles."

How could he know all this? She was the daughter of a proprietor and didn't know as much!

"And so they pooled their money and their resources to finance Charles Towne when all along, what they really wanted, was your fur?"

"It certainly looks that way, doesn't it?" Beau leaned back, casually sucked on his pipe for a few minutes, and watched the sky through the treetops. Dense gray clouds were gathering. It would rain tonight. "But it never really worked, not from the very start. In our own primitive way, I suppose our method of mining and selling Carolina fur was too well established to be interrupted by the whims of some foreign king. And it certainly wasn't our fault their stranded colonists decided to become a part of the existing fur business instead of whatever England planned. We forced no one's hand, Maria. The colonists made their own choice, even though the Crown insists on blaming the traders for seducing them away from the royal plan."

Maria looked up from where she was bending over Matthew in the stream. "But all the royal families of Europe wear Carolina fur. It's as precious to them as their jewels. Aren't you afraid of what they'll do to get it?"

They've already done it, Beau thought, but couldn't say as much to the winsome creature in the water below. It would crush her. Especially now. She was happier than he had ever known her to be. The time to wonder about telling her the truth was gone. It was just too late now.

"They can't get it, Maria," he said with a resigned sigh, "at least not without destroying half the native population in the territory . . . inciting the Spaniards who also mine their fur from the fringes of our market . . . or hauling the traders to England for trial only to learn we're descendants of

France." He grinned at her, hopped off the overhang, and started sliding down the muddy bank. "So after all their trouble, King Charles would have to relinquish his bounty to a Bourbon!"

Maria burst into a fit of naughty giggles. "You're positively invincible, Mr. Gardiner! Now I know why the Westoe Indians say you're divine. I half think it myself!" She laughed gaily, until Matthew threw a fistful of stones at Beau. "Oh, heavens! You mustn't throw things at your father. He has powerful friends, you know!"

And enemies, Beau added to himself.

He tossed a hatful of water over his head, then climbed a cluster of rocks where he could recline and watch Maria. A strong wind gusted through the forest, making the foliage hiss and swirl, a distant rumble of thunder carried in its flushing wake. He could feel the rain clinging to the air. The dampness brought out the forest aromas, bottling them beneath a thick layer of low-hanging clouds. It would be a lusty storm but he didn't care. It was a pleasure to escape the boiling sun for an afternoon, to lie there and listen to his son happily chirping and Maria humming under her breath.

He rolled onto his side and propped himself up so he could take pleasure in the sight of her beneath the low swoop of his hat brim.

What a changeling she had proved herself to be these last few weeks, the shy and reserved convent girl suddenly carefree and brimming with life. Even her manner of dress changed. The dainty London lady grew tired of suffocating herself beneath layers of clothing, stockings and garters, petticoats, and long-sleeved linen dresses. The heat made her resort to wearing just her chemises. They were modest little affairs like the one she wore now, white linen, sleeveless, lightweight, and without a trailing hem. Her legs were bare underneath. The shifts were blousy and full skirted so he made her a belt of braided jute to snuggle the dress around her waist and keep it from snagging on the foliage. She used a piece of blue satin ribbon to string her palmetto basket from the belt and keep her hands free. A hat made of broad magnolia leaves always sat on her head, wide-brimmed and flat-topped except for the cup-shaped contour on the back where it fit to her head. A thick cord of auburn hair was always dangling down her back. He liked the way it swayed from side to side on her rump when she walked in that graceful, flowing gait of hers.

Yet underneath her wilderness garb, Maria was still the perfect lady. Everything about her was distinctly feminine, every manner and movement whispering of an inbred daintiness that Beau found oddly seductive.

Like now, when Matthew sent a splatter of mud across her ankle. Without interrupting his play, she dipped her foot in the water and gave it a little swish until all the offensive matter was gone.

A rumble of thunder brought her head up. "Oh! Is that thunder?"

She hated New World storms, especially the violence of the lightning. "It's miles away yet," he said calmly. She wasn't convinced. Her eyes lifted to the sky, widening slightly with a first trace of fear. "Maria, you have plenty of time to finish," he insisted.

"Oh, but we're long done," she quickly announced as she plucked Matthew out of the water and carried him naked to the shore. She made speedy work of gathering his belongings, bending over the banks, and providing Beau with an exceptional view of her raised derriere. She popped upright, baby and gear clasped to her belly, as she rushed across the stream and nearly fell twice.

"What are you grinning at?" she asked as she slid to a halt beneath his throne of stones.

"You."

"Why?"

"Because you're such an Englishwoman sometimes. Here, give me your hand."

He sat up to give her room on his ledge, watching her plop down between his sprawled thighs to present his bundled son. "His hair needs drying." Matthew screamed in laughter when Beau gave him a frisky dry with a clean diaper. "I hate when you call me that. What exactly is an *Englishwoman,* as you say?"

"A pretty little thing who screeches at mice."

"I think I've been much braver than that!" she sniffed, turning up her chin in that haughty way of hers. "Humph! I wager you enjoyed one or two of those pretty little things while you were spying on my father in England . . ."

"One or two? Lord! What do you take me for, a feeble old man?"

"Oh, go on!" she scoffed, taking a swing at him. "How many then?"

"Several, actually, but there was one maid who caught my fancy so I . . . er . . . consorted with her for the rest of my visit."

"Oh?" Maria was interested although she acted aloof. Her eyes gave away her every thought, another trait he found most charming. "What was her name?"

"Polly."

"What a dreadful name."

"Common, isn't it? But she was quite fetching to look upon."

"Really? What did she look like?"

He leaned back against the rocks, crossed his arms behind his head, and pretended to be thinking of Polly with great longing. Even though his hat brim was pulled low, he could see her eyes narrow with jealousy. "She had long dark hair and very large mysterious eyes . . . and there was always the scent of roses about her . . ."

He winked at the smile curling across her lips. "You're teasing!" she blushed.

"And you're jealous."

"I'm not," she said with a pout, then gasped when he suddenly snatched her close. He swept off her hat as he pulled her near until he could feel the fullness of her breasts against his chest. His hand slid up the slender curve of her spine, massaging it the way she liked, until a sigh brought her face tilting up into his own. There was no resisting the sensual delights in her soft pink mouth. He sampled her flavor until they were both breathless and throbbing. "There's not a woman on earth who merits your jealousy, Lady Vandenburgh. I am like a man struck blind by your radiance—"

"Oh! don't poke fun at me," she moaned as he nibbled at the tender skin on the curve of her neck. Her fingers slid into his hair, raking his tether loose.

Her aggression thrilled him, the feel of her pure and untasted passions, womanly needs too strong for a virgin's body. His desire to bring her over that tender threshold made his loins thicken with hunger. "I'm not making fun." He sighed, letting her swallow his words in a long and sumptuous kiss that stirred him to his breaking point.

As she had that day in the pond. Maria was too innocent to know the limits she had forced him to that day. Had Matthew not interrupted, he would have taken her right there on the bank.

"Enough now . . ." he groaned, freeing his mouth from her thirsty lips and snatching her close in his arms. He said nothing, just held her for a long moment, until this fever of theirs dwindled. "You press me too far sometimes, Englishwoman. You may not want to learn the ways of men in the manner that I'll teach them . . ."

"From you, I would learn anything." She sighed, her soft voice breathless in his ears. "Because your way is so kind and patient. I fear nothing that comes from you."

He appreciated the sincerity in her, but it did not dispel his own guilt in allowing her to fall in love with him. He should stop this but he knew he wouldn't. He needed her, in some yet unnamed way, there was something about her points of pain that too exactly matched his own.

Beau smoothed her cheek, brought her face away from his breast, and looked into her simmering brown eyes. "Your heart is full of intentions your mind may not accept." She frowned at him, not understanding. "I want you in my bed, Maria." He felt a little quiver rush through her, the shade of her eyes darken like a muddy pool caught sparkling in the sunlight. "And if you take me into it, you must do so knowing we're not blessed. There are no men of the cloth here to bless us . . . nothing I can do to make this sacred enough for you . . ."

"There must be a man of the cloth somewhere who can bless us! Take me to him, Beau!"

"There is no one."

And even if there was, he thought with a pang of conscience, I can't marry you, bring you home to your father with your belly full of my seed.

Her eyes dropped in disappointment. "What do men and women of the frontier do then, Beau?"

"They either cohabit until a man of the cloth wanders by or join in Indian fashion."

"Which is?"

He chuckled at her hopeful expression. "It means erecting a tent, standing in front of the flap, and listening to the tribal chief bestow his wishes that the union of your bodies will bring forth many fruits."

Her face turned scarlet, her hopes dashed in the

shock of this godless practice. "Oh," she muttered dismally. "There it is then, eh?"

"There it is."

She turned thoughtful, perhaps contemplating religious philosophies. Hers and theirs. Once again, he chided himself for refusing her the other facts in the matter, more important reasons to resist intimacy with her.

Because he had kidnapped her. Because a second ransom note to Arthur was soon to be published in London. Because he couldn't very well return her pregnant to England.

Frustration brought forth a deep and bitter sigh from his lungs. But she didn't hear it. Growling thunder had her attention and once again she looked to him for protection.

He gathered her and Matthew and led them into safer shelter for the night.

It had been a hard, soaking rain. Maria wondered how such an angry night of storms could give way to this spectacular morning. The sun rose brilliantly, towering golden beams slashing through the timber, illuminating the wetness and making every surface gleam as if freshly waxed. The air was thick with the musky fragrance of soggy earth, a filmy mist clinging to the forest floor and lending the woods an almost mystical beauty.

She had an urge for a bath, to plunge herself into this earthy place and continue to deliberate on what Beau had told her yesterday about the ways of men and women here. It seemed so godless but at the same time, in a world so unadorned and natural, there was a kind of primitive logic to it.

Maria decided to be alone with her thoughts, gathered soap and a comb, and padded barefoot from the camp. The earth was damp and spongy under her feet as she followed the roaming banks of the stream, winding through the forest until she found a place where the water was deep enough.

She tossed aside her bundle, unbuttoned her chemise, and let it flutter down her arms. The simple act of baring her breasts out here in this flourishing cradle of life sent a wicked sensation of pleasure through her body. She shook off the dress, stepped naked to the banks of the stream, and started wading into the water.

It felt deliciously cold. She shuddered as the water licked at the soft flesh of her thighs. She submerged herself to the neck, let out a shivering gasp as her skin puckered in a rush of gooseflesh. In a moment she adjusted to the cold, fanned out her arms, and enjoyed a lazy float.

She rolled over, smiled at the sky in sheer delight. High overhead, sparrows swooped through the treetops, their songs trumpeting praise at the new sun. Willows sheltered her bath with a green lace curtain of feathery limbs. Maria fancied herself to be a part of this neolithic place, a child of its primal majesty and all the beautiful creatures that lived within it.

A rustling noise sounded in the reeds beside her. Maria feared an animal and knew it was best to be still until it passed.

It didn't go away. It was there, a dark form huddling behind the long thin stems of a stand of milkweed.

Without turning her head, she looked toward the bank out of the corner of her eye.

There was someone there. A man. He was squatting just inside the brush, watching her.

"Beau?"

No answer.

Of course it wasn't him. Beau never violated the privacy of her baths. He was always respectful of her modesty.

There was an Indian here.

Dear God!

The figure rose, unfolding from behind the reeds like some dreadful apparition from a nightmare.

It was a native all right, a short man who stood no taller than five feet. His red-brown chest was hairless, a large and garishly painted symbol etched in his flesh. He wore a collar of feathers and teeth, as well as a thin strand of bright-colored beads around his high protruding forehead. His features were broad and thick, and mats of dense black hair hung to his waist, fluttering in the morning breeze. He was naked except for a cloth of animal skin that bound his loins and the same style of moccasins that Beau wore.

Maria realized she was gawking at him and quickly looked away.

He started moving along the banks, following her drift.

Panic made her hang paralyzed in the water. She

couldn't think of what to do, how to get out of here without this man running her down in the woods.

He spoke then, a series of grunts that sounded like, "Ya keeta paw."

Dear Lord! He was trying to talk to her.

She didn't answer or look at him, but lay there in an almost hypnotic state of indecision.

Why hadn't Beau prepared her for this? He always said there were Indians about, but never once did he instruct her on how to behave if she ever encountered one. And so she continued to let herself float on the current, inching downstream with the desperate hope that it might bring her alongside their camp.

But she knew she was too far away.

The Indian grunted at her again, but this time his tone of voice was harsh, demanding. She looked at him, frantically shaking her head to tell him she didn't understand his strange, chopped language. The expression on his face hardened, turned grim and severe. He jabbed a finger at her, then pointed to the bank at his feet. He wanted her to come to him.

Again she shook her head, terrified tears filling her eyes just as he bounded off the banks and dove into the water. He disappeared in the deep pool, completely submerged. Seconds later, two clutching hands wrapped around her ankles.

Maria never knew she was capable of emitting such a sound as the scream that tore out of her throat at that moment. It was piercing enough to make all the birds fly away in a sudden frenzy. She kicked her legs powerfully and managed to wrest one ankle free. The Indian splashed through the surface, whipped his ragged hair out of his face, and jerked on her foot.

She flailed backward, screamed again, this time her mouth filling with water.

"NO!" she cried, "leave me be! Go away!"

His hand wrapped around her hair, ruthlessly yanking her upward until her breasts cleared the surface. He held her like that, hanging by her hair, while raking his eyes over her naked bosom until his face filled with lust.

She screamed again but this time the sound was dwarfed by another; a chilling, guttural howl that seemed to roar out of the sky directly above her head.

Beau's body was suddenly slamming against the Indian's shoulder, pitching him sideways into the water. Maria leapt free, dazed and horrified, watching both men tumble underwater and come up in a splashing fury only a few yards away. They had each other by the throat. Beau was on his back, the native atop him.

Then they stopped, looked at one another, and sprang apart.

Beau found his footing in the stream and rose out of the water, towering above the coiled native with a hunting blade clenched in his fist. For a long tense moment they just stood there glaring at each other, poised to attack, until the Indian finally relented to Beau's superior strength. They relaxed, stood upright, still watching each other warily as they shook their drenched manes and sent sprays of water tumbling through the sunlight.

Beau spoke to the brave then, his voice rough and hoarse, pointing at her and then himself. The Indian understood, nodded abruptly, then followed Beau out of the stream. As he scaled the banks, Beau gave Maria a chilling glance over his shoulder.

He was angry at her.

And she deserved it for straying so far.

Feeling suddenly sheepish, she sank deeper in the water and clung to the rocky streambed with her toes. Beau and the native proceeded into a much more friendly conversation on the banks.

While they seemed to forget her, Maria began to grow cold, her skin wrinkling and turning pink in the cool water. Not wanting to interrupt, she paddled around in an attempt to stay warm but the effort failed after only a few minutes.

"Beau," she gingerly called to him. He looked over at her, his gaze cold and hard. "Could you fetch my clothes? I need to get out of the water."

"I'm not your servant, madam!" he snapped and returned to his conversation. Only when he and the native parted peacefully, did Beau return his full attention to her.

He came to the edge of the stream, crossed his arms over his chest, and wordlessly demanded an explanation.

"How was I to know the Indian would be here!" she blurted defensively. "I was minding my own affairs, just taking a bath and enjoying the morning!"

"I hardly think it was necessary to venture this

far from camp for the privacy of a bath!" A long brown finger pointed at her then, his eyes blazing with blue fire as he demanded, "Don't you ever do this again. Do you hear me? You stay *at my side* at all times. Dammit Maria!" He shot his hands through his hair, trying to control himself. "These woods are infested with Creek. That brave was about to take you, thus marking you as his own and carrying you off with him to his village."

"Oh!" she gasped, instantly distressed at the thought of what could have happened to her. "What did you tell him?"

"That you were my woman, is what! And he had every right to challenge me because you don't wear a mark of mine. If I wasn't so respected among the Creek, we would have fought for your possession, which is the custom among red men."

"But I've not seen a native since we landed!"

"That means nothing! They're here . . . they know we're here . . . they allow us free passage because they know me . . . know that I'm a frequent wanderer here and am a man of peace." Beau stopped, looked at her more closely, and said, "We'll continue this discussion when you get out of the water. Your lips are turning blue."

"I'll get out when you turn around."

Beau whipped around impatiently and stood with his back to her, his narrow hips cocked, one foot tapping in annoyance.

Maria scrambled out of the stream and dove for her clothes. She dressed hurriedly, her fingers nervous and fumbling as she buttoned her dress far enough to cover her breasts. Beau was angry at her and she dreaded his disapproval.

When decent, she came out of the foliage and presented herself to his angry perusal. He seemed to see every place where her dress stuck to her wet, naked body but she didn't dare look at him, just hung her head in shame while he unleashed his justified wrath.

"I did not deserve to be awakened like this today . . . by the sound of your scream coming from somewhere deep in the woods . . . not a clue as to where I might find you and help. I had to wrench my son out of sleep and tie him up in his harness to come after you! You can apologize to us both for that!"

"I'm sorry," she said softly.

"Come here," he growled, taking her by the arm and leading her to a patch of wet dirt. He picked up a stick and drew a symbol there, a circle with an *X* through it.

"This is my symbol, the equivalent of a written name to the natives here. Every man has a mark and this is mine. The lines of the *X* symbolize the two paths I walk in life, one amongst my white ancestors, the other amongst the natives of the land where I was born. The paths intersect because I am part of both people, and the circle denotes the harmony with which I walk in both worlds.

"This is the mark you will wear from here on but I'll spare you the way it's normally done—by carving it into your skin with a knife—and fashion you some kind of pendant to wear. Until now, there was no need for this safeguard. You never wandered off like this before. But should it happen again, you'll be protected. I don't ever want to see you without my symbol displayed around your neck. Promise me, Maria. Don't make me mark you. It would sicken me to scar you but I'll do it if it keeps you safe."

Maria gulped, glad to be spared the cutting he described. She nodded at once, keeping her eyes pinned to a bright red ladybug that was perched on the tip of a reed only inches from her hand. After hearing of this barbaric custom, she was happy to look anywhere but at his face.

"Answer me," he implored.

"I'll wear it always, Beau."

"And promise me you'll never go off like this again . . . that you'll stay with me and keep your place beside my son."

"Place," she repeated, watching the ladybug inch down the other side of the reed. What a queer way to describe her relationship with him. "What do you mean?"

"You're supposed to stay with Matthew, Maria. That's what I hired you to do, remember?"

She nodded. "I didn't mean to neglect my duties."

"Of course you didn't. Forgive me for being so hard on you but you've done nothing like this before. You've always been mindful of your duties here."

"What do you mean by this . . . place . . .

duties?" She didn't like the terms he was using. Not one bit.

"With me and Matthew, is what. You agreed to tend him in exchange for my protection, your food and lodging in the New World."

Indenture. That's what he was describing.

"Are you suggesting that I'm indentured to you, Beau?"

He thought for a moment, stopped by the affronted tone in her voice. "According to English law, I suppose that's what you are, yes, an indentured servant."

"I see." She watched the ladybug drop off the reed. "You must remind me more often of my station."

How dare he suggest she was a mere indentured servant to him! He had no right!

Before she lost her composure, she brushed passed him, her injured pride swelling into indignant anger.

"Maria . . ." he called after her. "What the devil . . ." He marched up behind her and tried to take her arm but she whipped it away. "What's gotten into you?"

"I'm not your servant, Mr. Gardiner!" she snapped, her legs moving faster as her anger rose, until she was running outright through the woods.

He was right! Passage to the New World was commonly acquired through indenture, and no matter what else there was between her and Beau, she was still a servant.

Fool! You stupid, foolish girl! To escape the captivity of Arthur, she'd run straight into another!

"Maria! Stop it!"

His command only pricked her pride more, made her run all the harder as if trying to outrace the truth. Once she had been a member of the powerful upper class of London. Now she was the lowest class, a slave, bought and paid for in the eyes of the law. Was there no escaping her miserable lot in life? Must she always be a beggar for love, attention, a place to belong?

"Stop, I say!" Beau barked. He caught her arm and spun her around to face him. He was not prepared for what he saw. Normally docile eyes sparked with breathtaking rage. Her chin rose in defiance, her shoulders squared into a regal posture.

"You're sorely mistaken about this arrangement. If you remember correctly, I offered you my diamonds in exchange for passage. You refused them! I could have bought my own passage, sir!"

"All right then, you could! I saw no need for it—"

"Then you'll not refer to me as a servant."

"I never said that—"

"You implied it. Don't deny it! Mind your place, Maria!" she mimicked, yanking her arm free as she spun away from him.

What a mesmerizing woman, Beau thought, so cool and reserved except where her passions were concerned.

He trotted after her. "Whether it's by indenture

or not, you still belong to me, Maria! That's the only point I'm trying to make."

"Is that so?" She whirled around to confront him squarely. "I am not owned by you or any man, save the Lord. He is my only master, the only man in my life who never humiliated me or rejected me or degraded me. To Him I bow in service, but *only* Him! Think what you will, Beau, but I'll not be a party to this arrangement if it costs me my dignity as a human being!"

"Oh, for God's sake, Maria . . ."

"To be owned by another is the definition of servitude. Can you deny that?"

"No."

"Very well. Then I ask you to escort me to the nearest port where I can find passage back to England and serve as a proper governess in my own country."

Beau stopped admiring the view.

If she ran from Arthur, she could run from him.

The ransom scheme depended on keeping her happy and content with her fictitious position in his life.

Without realizing it, Beau had her by the shoulders now, had pulled her against his body until the contact with him made her start.

"I'm not taking you anywhere, Maria."

"You can't hold me here against my will!" she cried. She tried to wriggle out of his grasp, but the movement only brought an even warmer hue to his simmering blue gaze.

"Against your will? I don't think that's the case.

Shall I prove it?" She knew exactly what he was talking about. Her feelings for him.

Outraged by his arrogance, humiliated to the depths of her soul, she slapped his cheek with enough fury to make his head snap backward. "How dare you mock me!"

He released her and stood there staring at her in complete astonishment.

"The only thing you can prove to me now, Beau Gardiner, is how quickly you can get both myself and my possessions—which are aboard the *Savannah Wind*—back to England!"

With that, she turned on her heels and flew away.

He was after her in an instant, like a wild boar, charging through the woodland with a speed she could never hope to beat. With an angry cry of dismay, she felt his arm wrap around her waist and drag her down with him to the ground.

They sprawled in the leaves, clumps of dirt and debris fluttering around them as Maria fought him with all her might. But it was like pummeling an iron wall as he easily pinned her beneath his weight. Her flailing hands were gathered together at the wrist, held to the ground above her head.

From behind the tousled mass of his mahogany mane, two piercing blue eyes leveled directly into her own. His voice was a hard, rasping baritone as he growled, "Put these thoughts of running out of your head, woman, because there is no power on earth that will take you from me . . . *none!* Call yourself whatever you want, a slave, a governess, a servant. But to me, you're more than all those titles

. . . much more. And one day, you'll serve a greater purpose to me than that of a governess."

She stared at him, panting and breathless, her belly heaving into his in a way that made her entirely aware of how much of a man he was.

"What purpose? What are you talking about?"

"In time, you'll know. Until then, you belong to me and I will guard you jealously, possess you as I have never wanted to possess a woman."

An hour later, Maria was sitting with Matthew on a stump in camp, silent and sullen while Beau finished carving the pendant out of a piece of bark. He used a tether to make a cord for it, didn't speak to her or even look at her when he knotted it around her neck.

"Let's go," he said as he picked up their gear and brought it to a grunting halt on his back.

The air between them was strained for most of the day. Beau made a few attempts at conversation but Maria would not rise to it. She was too disturbed by the morning's incident, reminded of it every time his heavy pendant bounced on her breast. She wanted to rail at him in anger and confusion, to demand an explanation. But she didn't. Humility kept her wounds hidden beneath a reserved and practiced facade, her usual hiding place. No matter how many attempts Beau made to whisk away her mask, she kept it firmly in place. She was good at that.

Beau led her up the side of a steep ridge, the climb grueling with Matthew on her back. Her knees smarted against the rocks, the harness cutting ridges in her shoulders by the time they reached the crest. She sank against a half-dead tree, winded and sweaty.

"Are you all right, Maria?"

"Of course." Dare the indentured one complain?

He didn't look convinced but finally shrugged and walked to the edge of the summit, pointed down into the valley. "We'll spend the night down there . . . in Cussitah. The chief of the Creek tribe, Running Dog, keeps his family here, and his larders are open for trade." He glanced back at her to see if she was afraid. Maria kept her eyes pinned to the village. "My father's camp is only a half-day journey from here. We'll need supplies."

The village squatted in a small natural clearing in the woodland below. Nearly thirty huts, dome-shaped and thatched, collected under the dusky light of waning day. Several open fires were lit, little orange balls of light around which she could see figures moving. It looked peaceful down there, cozy and sheltered in the fiery glow of a setting sun, but the morning's experience made her apprehensive about spending the night here.

"The brave who came upon you this morning is most likely from this village."

What a pleasant reminder, Maria thought dryly. She couldn't wait to get there now!

"We can rest here if you wish, Maria." Beau approached her at the tree and was met by the same gloomy expression she had worn all day. She had not spoken ten words to him since they left camp.

"I know you're anxious to go on," she said, and continued to stare at the village.

Matthew whined. His diaper needed changing. Maria wanted to tend him before he developed a rash. She spread a tarp on the ground and laid him down. Matthew cooed sweetly at her, a piece of beef jerky clutched in his fist. While she changed him, he teased her with the soggy snack and she feigned snatching bites from it.

She heard Beau settle against a tree near her, could feel him watching her every move while he lazily sucked on his pipe.

"Maria," he finally said, "we must talk." He was becoming annoyed at her silence. He missed her engaging company, the attention she gave him. Now she barely looked him in the eye.

"About what?" she asked without looking up from Matthew. Her smile was only for the boy, he noticed.

"This morning."

"I have little to say on the matter."

"I've noticed. It was not my intention to hurt your feelings or make you ashamed of anything we have between us. I was only trying to protect you."

"I've always found it particularly ennobling when a man treats his servants well," she said in her perfectly pronounced British syllables.

His patience left him. "I sorely regret ever mentioning that word."

"That makes two of us then, doesn't it?"

He grit his teeth so hard he nearly bit through his

pipe stem. "You just won't put this aside, will you?"

"No, I will not," she said firmly, stubbornly. "And if you remember, you asked me not to forget my *place*. I'm merely obeying your wishes."

"I've had enough of this, woman!"

"Then let's not discuss it anymore."

"Have it your way then," he snarled in complete frustration. He got up, angrily slapped the spent tobacco from his pipe, and grabbed their gear. Without waiting for her, he started to descend the ridge toward the village.

"Beau? Where are you going?"

"To Cussitah . . . where there might be some livelier company."

She hurriedly finished with the baby, took up her belongings, and scrambled after him.

Their appearance on the ridge caused a stir in the sleepy village. There was a collection of Creek waiting at the base of the hill when Beau cleared the woods. He was immediately encircled by friends. Maria stayed close behind him, intimidated by this crush of savages with their long, stringy hair and half-naked bodies. Many of the women in the crowd were bare-breasted, some with babies openly suckling them. Maria was embarrassed at first, could hardly lift her face when Beau took her hand and drew her around in front of him.

"Just be still and let them admire you," he whispered. "I never brought my wife here before and they're pleased to see my family."

She stood frozen, her face humbly bent as she

heard the braves guffawing over her in obvious pleasure.

"They think you're fetching," Beau continued to interpret from behind. His hand slid around her waist, his palm boldly caressing her belly. He said something in Creek, the language fast and fluent on his lips while he continued to fondle her. The way he was touching her produced a spark of warmth between them as he murmured huskily, "Let them think my son came from you, eh? Be his mother while we're here. Matthew thinks it anyway."

Matthew was removed from her harness and held aloft. Cheers rang out, many of the braves slapping his back and openly praising Matthew. The boy just looked around with big wide eyes, avidly sucking his thumb, afraid of nothing while his father held him. Pride filled Beau's face as he presented his firstborn son and Maria felt the air fill with celebration.

Beau tucked Matthew against his side, brought Maria close and whispered, "They will give us a hut for the night and we'll share it as a family. Now go with the women and don't be afraid. It is rare for them to see a white woman. They will treat you well."

Beau disappeared into a crowd of men and Maria was left to stand alone in a circle of women. They inspected her with awe and admiration, were especially intrigued by the white cotton fabric of her gown.

One of the women took Maria's arm and spoke in broken but understandable English. "I daughter to Running Dog, chief of Creek. I Yant'Ho. Say name."

"Maria," she said in a soft, timid voice that made Yant'Ho bend closer to hear.

"Mah-ree-ah," Yant'Ho repeated, her deep-set black eyes perusing the white face intently from beneath a thick headband of blue-and-white beads. "Come to hut now, Mah-ree-ah. I show you."

She was led into the village along a zigzagging path between the huts, passing by an enormous fire pit where Beau and the men were settling on the ground to smoke and talk. He gave her a brief steadying look beneath the brim of his hat.

Yant'Ho stopped at a hut, then bent over to peel back the canvas flap and display the interior. It was carpeted in woven mats and fur pelts, with a round area of open dirt in the middle where dry wood was arranged and ready for fire. After sleeping outdoors for so long, Maria found the idea of snuggling in here surprisingly inviting. She did not suppress her smile of pleasure.

Yant'Ho saw it and bobbed her head happily. "Plenty room to pleasure man." Maria gulped. Yant'Ho cackled in laughter. "Sit," she commanded and beckoned at a round straw mat that sat outside the entrance to the hut. Maria did as she was told, sat down, and curled her legs under her the way Beau always did. A dozen women dropped to the ground around her. They all started babbling at once. Maria motioned to her lips and shook her head to tell them she did not know their language.

Everyone paused, looked toward Yant'Ho for

advice. Maria noticed then how highly decorated Yant'Ho was in comparison to the others. All the women sported strands of beads around their necks and wrists, each seeming to have their own particular set of colors. But Yant'Ho was abundantly adorned in blue-and-white beads, a thick band cinched around her forehead, two on each wrist, one on each ankle. Her doeskin shift was belted in the same manner. Where the other women left their hair straight and mangy, Yant'Ho's was neatly combed and braided into two thick black plaits that hung to her thighs. She was the comeliest maid of all, Maria saw, the wide bones of her face stark and proud with authority.

"Sisters ask you tell of homeland across Great Water."

Maria nodded, then spoke slowly so Yant'Ho could translate as she told the Creek women about Europe and her great cities. She described the lovely English countryside and the customs of the people. The women listened raptly.

"Now tell of dress. Where you get?"

Maria described the dressing habits of European women, about broadcloth and lace and satins and silks and how ladies dressed their hair for special occasions. These descriptions made the Creek women gasp in delight, many of them reaching out to finger the hem of her dress and gaze at it as if it were fashioned in gold.

Their innocence was heartwarming. After just a short time, Maria could see there was no hostility here, only a good-natured curiosity between two very different people. Her reservations slipped away, her taut nerves finally relaxing, as she answered Yant'Ho's questions and watched the women around her thrill at her descriptions.

Someone introduced a leather flask into the crowd and Maria saw it pass from hand to hand. When everyone had taken a sip, Yant'Ho presented it to her. Drinking from the flask was obviously a ritual of friendship and Maria complied, swallowing a mouthful. It burned all the way down her throat. She nearly gagged, struggled to hold back a choke of distaste, while blinking the water out of her eyes. Yant'Ho grinned at her indulgence, her eyes warm with friendship. Maria had obviously passed some sort of indoctrination and managed a wobbly smile in return. The flask passed through the crowd again and again. Each time it came to her, Maria grit her teeth and drank more. It wasn't long before she felt a little dizzy and silly, her whole body light and airy. She finally realized what they were drinking. Whiskey. No wonder they called it "burning water"! Thankfully, it became much easier to swallow once her lips had turned numb.

Their talk turned to religion and Yant'Ho was particularly fascinated by Maria's story of Jesus Christ. She showed them her rosary beads, and they looked pained when she described the Crucifixion. When she described His Resurrection and everlasting life, their faces glowed in rapture.

But then it was her turn to be entertained, and Maria stretched out to listen to an enchanting description of the Creek beliefs.

The Indians believed all men were descended from animals, which was why their gods were depicted as birds and mammals. Forest creatures were given the utmost respect. Even though it was often necessary to kill them for nourishment, just as Beau had once described, the Creek always apologized to their victims before slaying them. Their remains were considered sacred.

Symbolism was also a large part of their faith. They believed in good luck charms, manitous. Everyone had a special symbol. It was usually chosen from a dream of particular significance and was most often an animal or plant figure. This was not a custom peculiar to the Creek, Yant'Ho explained, but was practiced among many Carolina tribes such as the Savannah, Stono, Sanchee, and Westoe.

Maria was particularly impressed by their strange but beautiful concept of death. To die was considered a high honor. It meant acceptance into the spiritual world. The Creek had no burial grounds. People were buried on the exact spot where they died, their graves marked with the deceased person's manitou. Any Indian who passed over the grave would cast a stick or stone atop it as a gesture of respect for the dead spirit.

Indians didn't seem so pagan anymore. Maria was enjoying herself, the gloom of the day forgotten in their interesting talk. She and Yant'Ho reclined on the mat outside her hut, watched the women disperse to tend their children for the night, and let the antics of the men momentarily entertain them.

A fire was raging in the pit now as a large group

of men assembled around it. They were noisy and rambunctious, many pipes and flasks passing among the men while the boys kept to their own circles. The adolescents did not interfere with the men but they were just as loud, hooting over some game they played in the dirt with sticks and pebbles. Music emanated from the group, thumped out of small canvas drums held between the thighs. The rhythm was swift and wild. Several braves rose to dance, while others chanted strange songs.

And there was Beau, sitting in the center of their play, wares of food and fur being shown to him in exchange for the wampum in his casket. A keen eye assessed each offering. Deals waged, wampum passed from hand to hand, a pile of goods mounted behind him. All the while, jugs of whiskey and pipes of smoke were drawn in and out of his mouth. She could tell by the merry look on his face that he was having a grand time and getting quite drunk in the process.

But Maria was in no position to cast aspersions. She had a belly full of whiskey herself and was rather enjoying the effect it had on her. Until tonight, she'd never tasted any liquor stronger than sherry. It was not proper for English ladies to indulge in the more powerful drinks enjoyed by men. The custom was regrettable, she decided. Women should have the right to enjoy the wonderful listless state inspired by a good draft of whiskey.

It was time to put Matthew to bed and she watched Beau rise on unsteady legs with the boy clasped to his chest. Matthew wailed in disappointment as Beau looked around for her, his lazy gaze finally settling on the place where she and Yant'Ho were relaxing.

Maria's spirits sank as she watched him approach, suddenly remembering everything that had passed between them today. But the whiskey dulled the ache of it, left her more eager to peruse the handsome figure he presented as he swaggered up the path. Beau was stripped to the waist, his magnificent physique displayed in all its rugged glory. His skin gleamed with sweat in the firelight and there was power in his easy gait, a titanic grace in the stride of his long legs. Tight fawn britches rode low on his hips, hugging his taut belly, letting her see how the hair on his torso thinned and disappeared behind his lacings. There was little left to wonder about in those snug leggings. Just to look upon such an ample endowment of manhood made Maria blush crimson.

She looked away, glad for the darkness, relieved he couldn't detect the flush of her desire for him. What woman couldn't want this man? One glance from his startling blue eyes made every part of her womanhood come alive. Who could not be flattered by how adamantly he spoke for her today, lying atop her in the brush, refusing to let any power on earth take her away from him.

A woman who had been scorned and degraded too many times, Maria realized, and one whose fractured pride could not bear the rebuke of his angry words.

She kept her eyes averted when he handed Matthew down to her, taking notice of the whiskey flask lying beside her but saying nothing as he turned and walked away. She took Matthew into the hut and sat with him until he fell asleep.

By then, her mood was sunken. She decided to busy herself with the day's laundry and made no comment to Beau as she fetched it out of his gear. Yant'Ho showed her to the path that led to the Savannah River and Maria followed hastily. Her legs were oddly unstable. Twice she bumped into a tree but felt no injury, just a little foolish. With a giggle, she meandered down the path until it ended at the river.

The Savannah spread before her, wide and mighty and deep. It was a breathtaking sight, especially with a full moon hanging high and bright above it. The water was still, its glassy surface reflecting a brilliant canopy of light from the stars above. Here and there the surface broke as fish leapt and fed upon hovering insects. Their hungry gulps left silver rings in the water, ever-widening circles that fanned outward, then disappeared. A collection of water lilies swirled around her ankles as she waded into the water. A frog leapt and splashed away from her intrusion. She listened to the rustle of willow branches behind her, lazily swaying in the moist and sweet-smelling breezes.

Maria took the flask from her pocket and drank a few healthy swallows. She looked up into the sky, sought a bright star, and thanked God for the gift of this beautiful paradise.

If only she and Beau had not shared those angry words today!

Maria grimaced at the soiled diapers in her hand. She began to wash them in the cold water, slapping them against the rocks piled along the shore.

"Maria?"

Beau. She should have known he wouldn't let her wander far.

"I'm just doing the laundry," she said without looking at him.

Perhaps to Maria, her voice sounded perfectly normal, but not to Beau. Her tone was unusually deep, her speech slurred. "You're laundering at this hour of the night," he remarked, then noticed the whiskey flask by her side.

No wonder she had looked so loose beside the hut. She and Yant'Ho were sprawled on the mat as if they'd just been trampled by a horse. As impossible as it was to believe, the ever-proper Maria had apparently been drinking tonight.

"I'm not tired enough for sleep yet," she was saying.

"You've been drinking, haven't you?"

"Just a little," she drawled as she tried to press a garment against a rock but missed and nearly threw herself in the river. She giggled, caught herself, then replaced her smile with a grim look.

Amused, Beau sat down on the rocks behind her and watched her clumsy progress with laughter brimming in his eyes. He'd never seen her like this, all fumbling and awkward, devoid of her usual grace. It took her a few minutes to realize he was still there. She turned around and looked at him curiously.

There was a lazy droop to her eyelids, which gave her gaze a seductive, sultry look. Her cheeks were flushed, her lips parted and breathless. The top few buttons of her chemise were undone, teasing his eye with a healthy view of the deep cleavage between her breasts. Through the thin, blousy fabric, he could see the outline of tender pink tips. Drunkenness made him forget her chastity. He feasted on the sight of her as he had never allowed himself to do before. The surge in his loins was fierce and quick.

It felt good, what she did to him.

"If you want me to return to camp, just say so and I'll do as you bid."

Maria had to struggle to keep her voice stern. The way he was looking at her sent a chill racing up her spine. She had never seen his passion so intensely displayed as it was at that moment.

"Stop pretending you're a servant," he said and she noticed his voice was a few octaves lower.

Maria threw down the diaper and splashed out of the water to confront the figure lounging loftily on the rocks above her. "Then how am I supposed to act? You say I'm a governess, a person you claim through indenture, yet propose that one day I'll be much more than this to you. You're a very difficult man to understand sometimes, Beau."

"I want you to be the way you were before our argument."

"Well, I can't! You've reminded me of my 'position' in life, this lot of mine I can't seem to escape no matter where I run. For a time, I was happy here, Beau, happier than I ever was . . ."

She retrieved the diaper then, hiding her upset in the scrubbing of it while a lump of self-pity swelled in her throat. Every sad thought she'd entertained today came back with stunning clarity, making her feel a strong urge to cry but she resisted it. The whiskey had weakened her resolve, she decided, quickly wiping away a droplet that strayed down her cheek.

"What is your lot in life?"

"To be unwanted," she blurted, then wished she hadn't. "But never mind it. I'm long resigned to this fate. I've had years of practice, you see, and I can hide anything. Just hand me a pretty silk fan to cover my frown and listen to how gaily I can chatter while my heart breaks." Why was she saying this? Where were these words coming from? "I don't want to say anymore! It's not right! A lady is never offensive or aggressive or obtrusive because such behavior does not become one. Especially not a lady so well bred as I. I'm the wealthiest debutante in London, you know, raised in glamour and luxury, one whose life never shows the scars of hardship or hurt or rejection or the queer insanities of men—"

"Stop this." Beau slid down the rocks, snatched her off the banks, drew her backward into his lap. At first, she fought the arms that encircled her, the thighs that snuggled around her, but the effort failed.

A soft sob spilled from her lips. "Forgive me. I've been offensive."

"No, you've not offended me," he said soothingly, sliding her downy crown beneath his chin and tenderly nestling her there. "It was I who offended you today with words not meant for a heart so fragile. My ways are too brutish for so genuine a lady as you. Forgive me. Let me take back those angry words."

She turned in his arms, the moonlight flooding her face with a mystical silver light. It made her eyes glisten so brightly, so sadly. Beau's heart ached for her.

"I wish you would, Beau. I don't want to live in pain anymore . . . with so many regrets for a life still so short . . ."

Her soft mouth trembled, her sweet breath touching his face.

No thought occupied his mind now except a compelling need to comfort her, this exquisite creature who was so deeply and unjustly wounded by a cold world. He bent, pressed his lips against her brow. Her skin felt so smooth and inviting. "I don't want to be like the others in your life . . . who hurt you and degraded you . . . I don't belong there . . . not with them, Maria. You've never been unwanted by me. You know that. You know how much I want you . . . need you . . . those shattered pieces of you that lie in the same broken pile as mine."

Oh! How she adored his words, the way his lips moved so meticulously along the path of her every tear. He wiped them all away, erased her sorrow, replaced it with the genuine comfort she took from the mighty tenderness of his touch. Desire blossomed warm and deep within her. His name sighed from her lips, her fingers snaking into his hair, wanting his warm mouth to come and claim her own. She turned in his arms, letting her breasts press into the hard expanse of his naked chest. He groaned some unintelligible words of protest as the last of his resistance crumbled.

He captured her lips beneath his own and ravished her with a crushing, bruising kiss that demanded an end to every pain that haunted their souls. Maria groped for him, her body moving against his as if wanting to be swallowed by the fierce pleasure he brought. Arousal became like some invisible warrior that rose to slay every sorry emotion of theirs until desire became their most glorious victory. At this moment in time, she loved him so completely, so desperately, she became utterly selfless in his storming wake, her whole being absorbed by his.

It became a slow, entrancing dream, the way their bodies entwined, tumbled from the rocks, landed upon the soft moss beneath the sheltering willows. The distant drums of Cussitah beat an erotic rhythm in the air around them and gave her body a reckless sensation of throbbing, pulsing warmth. The urge for him turned delicious; she wanted to be consumed by the ardor of this beloved man.

Pinned under him, she lay mesmerized by the

sight of his fingers unbuttoning her chemise, his warm palms sliding away her gown to expose her breasts. They rose round and swollen in the moonlight, bathed in stars and the hoarse whispers of praise that flowed from his lips as he cupped his hands around her untouched flesh. How gentle was his touch, yet how wild was the fire it lit in her body. His eyes raked over her, took bold possession of every inch. There was only a whisper of virginal timidity in her spirit, but even that was quickly dissolved in her fierce want of him, to join with him in the way God meant it to be, an act of perfect love.

Maria gasped as his hungry mouth slid down her throat and traveled across the soft white flesh of her breasts. He tasted from her, his lips exploring her unveiled beauty, sampling from the rosy peaks that thrust out at him. She groaned, her hands fisting in his hair, her back arching toward the warm mouth that so intimately discovered her. Love raged into a hot and frantic new life. The heat between her legs turned to fire, making her hips writhe and squirm as it became more and more unbearable. She could feel his hot breath on her skin, his manly excitement stiff and unyielding between their straining bodies. He seemed to touch her everywhere, with his hands, his fingers, his lips, scorching her flesh, deliberately tossing her into a dazed delirium.

He reached for the stays of his britches and Maria was only vaguely aware of her own hand following him there, tugging at the ties with wildly trembling fingers. It was instinct that told her body it could only be relieved by his, an instinct she never knew she had before. From somewhere within this whirling, sensual world, her brain registered the feel of his engorged manhood, then the sharp intake of his breath. He murmured something incoherent against her hair as he spread her thighs and plunged his body deep inside her own.

The pain of her deflowering was diminished by a rush of new sensations, the glorious fullness that bloomed in her womanhood. She shuddered in the strong arms that held her, a ferocious fever spreading its heat between them, joining the frantic hammering of their hearts. His hands slid under her buttocks, lifting her off the ground until he claimed her deepest places. It made her cry out, her head tossing wildly, her hands clenching at his flesh. Beau's body swelled within her, until she could feel him twist in a kind of excruciating agony. The sight of him dazed her, filling her with a sudden spark that seemed to shoot clear through her flesh.

Her eyes popped open and she stared into his burning eyes in a state of suspended awe, unable to stop this rush of blinding heat. It was wicked, the spasms fast and furious, making her body leap into a strange new dance of the most divine pleasure she had ever felt.

And he watched her, his expression turned suddenly soft with love, so warm and tender behind the pitch black tumble of his disheveled hair.

Then his eyes closed, a kind of strained serenity washing over his gleaming face as he relinquished his strength to the greater needs of his body. His head dropped into her hair, his body shuddering in her arms as he filled her with his essence.

She was suddenly holding him, kissing his shoulders, his neck, his hair. Their fires slowly ebbed into a simmering warmth. They cuddled close, no part of them wanting to leave the tender aftermath of this profoundly intimate experience. Maria wanted to die there, locked in those big strong arms, basking in the rapture of having so thoroughly satisfied a man. The moment should be forever and she knew in her heart that this night would live in her memory for all her days on earth.

Beau was suddenly smiling down at her. "Proud of yourself, eh?"

"Indeed . . ." she whispered dreamily.

He bent down to nibble at her lips and inhale the sweet fragrance of her. "You should be. You took my breath away, Maria," he said, his voice thick with emotion. He cupped her face in his hands, kissing her deeply, until she was stirring again. "I cherish what you gave me."

"It belongs to you," she admitted, reaching up to smooth the hair from his brow and let him see the love shining in her eyes. "I love you, Beau, love you as I have never loved a man. All that I am belongs to you . . ."

Her words moved him, turning his kiss intimate and penetrating, making their bodies once again bloom in want. "You're mine now. Say it. No matter what happens, you'll always be mine, Lady Vandenburgh."

"Yes . . . yes . . . you know it's true."

He wanted her again and she reveled in it, this greatest compliment a man could pay a woman. She let him pick her off the ground, snatch up their garments, and cover her nakedness as they returned to the village and ducked into their tent.

By the time the flap fluttered closed, they were in each other's arms, craving again the rapture of joining their bodies and spirits. The night was old by the time they fell asleep.

Maria opened one eye, saw the sunlight pouring through the crack in the hut flap, and winced. It was awfully bright for such a tiny beam. She turned away, her breath catching in her throat as she took in the magnificent sight beside her.

Beau was lying flat on his back, one arm stretched over his head where it lay in a wavy pool of jet black hair. He was sound asleep, his face turned toward her, a luxurious net of dark lashes fanning across the high tips of his cheeks.

He was stark naked.

Reality jolted her awake, her mind flooding with a rush of erotic images from the night before.

Her snowy white skin entwined with his rugged

brown, their bodies writhing and pulsing, bathed in sweat and the musky moisture of love. Mouths seeking and searching private places, kisses deep and penetrating, the feel of her body when he was inside her. It all came back to her now, what they had done in here. It overwhelmed her, suspended her somewhere between being enthralled and appalled as she savored the taste of him in her mouth, the scent of him on her skin. The flesh between her legs ached where he had been.

She felt dizzy, and suddenly realized her head was pounding. Her mouth was so dry it felt like it was stuffed with linen.

Whiskey.

Dear God! What had she done?

Maria clamped her eyes shut and drew a pelt across his hips to avoid being tempted by his bare loins.

The movement brought a smart from her own loins. Lord! What he must think of her after what she had let him do last night. Just the thought of having Beau inside her made her shudder wickedly, but there was shame in it now. She was not his wife. Their union was not blessed.

"Oh, God," she groaned, snatched up her dress, and pulled it over her head.

Beau stirred, a long muscular leg bending up at the knee as he opened his eyes.

"Maria?"

"I was just getting dressed," she said, trying not to look as bewildered as she felt.

Beau sat up, ran his hands through his hair, and

looked at the woman fumbling with her buttons beside him. There was no mistaking the tremble in her hands, the distress she was hiding.

Something was wrong.

Alarmed that he might have hurt her last night, he slid across her pelt and pushed the hair out of her face. "Look up here at me." She did so, sad brown eyes barely meeting his own as they found something on the wall behind him to stare at. She was pale, drawn. "I hurt you, didn't I?" She shook her head. "Tell me the truth. . . . Don't be timid."

"No, I'm fine. But my head feels terrible."

He remembered the whiskey and sighed in relief. "The blessing of burning water is only surpassed by its curse. Food will ease you."

When he reached for his britches, Maria quickly dropped her eyes. Her shyness was an intriguing contradiction after the way she seduced him, so innocently eager, so urgently natural. His body had responded in ways he hardly recognized. Just to think of it aroused him, made him glad the pelt covered him. He left it there while he dressed so as not to offend her modesty.

She was still staring at her lap when he bent toward the flap, then stopped and looked at her more closely.

"Maria, are you sure you're all right?"

"Yes, I'm fine." Her voice was shaking.

He had a sudden sinking sensation in his gut. She was not fine. There was regret in her stiff posture. He was sure of it.

"You're troubled about last night . . ."

She didn't say anything but he saw her bite her bottom lip.

"Look at me," he urged. "Was it only the whiskey that brought you into my arms?"

She shook her head with surprising conviction. "No . . . you know it was more than that."

"Then what troubles you?"

"That we—we're not wed!" Her eyes rose, suddenly tearful and beseeching. "I can't reconcile myself to what I've done!"

He dropped the flap, returned to her pelt, and covered her fisted hands with his own. "To what *we* did."

"We've sinned," she gasped, sliding her fingers through his and holding them tightly. "We must set this aright, Beau!"

"Maria, there are no priests in the wilderness. Out here, a man and woman who wish to join must do so with only the blessing of nature."

Her sultry eyes brimmed with anxious tears. "Did you marry Julia like this?"

The question surprised him. He thought for a moment, chose his words carefully. "No. There was a man of the cloth in the colony. We exchanged our vows before him."

"Then take me to him and see us blessed!" She was frantic now, squeezing his hands, imploring him to ease her conscience.

"I . . . we can't do that, Maria. For God's sake, Charles Towne is quite a journey from here and there's no telling if a clergyman will be there when we arrive." He was lying and loathed himself for it.

"We'd be just as well off waiting for one to pass through the frontier . . ."

"Then we'll do it."

"Very good. Do you feel better now?"

"Yes! Knowing we'll soon be blessed will make the wait much less taxing."

"The what?"

"The wait."

"What wait?"

She looked at him strangely, as if he should know what she was talking about. "To be with you again." A blush brought new radiance to her pallid skin. Shy once more, she murmured, "You are a Christian, Beau. You know we cannot perpetuate this sin until our vows are sealed."

She couldn't be serious. He stared at her bent head, utterly stupefied. "Are you asking me not to touch you until we wed?"

She nodded solemnly.

He felt like a man who suddenly found himself crushed under a tree. The mere idea of abstaining from her after such a long-awaited and thrilling union made him want to drop to his knees and beg her to give up her convent ways.

But she wouldn't. Maria was a woman of faith. He had known this from the beginning, knew her faith was strong enough that she once considered taking the cloth herself.

Before he said something he would regret, Beau picked up his hat, rolled to the entrance, and slid through the flap of the tent.

Maria saw the look on his face just before he

made the abrupt exit. Pain. She'd hurt him. The mere thought was wrenching. She hurriedly plaited her hair, shoved her feet in her shoes, and started after him. The minute her hand rustled through the flap of the tent, Matthew came awake and giggled with happiness to see her near.

"Oh, dear," she wailed. "Why don't you be a big boy and go back to sleep for a few more minutes, eh?"

He thought she was teasing him, kicked up his feet, and pumped them briskly. A wide grin made his cheeks dimple beneath his twinkling blue eyes.

"Oh! Why must you be so adorable?" She tore into the pack, found a clean diaper, a fresh bunting, a pair of booties and dressed him in record time. He clung to her neck as she ducked through the flap and came to her feet. There were only a few people stirring, women mostly, feeding their children maize cakes that were warmed over last night's fire. In the light of day, the camp looked so much smaller, the cleared lanes between the huts littered with wooden trenchers and baskets, looms, and earthen pottery. She picked her way around them, finally stopping beside a young girl.

"Have you seen Beau?"

She smiled cheerfully, pointed at a path, and said, "Savannah."

Maria gave Matthew a jolting ride as she ran down the path, following its winding course through the brush until it brought her to the exact place where she'd lain with him last night.

He was there, alone, quietly filling a pair of canoes with last night's purchases. She approached him cautiously, watched him glance at her over his shoulder, then continue packing their supplies.

"Are you angry with me, Beau?"

"No, I'm not." His voice was soft, tired.

"I've hurt you, haven't I?"

He stopped then, stood upright, and looked at her squarely from across the canoe. "No. What ails me are the private woes of men. In time, it will pass."

"I can't bear to see you unhappy." He said nothing, just went back to his work, hefting sacks and satchels and woven baskets of food into the narrow concave inside the canoe. "If I displeased you, I didn't mean it."

"At the moment, I'm far from displeased with you."

Blue eyes peered up at her from beneath the deep black shadows of his hat. She thought him magnificently handsome just then. The pleasure of having known him so intimately last night made her shiver in private places.

He could see she would persist until he gave her an explanation. He stood upright and turned to look out over the water. A long, pensive moment passed before he spoke again.

"What you ask of me is very difficult and I'm struggling with myself to honor your wishes. You're too unfamiliar with men to understand it, but to ask a man to abstain from a woman who gave him such a night as we shared is like asking him to unman himself." He glanced at her just in time to see the hot blush on her cheeks. He sighed, frustrated with her innocence. "Never mind. Just leave me be on this subject for a time, eh?"

He turned away, used his hat to splash some water over his face and hair, then went back to loading the canoes. When everything was off the shore, he climbed into one and savagely rearranged it.

Maria stood there feeling terribly torn inside, her religion pulling her one way, her love for Beau yanking her in the opposite direction. She couldn't bear it and stood wringing her dress in one hand while balancing Matthew on her hip with the other.

"I don't want to leave it this way between us, Beau. What should I do?"

"Be true to your conscience. I don't want you unless you're willing. Until then, I'll do as you bid. You'll not feel my touch upon your body until this God of yours deems it right."

Beau was distant and detached when they left Cussitah, his expression dark and brooding. Maria respected his chagrin with silence, sat at his feet in the canoe with Matthew on her lap, and watched him work his oar with harsh, stabbing precision. Why was she allowing it to get so complicated? Her place was precisely here, tucked possessively between the legs of her man, his seed in her body, his son on her lap, on their way to their first home. Godliness should not make something so wrong out of something so right. There was little else to do but ply her rosary beads and beg God for guidance.

Beau chafed at himself more than her. Langdon's warning on the beach became a prophecy now, and he cursed himself for touching her in the first place. Not only would he betray her, but return her to England with a stained body, perhaps ripe with his child. As his oar slashed at the lazy Savannah, he half wished for an end to this scheme, for some other way to avenge his family other than that which would stand between her and him. But it was too late now. The forbidden fruit had been plucked, her taste more delicious than any other, dooming him to crave her nectar even more.

Beau was baffled by his own behavior. He had never been a man to feel such a witless and reckless passion for a woman. And absolutely never had he allowed a woman to take so much from him as Maria had last night. He gave her everything, from both his body and his spirit, holding nothing back from her. And in return, she had given him a pleasure so total, so complete, it made every other union with a woman pale in comparison.

Julia.

It occurred to him then, suddenly, regrettably.

This was what she had wanted, what he gave to Maria. All of him.

How could he have denied her this tender wish, to share such an intimate moment with her husband, to love him until he writhed and shuddered in her arms? He cursed himself for it, resigned himself to Maria's wishes as if it were a just punishment for making Julia turn in her grave last night.

The canoe stabbed into the banks of the Savannah just a hundred feet from the Gardiner trapping lodge. It faced the water, the windows shuttered inside the eaves of the porch. Sunlight slashed at the low sloping roof, which made the thatching look furry and dense. The cleared yard was overgrown with grass and weed, only a faint trace left of the path leading from the river to the front stoop.

Maria flew out of the canoe and went running up the yard, shouting with excitement as she inspected the place. Her feet danced across the porch, leaping once or twice as she tested the shutters and tried to look inside.

"Oh, Beau! It's beautiful! It's so big! You didn't tell me it was so big! And what a marvelous view! I can't wait to see the inside!"

He'd never seen her so excited. He fell victim to the enchantment of this suddenly vivacious creature and let himself enjoy her pleasure. He unjammed the door and let her flutter around inside like a butterfly in a spring garden.

The living area was one big room with a single ladder leading up to the sleeping loft. Although Maria had known far grander establishments in her life, none held the magic of this unpretentious wilderness cottage. It was her first real home. She couldn't hide her excitement as she danced through it, admiring it as if it were a mansion. And all the while, Beau stood in the doorway, quietly watching her delight.

The furnishings were sparse, consisting of a large wooden table, a man's arm chair draped in an old pelt, two ladies' chairs, a settle beside the back door, and a bench along the wall facing a giant stone hearth. There was a cupboard built into one corner, its shelves stacked with wooden bowls and pewter plates, clay crocks, and utensils. The walls were covered with the purpose of this place, chain link traps, metal cages, hunting spears, archery bows. It was a man's cabin, Maria surmised, and set her mind upon making it more feminine.

Within an hour, Beau had all the traps off the wall and had disappeared with them into the woods. Maria spent the afternoon indoors, scrubbing the floors, rearranging the furniture, airing the dusty stuffiness from the interior. She chose an expensively laced chemise to fashion into curtains and dressed the shuttered windows. The colorful Indian mats Beau had bought in Cussitah were carefully placed around the floor after the old rushes were removed and tossed into the huge outdoor fire pit behind the cabin. Next, she climbed into the loft, cleaned the floors, draped them in a thick layer of pelts. Matthew's harness was hung over the loft rail with the rest of their skins.

By the dinner hour, Maria was satisfied with the tidy appearance of her new home and presented it proudly when Beau returned.

"Is it to your liking?"

He just chuckled, amused at her exuberance.

"We can use real plates tonight for dinner! Look! I've cleaned them all! And I found a giant barrel out back for bathing! It's already filled with water but I can't seem to move it . . ."

"Never mind moving something so heavy. Let me do that. Where do you want it?" She had an exact location in mind and pointed at a spot near the hearth where they could bathe by the warmth of the fire.

"Perfect! A real bath! Oh, Beau! What a happy day this is!" She flew across the room, threw her arms around his neck, and hugged him tight. The feel of her plush young body made him grit his teeth for control. Without spoiling her mood, he disengaged himself and sought safer distances.

He prepared a feast for her that night from the variety of foodstuffs he had bought in Cussitah. Corn cakes, fried fish, carrots with celery, and spicy beets. While the meal simmered, they walked Matthew around the grounds, letting him inspect the overgrown gardens and their newly stocked root cellar. She praised the wisdom of Beau's purchases, boasted about having enough food for two winters.

She won't be here long enough to prove it, Beau thought.

Throughout dinner she entertained him with a breathless serenade of plans for the gardens and the interior of the house. While she spoke, her eyes danced and her lips smiled so infectiously he found himself even more drawn into her alluring magic. She had never looked so beautiful to him as she did tonight, so alive and happy, so newly a woman, so full of life's promise.

And he would take it from her, this first real home of hers, crush this winsome creature with the same hands that adored her last night. Just the thought of it filled him with a dread so genuine he began to seriously doubt if he could go through with this scheme.

After dinner, he sat alone beside the fire, smoked his pipe, and wrestled with his conscience. He just couldn't stomach the deception of this anymore. It would be easier if he just told her the truth and took his chances with the failure of the scheme if she decided to run off. Where could she go? She had no choice but to stay here with him, but she'd be miserable then, her happiness cheated by the truth. Which was more compassionate, to let her enjoy as many happy days as she could or fling her back into the cold and lonely world where he had found her?

A strange sensation came over him then, bringing the deliberations in his mind to an abrupt halt.

There was a prickling sensation on the back of his neck. His hair was standing up.

Someone was watching him.

Beau got up, walked to the middle of the backyard, and fell still as he tried to determine what was near, whether it was threatening.

A bird song pealed through the woods, lilting and thoroughly familiar.

Indigo!

"Show yourself, brother!" he commanded in Savannah.

The leaves rustled nearby.

Beau looked there, grinning broadly, his torn spirit easing in the gladness of this unexpected event.

Indigo came trotting out of the foliage, his red face split with a joyous grin.

Beau let out a howl of pleasure that brought Maria running to the back door and made Matthew giggle and point.

Their greeting was ripe with welcome, as they clasped each other by the arms and enjoyed the reunion of their friendship.

"You look well, trapper," Indigo said, "better than I expected. My heart has been heavy for you."

It passed between them then, a memory of the last time they had seen each other.

Standing in the backyard of a house full of death.

"Come and drink with me," Beau said, disengaging his eyes, his thoughts, from the tragedy in their minds. He motioned Indigo to the fire pit. "There are too many days between us."

Maria watched Beau bring a jug of whiskey out of the root cellar and join the Indian on the ground beside the fire. While they conversed in the Savannah tongue, Maria studied this dear friend of Beau's whose name she had heard so often.

In comparison to the sinewy Creek, this Savannah tribesman was quite tall and muscular, his black hair braided and elaborately decorated with bright blue feathers. He had a large flowering plant painted on his breast, obviously representing his name and his manitou, indigo. Two strips of vivid yellow were painted across high and severe cheekbones. He sported an extensive collection of decoration in his ears, around his throat, wrists, ankles, every limb strung with beads and silver disks and chunks of colored stones. He was so cluttered with ornaments Maria wondered if this Indian had some special status within the hierarchy of his tribe.

"I rejoice to find you well," Indigo applauded in Savannah. "Langdon came to my village and told of your travels across the great water. He said you found the killer of your kin but that you didn't slay him. Instead, you took a woman from him and you intend to kill his spirit by doing this."

Beau briefly explained the strategy behind his scheme.

Indigo absorbed his words without reaction except for an occasional nod of his head.

"Great suffering plagues your race." Indigo fixed him with a level and serious gaze. "The news I bring from the white man's village is not good."

Beau was stunned to learn that the Westoe tribe had attacked Charles Towne twice during his absence. The raid was led by the chief himself, Tomawausau. Although he forbade bloodshed, several homes were burned and many families driven out into the savannas.

"The first raid was retaliation for your death, Beau. Westoe permit no earthly hand to strike one whose origins are among the divine."

Beau understood this with guilty remorse. He hated deceiving Charles Towne, making them believe he was dead, but what choice did he have?

"The second raid was a warning. The white men sent by the English king to the Congaree spit lies at the Westoe. They tell them the traders made bad deals for skins. They speak from greed, Beau. They want the skins for themselves."

Beau was outraged by the danger these two naive Englishmen were creating for Charles Towne.

Tomawausau did not know the difference between one white man and another. Just as the raid proved, he would now assume them all to be dishonest, the traders, Charles Towne, Arthur's explorers on the Congaree. There was no doubt in Beau's mind that Tomawausau had given those two simpletons just as vivid a warning.

Indigo went on to tell him about Charles Towne, how they had discovered the death of the Gardiner family and reacted in rage and shock. Tension in the colony rose to unprecedented heights and had already caused three riots in the governor's square. Additional troops from England were summoned to police the streets and enforce stricter curfews. The governor rarely left his home now without an armed escort. He forbade the gathering of ten or more people in one group. The docks were closed to anyone not doing business there. Only one section of the colony was permitted to shop the weekly market at one time. The traders were followed the entire time they were in the colony. Indigo heard talk in the dram shops that many families wanted to leave Charles Towne and move to Oyster Point, which was several miles downriver.

Beau was pained to hear how the once peaceful life of the settlers had been disrupted. Without the stable leadership of Matthew Gardiner, the colonists could have little hope that Charles Towne would ever regain her former peaceful days. It made him yearn to return home, to take his father's place, to somehow lead them back to security.

But his time had not yet come. Vandenburgh, the

source of their trouble, would have to be destroyed first. And if Beau remained cloaked in security, he could complete his mission. He would be serving his people better if he stayed here and ensured their future rather than coming home to offer some temporary restoration. Years of tranquillity rested on the outcome of his plans.

And then, as he watched Maria carry a tray of food across the backyard, his earlier thoughts reached the same sad conclusion.

He would not forsake so many for the good of only one.

Maria stopped in midstride, intimidated by the way Indigo was staring at her. His gaze became too intense, as if he was trying to violate her very thoughts.

Beau read her fear, came to her side, and leaned closed to whisper, "Don't fear him. Let him make his peace with you."

"Why is he staring like that?"

"Because among the tribes of Carolina, Indigo is known as an oracle, a man gifted with second sight. He is a healer of the spirit, of troubled souls like yours and mine. He can teach us how to regain harmony in our inner lives. When he stares, he sees, and will no doubt say something quite uncanny when he's ready." She gulped hard and tried to look brave. "That's better. He won't scare you as much once you get to know him. My friendship with him is long and lasting. He is the wind at my side . . . has walked with me since we were Matthew's age."

This made her smile, and when he stepped away she let Indigo approach.

In Savannah tradition, Indigo placed his palm on his heart, a symbol of peace. He moved his hand from his breast to hers, then quietly spoke to her in English. "Your heart flutters like a dove caught in a web. A spirit so pure need not thrash. It is noble and deserving of honor."

Maria realized the Indian was paying her a high compliment. She smiled nervously, glad to feel Beau's arm snake around her shoulder in comforting support.

Indigo withdrew his hand, looked at her with dark and distant eyes as his voice began to chant softly, "You were not raised in the home of your family but were banished by an evil hand. Strangers raised you. They were kind but never gave enough to spare you loneliness. Even here, the clench of the evil hand remains around your heart. You cannot be free of its clutch until you accept the origin of your life. It came from evil. You must accept this.

"But do not fear because the goodness within you is more powerful. It will be your hand that crushes the wicked. The time will come. It is fast approaching. When the sun has circled the earth and come again to this place in the sky, your battle will have been waged and won."

Maria was so stunned by his prophecy she stood in speechless bewilderment. Worse, she understood every word, identified the evil hand as her father, realized the prophecy of having to face him one more time.

She felt suddenly exposed, deeply and profoundly disturbed. She handed her tray to Beau and ran into the house.

Beau attempted to go after her but Indigo held him back. "She must fight this battle alone, Beau."

"She's too tender for—"

"She is tender but not weak. A great pain lingers in her, one from long ago. She will not face this suffering until some time in her future and only then will she overcome it. In the present, her heart is light and filled with a strong and growing love. That love will one day be the strength that saves her. It is her love for you, Beau."

Although he'd known Indigo all his life, Beau could never get used to the uncanny accuracy with which Indigo could read a person. There was no point in arguing about it. He sat down on the hearth and told Indigo about the silent war he fought with himself over Maria and the scheme.

Indigo listened intently, his jewelry clanking as he puffed at Beau's pipe. Beneath the deep cleft of his brow, his severe eyes squinted in thought, tiny lines of age crinkling to life on his wind-burned face.

When Beau was finished, Indigo spoke, using the stem of the pipe to draw circles in the air.

"Your heart is divided into three spheres. One sphere holds your sorrow for a lost family. The second sphere holds your vengeance for their killer. The third sphere holds your hope for renewed life.

"The woman is like a dancer in your heart. She flits from sphere to sphere because inside each there is room for her. She gives you comfort in your grief. She is the vehicle of your revenge. If you return her love, she will give you new life.

"As time passes, so will two of the spheres. Only one will remain. Until then, she dances in the dark, and only you can bring to light the sphere where she can finally settle."

"But what should I do in the meantime?"

"Do? You have already done it, brother. The time to wonder has passed. You must decide what to do with her love now that you've taken what she gives. If her love heals you, it is good and you will not resist."

"Yes, but if I encourage her it will only hurt her more when—"

Indigo slashed a hand through the air, impatient with Beau's stubbornness. "Listen until you hear my words, trapper. You will hurt the woman no matter what you do. Accept this. You cannot spare her fate."

Beau said nothing. Indigo made too much sense. There was no point in arguing. She was already doomed. There was nothing he could do.

He decided to change the subject.

London, England
August 22, 1674

Gaylord Simmes parted the drapes in his private study and checked the street. It was clear. He went back to his desk and the hefty snifter of brandy waiting there. One last drink to settle his nerves, he told himself as he sat down. Lord Ashley's liveryman would be here any minute. He had to collect his thoughts, calm down, make himself appear relaxed and controlled when he met with Ashley. After all, he had expected this summons ever since the day the second ransom note was published.

He would never forget that black day, how shocked he was to read about the kidnap of Maria in that notorious and rebellious rag, the London

Chronicle. From that day forward, the abduction of Lady Maria Loretta Vandenburgh became the biggest scandal to hit London since the Dark Ages.

And because Arthur was in Paris, the outrage of the city fell full upon Gaylord. He was besieged with angry protests from both the citizens and the high-society invitees who were present the night of Maria's ball. The latter were particularly furious about the kidnap, now knowing Arthur had duped them that night with a lie about Maria's taking suddenly ill. Worse, the second ransom note clearly mentioned the first one, told how it was delivered the morning after the ball, and protested a lack of response from Arthur.

This made the public outrage swell even further. How could Arthur so cruelly disregard his own daughter's safety, be coldhearted enough to leave London on business only a few days later without even ordering a search for her! His behavior was appalling. Years of silent slurs about Arthur's heartless business practices became outright accusations. His reputation was in serious trouble.

Then there were the accounts of Maria, the details of her pathetic history as Arthur's neglected daughter which were gradually unearthed by the probing press and published broadly. People who had known her in the past made statements about her, how kind and generous she was to all, how they had never heard her complain about Arthur's neglect. She was touted as a devout Catholic who had excelled academically. A nun named Sister Eustace from the convent in Herefordshire County claimed Maria was considering taking the cloth at the time she was summoned home to London.

As if these details were not enough to make Maria the darling of London, one clever pressmen managed to get inside the Vandenburgh mansion and sketch a likeness of Maria from a parlor portrait of her late mother. Before long, all of London was familiar with the hauntingly beautiful face of this lonely woman. Englishwomen lamented her joyless life, and many a chivalrous gentleman came forward to offer his aid in searching for this lovely, melancholic lady. Every wealthy parlor in London hummed with talk of her, the mysterious Maria Loretta Vandenburgh.

What a nightmare!

Gaylord's hands shook as he sipped his brandy. Liquor was the only thing that eased him in the face of the trouble they were in.

Why had they lied about her? They should have told the truth, done something to find her. But how were they to know this April Fool would have the gall to publish the second note for all of England to read? This is what would infuriate Ashley, that they had allowed a scandal to arise about one of the proprietors. He wanted their reputations to remain sterling because to scorn one was to scorn them all.

For the last time, Gaylord looked over the notes he'd been keeping since the second note was published. It was written in French, delivered to Moineau by a commoner who paid him in pure gold. The sum was staggering and Gaylord was shocked to hear it. Whoever this April Fool was, the man was of substantial wealth. That spelled trouble to Gaylord. Money gave men power and this man knew how to use it.

Indeed he did. He had Gaylord completely stumped as to how to find him. The commoner who delivered the note had long since disappeared into the streets of London. Each note was written in a different language. Should he search for him in France? Just in case, he wrote Arthur who was staying in Paris and told him to be wary of his associates there. A copy of this correspondence was in Gaylord's file. It was one of the few items he could offer Ashley to prove they were trying to find Maria.

He rolled his notes into a tight scroll and placed them in his satchel just as Ashley's coach arrived out front. Weary from so many days of too little sleep and too much anxiety, Gaylord forced himself to rise to the gigantic task at hand.

Gaylord received him in the formal antechamber of his London residence and wasted no time getting down to business. Before Gaylord was seated the questioning began.

"Why didn't you come to me when Maria was first kidnapped?" the elderly Ashley asked in a clearly insulted tone.

Approaching sixty, the chief justice of Carolina was bent of body and white of hair but his mind was as shrewd as ever. His speech was lightning quick, and he expressed his thoughts with crystalline clarity.

"Arthur considered Maria's kidnap to be a personal matter and not worthy of your trouble, my lord."

"Nonsense," Ashley scoffed, waving a handful of bejeweled rings at him and assuming a stately pose on a nearby settee. "Vandenburgh is a member of a royal proprietorship and when his personal affairs become public news, we're all affected. When the aristocracy gossips, it's not about business, young man. It's about personal lives. Many a career has been ruined by the indiscreet actions of family."

"Your knowledge of such affairs surpasses my own, sir," Gaylord admitted. "My expertise lies only in the letter of the law and I find myself deficient in other areas."

"Which is only natural," Ashley generously allowed, "because you're too young to have developed in other areas. How old are you, Gaylord?"

"Twenty-seven, my lord."

"Twenty-seven. A mere child compared to men of Arthur's caliber. Don't you find it a bit distressing to be left here to manage this horrendous scandal while he dallies in France?"

"It's been most overwhelming, my lord. I implore him daily to return to London," Gaylord admitted only because Ashley seemed to care.

"Which is just another reason why you should have sought my aid. This business is far too weighty for one man to manage alone. I'll do everything in my power to help you, Gaylord, because you're in very dire trouble. Lord Clarendon has already been approached by the king about this affair."

Gaylord was not surprised. Coupled with the avalanche of protest letters being sent by Charles Towne settlers about the murder of Matthew Gardiner, this kidnap was bringing even more attention to their affairs.

"Let's start from the beginning, shall we, Gaylord? When did you first learn of Maria's kidnap?"

"The morning after the ball. This note was sent to Arthur's residence by common courier." Gaylord handed him the first ransom note. "Prior to receiving this, we had assumed the girl ran off."

"Oh? Why is that?"

"She and Arthur had a row, according to the servants."

"About what?"

"Lady Vandenburgh was distressed about being rushed into the ball so soon after her arrival in London. This argument led to a confrontation about their rather . . . er . . . distant relationship over the years. My lady was scorned by the truth when it was told."

"What was the truth?"

Gaylord was surprised at how embarrassed he suddenly felt about his employer's personal life. "He had no love for Maria, my lord. Her presence in London was a gross inconvenience. His plans were to marry her off as quickly as possible."

Ashley put aside the note, leaned into the seat cushion, and folded his arms over his chest. He stared at Gaylord, deep in thought.

"May I speak with you in confidence, Gaylord?"

"Of course, my lord."

"Arthur Vandenburgh is one of the most terrifying men I've ever known. Does that sound foolish? I'm not the only one who thinks it. The man's evil, Gaylord. Nothing about him is human. I daresay, if Satan could be reincarnated as a man, I'm certain he'd walk the earth as Arthur Vandenburgh."

Gaylord didn't know what to say. He sat speechless, profoundly disturbed by this chilling admission.

"I suppose you're wondering why I consort with him, eh? Like everyone else, we use Arthur's heartless business practices to get the job done for us. His enormous wealth lends him an equal dose of power, which serves our purposes quite well. Other than that, we have little to do with him. So tell me, what was Arthur's reaction to this first ransom note?"

"He was annoyed, sir."

"Annoyed. Is that all?"

"Yes, sir, that's all."

"Do you think she's still alive?"

"The second ransom note suggests this, my lord . . ."

"If the April Fool isn't lying. What about these evil deeds mentioned in the letters. What do you suppose they are?"

Gaylord immediately averted his eyes. He could think of a thousand evil deeds but, as always, only one stood paramount in his mind. It was the most wicked of all. The murder of the Gardiner family. "That accusation is entirely too ambiguous for me to deal with, my lord."

Ashley let out a delighted laugh, then leaned forward, still chuckling. "Now you see why no one trusts him, eh? I doubt he's done an honest deed in his entire life. Nonetheless, I'm holding you responsible for deciding which evil deed has gotten him into this much trouble."

"I find that assignment most impossible, sir!" Gaylord protested.

"Do you? Let me give you some direction. Carolina. Charles Towne. We'll start there. As chief justice of Carolina, I'm hereby seizing those records."

Gaylord sank in his chair and had the feeling all his blood was running into his feet. "Sir," he said quietly, "forgive me for asking, but what relevance is there between the kidnap and Carolina?"

"Perhaps none, but let's be sure about it, eh? There's been a lot of trouble over there and you know how I feel about Charles Towne. It's precious to me. It's also the most potentially lucrative colony in the New World. We struck gold over there, Gaylord. Gardiner gold. Fur. But it isn't ours yet, is it? I begged King Charles to grant me a monopoly over Charles Towne for nearly ten years, and it won't be jeopardized by this scandal. I'm not about to overlook any gossip associated with one of my proprietors. King Charles could decide we're all a lot of incompetent bunglers and take back control of Carolina. Absolutely not. Surely you can understand my position, Gaylord."

"I do, my lord."

"Very good. Officials will be sent to confiscate the records and you'll turn them over at once. I'll review them personally, then you and I will meet for further discussions. I'm sure I'll have many questions. You'll cooperate with me, won't you, Gaylord?"

"Absolutely, my lord."

"And you'll help me prepare for my upcoming meeting with Lord Clarendon about these protest letters from the settlers. You are aware of them, aren't you?"

"I've received many myself, sir."

Gaylord stiffened. Those letters pertained exclusively to the Gardiner murders. No matter how shaken he was, Gaylord allowed not a single suspicious expression to cross his face. Under no condition would he reveal the truth. This was murder. Gaylord was a lawyer. He knew the punishment given to murderers. Death.

"Have you any idea who might have slain Matthew Gardiner, Gaylord?"

"The governor insists the Westoe were more than likely responsible for—"

"Lord Clarendon doesn't believe that any more than I do, Gaylord," Ashley interrupted, "especially since the Westoe attacked Charles Towne twice this spring without killing anyone."

Good point. "Yes, but those savages are unpredictable, my lord. They could have been feuding with Matthew—"

"Perhaps, but even that's doubtful. I have a letter here from George Moore, one of the traders, who claim the Westoe have long considered Matt Gardiner's son to be a god of theirs. Did you know that? This son apparently survived some kind of indoctrination ritual into the tribe—a pagan rite of passage, so to speak, and one which few men have ever survived. It involves the endurance of excruciating pain, the consumption of poisonous liquids, and the like. Gardiner's son somehow lived through this in a way that struck awe in those pagan breasts. To this day, the Westoe revere him as a man of divine origin, lay themselves prostrate at his feet, are not permitted to make eye contact with him, and only the chief of the tribe is considered worthy enough to engage in speech with him."

Ashley stopped and looked at Gaylord. It was obvious he had never heard this peculiar situation described in such detail. Gaylord didn't bother to disguise his interest, thinking it might help his position to appear innocent of these facts.

"The Westoe did as this son commanded. You realize what that means, don't you? Gardiner's son was a renowned trapper, very much a part of the traders' inner circle. I'm sure he had a large part in setting up this network among the natives. His death could one day play in our favor, but it doesn't help us now, does it? You see, it only makes it more unlikely that the Westoe would slay such a man."

"Indeed, my lord, unless he somehow fell from grace . . ."

"A possibility," Ashley nodded, then sat back to sigh himself into his plush satin settee. "It dismays me how the settlers despise us, Simmes. It embarrasses me. I have such splendid and righteous plans for Charles Towne and can hardly understand why Yeamans doesn't promote them to the people. It could help them to understand that all of us can gain from the fur market over there, that we're not about to steal their livelihood and toss the lot of them into abject poverty."

Gaylord didn't mention how differently Arthur viewed the subject. He wanted all the fur, every last pelt, and his mind was set to get it.

"They just don't trust us, my lord."

"And why should they, eh? England is the throne for all the greed of mankind, isn't she? Ah well, perhaps they'll be somewhat appeased when they learn I plan to assume personal responsibility for investigating the murder of Matthew Gardiner. An edict to that effect has already been dispatched to Charles Towne."

Gaylord panicked. He suddenly felt that there wasn't enough air in the room. Ashley rose, quiet and thoughtful as he strolled to the magnificent white marble hearth across the room. Thankfully, he couldn't see Gaylord gripping the chair arms so tightly his fingernails nearly pierced the cloth.

"I pity you, Gaylord," Ashley said after a long pause. "I would not want to be in your position. You're too young to be tangled in such a twisted web, too innocent to realize how deadly a mistake it would be to underestimate your employer right now."

"My lord?"

Ashley turned and looked at Gaylord with compassion. "No matter what he's done, Gaylord, you'll take the blame for it. I hope you realize this. It's a common practice of Arthur's—framing others to take his blame. He used your father like this, business associates, now you. He may appear to be on your side but in truth, Arthur's schemes have only one side: his own. If he's caught, you'll be punished, not him."

"But I do nothing beyond what he directs me to do!" Gaylord blurted as he came to his feet in desperate defense.

"I hope you can prove that."

"I can!" Gaylord said as he frantically held open the parchments. "Everything about the kidnap is documented here!"

"And I'll give those documents a just review, Gaylord. You can be sure of that. Believe me, I've spared many an innocent lamb from his slaughter."

"Will you help me, my lord?" Gaylord knew he was pleading but he didn't care. His nerve was completely gone.

"Of course. But I must ask a favor of you first."

"Anything, my lord."

"Play along with Arthur and breathe not a word of this meeting to him. Document everything he says and does. Do you hear me? All of it! No matter what he's done to bring this about, it can't be worse than what will happen to you if you refuse complete cooperation with me. You are privy to information I need to ensure my own political survival if this kidnap affair does indeed prick the ears of the king. It's already with Clarendon, which is close enough for me. We're going to find Lady Vandenburgh and put an end to all of this. She must be brought safely home, Gaylord, for all our sakes, or the entire city will turn against us. Do you understand the enormity of the situation you're in?"

"I do, my lord."

"Then I can count on you to serve as my agent from here on without Arthur's knowledge."

"Stake your life on it, my lord."

"No, Gaylord, I'm staking *your* life on it."

The Savannah River
September 15, 1674

"Where are you going, Indigo?"

"To Cussitah."

"At this hour?"

"The Creek will be better company for me tonight," Indigo said as he finished loading a pile of pelts into the canoe. "Your mood is better suited for a woman's company."

"Indigo, I—"

"You fight the inevitable, Beau. You ache for the woman."

"This is not the way of her people. She must be my wife before I can lie with her."

"Her people deny you your manhood."

"They consider her honor more important. Besides, Maria's time here is short. Why encourage a relationship that will not last?"

"Life itself is short, Beau. That's no reason to deny yourself a chance to live it."

Beau opened his mouth to protest but Indigo was already hopping into the canoe.

He kicked a tree and cursed in frustration. Why was the Indian so blasted sensible?

He swung through the back door of the cabin to put another load of wood beside the hearth. Maria was playing with Matthew, dancing and giggling at the songs the boy sang to her. They twirled around Beau in a wide circle.

"Where's Indigo?" she asked.

"He's gone to Cussitah."

"At this hour?"

He sighed in exasperation. "The Savannah recognize the month of September as a time for romance. He's gone to the village to find some."

"But I thought he was married and had several sons."

"He is but—well, never mind . . ." She wouldn't understand. She was too godforsaken pure to understand the needs of men.

Maria watched him finish slamming the wood into a neat pile, then retreat to his nearby chair. He sat down and started furiously carving at a block of wood.

She frowned at his edgy mood, the way he always acted on those few occasions when Indigo left them alone for an evening. Beau always found somewhere else to be, anything to do other than closet himself in here with Maria.

She knew why. Their forced abstinence. Beau suffered it sorely at times like this, when they were alone and the temptation was ripe. She felt guilty but flattered at the same time and knew to behave discreetly when he was in this particular mood. There was no need to taunt him. She already knew he cared about her. Beau had made that perfectly clear.

He denied her nothing. She had only to mention something she wanted and it was immediately brought to her. If Beau couldn't trade for it in Cussitah, he made it himself. A loom, a spinning wheel, a rack for drying clothes, a bench to sit by the river. Sooner or later, the object of her desire would appear and she'd marvel at it, wondering how he had managed to get it. And when she ran to him, gushing with gratitude, he'd just look at her as if wondering why she was so surprised. In his own unpretentious way, this backwoods trapper could make her feel more adored and deserving than anyone ever had. And she loved him for it, more every day, every hour.

She put Matthew down and watched him waddle toward his pile of toys in the corner. He was still wobbly and unsure of his chubby legs, plowing into everything as he tried to be as fast a walker as he was once a crawler. He sprawled into his pile of toys and sent them scattering everywhere.

Beau reached him before she did. "Take your time, boy . . . slow . . . like this . . ." He held

Matthew's hands and slowly walked him a few feet forward.

"Papa pay . . ."

"What do you want to play?"

Matthew fussed for his toys and Beau let him crawl back into the pile. The boy picked up his favorite figurine and made a gobbling sound.

"Very well," Beau said, giving Matthew a quick smile. A moment later, he was sitting cross-legged on the floor, a figurine of a bear in his hand. "What horrible death will the vicious turkey contrive for the poor bear tonight?"

Matthew thrust the toy toward Maria and made it gobble at her. "Ree! Ree pay!" He wanted their undivided attention.

She joined them on the floor in the corner and selected a toy fox. The game commenced at once, Matthew stabbing at her fox with his turkey, then squealing when she hid it behind herself. In a moment, they were both romping their figurines across the floor with Matthew's turkey in pursuit. They lost themselves in the childish game, laughing at one another as they dove away from the screeching boy and his ferocious turkey. Matthew insisted that they make the sounds of their appointed animals and act out a painful death when his bird caught them.

Like all year-old toddlers with more energy than strength, Matthew began to tire just as the scorching August sun lost its fire to dusk. The boy stopped climbing in and out of his father's crossed legs. Soon the back of his head nestled against Beau's thigh, where he could gaze up at his father and babble softly between broad yawns.

Beau looked almost as tired as his son, she noticed. His eyelids were heavy, the day's sweat still clinging to his sun-burnished arms. The muscles of his back flexed beneath his rawhide vest as he stretched out the stiffness, his shoulders broad and brown in the soft light.

A cool drink would refresh him, Maria decided. She lit a few lanterns and used one to light her way into the root cellar outside. She drew a small kettle of cool cider, brought it inside, and left a few sticks of cinnamon to steep in it while she put Matthew to bed. She tucked the boy into his crib, acutely aware of Beau's movements downstairs, how alone they were for the night.

But he was gone when she returned, the back door ajar, only his shadow visible in the fading light as he moved between his giant racks of drying pelts. With two cups of cider in her hands, she went outside to offer him one.

"Have some cider, Beau. It will cool you," she said from behind him, watching him shift a few pelts on the rack before he turned for the cup. He didn't look at her, swallowed the brew in three gulps, and handed it back. "More?"

"In a minute."

She let him work, refilled his cup, and strolled through the yard with it. Beau's figure dipped in and out of the dozen wooden racks as he drew off dry pelts, folded them into baskets, made sure the fresh ones were spread open for tomorrow's sun. Minutes passed and he did not come for his cider.

Maria read the message in his tension. Perhaps her company was too tempting for him to resist tonight. She wouldn't plague him. She took her cups of cider to the river and sat on the log bench he had made for her.

Darkness fell over the Savannah and she watched the distant shore melt out of sight. It was a clear night with a strong, wet breeze, making her sigh every time it blew across her face. Just swift enough to keep away the bugs, it felt rejuvenating.

There was a faint rustling sound behind her and she knew it was Beau, her ear practiced enough now to detect this man who could move silently through the woods. She was even getting used to the way the natives could just materialize out of the woods, like so many vapors of steam. It used to scare the wits from her, still did sometimes.

He bypassed the bench, walked straight into the river until the water lapped around his thighs. In one graceful motion, his body lunged forward, his full length spread across the surface for just an instant before he dove out of sight. He resurfaced in the middle of the river, on his back, floating for a long, languid moment, until the current started to drag him downstream. Once again he disappeared beneath the starlit water, emerging only a few yards offshore. He walked toward the riverbank, rising out of the water like some magnificent godlike apparition, bathed in water and moonlight. He shook his hair in a reckless spray of water, pushing it back with his hands as he came to the bench.

"Where's that cider you promised?"

She handed it to him. His fingers were wet and cold as they brushed her own. "You've had a long day, Beau."

"A good one." He sighed, straddled the bench, and faced her. She liked the feel of his undivided attention, the way his eyes roamed her for a brief instant before they disappeared into his upturned mug. His nearness made her feel very warm and aware of him, subtly alive in private places. "The racks are full now," he said between gulps of cider. "If I trap any more, the meat will go to waste."

"I thought Indigo took the meat to Running Dog."

"He did, but there's plenty more."

"Take a rest then," she suggested, reaching for his empty mug and offering him a sip from her own cup. Of course, he didn't take it. "You labor at your traps all day . . . for weeks now . . ."

"The fall is the best harvest. The animals are fat from a summer's feed." He stretched then, arching his back and yawning broadly at the sky. "But we've months left, I suppose." She watched him round his shoulders in a quick flex.

"Your back aches. Turn around . . . let me rub it."

A dubious look crossed his face but she scoffed at it.

"Go on, trapper. You could use a whit of care sometimes too."

He turned around and straddled the bench the other way. She slid her hands beneath his soggy vest, his skin warm and wet as she eased it off his shoulders.

"Where do you ache?"

He reached around and pointed to the lower curve in his back. "Gently, princess . . ."

"You've a knot back here, Beau. What happened?"

"Tree branch snapped." He arched when she pressed her fingers there. "The one I was sitting on."

"You fell? Oh, for heavens sake! Why didn't you say something?"

"Like what?"

"Like you fell and got hurt, is what! Stubborn man. I should fix a poultice for this."

"Don't fuss over me, just rub it . . . gently."

She clucked her tongue at him. "When did this happen?"

"Yesterday—ah! Don't press so hard."

Concerned now, she straddled the bench behind him and paid full attention to the ball of swollen flesh half-hidden under his belt. She used only her fingertips on the spot and applied the gentlest pressure, just enough to soothe him. Beau sighed with pleasure, leaned forward, and presented the full expanse of his back to her.

Maria was only too happy to oblige. They usually just sat on the stoop and talked at the end of the day. She didn't often have the opportunity to ease his aches like this. His every rapturous sound brought a satisfied smile to her lips, as he drooped forward on the bench in total submission to her hands.

For some reason, it reminded her of Cussitah.

Visions of him in the hut came back to titillate her: the sight of him lying under her while she explored him with her hands, her lips. She could make this brutally strong body writhe, feel its power and potency. And like now, without resistance or a moment's struggle, he relinquished himself to the pleasure she made him feel.

These thoughts were dangerous. She should push them away, not allow this dull, pulsing warmth to spread between her legs. His senses were too acute. He would read her mind the way he always did, look at her with eyes that spoke a strange and wordless language only understood between a man and a woman who had known each other intimately. It would flash between them, the memories of Cussitah, the white-hot passion they had found within the crude thatched walls of a Creek hut, a single wild night that neither would ever forget.

Beau's hand reached back, cinched around her arm. She jumped, startled out of her forbidden dreams, made some vain attempt to get off the bench before he saw the evidence of her thoughts.

But it was too late. She could feel the heat of his gaze on her face as she tried to walk past. "I should check Matthew."

"Maria . . ." he whispered, that telltale huskiness in his voice. "Don't go."

What woman could deny such a man, could escape the brawny arm that was sliding around her waist, pulling her between his thighs.

"Beau . . ." She breathed his name, felt his head come to rest against her belly, and just stood there raking his hair in her fingers. "I'll not tempt you."

"Everything about you tempts me."

"Don't say that."

"I can't forget Cussitah . . . I'll never forget it." He was pulling her down, his words as arousing as the reckless passion of his lips as they scampered up the front of her body. She gasped, her eyes closing in a sudden dizzy wave of want. Her attention was stolen from everything but the feel of his hungry mouth on her breasts, her throat, running up the side of her face. She felt consumed by it, this ever-present desire of theirs, suddenly wanting it to crash through their stubborn barriers and swallow them both.

His tolerance snapped at the same time as hers, a groan of dismay escaping his throat as he turned her face and covered her mouth with his own. This first kiss in such a long time turned instantly hot and hard. It inflamed them like a flash fire, infused them with a heat that made them clutch at each other in sudden, desperate need.

It had been too long since he'd touched her and Maria drank from him greedily, controlled by nothing but her craving for this beloved man. Trembling hands cupped his face as she parted his lips and took a deep taste of him, shuddering at his deliciousness. A wicked tremble coursed through him.

His arms cinched around her like a vise while she ravished him, thrilled him.

He fell back on the bench and she rolled atop him. She plunged her hands deep into his thick wet hair as if she couldn't bear the feel of his swollen manhood pressing against that place where she ached the most for him. And he knew it, his hand sweeping down her back, sliding over her bottom, pressing her even closer until she wanted to cry out for mercy.

But he did instead, his fisted hand pulling on her hair until he could free his mouth from her thirsty lips. "Dear God! Have mercy on me." His blue eyes focused hard on her face. "Has this God of yours no compassion? Tell me that! Tell me what He means by forcing us to burn in want for each other without relief. What is this proving?"

She wanted to wail aloud in frustration. "I don't know . . . but our love is forbidden until it's blessed, Beau! This much I do know!"

He cursed viciously, sprang upright on the bench, and suddenly deposited her on the seat beside him. He got up, stalked to the river, fell into an agitated pace at its edge. Maria hugged herself, shivering despite the heat.

"Please don't be angry with me, Beau."

"I'm not angry." He sighed heavily. "But this is inhuman, Maria! I work until I drop just so I don't have to lie awake in the loft beside you, gritting my teeth until dawn!"

She winced to hear how he had suffered, remaining silent about it. Until now. "This is my fault."

"It's not. There is no one to blame for this but me. I knew better but I did it anyway. And now I pay for taking what did not belong to me."

"But I do belong to you!" she moaned, coming to her feet and wringing her dress in her hands. "You must know that by now."

He stopped pacing and turned to face her from the shore, his shadowed face drawn and desperate. This was a rare glimpse of emotion from him. For a moment, she felt certain he was about to say something, utter a secret.

But he didn't, just murmured something about seeing her inside. He walked ahead of her on the path, silent again, led her to the back stoop, and paused with his hand on the latch.

Once again he stared at her hard, making her feel that he wanted to say something important.

"Beau? What's wrong?"

"Everything," he whispered more to himself than her. He met her startled expression with a quick shake of his head. "But I'll make things right between us, Maria. One day. I promise."

She was in his arms then, holding him tightly for a moment before he let her go and opened the back door.

"I'll be up later," he whispered. Then he stepped off the stoop and strolled back into the night.

Maria awoke the following morning to find herself alone with Matthew. Both canoes were gone and she assumed Beau had taken another load of meat to Running Dog in Cussitah. Thoughts of last night preoccupied her as she worked through the morning, her spirit thrilling just to remember those few exhilarating moments in his arms. And then later, when he had promised to make everything right, Maria was certain he had meant to marry her soon. What a wonderful day that would be. Mrs. Maria Gardiner. The mere idea made her want to break into a song of joy right there in the middle of the backyard.

Indigo returned to the camp at midday. Maria half expected to see Beau with him but the Indian was alone.

"Did you see Beau this morning?" she asked, setting out a plate of food for him.

"He came last night."

"Oh?" This surprised her. It was not Beau's habit to leave her and Matthew alone at night. If one man left, the other stayed. "Ah well." She sighed, then filled Indigo's mug from a kettle of cider. "His spirits were low last night. Perhaps the visit cheered him."

"His spirits are low because he is constricted," Indigo said. He took a bite out of a stalk of celery and munched it contentedly. "He came there to heal himself."

"Constricted? What sort of illness is that?"

Indigo chuckled at her, his eyes dancing with affection as he explained. "It is the illness you bring upon him, innocent one."

"Me?"

"He has made you a woman but he hasn't taught you enough about men." A telltale flush of color crept up her neck, making Indigo's expression soften with warm regard. "A man suffers when he lives so many months without a woman. It is even worse for Beau because he closets himself with a woman he desires but refuses to take."

"Oh, dear," she murmured in acute discomfort. She turned around and started shifting the bowls of vegetables on her worktable.

Indigo's chuckle was gentle as he watched her. There was not a hint of mockery in his tone when he mused aloud, "This religion of yours is strange. Your God makes you human, then condemns you for it. Beau decided that to lie with you in love was wrong, but to lie with an unknown woman in Cussitah was right."

Maria dropped a bowl. "What?" She whirled around, gaping at the Indian in slack-jawed surprise.

"He eased himself on a maid last night . . . and part of the morning. He was still in the tent with her when I left," Indigo explained as if telling her something she should already know.

"But—but he . . ." she stammered, feeling the outrage smother her voice. Before she said something regrettable, she snatched up her kettle and rushed outside with it.

Indigo went to the doorway and watched her plow in and out of the root cellar with a murderous rage pinching her pretty face. "What ails you, woman?"

"How dare he!" she fumed, stomping past Indigo and slamming a full kettle down on the table.

"What choice had he?"

"I can think of plenty of choices, Indigo!" she said, her voice rising into a near screech.

Indigo stared at her in utter bemusement. It was obvious he did not understand her sudden wrath. Maria was not given to foul tempers but he could see that something very black had taken hold of her spirit. He was at a loss to dispel it and finally just shrugged at her and said, "I'll go and turn the skins now."

"Yes, why don't you!" she snapped unkindly, then felt suddenly guilty for venting her anger on Indigo. It wasn't his fault. "Forgive me, Indigo, but I—" she began, then turned to find the doorway empty. He was gone.

She just stood there for a moment, alone with the tormenting visions that engulfed her mind. Beau had spent the night in another woman's arms, touching her, kissing her, filling her body with a love meant for her.

Her heart ached with hurt. Hot tears flooded her eyes, spilling down her flushed cheeks. Before she lost the last shred of composure, she gathered Matthew off the floor and took him into the loft for a nap. She laid him down, stretched out beside him, and burst into tears.

She sobbed the whole time he slept. Then she listened to him gurgle awake and coo to himself for a while before he started whining for dinner. She knew she should tend him, stop lying here despondent with jealousy. She forced herself to rise, rinse her face, and try to concentrate on what to make for dinner. There was no sense in tormenting herself over this. After all, it was her religion that had made him seek another.

But if it bothered Beau so much, why didn't he take her to a man of the cloth? Why resort to whoring instead? And then, as she carried Matthew downstairs, a new burst of enlightenment made her realize Beau had never once spoken of love to her. Not even in the grips of passion. Throughout that entire night in Cussitah he never once said he loved her.

Maybe he never spoke of love because he didn't feel that way about her.

Why hadn't she noticed this before? She felt suddenly cheap, used.

Dear God, what had she done?

She opened the back door and looked outside, at this place where she had spent the happiest days of her life. It looked so different now, as she wondered about Beau's intentions.

Then she saw him, sitting near the fire pit, propped against a tree, his long legs stretched and crossed at the ankles. The brim of his black hat was drawn low over his face, hiding it while he languidly puffed on his pipe. The mere sight of him in such a calm and relaxed state only clarified the success of his mission last night. Renewed anger made her cringe inside.

"Humph! She must have pleased him well," she muttered to herself, hugging Matthew close as she whipped off the stoop.

She walked a wide circle around Beau and went to the other side of the fire pit.

"Good evening, princess," he said in an unusually soft and contented voice.

She completely ignored him and feigned great concentration on fixing dinner. Out of the corner of her eye, she saw him push up his hat brim to reveal a pair of brilliantly blue and relaxed eyes. The mere sight of him taunted her. She threw a handful of crushed maize in a crock, added water and lard, and furiously formed a pile of cakes.

Beau continued to watch her, took notice of her sour mood, and frowned. At the moment, she didn't care what he noticed. She turned to the fire and filled the griddle with fresh cakes. One dropped into the fire. She reached for it and burned her hand. It stung so badly she cradled the scorched fingers in her lap and desperately fought off the tears that threatened to fill her sore eyes again.

Beau reached to help her. "Leave me be!" she snapped venomously and jerked away from his hand.

"What the devil . . . ?" Beau stared at her in confusion. From across the yard, Indigo made a cradling gesture with his arms, then threw him a sheepish shrug. Beau deciphered the sign language at once. That fool Indian told her what he did in Cussitah last night! No wonder Maria was mad! Indigo was awarded a scalding look.

How could he broach the subject now, when her tender feelings were already pricked? She looked ready to kill at the utterance of one wrong word.

A few tense minutes later, she offered them dinner.

"I'm starved," he said.

"I'm sure you are," she bristled, then grit her teeth so hard her gums hurt.

"Are you angry at me?"

She didn't answer, just turned her back on him to feed Matthew. Indigo ate much more quickly than usual, put aside his plate, and casually sauntered out of sight.

Coward! Beau mentally hurled at him.

"I'm taking Matthew for a walk at the river," Maria announced, getting up.

"No, you're not," he retorted, leaping up and grabbing her arm.

"Unhand me."

"Out with it, woman! Say what's on your mind!"

She fixed him with the ugliest look he'd ever seen on her winsome face. "Why don't you go to hell," she said, crisply pronouncing each syllable as if wishing they were blades slashing at his flesh. "Now leave go of me . . ."

"No."

Their stubborn spirits collided head-on. She just stood there glaring at him in stunning defiance.

"Why are you angry with me?" he demanded.

"You know why!" she spat.

"I don't," he shot back.

"I hope she pleased you well!" She yanked her arm free and stomped across the yard.

"Blasted Indian," he cursed under his breath and went after her. "I did what was best for us, Maria," he said to her retreating back. "What you wanted."

"Me?" She whirled around, her face shining red with anger and sweat as she clutched Matthew to her breast.

"Yes, you," he said, taking the child from her and setting Matthew on the ground at his feet. The boy just sat there, staring up at them, sucking his thumb and wondering what they were doing. "What would you have me do? I can't eat or sleep for want of you!" It made him suddenly angry, what she could do to him. This innocent young girl reduced him to a rutting stallion and his pride was pricked. "There's a limit to what I can tolerate. For God's sake, I'm just a man, like any other—"

"Oh?" she taunted. She crossed her arms over her breasts and quipped, "But I thought you were divine!"

"Believe me, there were a thousand times this past year when I wished I was!"

She shouldn't mock him. It wasn't fair. She'd seen this man suffer. Some of the fire in her anger died. "I just don't understand you!" she wailed, turning her back on him and staring at the woods where he couldn't see the new batch of tears welling in her eyes. "If this arrangement of ours is so hard on you—and you do nothing to find a man of the cloth—then why endure it? Why don't you just find someone else to tend your son and let me—oh!" She was spun around so fast it made her dizzy. Of a sudden, she found herself cinched against a long hard body, a pair of vivid blue eyes filling her line of vision until she could see nothing but him.

"I want no one else for him but you . . . no other woman!"

The slightest mention of her leaving him always caused this same reaction in him. Why? "You befuddle the wits from me, Beau Gardiner!" she cried. "You won't have me but you won't let me go either! What do you want from me? Why are you playing with me like this?"

"I'm not playing with you!"

"Then why are you doing this to us . . . leaving us to remain unblessed even though you know it's the only thing that stands between us! If you really wanted me, Beau, you would never let this go on so long."

"I do really want you," he said as insistently as he could. She was wandering much to close to the place where the scheme stood between them. He would have to tell her soon. They couldn't go on like this.

"Then why did you take another in my place?"

"No other woman can take your place with me, Maria," he whispered fiercely as he cupped her face in his hands. "She could only ease my physical discomfort, nothing else. When I was inside her, I thought only of you, of the way you satisfied me." How she longed for these words of his, to watch his emotions surface as they so rarely did. She melted against him, her eyes pleading for more of the truth. "Forgive my oafish ways, how I fumble with you—"

"No . . . no," she whispered, her hands reaching for him, adoring every rugged line of his face.

"No man has ever made me so happy, Beau, you know that." Their lips met in a fleeting, tender kiss, his arms closing tighter until she could feel the emotion trembling in his body. "You leave me to want nothing."

"I'm not accustomed to this, to the way you make me feel. . . . It overwhelms me, Maria, all of this. You're in my blood and I don't know how you got there . . . why I let it happen . . . when my life lies in ruin at my feet. Why now? Why you?"

Maria hung in his arms, bathed in his river of words and the torrent of emotions he spilled. "Oh, Beau . . . I love you . . . I love you so much . . ." Her lips fled across his face.

"I could deny my wife but not you. This is what she wanted, this is all she wanted from me, but I couldn't give it. Yet to you it comes without effort."

He let go of his ever-present control, snatched her off the ground where she hung powerless in his mighty arms, his lips showering his unspoken love across her face, her hair, her throat. Fire leapt between them, spread through them, engulfed them in the storming tides of their relentless passion. Maria sighed in the rapture of it, clinging to him, adoring the way his ardor turned his voice husky and hard.

"I need you, can't you see that? Every dark place in us that comes to light when we touch . . . your pain and mine . . . how we can make ecstasy from agony . . . don't take that from me. I need it . . . everything you make me feel . . . everything about you that I can't stop reaching for. Stay with me

. . . promise me . . . no matter what happens . . . you'll always be the heaven in my hell."

Langdon steered the canoe around the last bend in the river and saw the Gardiner lodge bloom into view.

"There it is," his father announced quietly, then looked away as if the sight of it pained him. "Last time I saw this place the whole family was here. Remember? Last summer?"

"I remember," Langdon said dismally as he turned the canoe toward the banks and caught a glimpse of the backyard.

What he saw there made his oar pause in midair.

Beau and Maria. They were locked in an embrace, their bodies clasped so tightly together they appeared as one form. Before Franklin saw them, Langdon punched his oar into the river bottom and jerked the canoe around until it approached the bank backward. He looked over his shoulder just in time to see Indigo disappear around back. A door slammed. He prayed the two had separated, but just in case he stalled Franklin at the bank for as long as he could.

His father was anxious to see Beau and hopped out of the canoe, took off his hat, and wiped the sweat from his brow as he trudged up the path. His long brown fingers snaked through his damp blond hair as he attempted to straighten himself before meeting the lovely lady who had all of London talking these days.

Langdon hurried after him, turned the corner, and squinted at the backyard.

They weren't there. The yard was empty except for a sprawling collection of wooden racks where scores of pelts hung drying in the sun.

Ermine. Beaver. Red fox. Sable.

"By the grace of God!" Franklin exclaimed, staring at the racks as if they were mountains of gold. It was an awesome sight. Every pelt was of the finest quality, expertly cut, neatly stretched, the fur brushed to a healthy sheen. "No one can trap like a Gardiner, eh Lang? Look at it all! Magnificent! No matter what hell he's been through, the man still traps as good as ever!"

"Have you ever known a Gardiner to do anything else?" taunted a familiar voice from close behind.

Beau was standing in the doorway of his cabin, watching them with a quiet smile on his tanned face. Langdon was amazed at how good he looked compared to when they'd parted on the beach at Cape Fear. The drawn and brooding expression was gone from his face. His figure glowed with robust good health, his azure blue eyes bright and sparkling in the radiant sunlight.

"Beau," Franklin said as he dropped his gear and ran toward the stoop as if the man might disappear at any moment. He took Beau by the shoulders, looked him over, and grinned broadly. "By God it's a relief to see your face again, man. You look well! Better than I expected. Much better! Langdon told me the trip was hard on you . . ."

"Franklin, you're babbling like a long lost father." Beau chuckled.

"That I am," Franklin cheerfully admitted. "But allow an old trapper his weaknesses, eh? Not a day's past without a thought of you, Beau." Some of the cheer dropped out of his face, his expression dimming considerably as the two of them remembered the last time they'd seen each other.

On that horrible night ten months ago, when Beau stood on the threshold of their Charles Towne home. He wore the last blood of his kin on his clothes, his face still dazed with the shock of the carnage he'd found. Franklin was the only other man in the world who knew what Beau found in there that night and it came back to them now. Langdon could feel it, sense it in the long and silent embrace the two men shared and was almost glad he was not a part of it.

No, he didn't want to remember what they did. He'd seen enough the day he finally drew up the courage to ride out to the Gardiner homestead. It was weeks after his return from England, his nerve stoked by the way everyone avoided the place now. The children claimed it was haunted, that Matt's ghost prowled the grounds. Langdon hated this talk. Such good-natured people didn't deserve to become the phantoms in a child's nightmare.

If Beau saw the place now he would fall to pieces. It was boarded, the animals set free, the fields left to fallow. But that wasn't the worst of it.

The greatest horror was tucked into that quiet corner on the edge of the savanna where five wooden crosses stood like eerie sentinels on the horizon, beneath them buried the remains of one murderous November night.

Langdon had cried then, like he hadn't done since becoming a man, so overwhelmed by it all that he could do nothing but hide his face from the knowing eyes of his father, who had accompanied him that afternoon.

He felt sheepish later, afraid to face his father, who had suffered the additional agony of having to bury them. To this day, Franklin never spoke about what he had found in the dining room.

Beau broke away from Franklin, and Langdon could see the grief in him now, understand it as he never had before. Seeing Franklin again reminded Beau of the past, of the life none of them would ever know again. Ever so briefly, Langdon caught a glimpse of the stony expression Beau had worn throughout their entire visit in England.

Langdon couldn't stand the sight of it. "We've good news for you, Beau," he said quickly. "Far better news than even you expect!" Beau's expression brightened immediately. "Is she here? Maybe we should talk later."

"She's up in the loft," Beau said, giving Langdon's back a hearty swat. "Good to see you again, man."

"Here, here."

"Did Zachariah get back?"

Langdon nodded. "That's why we came." He lowered his voice and said, "It worked, Beau, the second note . . . I tell you, she's the talk of London!"

"Maria?"

Franklin joined them, steered them across the backyard, and bragged, "You read Vandenburgh well . . . very well. As you predicted, he got caught in his lies about her disappearance."

Langdon nervously glanced at the back door. "How is she, Beau?"

"Never better."

"Oh?"

"She loves it here, Lang, the gardens, the river, the house. Amazing, isn't it? Considering where she came from. I tell you, the woman's changed. She's happier than we've ever seen her. And she's adapted well to it all . . . the frontier . . . even the natives that come here to buy my pelts. She's befriended Yant'Ho, Running Dog's daughter, canoes to Cussitah herself on occasion. Even Indigo adores her. You should see how he dotes on her."

And you? Langdon wanted to ask but he didn't. There'd be time for that kind of private talk later.

"Paw-Paw!"

A child's excited voice sounded from the woods. Matthew burst out of the foliage with Indigo right behind. The babe ran toward his father at a breakneck speed, so fast he lost control and collided headlong into Beau's legs. He fell back on his rump but was too excited to be ruffled by the fall. Instead, he thrust out his fist with a squeal of excitement, "Tokee!" and showed his father the ragged remains of a turkey feather squashed in his hand.

Beau grinned at his son, scooped him off the ground, and tossed him in the air until he shrieked with laughter.

"I can't believe this is the same baby I last saw in Charles Towne!" Franklin exclaimed.

"He's no baby anymore, Franklin." Beau righted his son, let the boy straddle his hip, and presented him to the guests. "He's sixteen months old now. Hard to believe, isn't it? They've been gone nearly a year now."

Matthew clung to his father's vest and inspected the newcomers with wide blue eyes. His black hair hung in deep thick waves to his shoulders, only a small portion of it still gathered in a loose tether. His gaze settled on Langdon and he could almost feel how hard the boy was trying to remember him.

"Don't you remember me?" Langdon coaxed, then glanced up at Beau. "How long has he been walking?"

"You call that walking?"

They all laughed.

"One morning he was sitting on the stoop with Maria when his favorite creature, a turkey, walked across the backyard. Lo and behold, I turned around just in time to see my son tear across the yard on his feet rather than his knees!" He chuckled. "Maria congratulated me on my son's first run!"

"Are you boasting about him again?" Maria called softly from the doorway.

They all turned, watched her glide off the stoop and cross the yard toward them, the delicate features of her face radiant and warm with welcome. She was dressed in a yellow shift, her beautiful auburn hair neatly braided and wrapped around the crown of her head. Even out here, ensconced in the wilderness, she carried herself with an aristocratic poise, so tall and slender and graceful while moving through the vibrant green landscape. She was breathtaking, a timeless beauty with smiling eyes and blooms of peach color on her high cheekbones. She held her hands together in front of her narrow waist, so sophisticated and well bred in the midst of her frontier home.

Franklin immediately swiped off his hat. Langdon met her approach, took one of her soft hands, and bowed low over it. "You're even more beautiful than I remember," he murmured, delivering a gallant kiss to her fingertips. Her eyes shone with genuine affection when he faced her. "I missed you, Maria."

"And I you, my dear friend," she said in her melodious voice. "Welcome to our home." And then to Franklin, she said, "You must be his father. The resemblance is striking."

"My lady," Franklin said and bowed over her hand.

Beau caught her eyes and Langdon saw the strong message he flashed to her. Pride. The kind of masculine satisfaction a man found in presenting such a beautiful woman as his own.

They'd been intimate. Langdon was certain of it, thought it was obvious in the way they looked at each other just then. He was startled by the idea but not really surprised. It had always been there between these two, a kind of sensual tension that was so strong at times it had made the cabin feel much too small for the three of them.

"I do hope you plan to stay," Maria was saying as if offering a palace to them. "We've plenty of room and our cellar is full of food!"

Franklin found it hard to hide the sorrow he felt to look upon this tragic lady, to think a father could turn on such a radiant creature in the cruel way Arthur had. Her whole being seemed to radiate sweetness, a kind of soft and tender glow about her that bespoke a gentle and good heart. And how kind and gracious she was while fetching them a tray of refreshment, then smiling so shyly at their compliments to her fine cooking. She was too glamorous a hostess for this primitive setting; she belonged in the parlor of a prince instead of this trapper's cabin. But she was clearly at home here, offering the comforts of her simple dwelling with pride and utter selflessness. It wasn't long before Franklin was as beguiled by her graces as the younger men obviously were.

Later, when she retired for the evening, they brought a lantern to the river's edge and sat down to smoke and talk. Beau was anxious for the details and listened in quiet amazement to what Zachariah Deane had found upon his return to England.

The kidnap of Maria Vandenburgh was still unknown to the public. Her absence was excused as an illness that sent her to southern Italy for recuperation. Arthur was not in London. He'd left for

France just a few days after the ball, and from what Zachariah could see, life was normal on Dabney Street.

Hearing how Arthur had left England so soon after Maria's kidnap drew an embittered comment from Beau. "Heartless bastard," he cursed under his breath. "I knew he would do this—nothing—lift not a finger to help his abducted daughter, his only kin, go traipsing off to Paris while knowing damn well what kind of danger she's in. He cares not a whit for her and it tears her apart."

"The man's inhuman," Franklin sadly agreed. "But remember, you and Maria are surviving him, aren't you? It's obvious that you're happy together."

"Yes, when our memories are quiet!"

Langdon hurried on and appeased Beau's anger with a rendition of how enormously easy it was for Deane to gain the cooperation of the printer, Jacques Moineau. "Just like you said, the man tossed aside his scruples the moment he saw your sack of gold, Beau. According to Zach, he didn't hesitate for a minute, took the money and did what he got paid for the very next day. He published a translation of the ransom note and by midday, Zach claims there were so many people lined up to get a copy he had to print more!"

This brought a smile of satisfaction to Beau's face, an expression that widened into a broad grin when he looked at one of the pamphlets about Maria that Zachariah had brought back from London.

Beau shifted the picture of her into the lantern

light, remembered the way that regal face looked today, when she was in his arms, so full of bliss to hear him lay his soul at her feet. It amazed him then, very suddenly and unexpectedly, how they could know so much of heaven after the hell they'd both suffered in their young lives. It was a miracle, whatever they had between them, an absolute miracle.

"I'm sure your memories are black, Beau, but now you have the comfort of knowing your scheme is working," Franklin said. "I daresay, you're getting the revenge you want! London is as outraged by his behavior as we all are. I tell you, there might already be enough damage done to see the public hang him."

"No," Beau said adamantly. "It's not enough yet. I want another note published. Take it back to Charles Towne and send Zach to England at once. This note will tell Arthur he is to pay the ransom to Lord Clarendon within twenty-four hours or all of England will know *exactly* what crimes of Arthur's drove me to this. Let them all pay for Arthur's crimes then, the king, his ministers, Ashley, and the proprietors. The people of England deserve to know what manner of men they are!"

Franklin's face lit up with wicked delight. "Yes! Perfect! Force him to reply by putting the pressure on his superiors! They'll make him answer you, Beau!"

"No, they'll publish something to pacify me, then delve into this matter themselves. Believe me, they'll try to find out what I know long before it gets to the public eye! Which is precisely what I want. I'll write the note tonight . . . in Spanish this time . . . just to confuse them a little more. That will keep the pressure on Arthur while they run around in circles trying to find me. They'll give up, know Arthur's the only one who can get them out of this . . ."

"But what if he agrees to pay the ransom?"

"Oh, come on, Franklin!" Beau snorted, threw back his head, and laughed. The evil in his laugh made the hair on Langdon's arm stand up. "Arthur's money is his lifeblood! He'll die before he parts with it!"

"But what if the Crown pressures him into it?"

"That's when we take her back, Franklin. When the king himself is ordering Arthur to do something about this daughter of his that he thinks is so damned insignificant! That will be Maria's revenge, won't it? To see her father stripped of everything he thought was more important than her! Ha! I plan to live long enough to see it."

"You better start thinking about that, son," Franklin said, leaning through the darkness to cinch a firm hold of Beau's arms. "How do you plan to stay alive, eh? What do you think they're going to do to you over there?"

Beau leaned forward until he could look Franklin in the eye and said, "There's only one way to do that, Franklin. Charles Towne will have to be told . . . before I arrive in England. Go to the governor, arrange a town meeting, and tell the people the whole truth."

"What?"

"You heard me. Tell them I'm alive, that I have proof Arthur killed my family, that I abducted his daughter, and have blackmailed him into the hands of the king."

Silence. They all just sat there and stared at him in utter disbelief.

Why hadn't they thought of it before? Clarendon wouldn't dare kill the last of the Gardiners, not when the entire colony was rioting in the streets over the murders. Besides, Beau was his only link to the gold mine of fur in Carolina, and Clarendon was sharp enough to know it. If he killed Beau, both Charles Towne and the fur could be lost forever.

It was Franklin who finally spoke, his voice sounding oddly diminished and heavy. "I wish Matt was alive to see you now, Beau. He always knew you were special . . . that there was something about you greater than the rest of us. I can see why. Matt wasn't just bragging about you all those years. He knew what he was talking about."

Beau sat back, a smoking pipe left to dangle out of the corner of his mouth. "I am only what he made me. Don't ever forget that, Franklin. He was the great one, not I. Remember him every time you look at me because that's where Matt put the best of himself . . . in me. The shadow my figure casts upon the ground might just as well be his."

"He loved you, Beau," Franklin said, emotion trembling in his voice. "I hope to God he told you that once in a while."

"He didn't have to."

"Well, he told me. You were the pride of his manhood, Beau. Sometimes he'd look at you, shake his head, and mutter, 'Franklin, if I could piece together the perfect son, he'd turn out just like him.' Oh, he loved Michael all right, but you, well, you had a way of stirring up the pride in that hard old trapper. I just want you to know that. You had a special place in his heart."

Langdon could see Beau was caught off guard by the admission, touched and disturbed by it. It was a long moment before he said anything but when he did, the grief was thick in his throat. "Thank you for that, Franklin."

His father nodded, then stood up. "My limbs are weary. I'll take my rest in your loft."

"Go on then. Maria will see to you."

The minute Franklin was beyond hearing range, Langdon sat up and faced his friend. "I saw you two in the yard today . . ." He let the sentence hang.

"I see," Beau muttered.

"What's going on between you?"

"Everything, Langdon," Beau said, looking him square in the eye and knowing Langdon understood what he meant.

He watched Langdon attempt to hide the tension that stiffened his features, that made his thin lips press tightly together. "Why?" he asked. "Why are you doing this, Beau? She's your captive here! How can you just dismiss that?"

"The man in me dismisses it . . . not my mind. I know it's wrong."

"Then why?"

He sighed, not really in the mood to be chastised for this but knowing he owed Langdon an explanation. After all, they had promised not to hurt Maria any more than necessary and Beau had violated the rules.

He spared Langdon few details in telling him everything that had happened after they parted on Cape Fear. Travel with Maria was swift and easy. She denied her own aches and saw to his comfort and Matthew's with selfless efficiency.

But it was the darker moments that brought them together, found them alone except for each other. They had no one else to cling to when their hearts spilled over, and every sorry admission brought them closer together. In their grief, there was a mutual understanding, a common ground. They understood each other as no one else could.

She was inside him now, a part of his inner life, the closest he had ever been to a woman. They shared everything, their pain, their hopes, their needs. And, eventually, their bodies. Although Julia had worn his ring and taken his name, Maria knew him the way a woman was supposed to know her man.

"Is she in love with you, Beau?"

"Yes."

"Can you imagine how much more this will hurt her now . . . when she learns the truth?"

"The truth? The truth is our relationship has absolutely nothing to do with this scheme."

"You don't expect her to believe that, do you? She'll think it was all a ruse, Beau . . . everything!"

"I won't let her!" Beau stubbornly vowed.

"Think of yourself then! Haven't you lost enough of what you cherish in this life? Can you bear to lose her too?"

"So long as we're both alive, I'll fight for her, Langdon . . . the way I would have fought for my family if only I had had the chance."

"You sound so desperate about this, Beau."

"I want her, Langdon."

Beau looked across the flickering light, into the level eyes of his friend. He saw bewilderment on Langdon's face, heard a trace of amazement in his voice when he asked, "You're in love with her, aren't you Beau?"

Beau started to scoff but the words stuck in his throat. He suddenly didn't know what to say, what to think. Who but poets could put such romantic labels on the affairs of men and women?

"I'm too tired for this kind of prattle," he muttered, grabbed the lantern, and stood up. "Let's go to bed."

14

London, England
October 24, 1674

"I want this April Fool stopped, Arthur . . . immediately!" Lord Ashley demanded. From across the luxurious palace chamber, Lord Clarendon's clerk looked up from his appointment desk and frowned. Ashley lowered his voice and hissed, "I'm outraged at your indifference to this affair!"

Gaylord had never seen the stately Lord Ashley so disturbed. The sight of him momentarily distracted Gaylord from the numbing sense of dread he had felt since riding over here in the coach. Arthur would find out about the seizure of his records today and Gaylord found it difficult to concentrate on anything else.

Not even the third ransom note, this one written

in Spanish, then gleefully translated by Moineau for all of London to read over their morning tea today. Not only did the third note add more fuel to the fiery scandal, but it demanded that Arthur make his confession to Lord Clarendon. Arthur had coldly dismissed this particular request.

Until the court summons had arrived that morning.

This presented a change of venue. The scandalous kidnap of Maria Loretta Vandenburgh had reached the venerable offices of Buckingham Palace.

Arthur wasn't just livid about that. He was downright malevolent.

This was not the kind of mood Gaylord wanted his employer to be in when he found out about the records. Arthur would have him killed over it. Gaylord was certain about that. He wondered how quickly he could get himself out of London, never to be seen or heard from again.

"I've done everything in my power to find her, my lord," Arthur lied calmly. "I had every intention of soliciting your help in finding her just as soon as my business in France was concluded. You should know my delay in returning to London had everything to do with this kidnap. I suspected a group of Frenchmen might be responsible for this affair and spent considerable time investigating them."

"What made you suspect the French?"

"Surely you know the second ransom note was written in French."

"Yes, but you left for France months before it was printed."

"Because the first note, the one I received the morning after Maria's ball, was also written in French."

"Was it?" Ashley's eyes met Gaylord's with a level stare. Arthur was lying and they both knew it.

"I'm distraught with worry for her, Lord Ashley," Arthur continued, opening a miniature porcelain box and putting a pinch of snuff to his nostrils. He inhaled deeply, then sighed contentedly. "Which is why I intended to come to you and request your assistance."

"Really!" Ashley exclaimed indignantly. "You should have done that long ago, Arthur, before subjecting me to this kind of embarrassment before ministers of the Crown!"

"But this has nothing to do with our proprietorship," Arthur said. "I don't know why my lord Clarendon is involving you in this . . ."

"Because there's been so much bloody trouble in Charles Towne, is why!" Ashley snapped. "He's suspicious of those affairs, Arthur! And you better have a few answers for him in there . . . such as why you are continually unable to glean more than a ton of fur out of Carolina! It's the height of the fur season over there and we've but a half ton to show for it!"

Arthur looked directly at Gaylord. "Did you provide my lord with those figures?"

Gaylord looked up, saw Arthur's cold scrutiny, and felt a shrinking sensation. Before he could force an answer through his frozen lips, Ashley interrupted, "You've been so tardy about this affair I took it upon myself to look into the matter."

Gaylord fell still, poised on the brink of discovery.

"Oh? Wherever did you find those figures?"

"In your records."

"My records?"

"Yes. I seized them two months ago, Arthur," Ashley said with cruel nonchalance. "They were in my possession until yesterday afternoon when Lord Clarendon requested them. He's been studying them ever since."

Arthur shot to his feet and whirled upon Gaylord. "Why didn't you tell me about this?"

The minister's clerk looked up from his appointment desk again, cleared his throat, and awarded them a withering eye.

"Never mind blaming Gaylord," Ashley said smugly, then lowered his voice to explain. "He had no choice, you see. It was either turn over the records or be arrested."

"I shall officially complain to Lord Clarendon about this outrageous invasion of my privacy! In addition, I'll state my own case to him and put this entire scandal behind me!"

"Good heavens, no!" Ashley chuckled. "I'm doing the talking in there, Arthur, not you. If you think I believe a word of what you tell me about it, you're sorely mistaken. I think you're hiding something!"

"What?" Arthur gasped. He was just about to

attack when the huge mahogany doors of Clarendon's inner chamber swung open.

"Lord Clarendon," a guard announced.

Clarendon stood on the threshold, tall and stately in his brilliant red satin attire. Expensive white lace fluttered around his wrist as he waved them in.

The three of them followed the minister, silently following him to stand by the chairs positioned in front of Clarendon's massive desk. Clarendon extended his arm across the desk and each of them kissed his ring with proper respect.

Clarendon sat down at once and motioned for them to sit. His long thin face was pale and expressionless as he turned his attention to the papers before him.

They braced themselves. Clarendon was not only the shrewdest man in England, he was also a ruthless interrogator.

"Let's get down to business," the minister said in his crisp, impersonal voice. "Arthur, I want your daughter found immediately and an end put to this horrendous scandal. The April Fool wants a reply by sundown today and has shifted the public pressure in my direction. I'm to hear your confession, it seems. Kindly make it."

"My liege, I have no idea what he's talking about."

"No? Think of something, Vandenburgh. I don't want the people to think I'm consorting with you in this affair. Get on with it."

Silence. Arthur looked at Simmes, a scalding threat in his eyes.

"My liege," Gaylord ventured, "perhaps we should make some reply that will pacify the man until we can determine what sins he's referring to."

"Perhaps," Clarendon said without looking at him. His attention was squarely focused on Arthur. "What steps have you taken to find your daughter?"

Arthur made a brilliant presentation of facts that were, of course, completely unsubstantiated. "To date, he has led us all on a most baffling hunt," he concluded.

"Did you expect him to lead you to his door?" Clarendon mocked.

"Of course not, my liege," Arthur played along.

"Then why can't you respond to his accusations?"

"Because I believe he's merely a shunted competitor and—"

"He's nothing of the kind," Clarendon interrupted brutally. "He claims you committed a crime against him and it must have been quite horrendous to make him resort to such a dangerous plot as this. I don't believe money is the substance of this affair. You've done something far more despicable than cheat him out of a few coins."

"But, my liege—"

"Never mind, Arthur." Clarendon brushed him aside as if he were nothing more than a nagging insect. "You're obviously more concerned with yourself than the Lady Vandenburgh, so I shall take over from here, eh? I'll find her. And quickly. Now then . . ." He unrolled a set of parchments Gaylord instantly recognized. "There's been so much trouble in Charles Towne of late I simply can't overlook it as suspect . . ."

"Allow me to speak for Sir Arthur," Ashley interjected. "Although our margin of profit in Charles Towne is quite slim to date, those affairs are in order and quite legitimate. I'm in doubt as to whether the kidnap has anything at all to do with Carolina despite all the problems there."

"No? I'm not convinced, Lord Ashley." Clarendon's tone was far more pleasant with Ashley. "Allow me to reiterate a few facts I managed to glean from these records. First, I can interpret Arthur's duties as those concerning the financial business of the colony, purchasing supplies, collecting payment of stipends and taxes, funding the internal penetration of the territory by our explorers, Dr. Woodward and Sir Peter Colleton. Is that correct?" Ashley nodded. "And last, but not at all least, Sir Vandenburgh is in charge of the importation of Carolina fur."

"Yes, my liege, that has been his primary concern."

"As well it should be. It is also the area that raises the most questions in my mind." He shifted his eyes to Arthur again. "You are known to be one of the shrewdest businessmen in the world, Arthur. How could it possibly be that you have acquired nothing but one failure after another when it concerns the Charles Towne Traders?"

Again, Ashley spoke on Arthur's behalf and Clarendon allowed it due to whatever private relationship he had with the chief proprietor. "The traders are a powerful obstacle, my liege. Their control of the area and the settlers is quite formidable and we have little to counter it with."

"This much I can see for myself, Lord Ashley. And, consequently, the fur business remains the source of every problem that plagues Charles Towne, except for the Westoe attacks."

"There was no bloodshed."

"No, but those attacks puzzle me. First, I see by these records that Arthur has been pressuring the explorers to disrupt the relationship between the tribes and the traders. I wonder if they're not overzealous and unwittingly brought about these attacks."

Arthur spoke up this time. "They have been strictly cautioned against causing hostility . . . only suspicion. I am in constant communication with them and closely monitor their conduct."

"Very good, but just in case, I shall pen a letter to the explorers myself and warn them against volatile conduct that could inspire the tribes against the colony instead of just the traders."

"As you wish, my liege." Ashley bowed his head obediently.

"And the second reason why the attacks perplex me is because these Indians were blamed for the death of Matthew Gardiner and his family. It just doesn't seem right that they'd kill the Gardiners but twice attack the colony and shed not a drop of blood."

Ashley opened his mouth to reply but this time Clarendon put up his hand for silence. "I already know what you're going to say . . . that the Westoe may have had a private grudge against the Gardiners and so on. Unfortunately, I just can't be satisfied with that. I've tried, mind you, but something doesn't fit here. What can you tell me about that affair, Arthur?"

"Only what Governor Yeamans reports. He claims it was a typical Indian massacre—"

"Arthur, Indian massacres are not typical in Charles Towne. Furthermore, I see no record of Yeamans reporting this to you. It's the other way around, isn't it? *You* told him the Westoe were responsible. Isn't that true?"

"After Yeamans gave me the facts, I offered it as a solution to the mystery, is all."

"I see," Clarendon said, still watching Arthur closely. "Considering the amount of tension these murders caused in the colony, I'm amazed at your rather weak response. Especially because the fur is *your* business. Why, Matthew Gardiner was the leader of the Charles Towne Traders, the unspoken master of the colony and every trapper in it, the most respected furrier in North America. It puzzles me that you made such an indifferent investigation into his murder. In fact, this is what makes me the most suspicious."

"Suspicious? There was little to be revealed in an investigation, my liege. Why waste the coin? If the

Indians didn't kill him, who would?" Arthur's flesh crawled. Had he made a mistake by so completely masking the details of that affair last November? "I can assure you, I questioned everyone about it . . . Yeamans, Woodward, Colleton, even Edinburgh, one of the traders . . ."

Ashley recalled no mention of any such correspondence. Even if most had escaped the ledgers, surely one letter would have found its way into the documentation.

He was lying. He had lied about the first ransom note and he was lying to Clarendon now. What had the man done over there?

"Matthew Gardiner was killed at the height of the tension between England and the settlers," Clarendon continued, "at precisely the time when Arthur was under the most pressure about the troublesome fur market. Suddenly, the head of the Charles Towne Traders turns up dead, his murder blamed on the Westoe. Shortly thereafter, the Westoe attack the settlement twice but kill no one. Suddenly, Arthur's daughter is kidnapped by a man accusing him of foul deeds so reprehensible they would shock the devil himself."

Arthur could feel Ashley's eyes staring at him in disbelief. Clarendon was reaching all the right conclusions.

"And if you are responsible for this heinous crime, that would certainly give a man just motive, would it not?"

"Impossible!" Ashley blurted. He came to his feet in unchecked rage. He glared at Arthur as if every accusation was already proven true. "You wouldn't dare set afoul the meticulous planning I devoted to that colony!"

"You're all jumping to conclusions," Arthur scoffed. "These events are pure coincidence."

"I don't think so," Clarendon said and for the first time since the meeting began, he smiled. This was a rare opportunity to prick the infamous Vandenburgh. "Events of coincidence are usually isolated. They don't recur throughout an entire year, do they? No." Clarendon jabbed his finger into the Carolina parchments spread open on his desk. "I think we might be close to discovering the 'sin' this April Fool wants confessed, eh? I'll pen him a note and beg him for more time."

"I'm sure you're mistaken, my liege." Arthur continued to make light of the situation. "But I invite you to investigate the affair which will only uncover my innocence."

"I don't need your invitation to investigate anything, Arthur," Clarendon said. "Now then, Gaylord, I understand you've given Lord Ashley your faultless cooperation."

"I've done my best, sir."

"Pray do continue. I've hired a group of mercenaries who will accompany you to Carolina. I want you to search the area and determine if the lady is there."

"As you wish, sire."

Arthur instantly relaxed and Gaylord knew why. If the kidnapper was indeed connected to the murder of Gardiner, Arthur knew his lawyer couldn't reveal it. Gaylord would have no choice but to cover up the evidence and manipulate the investigation away from the guilty parties.

"Arthur, I will take it upon myself to make a public response to the third ransom note on your behalf."

"I'm grateful, my liege."

"Oh? You'll have plenty of time to show me your gratitude then, won't you? Until I've investigated these rather formidable conclusions I'm drawing about you, you will remain in the custody of the court . . . where I can keep an eye on you."

"But I have business to tend!"

"Your quarters will be most comfortable," Clarendon said, ignoring his protests. "You're not a prisoner here, merely a resident. Unfortunately, I'll have to make this arrangement public knowledge because I want your daughter's kidnapper to know how serious I am about this affair. In the interim, you may conduct whatever affairs you wish . . . under the watchful eyes of one of my guards. If my accusations prove gainful, your room in the Tower won't be as pretty. Until then, enjoy the palace, won't you?"

Gaylord rode home from the palace like a man who'd just had his blood drained. He was numb with panic. The worst was happening. They would be found out. Arthur was in court custody and Gaylord was responsible for an investigation he would have no choice but to tamper with. But doing so would only sink him deeper into trouble. He was trapped, caught between duty to justice and the need to protect his own neck.

Without speaking to his servants, Gaylord walked into his parlor. He wasn't surprised to find someone waiting there. Clarendon had said a group of mercenaries had been hired, and this was probably their representative.

The man by the window didn't turn or acknowledge his entrance in any way. He just stood there staring outside, almost serene as he watched the busy street, both hands casually thrust into his pockets.

"Allow me to introduce myself," he said to the man's back. The man finally turned around. "As I'm sure you know, I'm Gaylord—" He stopped in midsentence to look upon a face he would never forget. Gaylord's satchel dropped to the floor with a heavy thud.

"We meet again, eh, Simmes?"

"You!" This couldn't be! This was the same man he'd hired to kill Gardiner!

"O'Keefe! What the devil are you doing here?"

"Don't you know? I've been hired to assist you in searching for Maria Vandenburgh." A devious smile spread across his pocked face. "And to find out who killed Matt Gardiner," he said, pointing at himself. "Imagine that! I've been hired to investigate myself!" He laughed then, his short, stout body jiggling with an evil mirth.

"You didn't tell Clarendon the truth, did you?" Gaylord ran to shut the parlor door.

"Whyever would I do that? I live quite comfortably by the Crown's hire. You don't think I'd ruin my standing with Clarendon by admitting I sometimes work against him."

Gaylord stood in the center of the room, dumbstruck. He actually wanted to lose his nerve just then, to drop to the floor in a fit of madness and spend the rest of his life in an institution. Anything was better than going through with this.

Michael O'Keefe stood before the window, the pale gray light illuminating the smallpox scars on his weathered cheeks and accentuating the streaks of silver in his dull brown hair. Gaylord found it hard to believe a man of such meager stature was capable of being a master assassin.

"I suppose I should have told you I sometimes work for the Crown at the time you hired me for the Gardiner job."

"Yes, you should have. I wouldn't have hired you if I had known."

"But I suppose you're glad now, eh? Otherwise, think how hard your investigation might have been. You would have had to hide your involvement in Matt's death from the members of your own team."

The man was right. This preposterous coincidence might work out in his favor after all. "Then what sense is there in conducting the investigation . . . traveling all that way when we already know the outcome?"

"Why, to find the girl, of course."

"You don't really think she's over there, do you?"

"If my theories prove correct, that's exactly where she is."

"Are you suggesting—"

"The traders are definitely behind this. They know who this April Fool is—perhaps one of them —and are covering for him at this very moment. Her abduction was retaliation for Matt's murder. They'll destroy Vandenburgh over this, Gaylord. Those men will bring him to his knees, then crush him."

"But they haven't a bit of proof. I never documented anything."

"Let's hope they don't have any substantial evidence, Simmes, because if they do, we'll have no choice but to expose both you and Vandenburgh."

"But why?"

"Because Clarendon wants the April Fool brought back alive, is why."

"No!" Gaylord cried. "We can't! If we find him, we'll just make his death look like an accident."

Michael chortled aloud and shook his head. "Clarendon knows me too well. Accidents don't happen with the likes of me." He turned back to the window, smiling to himself as he gazed outside. "We have quite a challenge ahead of us. On both sides, we play with high stakes, each with men of equal power and greatness but from two entirely different worlds. I'm enormously impatient to begin this assignment."

"I don't share your enthusiasm," Gaylord said glumly.

"Of course you don't. You're scared and I'm not.

Which is why you should let me control this mission."

"Gladly."

"Very well, we leave in the morning."

"Tomorrow? I need time to pack."

Again the mercenary laughed. "Packing is easy when you're destined for the New World. Leave your lacy blouses behind, Simmes. You'll need nothing but a pair of rugged britches, a well-honed blade, and a breastplate of iron."

Michael turned around, the humor gone from his face as he said, "You'd best gather your wits, Gaylord, for these are no simple foes we hunt. They are tough, fearless men and we're going to try to hunt them on their own territory. It won't be easy. Now get yourself packed. I'll be back for you at dawn."

Zachariah Deane watched the activity on Blackwell's rig only two berths away. Something was going on over there. He kept his glass pinned to the English rig until he saw a coach pull up.

"Well, what do you know," he muttered to himself as Gaylord Simmes exited the vehicle. "If it ain't the fancy lawyer." He wasn't fancy now, though. He was dressed in the rugged gear of a soldier, high leather boots, broadcloth tunic, heavy wool britches.

Wonder where he's going dressed like that, Zachariah thought with a knowing grin.

"Hoist sail!" he barked from the bow. He listened to his men grumbling as they went about their duties.

It was obvious where Gaylord was headed; to a place where there wouldn't be any fancy balls, luxurious parlors, high society teas. A less civilized place, a British colony overseas. Gaylord Simmes was only involved in one overseas settlement. Charles Towne.

Zachariah laughed as his rig jerked out of the berth and headed toward open sea.

Wouldn't the traders be intrigued to learn this news?

Arthur Vandenburgh was in court custody and Gaylord Simmes was going to the New World.

The Savannah River
November 6, 1674

On her hands and knees, Maria leaned across the turnip rows to grab at the weeds in the onion section. It had rained for nearly a week and the garden was already overgrown. Worthless weeds or not, it was amazing how quickly everything grew here, even so late in the season.

"Yummmm," Matthew exclaimed from behind her.

She turned around, pushed her hat up and watched him shove a fistful of weeds in his mouth. "No, don't eat that." She carefully backed out of the garden while the child munched happily. "Spit that out, all of it." With the hem of her dress, she wiped off his hand. Now she could add grass stains to the mud. "How can you still be hungry? You just ate a full bowl of oats!"

Matthew looked up at her, coyly fluttered his lashes, and awarded her a wide dimpled smile. "Pie."

"Oh, no!" She wagged her finger at him. "That's for dinner. It's your papa's favorite." She gave his black pate a conciliatory kiss. It made a loud smacking sound that drew a bubbling laugh out of him.

"Paw-Paw pie . . ."

"Smart boy."

"Maffew smart!"

"You certainly are." She grinned, caught a whiff of something odorous around the boy, and sighed, "Do you need a clean diaper?"

"NO!" He started crawling away. Matthew had a new aversion to diaper changes. She had to crawl after him to check the diaper herself. It was clean. "All right then, but stay over here with me."

She returned to weeding, beginning to make some headway in the onion patch. That strange odor was getting stronger. It was a foul, fecal stench. She took off her hat and fanned the air around her head. Maybe some food was rotting in the cellar.

But Beau was always careful about food. Nothing went to waste if he could help it.

"Bad."

"What's bad, dear?"

"Dem."

"Hmm? You smell it too?"

"Bad . . . bad . . . bad . . ."

"It certainly is. I can hardly stand it."

"Maffew scared."

"Of what, darling?"

"Dem."

"Who?"

"Dem!"

She glanced back at him and followed the tiny finger that pointed across the yard. What she saw made her freeze in terror.

Indians.

They were standing all over the backyard, more than a dozen of them. They were hideously painted and smelled unclean. One glance told her they were not members of the local tribes she was accustomed to seeing in these parts. Oh no. These were not the amiable Creek farmers or the meadow-dwelling Savannahs. There wasn't a hint of friendliness about these visitors. They just stood there staring, so still and silent that Maria instantly sensed danger.

"Who are you?" she asked. No one answered. "What do you want?"

There was a native standing only three feet away from Matthew. The boy looked up at him, his head tilted way back, his tiny body moving not an inch except for the big round O he made with his lips.

"Come to Ree, Matthew," she said quietly. The boy turned and started toward her. She kept her eyes pinned to the native looming over him.

He was bared to the waist, his flesh was decorated with garish black-and-white symbols. A bizarre collection of animal bones hung around his neck and decorated his forearms. From what she could see, they were woven with hair. Human hair. He didn't move when Matthew inched into the garden, just stared down at him, his face hidden behind matted clumps of black hair.

"Paw-Paw," Matthew whimpered.

Beau.

The pendant.

With painstaking care, she reached for the leather cord around her neck, tugged it, felt the heavy wooden pendant slip out of her bodice. It dropped free, swaying over her lap.

The native saw it, suddenly jumping away and shouting at the others. His arm shot into the air, which sent all the natives scrambling at the same time. They swooped into the woods, hulked low in the foliage, and peered at her from the cover of the woods.

Maria leapt for Matthew, crushing half the potatoes as she dragged him into her arms. His little body was trembling as hard as hers. She clutched him close, inched off her knees, her eyes wildly scanning the half-hidden audience in the woods. The minute her feet felt the soggy ground she bolted out of the garden, across the yard, flew into the house and slammed the door behind her.

"Oh, my God," she was gasping under her breath. "Don't cry. . . . Ree has you. . . . Papa will come soon. . . ." She shoved the table up against the back door. Every shutter was closed, latched. The front door was jammed with Beau's chair. Satisfied the cabin was as secure as she could make it, she grabbed a spear off the wall, and with Matthew on her hip she scrambled up the loft ladder.

They hid in the farthest corner, under a pelt where she could only sit and pray Beau would come home soon.

Indigo pitched the canoe against the shore and they hopped out, tired and hungry. They both grimaced at the prospect of unloading the pile of supplies.

"It'll be our last effort of the day," Beau said, taking up the first load.

Indigo followed. "You spoil this new family of yours, trapper."

"Bah! My boy is growing strong. Besides, you eat from the same table, brother."

Indigo shifted the basket full of raw vegetables on his back and laughed. "My whole village feeds on less. This is why I stay."

With the first load stored in the cellar, they climbed out and started for the next.

Somewhere in the middle of the backyard was where they noticed it, suddenly, both stopping in midstride to look around.

Silence.

Maria was not busy cooking at the fire pit. There were no giggles from Matthew.

An eerie chill raced through his body. This was the same kind of silence Beau had come upon a year ago, the same quiet hanging over a house filled with death.

Indigo sensed his ominous thoughts, his face slack and expressionless as he looked at Beau through the shadows of twilight.

"Someone is here . . . near to us now."

Beau spun around, faced the house, saw that all the shutters were closed. It looked dark, abandoned.

Her name burst from his throat as he ran toward the back door.

"MARIA!" His shoulders slammed into the door. It wouldn't budge. "MATT!"

Panic slashed through him like the crack of a whip. He broke into a sudden wild run, punching at the shutters as he skidded around the house. "ARE YOU IN THERE? MARIA!" He slid in the mud, careened over the porch rail, and threw himself at the front door.

It was also jammed, but fear lent his strength a new, brutal force. He hurled his full weight against the door and it gave way.

He fell into the cabin, tripped over his chair, and stumbled around in the dark.

Where were they? Oh, dear God. Please no! Not again.

He tried to holler but no sound came out of his throat. He could hear nothing but the sound of his heart slamming against his ribs.

They were not downstairs.

The loft.

He scaled the ladder three rungs at a time, his

hands trembling as he lit the lantern and brought the chamber to light.

He saw them then, curled in a ball in the far corner, only their faces visible under a thick fur cover.

They were sound asleep.

He stared at them for a moment in absolute wonder. They were sleeping! That's all. Just sleeping!

He dropped to the floor, his knees banging hard against the planks. But he felt no pain. Nothing would ever hurt him again. They were alive.

"They're here," he called to Indigo. "Sleeping . . . that's all. Look at them."

Indigo was breathing hard behind him. He felt the Indian's hand clench his shoulder very tightly. "The gods play evil games. Even I thought darkness had come to you again."

Beau just gazed at Maria and Matthew with such fierce love in his heart he could find no words to describe it.

"Yet I saw nothing this time," Indigo went on. "Last time, I saw something in my mind when we approached the house on the night of the murders."

Beau looked up at him then, oddly unaffected by talk of last November. Normally it would bother him. But not now. No. He felt too exalted to care. "What did you see?"

"An omen."

"Like what?"

"A long dark tunnel that led into the earth."

"You never told me this before."

"Because you were not healed enough to hear it.

Besides, at the time, I could make no sense of it. Sometimes my visions are not clear."

Beau returned his gaze to his loved ones. "This time, they're just sleeping," he said again, shook his head, and laughed.

Beau finally went to rouse them, realizing that he had to ask what they were doing up here, dozing at such a strange hour. Why had she shuttered the house, jammed the doors?

Something had happened here today.

He drew back the pelt and checked them for any sign of wounds. They were fine, except for Maria's muddy hands. Matthew was curled into the curve of her body, contentedly sucking his thumb in his sleep.

"Maria," he called softly, touching her soft hair as he leaned down to kiss her on the temple, where he could feel her slow, steady pulse. "Come awake, my love . . ."

Matthew stirred, wrinkled his nose, and rubbed his hand against it. Their combined warmth gave him a magnificent sensation of closeness, as if their spirits were fusing somewhere deep inside him.

Maria's eyes opened slowly.

"Maria," he whispered, "are you all right?"

His voice seemed to strike her like a thunderclap. She jumped up so fast it startled him. With her back against the wall of the loft, Matthew clutched tight in her arms, she stared at him with wide, frightened eyes.

"Beau!" she said, now fully awake. "Thank God

you're here!" She flew off the wall and straight into his arms. "Where were you? They frightened us!"

"Who? What are you talking about?"

"Those . . . those . . . savages who were here. Did you see them?"

He lifted her head off his breast, looked into her dark slanted eyes, and tried to concentrate on what she was saying instead of how beautiful she looked just then. Alive. Alert. So full of energy.

"I saw no one," he said. He brushed his cheek against the crown of her head and whispered, "Tell me what happened."

"I was weeding the garden by the root cellar and they crept into the yard behind me. Matthew saw them first. Oh! They were awful looking! They reeked, Beau! The stench of them was so terrible . . . and the way they stared at me . . . as if to kill me . . . until they saw the pendant. Then they ran off . . . into the woods . . . and hid behind the brush to stare at me from there! But I ran into the house then and latched every shutter. We sat up here for the longest time, and I suppose we eventually just dropped off. . . . Beau? Are you listening?"

"Yes . . ."

"Why are you smiling?"

"Am I?"

"Yes! Don't you think this is terrible?"

"I think it's godawful."

"Beau!"

He grinned then. He couldn't help it. She looked so pretty and vibrant and engrossed in her story, her words rushing out in a voice full of musical inflections.

"I don't find this to be the least bit funny," she scolded.

"Paw-Paw . . . pie . . ." Matthew was cooing. "Yummmmm . . ."

Maria looked at them, pouting at their indifference. "Never mind . . . I'll ask Indigo to check the yard then . . ."

"No, I'll do it," he said quietly. He hugged them close for an instant, then finally climbed out of the loft. Maria stared after him, thoroughly bemused by his strange mood.

Even stranger was what she swore she heard him say just as she was surfacing from sleep. "Come awake, my love . . ."

Did he really say that or had she been dreaming?

The sun had nearly set when he went outside. It was difficult to see more than a few feet into the woods in such bad light. But he looked around anyway. Maria had been quite adamant. Someone or something had indeed frightened her and he made a mental note to be more careful about leaving her alone out here. It wasn't the natives he feared; it was the animals. Bear, wild pig, boar, meadow dogs. He had traps set around the circumference of the camp, hidden in the woods beyond where Matthew would stumble into them. They kept most of the animals away but Beau left nothing to chance.

Especially not after tonight. He'd circled the yard three times already and still felt shaken inside.

There was a rustling sound to his right. He

stopped moving in the middle of the yard and looked there.

"Indigo?"

"Behind you."

The smell. It hit him then, full force. "Westoe."

There was movement just beyond where the light penetrated the woods, vague shadows slanting and swaying amid the deep underbrush.

Acting on his hunch, Beau called out in the Westoe tongue, "Show yourself. Come forward into the light."

Only one native obeyed.

Tomawausau.

Beau looked at him once, twice, unable to believe the Westoe warrior was here. How had Tomawausau found him? This was not good. Someone must have told him Beau was alive. Why else would he venture nearly a hundred miles from Westoe territory?

Beau watched Tomawausau move out of the woods, his head bent as he slowly backed himself to the fire pit. It was considered offensive to show one's back to a deity, and to look one in the eye was a grave sin. Tomawausau slowly folded himself to the ground and sat waiting for a discourse with Beau. He would not speak until Beau permitted it.

"Keep Maria in the house," he told Indigo, then came to the fire pit to stand over the Westoe chief.

Beau immediately noticed his manner of dress. Tomawausau was bedecked for war, his body painted in the death colors of black and white. Human scalps hung from his loin cloth, the decoration meant to display his ability to render death.

"Speak to me, Tomawausau. Tell me why you've come."

"The white-haired trapper sent me." Langdon. Tomawausau didn't hear Beau's sigh of relief. "I came to the altar of your sacrifice . . . where your earthly body was slain." He had been to the Gardiner home? Beau said nothing, but he felt a sudden heaviness. Is this what the Gardiner homestead was known as now, a sacrificial altar?

"And the white-haired one told me you had returned from the afterworld and resided here in secrecy." Thank God Langdon had added that part about secrecy. If his continued existence was meant to be kept secret, no amount of torture would make a Westoe talk. Forsaking a deity meant everlasting death.

"What has happened between our people, Tomawausau? My village wears the mark of Westoe rage."

"We are not at peace," Tomawausau said and grunted in distaste. "The white men who live on Westoe land speak to my people in riddles. They confuse the minds of my warriors. They say your village is evil and infested with hate."

"Who told you that?"

"The white men who now live on the Congaree."

Woodward and Colleton.

Those idiots! Beau seethed inwardly. He shook his head and said firmly, "These white men came from the kingdom across the Great Water. They do not understand our ways. Not your ways or the ways of my village. You have known the traders many years. Have they ever been evil?"

Tomawausau answered immediately, "No."

"Then why do you allow the newcomers to tell you about people you know better than they?"

"Because your village rose against you! Your dwelling place is restless with the spirits of those taken without consent!"

Beau looked at the chief incredulously. "These white men told you my family was killed by my own people?"

Tomawausau said nothing, just nodded his head.

"How dare they blame this massacre on my own village! It was the hand of *their* leader that spilled my people's blood!"

Tomawausau stiffened as he heard this. "What say you, Divine One?"

"I say they lie!" Beau spit out the words venomously. "I shroud my life from the eyes of the world because even now, as we speak, I am destroying him for what he's done to me."

How could Woodward and Colleton act so dangerously stupid? If they knew this land and its natives well enough, they wouldn't dare accuse Charles Towne of scorning a man considered divine by the Westoe. It was a miracle Tomawausau's warriors hadn't killed every living creature in the village during those attacks. The Westoe were the most volatile of any Carolina tribe and such a careless accusation might have cost nearly a thousand lives.

He had to get word to the traders.

Indigo.

It was the only way.

"Tomawausau, you must never converse with the newcomers again. Stay away from them and forbid your people to go to their camp on the Congaree. You must let me cleanse it of its evil."

Tomawausau nodded. "If you condemn them, then they are to be condemned. We will not war with your village because you have spoken for them. Your word brings me the purest truth. Let me go to the evil ones on the Congaree so I can slay them in your honor."

Beau mentally searched for a way to prevent the deaths of Woodward and Colleton without offending Tomawausau's honor. It was a great privilege to act for a god. But he knew the Englishmen were neophytes. They didn't know how close they'd come to destroying Charles Towne. Somehow, Beau must become a liaison with the men on the Congaree to ensure that this never happened again.

"Tomawausau, my spirit rises in joy for the offering of your aid. It is worthy." The chief bowed his head and accepted the homage gratefully. "But my word has been spoken. Do not consort with the white men on the Congaree."

"I give my word."

"After I visit those men, I will come to your village and we will speak again. Until that time, let our hearts be glad for the peace we have restored between our people."

Beau sat on the ground and continued to stare after Tomawausau for a long time. He wondered what had happened to their peaceful life here. He longed for those days before Charles Towne arrived with her ships full of English decrees. What a twisted mess they had made out of such a simple place.

The colonists knew Carolina's beauty, her serenity, her prolific soil and farming tribes and winding saltwater bays. What could men of Europe know about life here? Stockpiles of gold were not needed for joy here. Life was its own reward; another day, another harvest, another child. All that was human found glory here.

He sighed, pushed himself off the ground, and went inside for Indigo. Maria was busy at the table chopping vegetables. Matthew was under the table, at her feet, riding her rosary beads along a crack in the planks.

"You must go to Charles Towne at once," Beau said to Indigo in the Savannah tongue. He went on to relate his conversation with Tomawausau. Maria glanced at them once or twice, detecting the serious nature of their talk though she didn't understand the language. "I doubt Tomawausau told Langdon as much as he just told me. The people must be warned. Go to one of the traders with this. They'll know what to do."

Indigo nodded. "I'll go at first light . . . by canoe. It will be faster but you have spared them, Beau. Your people will not feel Westoe anger again."

"I hope you're right."

"I see this, trapper."

"Oh?" He looked toward Maria. Tonight had taught him a lesson. It had made him realize, even if for only a single panicked moment, what pain her loss could inspire in him. Something dark and desperate welled in his soul. Indigo sensed it, knew the question even before it left his lips. "What about . . ."

"Her time is soon to come, brother. She will see only two more moons in this part of the world."

Two months. Eight weeks.

It wasn't enough time.

Beau struggled to mask his sad heart during dinner, when she presented him with his favorite pie, perfectly baked, the mincemeat sweet and tender. They discussed Tomawausau's visit and her discourse with him was intelligent and insightful, their conversation flowing freely throughout the meal and continuing while she cleaned the dishes in a bucket on the back stoop. He sat with her there, smoking his pipe, noticing how familiar she was with everything here. The well, the cellar, the route to the river. This was her place, as was the spot she always took on the stoop just beside his own when they came out here at night to talk. Almost every day ended like this, on the stoop or the bench. There was always something to discuss about their closely interwoven lives.

He took particular notice of it all tonight, at the ease with which they shared their lives. They flowed together like a river, on the current of their shared pain, through the rapid water of their ever-present desire for each other. She was the perfect woman for a man like him, gentle enough to penetrate his toughness, woman enough to draw him out so that he could be loved without fearing any loss of his masculinity. She never scorned him, not even in his blackest moments when haunting dreams left him trembling and weak. She accepted him in every way that he was, good and bad. There was only one part of him that she had yet to see; the place where he hid the revenge for his lost kin.

Somehow, some way, she would accept this too. He felt certain of it now, as he sat smoking his pipe and watching every move of his gentle maid who danced so lightly through every corner of his heart.

He loved her. Fiercely, completely, and just recklessly enough to know that nothing in this world would ever take her from him now.

Nothing.

Except death.

Charles Towne
November 29, 1674

Gaylord Simmes and Michael O'Keefe came topside for the first time in a week and watched the calm waters of the Cooper River with tremendous relief. They had been seasick ever since reaching Hatteras, where this notorious stretch of the New World coast turned every legend into fact. Gales and ten-foot high seas tormented them with drenching rains and wind gusts that tore the sails to ribbons. When they finally cleared the shoals and slid into Charles Towne Bay, they fell to their knees in thanksgiving.

It was dusk. The setting sun spread a glowing path of firelight across the water, bathing the surrounding wilderness in a warm shade of orange.

Gaylord stood at the rails and scanned the terrain, his eyes wide and curious. He'd never seen forests so dense before. They seemed stuffed, crammed with an assortment of timber, all grown tall and bushy and green. The riverbanks were draped in deep pile mosses and lace ferns, overlooking water so clean and clear he could see fish feeding on the riverbed below.

Gaylord wished that Lord Ashley could see what a perfect location he'd picked for his model settlement. Even Gaylord felt proud to look at it, the way it nestled inside the mouth of the Charles River, where fresh water and saltwater blended into one, making the shores prolific in all that sustained life. Yes, he'd read plenty about this plush oasis, how bushels of mussels and oysters and clams washed ashore every day. The settlers could grow anything in this soil, red clay and black mold giving rise to hearty crops that flourished in the moderate climate. Winter never quite reached this place. The summers were fierce but the tradewinds brought frequent tropical rains and cool night breezes.

He watched the ship slope around a wide bend in the bay, presenting a full view of the small port of Charles Towne. It had only a few piers but they were clean and well built. Two merchant rigs were berthed at the docks, their sails furled, keels riding high on the water to suggest that they had already unloaded their holds. The place was otherwise deserted, not a human in sight as they slid between the two empty rigs. One was a Portuguese vessel, the other identified only as the *Savannah Wind*. Blackwell threw down his ropes and added their British vessel to the modest collection.

"Hard to believe this is the height of the fur season, eh Simmes?" O'Keefe shot him a sidelong glance. "Look at this place, barely a rig in sight . . . but I wager there's tons of fur on the way to Europe at this very moment. And most of it originates from somewhere in those woods over there."

He pointed upriver, beyond the place where the tall split-rail fence around the colony ended.

"Is that where the traders live?"

"Most of them. Franklin Miles lives in the colony but he's the only one. Word has it the British came and pitched the colony all over his front yard. He refused to leave. Said he was here first." O'Keefe chuckled under his breath. "Those laws you pen all day long . . . they mean nothing here, Simmes. Absolutely nothing."

Simmes trailed behind O'Keefe, carrying his own bags off the ship. The rest of the men in the party, nine armed mercenaries, would remain on board until needed. Their initial plan was to quietly take up lodging in the colony and conduct a discreet investigation about the woman they would identify only as a girl named Maria.

Michael hopped off the dock, his boots smacking in the muddy trail along the fence. Gaylord followed, trying to see into the colony between the rails. It seemed so quiet in there. The only noise they heard was a distant rumble from the south, which seemed to be coming from somewhere in the middle of Charles Towne. The trail led east, back toward the sea, and as they traveled it, Gaylord began to hear faint traces of music.

"Must be a gathering tonight," O'Keefe said more to himself than to Gaylord. "They're not supposed to gather, but like I said, they do what they want."

"But the soldiers—"

O'Keefe interrupted with a snort of laughter. "You waste the Crown's money sending them here. They spend most of their time swimming in the Wando." He pointed at the Cooper River. "These thousand settlers answer to only one authority—the land—and the traders who own it."

"They don't own it! This is British territory!"

"Over here, those who control are those who own." O'Keefe turned around to look Gaylord in the eye. "Better get this straight before we go in there. The traders are like gods to these people. They saved the colonists' necks long ago, back when British rigs couldn't get through Hatteras with supplies. That was your biggest mistake. You left them stranded without food, put them at the mercy of the four families who lived here, Mileses, Gardiners, Edinburghs, and Moores. You already know the rest of the story, don't you Simmes? The traders helped them all right, made world-class trappers out of the stoutest and damned good farmers out of the rest. By the time England got here, Charles Towne didn't need you anymore."

Gaylord didn't respond. He was sick of being treated like a fool by this top-lofty assassin. O'Keefe kept moving and Gaylord followed because he had no other choice. They trudged along in silence.

The path finally veered to the south, and when they rounded the bend, a wide-spread gate gave them an unobstructed view into the colony.

It was much larger than Gaylord had expected. A broad array of buildings started just inside the gate and closely lined the wide mud road that led through town. The buildings were short and squat, some with candles glowing through spread shutters, all of them arranged side-by-side with their front doors opening directly onto the street. It looked so peaceful, the buildings huddled there under the darkening sky, candlelight glistening in the puddles of rainwater in the narrow street.

"Welcome to Charles Towne, Englishmen," came a voice from the darkness.

O'Keefe spun around to see where it came from. He saw something before Gaylord did and fell very still, staring at a spot where the black foliage grew up the side of the colony wall.

The outline of a tall figure leaned against the fence only a few feet away. A small orange flame moved up and down before his face as he casually sucked on a pipe.

The man pushed off the fence and strolled toward them.

He was huge, a giant of a man. He walked straight up to O'Keefe and didn't stop until he was almost on top of him. The stranger towered over him, tall and commanding as he eyed O'Keefe from head to toe. He stuck his pipe in his mouth and dragged on it a moment before saying in a low, rumbling drawl, "What's your name?"

"Michael O'Keefe."

"Oh? Never heard of you. Just landed, eh?"

Michael nodded and had to bend his head way back to keep his eyes fixed on the man's face.

Gaylord didn't move. He took in this awesome figure of a man, noticing his strange manner of dress. His britches were made out of animal skins with thick fringes running up the outside seams. His shoes were made of the same wild fabric, laced up his shins to just below the knee. He wore no blouse, only a vest made of dense, plush fur that reached to his midriff. The man's muscles seemed to bulge everywhere, in thick round balls at his shoulders, rippling down the front of his fair-haired chest, tightly tapering toward his abdomen and hips. A thick black belt was cinched there, the metal buckle flashing silver.

He must be a native, Gaylord decided. Only this land could produce a man of such enormous proportions.

"And who are you?" the man rumbled at Gaylord.

He shrank when the giant turned toward him, and felt his breath come to a halt somewhere in the middle of his throat. "Why, I'm here on Crown business."

"I didn't ask what you're doing here, man. What's your name?"

"His name is Gaylord," Michael said in a quick

rush of words, warning Gaylord not to say any more with a sharp glance.

"Gaylord? Strange name. Moore here," the man said as he grabbed Michael's hand and clasped it in a viselike grip. "George Moore. Nobody you oughta pay any mind to. Just a trapper . . . simple man . . ." He let go of Michael's hand and tipped a big black hat toward Gaylord. "Gaylord."

George Moore. A trader. This was one of them, right here, in the flesh. A Charles Towne Trader. If they were all as imposing as this one, what chance did he stand against the likes of them?

"Call me George. We don't take to titles hereabouts."

"I see . . ." Gaylord mumbled.

"Need a place to stay, do you?" Even his voice was powerful, like the deep-toned bong of a cast-iron bell.

"We've made arrangements," Michael said stiffly.

The trader nodded his huge head, a pleasant smile making his sturdy face look almost handsome. His pale blond hair rustled in the wind as he turned back to his place in the weeds, pulling down the brim of his hat and leaning against the fence to continue smoking.

"Just stay on yonder road . . . take you straight to the taverns. Can have your pick. No travelers in town these days . . . they're all trapping the frontier this time of year." O'Keefe picked up the bags he'd dropped, but he didn't move on. He just stood there as if commanded to stay until the trader was done talking to him. "Just back myself . . . trapped the Congaree, I did." The Congaree. Where Woodward and Colleton were. "Go on along now!" he said with a wave of his massive arm. "Put your bags away and take the south lane past the governor's place. Winter market opened tonight. Everybody's there. Music. Whiskey. Have yourselves a time of it, eh?"

He grinned then, his eyes glinting as bright as his pure white teeth as he slid down the fence and sat cross-legged on the ground. His face turned away to the river, the pipe back in his mouth.

Michael walked a good distance into the settlement without speaking, so Gaylord kept quiet as he followed him. The colony was neat and orderly. Every house had spotlessly clean gables of masonry, individual yards fenced in split wood. The houses were built low to the ground, squatting close to the coolness of the earth. Plentiful stacks of hay and wood clung to the outer walls of each home. They could smell roasting meat and baking bread as they walked along.

"Dammit," Michael finally spoke.

"What's wrong?" Gaylord asked, coming alongside him.

"They know who we are."

"What?"

"Oh, come on, Gaylord! Use your head! You don't think we just happened upon a Charles Towne Trader at the gate, do you? They've been waiting for us. And George Moore just made sure we knew it."

"But why—"

"To intimidate us, you fool!"

"I was just asking," Gaylord snapped, furious with Michael all over again. "If you don't think we should go through with this—"

"Oh, for God's sake!" Michael hissed. "What are you going to tell Clarendon . . . that a trader spooked us at the gate so we ran off?"

"Oh, never mind . . ." Gaylord brushed past him.

"Never mind is right. Just shut up and let me think."

Gaylord stomped up the road, his fists curled around the straps of his satchel. He was scared, not only by this unexpected turn of events but because Michael was so obviously disturbed by it.

They were halfway into the colony when O'Keefe started issuing instructions. "Keep your last name to yourself, do you hear? Don't go bragging about being Vandenburgh's lawyer."

"Really!" Gaylord sniffed.

"And keep those pictures of Lady Vandenburgh hidden. Don't show them to anyone until I can determine just how much they know about us."

"It can't be much."

"Why not?"

"Because my own records don't reveal anything about your expedition last year, O'Keefe. I've told you that a hundred times already. There is no chance that anyone in Charles Towne suspects us. Perhaps they know we've come looking for Maria, but there is nothing to link us with the Gardiner murders."

"You better hope so, Simmes." Michael gave him a long, thorough look. "Until then, we split up . . . stay in different taverns . . . go our own way in the morning. You pretend you're here on some minor business of the Crown if anyone asks. If not, just mingle in the streets tomorrow, listen for any talk of Arthur's kidnapped daughter. Remember, these people are English. They've got relatives all over England. By now, someone has been told that Vandenburgh's daughter was kidnapped. Don't be obvious about it. Just let them tell you what they know." O'Keefe stopped in front of Tobias's Taverne. "I'll bed down here. You go to a place called Mierda's. It's about a block ahead on the left. You'll see it. I'll come there tomorrow night for a cup of ale. You be there."

Gaylord found himself stranded in the middle of the street. He looked around the dark road and suddenly saw all the shadows lurking between the houses, how the interior lanterns made eerie patterns of light in the puddles. Now the colony seemed dangerous. He took a deep breath in an attempt to calm down. There was no reason to feel so shaken. The most anyone could know of him was that he was Arthur's lawyer. Once he was safely quartered in the tavern, he could collect his wits.

Mierda's Taverne had an unpretentious face: a broad front porch fanning the length of the two-story wooden frame house. A single plank of wood was nailed to the wall beside a coarse wooden door. Mierda was all it said.

The door opened into a surprisingly large room with clean plank floors devoid of rushes. It was L-shaped, the long part to the left of him obviously being the tavern area. It was filled with rows of benches that stretched through the center of the space, surrounded by walls where giant kegs of ale rested in double stacks. Ahead of him was an eating area, a crude table carved out of a huge chunk of white oak with two long benches on either side. It was decorated with a group of pewter steins and a big basket full of green apples. Behind it was a hearth big enough for a man to stand in, made of stone with mud mortar holding it together. A collection of iron kettles, butter molds, bread pans, and skillets hung from the mantel.

This was a well-tended tavern, he decided, impressed by the tidy simplicity of it. Even if it was deserted. He was just about to go back outside to check the yard when a woman with a single candlestick inched down a ladder in the far corner of the room.

"You need lodging, sir?" she asked. Simmes was surprised at how young and lovely she was. Dressed in a plain muslin shift with a starched white bib and apron, she was slender and narrow waisted. Her thick black hair was tightly braided and wound around the back of her head. A thin white veil was pinned over it.

He inquired about lodging for an indefinite period of time and the girl's clear green eyes brightened prettily.

"We've plenty of room, sir! This time of year we get few visitors, just trappers on their way to the frontier. They only stay here long enough to fetch supplies. Did you just come to Charles Towne, then?"

"An hour ago," Gaylord said and smiled pleasantly. He liked the woman, who introduced herself as Marietta Mierda, the daughter of the tavernkeeper, Jacob.

"From where do you hail?"

"England."

"Oh! You must be on official business then."

Simmes simply nodded. He changed the subject to fees and was told a place in the sleeping loft cost one bit a night. He paid for a week in advance and accepted her cordial offer of a plate before he retired.

She showed him to the table, then lit a small fire in the hearth. A tray of pickled beets, sweetmeats, and a stalk of celery was soon placed before him along with a brimming leather mug of fresh-drawn dram.

"I hear there's a market tonight, Miss Mierda."

"Indeed! The whole town is still there . . . since this morning! The opening day of the winter market is a big event in Charles Towne. Why, the traders always come into the colony for it . . . bring their wives and children and their best whiskey for us to share! I daresay, the lot of them are reeling drunk by now!"

Except George Moore, Gaylord thought to himself. That man was completely in control of his wits.

Some of the light left Marietta's face then. She turned away, her back to him as she bent over the hearth, and said with a sigh, "They're trying especially hard this year to make the market festive. It's the first one without the Gardiners . . ." She let the sentence trail, tossed another piece of kindling into the firebed, then stood up to wipe her hands on her apron. "But I suppose you wouldn't know about them, being new to Charles Towne."

Gaylord thought this was a fine opportunity to ask a few probing questions, now that the subject had been raised. While Marietta settled into one of the cane chairs, he carefully formed questions in his mind.

"Gardiner . . ." he mused aloud. "Isn't that the clan the Westoe murdered last year about this time?"

"Oh, heavens!" Marietta scoffed, brushing at the air with her delicate white hand. "It wasn't the Westoe! The only one who believes that around here is the governor, but we know better. One of the Gardiner sons was particularly revered among the Westoe tribe. They would never have slaughtered him . . . nor his blood kin." Her eyes clouded with sorrow. "Such fine people they were. Louisa Gardiner was my best friend. I miss her so much—" Marietta stopped, momentarily struggled with her emotions. This surprised Gaylord. They were a year dead. "It was a godawful crime . . . some say the worst ever in Carolina. None of us can rest until the killer is brought to justice."

"Any clues?"

"A few, but the traders keep it to themselves."

"Oh?"

"They're a tight bunch, those families. Matthew Gardiner was sort of the leader amongst them . . . he and his son Beau." The mention of the latter man's name brought a more wistful look to her face. Then she turned toward Gaylord, her eyes sparkling with girlish delight. "Beau Gardiner was the handsomest man in these parts!"

She let out a whispery giggle that made him smile. When she noticed his pleasure, she blushed bashfully.

"I shouldn't go on so. Although I tried for him . . . but he chose Julia Wenceworth for his bride. We were so jealous! But Julia deserved him. She loved him for so long and he never even noticed her." She looked at the fire, sighing wistfully. "Then all of a sudden, one day, he did! Just like that! And it happened right out front. Julia was walking by as Beau came off the stoop and accidentally stepped on her train. Her dress ripped and he was ashamed of himself for being such a 'brute,' as he put it. Ah! I can still hear his voice . . . so soft and low it sent chills up a lady's spine, it did! He offered to replace the dress and that he did! Brought it to her house and immediately asked her father for permission to call on her. Imagine that! He never let on for a moment that he fancied her. Julia was thrilled. We were all so happy for her . . . if not a bit envious!"

But then she stopped, all the romance leaving her face as she whispered, "Their baby was only six months old when it happened . . . a little boy named for his grandfather . . . born only ten months after their wedding . . ."

Silence fell over the room. Gaylord stopped chewing and stared at the girl, then ever so gently he asked, "Was the infant killed too?"

Marietta nodded. "All of them were killed . . . every last one."

Later, when Gaylord lay down to sleep, he fell victim to the tender place inside him that was pricked by Marietta's tragic tale. Had he disobeyed Arthur and listened to his own heart instead, that young trapper, his bride, and their baby son would be alive today.

A pang of guilt slashed through his soul, so sharp and stinging that he clenched his fists against it.

"Forgive me," he whispered at the heavens where the slain family now rested in the peace of God. "Forgive what the hand of Satan has done to us all."

Mierda's was the most popular tavern in town. By the time Michael joined Gaylord the following night, there were already two dozen men crowding the benches. The ale flowed freely, and pipes of tobacco filled the eaves with great clouds of wafting smoke.

Gaylord and Michael huddled in a far corner where they could converse without notice and hear themselves beneath the din.

"Maria isn't in Charles Towne, Simmes," Michael said, noticing the robust figure of George Moore a few rows ahead of them. Moore acknowledged them with a tip of the hat, joined the chatter of his neighbors, and seemed to forget all about them. Michael kept a wary eye on him. "Her kidnap isn't general knowledge here. The few who knew about it were merely curious. They weren't hiding anything."

"I had the same impression," Gaylord agreed. "The most I could gather is that they know Arthur's daughter disappeared last spring. No one acted the least bit suspicious. If she was here, someone would have slipped. Clarendon must be wrong about the April Fool. Maria isn't here."

"Don't book your passage home yet," Michael snorted. "She could be held somewhere else in the territory."

"But Carolina is huge! We don't even know its boundaries yet! Surely you don't expect us to search the frontier!"

"We might have to. If the traders are involved in this, knowing the region the way they do, she's in a place where no one will find her until they're ready to let her be found."

"Poor lass," Gaylord breathed into the dregs of his jack, then held it aloft for a refill. Marietta gave him a special smile when she retrieved it, obviously liking him as much as he liked her. "Maria's not the kind who can survive a wilderness like this. She's so young and delicately reared."

"Yes, but she's probably alive."

"Some things are worse than death."

Michael clucked his tongue in disgust and turned away. Why was Simmes always so fatalistic about everything? It was tiresome and annoying.

"Relax, Simmes. These traders are not barbarians. If she's in their custody, I suspect she's being treated well."

The door to Mierda's swung open and an old man walked in. Shouts of welcome sprang from the crowd and the man grinned, tipping his hat. Marietta scolded him about his muddy shoes, paying not the least bit of attention to the armed guards who were following close behind the elderly man. The soldiers looked ridiculously young, almost silly in the way they tried to strike an intimidating pose. Their hard stares and glinting weapons were hardly noticed.

The old man pinched Marietta's cheek and asked if she would help him remove his shoes.

This made the young girl put her hands on her hips and reprimand him, "You're as old as the hills and just as stout, Mr. Edinburgh! If you can carry around a half ton of chain link, you can take off your own shoes!"

Edinburgh. Another trader.

Gaylord looked at the tall, thin man with new respect. Despite Edinburgh's shock of silver hair and untrimmed white beard and a face so hollow it looked skeletal, the man was far from his grave.

The energy of the land was in his sharp, blue-green eyes.

Now he understood why the guards were inside. There were two traders here now and they weren't permitted to loiter together without a Crown guard present.

Edinburgh stooped to remove his moccasins, then rudely shoved the guards aside to toss his shoes on the porch. One of the guards growled at him to behave.

Edmund cackled in amusement. "How old are you, boy?"

"Seventeen!" the guard snapped.

"Then it's past your bedtime," Edinburgh announced to the delight of the crowd. "You're not old enough to trail the likes of me, boy!"

"I'm old enough to serve my king!"

"Yeah, but your king doesn't have as much guts as me!"

Everyone howled and the guard looked embarrassed. A group of men rose off the front bench and threatened to throw the soldiers out.

This brought George Moore to his feet. The giant trapper stood between the guards and the men and said in a friendly tone of voice, "Go on outside now, boys. We're just here to drink and be neighborly is all. We're not having any meetings, see? Now just go on out and don't start trouble over nothing."

The guards looked dubious for a moment, then shrugged. What choice had they? They returned to their posts outside.

"How could you sell ermine so cheap?" The man in front of Gaylord was arguing with his neighbor.

"Because I need the wampum, Lang! We're heading west to trap the upper Savannah. I'll need supplies from Cussitah," the berated man said in his own defense.

"If I were you, I'd get that ermine back," the man snorted, taking his hat off and tossing it to the floor at his feet. He ran his fingers through his neatly trimmed blond hair and looked at the offended neighbor next to him. There was a sparkle of mischief in his hazel eyes as he quipped, "You could buy it back with a handful of buttons!"

This must be some kind of private joke, Gaylord guessed, because both men burst into laughter.

"God rest his soul," the second man said to the one named Lang. "Only Beau Gardiner could strike a deal like that, eh?"

"Indeed," the blonde grinned in secret amusement. "I'll never forget that night . . . how serious he was with Cowachee . . . explaining how the great kings of Europe fasten their garments with buttons instead of laces. He showed the Sanchee a button—probably from one of Julia's gowns—and they immediately laid three pelts at his feet in exchange for the button!"

"And the Sanchee still trade pelts for buttons!" A third man said, joining the conversation.

"Won't cost you a pence to get that ermine back," the blond man insisted. "Just pluck a button off your wife's gown, man!"

Everyone laughed for a moment at this pleasant

memory of the man named Beau Gardiner, the same young trapper Marietta had spoken of with such enchantment last night. He must have been quite a man, Gaylord mused.

A newcomer slid between the row of benches and nudged his way into a seat beside the blond man.

"Have a seat, Franklin," someone said.

Michael looked up sharply.

Franklin? His eye traveled between the newcomer and the man someone had called Lang. Yes, they did indeed resemble each other, both fair-haired and of the same stocky build.

Father and son.

Franklin and Langdon Miles.

Of course!

Michael looked at Gaylord to warn him. They were again the victim of a strange coincidence. All the Charles Towne Traders were here, in Mierda's, and they had all chosen seats in the rear of the tavern area, very near to where he and Gaylord sat.

Michael didn't like this. Not at all. It was too contrived.

He decided not to tell Gaylord. The man would no doubt panic and do something stupid.

"We've got to stop brooding over the Gardiners, men," Franklin Miles said to those around him. "They're dead a year now."

"Can hardly believe it's been that long," one man said, shaking his head dismally. "To think Matt ended up like that . . . with a hatchet in his head!"

Langdon grimaced, "Let's not remember him that way, eh?"

"He's right," George Moore said from the next row, swinging a long leg over the seat and turning half around. "I have better memories of Matt . . . can still see him sitting over there in his favorite place—" Moore pointed directly at the seat occupied by Gaylord. "He'd have his feet propped up real lazy like . . . look half-asleep . . . then he'd say the damndest things and we'd laugh so hard the floor would shake. Remember?"

Gaylord was squirming on the bench. Michael stabbed his foot with the toe of his boot.

Gaylord looked at him, leaned close, and whispered, "Am I mistaken, or all the traders here?"

"You're not mistaken."

"Let's get out of here."

"Don't panic. Just stay calm."

Edmund Edinburgh slid into the spot left open by George's half-turned body. He faced Langdon and Franklin and said in his high-pitched voice, "I miss the hell out of Matt and I don't mind saying it." He was looking directly at Gaylord now, his vision keen. "Beau too! You know, some of the excitement went out of this town when he was taken from us. Why, there's no one left to make the ladies swoon the way he could with those swaggering hips and big blue eyes."

O'Keefe stiffened on the bench beside him. Gaylord glanced at Michael and saw that he appeared to be deep in thought, and was looking down at the floor. Gaylord leaned forward, his jack between his spread knees, and pretended to study how it swished and frothed in his vibrating hand. He wanted to get out of there. Now.

"Face it, George, this town is never going to bury them until the killer is found. Until then, it's going to fester like an open wound."

Gaylord could feel Edmund's eyes on him and knew he couldn't stand much more of this. The mere mention of the Gardiner name brought instant misery to everyone in Charles Towne and his nagging conscience couldn't stand the truth. They were beloved, good people, and it was his hand that had helped to destroy them.

Two people on the bench in front of them rose and left the tavern. George Moore and Edmund Edinburgh leapt into the abandoned seats.

Michael suddenly found the four traders sitting directly in front of them.

It was time. They were moving in for the kill.

Why? What the hell did these men know? Deep in his gut, Michael sensed danger. Real danger. The kind he would face if the traders knew who they were, that Gaylord was the man who authorized the killings and Michael was the man who had carried them out.

But that was impossible!

Think! he commanded himself. Don't lose control of this situation.

Langdon turned on his bench, unable to resist a chance to take a long hard look at Gaylord Simmes. He'd only seen the man once, in England, exiting his coach and vanishing inside the Vandenburgh mansion. Langdon was surprised at how pale and fragile he now looked, the perfect London barrister. How could such an unimposing man have enough power to slaughter a whole family? Hate welled within him.

The lawyer looked up from his cup, his glance reaching Langdon just long enough to see the trapper's hatred. Gaylord averted his eyes. Langdon licked his lips, savoring Gaylord's obvious fear.

"You're new in town, eh?" Langdon asked him.

"I just arrived yesterday," Gaylord mumbled, taking another drink to avoid the murderous glint in the young trapper's eye.

"What's your business here?" Langdon persisted.

"It's official business." Gaylord was evasive, wishing Langdon would stop looking at him so coldly.

"Are you here about the new governor?"

"No, it's something else."

"Confidential business?"

"Yes . . . quite confidential."

Langdon grit his teeth. Zach was right. Simmes was here to find Maria. It was just about time for Arthur to start searching Carolina for the man who had kidnapped his daughter seven months ago. Charles Towne was certainly the most obvious enemy on Vandenburgh's list.

"I heard you were asking questions about Lady Vandenburgh." Langdon enjoyed the way Gaylord squirmed the minute her name was mentioned.

Michael looked at Gaylord, wondering whether he had been stupid enough to mention Maria's name today. Obviously, he had been. The lawyer was swirling his ale nervously. Some of it sloshed over the rim of his leather mug and splashed to the floor.

"Curious affair, isn't it?" Michael said quickly, trying to distract Langdon.

"You don't think she's here, do you?" Langdon asked innocently.

Before Michael could answer, Franklin turned around and grinned at his son.

"In Charles Towne?" Michael feigned stupidity.

Franklin chuckled from somewhere deep in his throat. "Well now, isn't that a preposterous notion."

Michael watched Franklin's grin broaden until it became an outright taunt.

They had her. There was no mistaking it.

And they wanted him to know it.

Why?

Damn! These men were shrewder than even he guessed.

"Is this what she looks like?" George Moore asked, stretching across the bench to hand Michael a folded sheet of paper.

He opened it and stared at an artist's rendering of the face of Maria Vandenburgh. Michael was so startled he dared not look up for fear they'd see his reaction.

Where the hell did they get this?

Anyone's relative could have sent the pamphlet, he tried to tell himself. This didn't mean anything, did it?

"Fetching, isn't she?" he said airily, and handed it back to George. "That's her all right. There's not a gent in London who hasn't offered his aid, his fortune, and his name to the lass! If she's ever found, she'll be the envy of every woman in England!"

"Good for her!" Langdon said and slapped his knee in delight.

"So why were you asking so many questions about her?" Franklin persisted.

"I wasn't," Michael said.

"No, but he was." Franklin pointed at Gaylord.

Michael couldn't believe Gaylord had already given himself away.

"Oh, he's just as infatuated with her as the rest of them," Michael scoffed.

"She's been missing a long time now," Edmund interjected. "Since April Fool's day, isn't that right?"

Gaylord's head snapped up, a look of complete terror flooding his face. Everyone saw it and the traders made no attempt to hide the enormous satisfaction they took from it. The traders had Maria. Michael was certain of it now. And that could only mean one thing. Her kidnap was directly related to the Gardiner murders.

They had the upper hand now and they began to use it, ruthlessly, brilliantly, sending a torrent of questions raining over them.

"Do you think she's still alive?" "Did Arthur send you here?" "Where do *YOU* think she is?"

"How come you brought all those soldiers with you?" "You ever been in these parts before?"

Michael felt suffocated, surrounded. These men knew something and they were taunting him with it, never quite saying what it was, just torturing them with questions.

Gaylord could feel a droplet of sweat running down the side of his face. Questions whirled past as the traders pressed their inquiries and Michael evaded the answers. Through a heavy haze of smoke, the four traders watched them with unwavering eyes.

Gaylord had a powerful urge to jump up and run out of the room. He wiped his brow, trying to stave off the hysteria. Langdon kept staring at him, his eyes cold and merciless and full of unspoken accusations. Langdon knew who he was. He didn't have to say it. He knew Gaylord had killed the Gardiners. He had to know it. Why else would he stare at him with such brutal hatred?

"We really must be going," O'Keefe said and rose abruptly. Gaylord leapt at the chance to get away.

George Moore reached out and cinched a mighty hold around Michael's arm. "What's your hurry, man? Drink with us for a spell."

"We've been here all evening."

"Yes, but you've not spent time with us! We traders like to get to know newcomers," Edinburgh mocked.

"Yes, but—" Michael began, but Gaylord had had enough. He left O'Keefe to talk his way out of it and stumbled outside. His stiff legs shuffled to the porch rail. He hung over it and drew in huge doses of air. He was sweating so hard there were big wet rings under his arms.

"Are you all right, man?"

Gaylord jumped, then swung around. One of the guards was standing right behind him.

"Yes, yes. I'm all right." He was shaken. "The air is so thick in there."

He walked off the porch just as the door opened and Langdon Miles strolled out. The young trapper leaned against the rail, slapped his hat on his head, and watched Simmes stumble into the street.

"Doesn't Arthur Vandenburgh have a lawyer named Gaylord?"

"What?" Gaylord turned and saw the man on the porch. Those eyes cut into his soul, accused him, blamed him for murdering the most beloved family in Charles Towne. "Yes, he does!" Gaylord cried. "His name is Gaylord Simmes!"

"Why did he send you here, Simmes? Haven't you done enough?"

"I'm not him!" Gaylord screamed. He started trotting away, down the dark street. He had to get away. They knew. Everyone knew he was a murderer.

He started running, wildly, blindly. The town was so dark. He rushed around a corner. Something hard and fleshy slammed into his face and knocked him back a step. He looked up to see a nightmarish face peering at him from the darkness. It was a painted man, bright yellow stripes of color glowing from his cheeks, a large blue flower glaring across his bare breast.

"From what do you run, stranger?" the Indian asked, and Gaylord backed away in horror. "Do demons chase you? Yes, they follow the strange tracks your boots leave in the dirt. It is the track of the jackal . . . one born to kill . . ."

"No!" Gaylord screamed and started running in the opposite direction. He didn't know where he was, what he was doing, where he was going. He just ran, ran until Michael appeared in the blur and shook his shoulders so hard it made his head snap back and forth.

"Get a grip on yourself, man!"

"They know . . . everyone knows . . . Langdon knows what I did!"

"Stop it! They all know it, dammit!" O'Keefe shouted as he dragged him out of the middle of the street and threw him up against the wall of a building. He leaned close to hiss into his face, "These men knew about us before we even got here. Tonight was a trap and you fell right into it! They were looking for guilt and that's exactly what you gave them!"

"I am guilty!" Gaylord cried, choking on the sob straining in his throat. "I killed them! And they know it. You can't deny it after what happened in there!"

"Nothing happened in there, Simmes! The traders didn't accuse us of anything!" He gave Gaylord another hard shake and waited until the stricken lawyer gulped enough air to calm himself. "Listen to me, Gaylord, and listen good. I discovered something in there . . . while you were busy panicking."

"What? What did you discover?"

O'Keefe looked around to be sure no one was near, took Gaylord's arm, and started leading him down the street. He leaned close to whisper in the lawyer's ear, "Beau Gardiner's alive."

"What?"

"The son we killed last year was brown-eyed. Edinburgh distinctly described this Beau Gardiner as having big blue eyes . . ."

Gaylord grew quiet, his eyes wide with sudden interest.

"That's right. Apparently, Matt Gardiner had more than one son. There was only one son at home the night of the killing. Do you understand what I'm saying? I missed someone!"

"But how—"

"You tell me! You never said there was more than one son!"

"I didn't know!"

"Well now you do! And this son named Beau is a legend in this town. You hear how they talk about him! They say he's a trapping phenomenon, a wizard when it comes to striking deals."

"Yes." Gaylord remembered his conversation with Marietta last night. "And he's probably the son the Westoe consider divine, which is why no one believes that tribe is responsible for the killing."

"That's right. And here's something else I found out about him today. He's fluent in French, which is his family's ancestral language, learned Spanish from trading in the Spanish port of Saint Ellens and knows all seven tribal languages! Fit the pieces together, Simmes. Now we know why the April Fool publishes his ransom notes in a different language every time."

"Dear God!"

"That's right. Beau Gardiner is still alive and he's the April Fool. I'd stake my life on it."

"But everyone thinks he's dead! Why would he lead his own people to believe he was dead?"

"For obscurity, you fool! The murders gave him the perfect cover. And if he manages to bring Vandenburgh down over this, do you really think Charles Towne will hold it against him? Ha! They'll likely crown him king over it!"

"Then the traders must know he's still alive."

"Of course they do . . . and they know where he's hiding the lady . . . you can wager on that one! This might have been a nerve-racking evening, but it was worth it. I think we just solved the mystery of the April Fool! Now let's go."

"Where?"

"We're going to follow the traders home tonight. I know where we can steal off with a few horses. You can ride, can't you?"

"Of course, but I can't go—"

"You're coming with me," Michael insisted, taking a firm hold of his arm. "Get control of yourself, Simmes. Otherwise, you'll never make it out of this mess alive, do you hear? You're nothing more than fishbait to men like these, especially if they know what you did to their beloved Gardiners. They'll kill you, Simmes, catch you in one of their traps and leave you to bleed somewhere out there where barely a man on earth has ever been."

The traders met on horseback on the road out of town. They trotted side by side, engrossed in the business at hand.

"It's back to the Savannah for you, Langdon," Franklin said.

"Tell Beau that Simmes is here. He's got to make his move now."

"They've tracked her down far enough," George decided. "Arthur's in Clarendon's custody so there's not much harm he can do now, not under Clarendon's watchful eyes."

"When should we tell Charles Towne what's going on?" Edmund wondered.

"As soon as I get back and we're sure Beau is safely on his way to England with Maria," Langdon said. "We can't risk some exuberant citizen leaping into the middle of this. Let's see it done first."

"Very well. We'll have Deane wait off the Cape Fear coast in a fortnight's time, near the beaches in Stono territory. It's as good a place as any . . . deserted enough for him to be safely picked up." George looked at Langdon, mentally making the final preparations for the end of this scheme. "You're sure he's got those letters Vandenburgh sent to Matt last year?"

"Yes, three of them . . . plus two of our own."

"Let's hope it's enough evidence to convict Arthur." Franklin was worried.

"It will be," Edmund said definitively. "And it's in writing."

"Which is better than the hearsay Beau managed to gather all those times he sat hiding in Vandenburgh's house. He heard plenty in there but I don't know how much we can use," Langdon said.

"Try it all, man!" Edmund suggested. "Try anything you got. It's Beau's life we're talking about here. I want it to be Vandenburgh's neck in the noose, not Beau's."

Langdon shuddered at the mere thought of what Beau would face when he landed in England with Maria. "Just keep your eye on those two and make sure they don't follow me. I've got to get to Beau safely."

"Those bumbling Englishmen couldn't catch you if they tried," George said.

"I will follow you," Indigo announced, "by a half day. I go to my village and gather Savannah hunters. They will come if I ask them."

Langdon liked this idea. He would feel much better if he knew Indigo was following. If anything stopped Langdon, they still had a chance with Indigo. He looked at Beau's cherished companion and nodded his head in gratitude.

Indigo's dark eyes glistened in the pale moonlight. "Their kind cannot match the Savannah . . . not here. We are too fleet-footed for men wearing boots and can—" He stopped in midsentence, drew on his rope, and turned full around on his mount. He fell as still as a statue on the dark trail.

"What is it?" Langdon asked as they all drew back on their reins.

Indigo put up his hand for silence. "Listen."

The traders strained to hear something odd beneath the usual din of crickets and buzzing gnats. They heard nothing.

"The jackal rides nearby. He hears us."

Edinburgh's eyes pierced the night, filled with a sudden burst of passion and hate. "Let the murderer scramble through the brush like the viper he is! His fate is sealed!"

Gaylord tossed and turned upon the fur-covered floor of Mierda's loft. Dreams plagued him through the night.

Langdon Miles droned, "All those times he sat hiding in Vandenburgh's house . . ." A painted man reared up in his slumbering mind, ". . . Jackal . . . born to kill . . ." The whining cackle of Edinburgh screamed hatefully, ". . . viper . . . his fate is sealed . . ."

Gaylord sprang awake and sat upright on his pallet. His body trembled; his teeth chattered violently. They had proof. The trapper had been to England! He had actually been inside the Vandenburgh house! Dear God, what *had* he overheard in the brush by the side of the road? Gaylord knew he was doomed. Caught. They'd trapped him just like some wild animal in a cage!

"God help me . . . please help me . . ."

He lifted his hands to his face and tried to dispel his wild thoughts. In the dark, he looked at his fingers. They were dripping blood. He screamed.

17

The Savannah River
December 24, 1674

Maria watched his face loom above her, close enough to see his features materialize in the swirling mists of this fabulous dream. His cool blue eyes were so striking in the dark. She sighed in her sleep, watching his mouth move as he spoke to her in that deep whispery voice, his lips so full and perfectly sculpted.

"Don't deny me anymore. You're my beloved . . . the bride of my manhood . . . give me all, sweet Maria . . . all of you . . ."

Oh! what a marvelous dream this was.

She didn't want it to end, ever. She let herself adore his words, the feel of his rough-skinned hands sliding so tenderly around her face. A sigh of utter bliss escaped her, made her arch against him, draw his body away from his lonely pallet until he joined her on her own.

"Oh Beau . . . my beloved Beau . . ." She sighed into the stillness of the night. His hair felt so luxurious in her hands, it was like plunging her fingers into the finest black satin. The scent of him engulfed her, a clean and musky aroma. "Make me your wife . . . let me be with you forevermore . . ."

His lips scampered up the front of her throat, fast and feverish. His hunger blended with her own. She didn't fight it. Not here. This was the only place where she could open her arms to him, invite him close. In her dreams. It was safe here, no need to worry about tempting him across the boundaries of faith and righteousness. Nothing mattered but letting her love burst through the spiritual barriers inside her and watching it shower over him with the fury of a summer cloudburst. She could feel his flesh shudder beneath her hands as he struggled for some last shred of control. But she showed him no mercy as her hands danced across his shoulders, his back, the thick muscles of his arms.

"I want you . . . oh God I want you . . ." he moaned against her throat.

She let her arms wrap around him, watching his face lift in the darkness, the color of his eyes change from pale blue to fiery smoke as he saw her desire and let it fuel his own.

"Love me," she whispered, her words soft and trembling, "as only you can love me."

Some hoarse, strangled moan escaped his throat just before he let down his guard, pulled her under him and covered her lips with his own.

His kiss was fierce with hunger, sending a reckless thrill through her veins. She shivered, clenched him tight as he pinned her beneath his weight. He took what he wanted now, ravished her with his long-suppressed desire until she was squirming and writhing under him, wanting nothing but to live in this moment until the end of time.

She was lost in him now, her mind spinning away from this world, this dream, this place in the loft where she had lain alone for so many months. She was aware of nothing but him, his taste, his scent, the feel of his swollen manhood moving against her, stoking her fires until they were burning out of control. Their pent-up passions erupted with breathtaking power. No force on earth could stop this deep and vibrant love.

As if from some other world, Maria realized she wasn't sleeping anymore, that this wasn't just a dream. She was really holding him, feeling him probe her between her thighs with his swollen body. She must have sought him for warmth on this chilly Christmas Eve because she was on his pelt, not hers, must have roused him unwittingly while in the blissful throes of this fabulous dream.

But it was too late to matter. They had gone too far. The floodgates had opened too far.

Her muslin nightdress was around her waist, her body completely open to him. She felt his hands on her hips, holding her still just long enough to find his way inside her.

Maria cried out his name, gasped at the feel of his complete penetration, the bliss of being joined with a man she loved so deeply. Rapture bloomed through this body of hers that was now his. And all the while, he filled her ears with words that made her soul swell with his private music.

"My beautiful Maria . . . live in me as I live in you . . . take life from me . . . all that you need . . . I'll give it . . . give you anything you want . . . just stay with me . . . stay with me . . ."

Ecstasy strained at the seams of their spirits, slowly breaking every tiny hidden thread until it burst and sent them soaring into a heaven meant only for them. They clung to each other, gasping and rocking in the throes of release, the sweet torture of it lasting just long enough to startle them, to make them gaze at each other in awe.

And then it ended, ever so slowly, his body and hers melting back to the floor where the fur pelt could snuggle around their breathless bodies.

Reality came back but it had no words. There was nothing to be said. No explanations. No apologies. No regrets.

Only peace.

She watched him doze in her arms, his face and hers close in the darkness. Her fingers looked so white and ghostly against the dark tan of his skin. "I love you, Beau," she whispered, watching a smile play at the corner of his lips, "love you until the end of time."

His black brows furled and his eyes suddenly popped open. Awake and alert now, he caught her dreamy gaze and held it tight. "No matter what happens, Maria, I'll never let you forget that."

"What?"

"You heard me."

"I don't understand . . ."

"You will." He reached, brushed the hair out of her eyes, and said, "But it doesn't matter now. Just this . . . what we have between us. You please me, Maria . . . the way you love me . . . it thrills me."

She sighed blissfully at his praise. It was even more satisfying when he rewarded her with a long and languid kiss that was just deep enough to stir new passion between them.

"Don't let us deny each other anymore, Beau."

"I only await your word."

"You have it."

"Yes, I have, Englishwoman. Who taught you how to wake a man up like that in the middle of the night, eh?"

She giggled despite herself. "I thought I was dreaming."

He laughed huskily as he rose on an elbow to watch her glowing happiness. Nothing in the world seemed to matter at that moment but seeing her smile, hearing her laugh. She basked in his adoring attention. But then it shifted, as some other thought invaded his mind, something that made a frown slowly drift across his brow.

"What is it, Beau? Something troubles you."

He just sighed as he shook his head and lay back down. "One day, I'm going to tell you some things you have to know, Maria, things that will hurt you . . . make you doubt me."

"Don't say that, Beau! I'll never doubt you! You changed my life . . . gave me the first happiness I've ever known."

"But I have more to give you," he whispered, "so much more . . . and I will . . . soon . . . very soon."

She didn't understand him, sensed some hidden meaning behind his words that she knew he wouldn't explain. She realized how often he spoke to her like this, in veiled syllables, riddles hidden in his words. She had the strangest sensation that whatever he hid was something bad, something she should know about.

"Beau, I—"

"No more talk," he said, silencing her with another kiss, this one full of new urgency. "There'll be time for talk later . . . not now . . . I waited too long for your bed, Lady Vandenburgh."

She didn't know what time it was, how long they'd been sleeping, spent and drained in each other's arms, when Beau came abruptly awake. He sat up, looked around.

"Beau?"

He put up his hand for silence, his figure falling very still and poised in the darkness. A moment later, he was on his feet, naked before her.

"I hear something . . . probably just an animal." His voice was rough, groggy. "I'll check. Go back to sleep, princess."

He was scaling the ladder, dropping out of sight, his bare feet making little noise on the floor below. The back door creaked open and then shut. She listened for some sound of him in the yard but she heard nothing. Wearily, she drew a pelt over Matthew and settled back down to sleep.

Beau didn't say anything when he first saw Langdon at the fire pit. He just stood there in the middle of the backyard, stark naked, half asleep, a deadly crossbow clenched in one hand.

"I knew you'd come awake if I sat here long enough," Langdon said. He looked tired and unkempt, like a man would who had spent the last fortnight in the hinterlands. Beau watched the glowing bucket of his pipe rise up and down before his face.

"You have news?"

Langdon nodded. "They've come for her, Beau. They're here . . . in Charles Towne."

His grip on the crossbow eased. "Who?"

"Simmes . . . and another man named O'Keefe."

Langdon finally rose out of the shadow of the woods, crossed the yard, and came upon the unmoving figure poised there. When he got close enough, he saw Beau's face in the vague light, so full of dread it robbed all the victory from Langdon's mood. This was supposed to be good news, that Arthur Vandenburgh was in court custody and Beau was close to accomplishing this impossible scheme of revenge. Langdon blinked and stared at him hard, unaccustomed to seeing so much emotion on that chiseled face.

But it was there, a compelling mixture of sadness and dread, of losses weighing more than gains.

Maria.

Langdon didn't need to ask why Beau took the news like this. After all, here he was in the yard of the home he shared with Maria and his son, his nakedness underscoring the relationship he had with her. They lived together, ate together, slept together.

And now she must go.

Langdon decided to curb his own jubilation for the moment.

But then Beau ran a hand through his wild hair and gave Langdon's shoulder a cuff of welcome. "You've come a long way. Have some whiskey and tell me what happened." He led Langdon to the fire pit and the jug of whiskey propped against a nearby tree.

They sat down, drank and smoked while Langdon told him everything that had happened after the publication of the third ransom note. They were looking for Maria in Charles Towne, had no doubt broadened their search into the surrounding area by now.

"I can hardly believe how far you've come with this, Beau. It seemed so impossible a year ago, when you first heard of Maria . . . heard she was coming home to London . . . then saw her that night. Remember? That's when it all started . . . when this whole idea was born. And now it's nearly over. You've done it. You can crush him, Beau. Do it now while he's under the scrutiny of the Crown."

"Yes, the time has come." Beau glanced at the window of the loft, where Maria and Matthew slept so unaware. Their fairy-tale life was about to come to an end. His heart sank. He looked at Langdon, grateful to him and everyone else involved in this scheme who had performed so much better than Beau could have hoped. He was the only one who had failed. He had defied his own rules and now he would pay the price.

"I'll have to tell her now, Lang . . ."

"Yes," Langdon muttered dismally.

"Not tonight," Beau said. He wanted to groan at the mere thought of it. How could he make love to a woman as fiercely as he had tonight, then crush her innocence with such a twisted tale? On the eve of Christmas no less. Was there no end to her suffering in this world? No route of escape for her? Compassion made his throat tighten, and his words sounded oddly choked when he whispered, "I've dreaded this for a long time. The truth will destroy her."

"She has no idea?"

"None," Beau said, "and I curse myself for that now. So many times I wanted to tell her just to spare her the shock of hearing it all at once but I stopped myself every time."

"Why?"

"Because she's so happy here . . . claims these are the happiest days of her life. What man could shatter that for her? Not I, Langdon. I wanted her to have all the happiness she could get from this life we made for ourselves here. Maybe it was wrong—"

"No," Langdon interrupted, "if those were your true reasons, then you did right. Who could blame such a good reason, eh? Not I. Were I in your shoes, I would have done the same."

"Would you? Would you have taken her heart the way I did?"

They looked at each other then. "If she'd offered her heart to me, I wouldn't have resisted. There was a time when I wanted her, Beau."

"I know."

"But her eyes saw only you . . . and whether you admit it or not, your eyes were firmly planted on her pretty head. She had a way of distracting you and perhaps I wanted her to. I was terrified for you in those months after the murders . . . afraid that at any moment it would snap you apart . . ."

"It almost did," Beau said, recalling that time when the pain was still so raw. He remembered the nightmares, the way voices had called out to him from the Sanchee woods, "Help us, Beau . . . help us . . . they're killing us . . ."

Agony ripped through his spirit then. "I'll see this done for their sake, Langdon," he said in a sudden rush of words. "I can't make a new family for myself until the old one is at peace. Somehow, I'll make her understand that." He stood up, stretched, seemed to brace himself for the task at hand. "But it's Christmas. She never had much of a Christmas while she was growing up. I wanted this to be good for her."

"Let's not tell her yet. We'll wait."

"How much time do I have?"

"Deane will anchor off the Cape Fear coast in a fortnight. You can meet him there any time."

"A few more days then. It can wait a few more days."

"If you want me to go . . . leave you alone for a while . . ."

"No. She'll be thrilled to see you. She's got a twenty-pound turkey ready to dress in the morning . . . all sorts of presents wrapped for Matthew and me. Stay. You were with me in the beginning . . . be with me in the end."

"Until the very end, Beau. I'm going to England with you. You won't face this alone."

This made Beau turn and look at him sharply. "You'll be considered an accomplice over there, Lang. They might decide not to care what the colonists think if they execute a trader."

"To die for this would be an honor, Beau. I mean that."

Beau was deeply moved by his words. Emotion making his voice tight as he whispered, "So be it, brother."

Maria huddled beside the smoking pit in the backyard, the predawn chill penetrating her old capuchin as she laid the turkey on a bed of embers. It would take all day to cook and she wanted it to be perfect.

Like this Christmas Day.

For the first time in her life, she was celebrating the Yule with a family, her family, in a home where she was loved and needed. Maria smiled, hugged herself, remembered last night, and felt her spirit leap with gladness. Joy and love filled her heart, blended with the shudder of pleasure in her body. She felt as if she were soaring just then, brimming with a warm, glowing radiance.

This was the happiest morning of her life.

She looked up to heaven and knew God was smiling down on her, telling her not to worry about the dictates of the old religion. In this new place, nature ruled with its own laws and she had obeyed them, giving her love to a man the way it was meant to be given. Completely. And if she was lucky, the parts of him left inside her today would bloom into new life, a child of theirs, sprung from the magic of it all.

The mere thought made her want to leap and dance through the woods.

"Careful . . . you'll catch a cold," a familiar voice whispered behind her.

She grinned, warming to the feel of Beau squatting down behind her. "Good morning, my love."

"Merry Christmas," he said softly, his hands sliding up her back, caressing her shoulders ever so tenderly as he draped her with something that felt exquisitely warm and luxurious. It felt so marvelous, in fact, that she knew at once it wasn't just another pelt. She looked down and watched the drape of pure white ermine flow around her huddled figure.

She gasped, felt his hands squeeze her shoulders, his words breathing close in her hair. "It's time you tossed that old cloak of yours, Maria."

"Oh! Oh, my goodness!"

She stood up and let the garment drop around her legs, enveloping her in pelts of ermine of such high quality that they gleamed even in the faint light of this cloudy morning. But there was more to it.

The inside was lined with sable, a deep ruddy red. It was folded back on the outside, stitched to trim the full length of the cloak and around the hem at the bottom. She sank into its downy interior, clutching it around herself and twirling around and around in the expensive luxury of it.

"Oh, Beau! It's beautiful, the most beautiful cloak in all the world! Not even the queen has a cloak as fine as mine!"

He chuckled, grinning at her giddiness, and looked at her in obvious appreciation.

"It looks beautiful on you," he said, reaching out and pulling her into his arms where he could feel every shiver in her body. His fingers rushed through her unbound hair, pulled it free of the cloak, and let it wash over her, the color as brilliant and rich as the sable lining. His face bent, captured her breathless lips beneath his own, and kissed her softly, leisurely, just long enough to repossess her. "I made it especially for you," he murmured, his blue eyes glowing with memories of their lusty union last night, ". . . for my sable-haired beauty . . . with her snow-white heart."

He made her want him again. She wrapped her arms around his neck and let her body melt against his. "Such fine pelts could fetch you gold, trapper."

His arms tightened around her and she sighed blissfully at the feel of his lips scampering up the side of her neck. "At the moment, my lady, a mountain of gold couldn't take my eyes off you. I want to treat you as you deserve to be treated and I will one day . . . lay all of my possessions at your feet . . . acres of land . . . trunks of gold and silver . . . the richest fur in the world . . . a mansion the likes of which the New World has never seen."

They lost themselves then, reeling into a whirlwind of rising emotions and a swift new soar of passion. Love turned vibrant, energized them, made their lips join and search for more of the thrilling intimacy they had found in the loft last night.

A door banged behind them, and a little boy's voice rang out, "Paw-Paw . . . wangon!"

They groaned through their groping lips, parted slowly, reluctantly. Beau set her feet back on the ground, unable to look away from the brilliant yearning in her eyes. Her willingness was breathtaking, made him ache with anticipation of how she'd thrill him later. "Tonight, you'll sleep in my arms, convent girl."

"Paw-Paw . . . wangon!" Matthew repeated, coming to a flying halt against his father's legs and clutching at Beau's fringes to stay upright. "Wangon!"

"Is Uncle Langdon here?" Beau asked as he bent over and scooped the toddler off the ground.

"Langdon?" Maria thought the child must have been dreaming about Uncle Langdon until she saw the man lazily propped in the back doorway. "Langdon!" she cried, bolting across the lawn in a rush of white ermine. "What a wonderful surprise! Merry Christmas!"

Langdon smiled, his hazel eyes tired and heavy as

he took both her hands. "You grow more beautiful every time I see you. Merry Christmas, Maria."

"I'm so glad to see you!" she smiled radiantly. It made Langdon's heart ache to see her, so flushed with happiness and the lingering bliss of Beau's embrace. And how elegant she looked in her pure white fur, the rich red sable trim matching the color of her hair. Her cheeks were rosy, her dark eyes danced, her lips colored with a vivacious smile. "When did you arrive?"

"Last night. You were sound asleep when I came up to the loft."

She hurried him inside. "You must be famished after the journey. Come inside. I've enough food prepared to feed twenty today!" She rushed around the table, so excited about having a guest it took her a moment to realize there was something strange about this unexpected visit.

Why would Langdon come here on Christmas? He was devoted to his family. Surely he'd want to spend the Yule with his kin.

Something must be amiss in Charles Towne, she decided as she laid out plates of food and watched the man eat hungrily. She filled his plate twice and prepared him a third cup of tea. He must have run all the way out here, she mused to herself, while the men indulged in their favorite topic: trapping the Savannah.

From the sounds of it, this had been a banner year for the Charles Towne Traders. They had already shipped more than eight tons of fur and the season was not yet over. The trader named Edinburgh had arranged for one shipment of fur to reach England.

"George wanted us to ship England a second load but we outvoted him," Langdon said. "If we do, the proprietors will think Woodward and Colleton are making headway and we can't let that happen. George spent a few days with the Westoe elders, just in time to stop them from raiding the English camp on the Congaree. Tomawausau hadn't returned from here yet with your advice on the matter. They were dressed for war, Beau. There's going to be trouble out there soon."

"I plan to meet with the Englishmen as soon as I can." Matthew was making a mess out of his father's breakfast, waving a stalk of celery in the air and enjoying Langdon's attention. "Give me that, Matt."

"Mine!" Matthew squealed, then poked the stalk at Beau's mouth. "Paw . . . eat . . ."

Beau took a voracious bite out of it, which made Matthew shriek with laughter. "He's showing off," Beau said, unable to hide his humor as Matthew bounced gaily on his lap, flailing the celery at his father. "Langdon thinks you have bad manners. Your grandmother turns in her grave over you, boy."

Langdon snorted into his cup. "Your mother was relentless about manners," he said. "Remember?"

Beau rolled his eyes to the ceiling, imitating his mother's voice in a way that made Maria giggle, "Beau, don't you dare come to this table with a dirty face . . . and I see a speck of mud on your hand . . . wash them again . . . don't tease your sister, and leave your brother alone . . . no roughhousing in the parlor . . . and never mind that foul language in my house . . . go wash your mouth out . . ."

Langdon threw back his head and laughed. "He spent half his childhood sleeping in the smokehouse for being offensive," he explained to Maria.

Maria laughed gaily, trying to imagine Beau as a child. "I admire her for that," she said, gazing into Beau's twinkling blue eyes. "To raise a boy into a gentleman on this continent is quite a feat."

"And torture for the boy," Beau added. "She even imposed her mannerly ways on Indigo . . . wouldn't let him eat at the table unless he used a spoon." He laughed, but a whisper of sadness was creeping into his voice. Beau rarely spoke of his family, his past life. It still pained him too much. He would change the subject now, she knew.

"Are you going to eat or play with your food, Matt?"

"Paw . . . eat . . ."

"No, I've had enough now. You eat it."

"Tokee . . . .pay!"

"The turkey's cooking now, son. You were lucky I let you play with it at all."

Maria smiled, remembering how triumphant Beau had looked yesterday when he came home after successfully hunting down a turkey. It took him all morning. But Matthew's delight made the labor of the hunt worthwhile, the way he squealed and danced around the dead bird in absolute joy when his father laid it at his feet.

And then later, when Matthew went to sleep for the night, Beau had worried with her about spoiling him. But she wouldn't hear of it. He was a good father, she insisted. What fault could be found with a man who so cherished his child? None that she could find. None that she would ever find.

Beau seemed to sense her warm thoughts as she hummed through the chore of cleaning up after breakfast. He stole away from Langdon just long enough to share a private moment with her in a far corner.

"I can't stop thinking about you." He drew her back against him, his arms snuggling around her waist, his hands caressing her with a titillating mixture of boldness and tenderness. She sighed, relaxing against him as she let him brush aside her hair and press his warm mouth against the thin skin of her neck. A sensual thrill made her body shudder in his arms.

"What manner of virgin are you . . . so pure yet so passionate . . . the way you love me . . . it makes my blood boil."

"Oh, Beau, I want you . . . love you . . ."

"I'm going to send Langdon to Cussitah tonight. He'll understand. . . . I want you all to myself."

"It's not right . . . he's come so far."

"So have I, my lady, so have I."

They eventually rejoined Langdon at the hearth, their moods flushed with contentment as they let the festivities of Christmas begin. Matthew was allowed to find his gifts, which were hidden under the pelt on Beau's chair. The boy squealed with delight to discover them there.

Beau made much of the boy's first pair of britches. "Enough with those dresses he wears," he said with masculine disdain. "No son of mine should be wearing dresses."

Langdon dressed Matthew in his new leggings while they watched from their snuggled position on the hearth step. Beau chuckled at his son's reaction to britches, the way he kept pulling at the fabric between his legs and grabbing at the fringes. But Maria's nearness kept him distracted and she basked in his close attention, adored the way his hand roamed up and down her arm and how he never let her venture beyond his reach.

Matthew was soon strutting around the room in his britches, an exact replica of his father's, complete with fringed seams and leather laces. The child beamed at himself; he obviously enjoyed being the center of attention.

But his next gift instantly became his favorite.

It was a tiny wooden pipe, fashioned out of a hunk of hickory. They were all amused to watch Matthew mimic his father as Beau smoked his own pipe. When he took a puff, Matthew did. When he tapped the spent tobacco in the fireplace, Matthew did the same.

Maria thought this was the perfect time to fetch Beau's gift from the loft. She wriggled out of his grasp and was just crossing the room when footsteps sounded on the front porch.

There was a loud knock.

Beau and Langdon stopped laughing, stood up. "Maria, wait—" Beau began but it was too late.

She opened the door and looked upon the visitor in shocked surprise. "Gaylord Simmes!" she cried. "Whatever brings you here?"

Gaylord was caught off guard when Maria answered the door. After all these months of worry, here she was, smiling as if nothing at all was amiss.

"Thank God we found you, Maria! You can't imagine how worried we've been!"

Her eyes dropped shyly. "I suppose it was unkind of me to run off the way I did . . . without leaving a note. Did Father send you?"

"No, Lord Clarendon ordered me to find you."

"Clarendon? Why would he be looking for me?"

Simmes and O'Keefe looked at each other in confusion. It was obvious Maria had no idea why they were here.

"What did you say about running off, my lady?" O'Keefe inquired politely.

"Why, I ran away the night of my announcement ball."

"What the devil is she talking about?" O'Keefe snapped at Simmes. No doubt the lawyer was still hiding facts from him.

A gust of wind made the door swing back on its hinges. Gaylord looked inside, saw the man who stood there, nonchalantly leaning on the hearth.

Beau Gardiner.

He had more than just Maria fooled.

"Allow me to congratulate you on a job well done, Simmes," Beau drawled softly. Just looking at the face of the man who had arranged the murders made Beau forget everything but the fierce hate he hid in his heart. Gaylord saw it, didn't move when Beau beckoned, "Come in, won't you?"

O'Keefe pushed past the frozen lawyer and came inside with his weapon drawn. An envoy of mercenaries followed and surrounded the hearth, their blades fixed on Beau and Langdon.

"What's going on, Beau? What's happening?" Maria gasped, pulling Matthew against the folds of her dress. No one seemed to hear her.

"You're a Gardiner all right," O'Keefe said, mentally connecting the bold features of this man and the mother of the brood he had slain a year ago. He sported the same pitch-black mane, his eyes so brilliantly blue, twins of those he would never forget. "Yes," he said with finality, "the one they call Beau." He felt victorious then, having caught him.

And because he was so well guarded, he had no reservations about taunting this giant woodsman. "You look just like her."

"Like who," Beau asked with perfect calm, his arms folded across his massive chest. There wasn't a hint of fear on his face. This piqued Michael.

"Why, like your mother, of course!"

"And how would you know that?"

A new light flashed in the trapper's eyes. Gardiner knew even before O'Keefe revealed his dark secret.

"I remember her eyes . . . looked into them just as my man was slitting her throat."

O'Keefe heard only a low, animallike growl from somewhere deep in the trapper's throat. It made Beau's whole body coil like a snake, his eyes narrow, his vision pierce Michael with a hatred so vicious it made him look almost demonic.

This pleased Michael. He could feel his lips curl upward into a sneer of intense satisfaction. But something stopped the motion of his mouth, a force that felt like an explosion against the side of his face. He was suddenly airborne, hurtling backward, hitting the far wall with such violence it made all the air rush out of his lungs.

Before he could recover, the trapper's body slammed into him, brutal enough to make Michael's head crack against the wall and he felt the room start spinning wildly. He couldn't think, react, unhinge his body from beneath the rapid-fire onslaught of the trapper's fists. He just hung there, helpless, powerless to stop the way those savage fists landed every blow, pounded and tore at his body.

He could hear men shouting, Maria screaming, the trapper grunting. All the while those crystal eyes spun before him, blue knives impaling him with the rage of demons.

A scream of agony came from Michael's throat. Michael put his hands over his face just as his men managed to wrench the trapper away.

Michael slumped to the floor. Blood gushed from his mouth, spilling down the front of his cloak. In a shocked stupor, he lay there staring at the trapper, unable to believe the inhuman strength of the man.

"Murdering bastard!" the trapper spat, his arms and legs still fighting as no less than six guards grappled with his powerful limbs. "I'll kill you . . . tear your throat out . . ."

A guard finally drew his blade, lunged as if he'd sink the tip into the trapper's belly, but Maria was suddenly there, throwing her arms around Beau's neck.

The soldier leapt away at the last moment to avoid hurting her.

Gaylord tugged at the lady's arm, "Come away before you're hurt."

"I don't understand!" she wailed, clutching Gaylord's arm as she beseeched him. "What is this about?"

"I barely understand it myself," he said. A soldier tried to help Michael off the floor. O'Keefe's jaw hung at an oddly crooked angle, his nose was flattened against his face, his eyes were swollen shut.

Maria's knees gave way and she started to slump to the floor. Gaylord caught her, looked into her shocked eyes, and tried to explain. "My lady, you say you ran away on the night of your ball . . . maybe you believe that . . . but it's not the whole truth. On the morning after the ball, your father received a ransom note demanding his assets and a public confession of some unnamed crime in order to see you safely returned. The man called himself the April Fool. I have every reason to believe the man who did this is Beau Gardiner."

"What?" Maria looked at Beau, whose bloodthirsty eyes were still pinned on Michael. "What is he talking about?"

"What he says is true," Beau rasped, the malice on his face softening slightly when he looked at her. It was as if he just now remembered she was there. "You were indeed running away but how I came to assist your flight was not so innocent. I kept us out here . . . in hiding . . . ransomed you to your father."

"But that can't be true!" she cried as she whirled out of Gaylord's grip and sat on the floor. She stared up at Beau as if he was suddenly a monster. "Why would you do such a thing, Beau?"

"I have good reason."

"You mean . . . all of this . . . hiring me as a governess . . . bringing me to live here . . . was all a lie?"

"Yes. It was a lie."

"Why?" Her voice became so faint Beau thought she didn't have the strength to hear the rest of it.

"I once told you my family died from a poison . . . a poison that came straight from hell. Remember? On the *Savannah Wind?*" She nodded mutely. "It was a symbolic way of telling you the truth. Your father was that poison . . . your father and his spineless lawyer! They arranged the murder and as I've just learned, this man and his hirelings carried them out."

Beau noticed several soldiers shaking their heads at him, as if to say they weren't involved. But there were three others who seemed to shrink when his eyes passed over them.

He would remember them.

And they knew it.

Maria's face drained of all color. Her trembling hand knotted into a fist and rose to her mouth in a desperate attempt to contain the horror she felt. "I can't believe this," she whispered. "Father wouldn't do such a thing, Beau . . . he couldn't have . . ." She looked at Gaylord then, her eyes begging him to deny it. "Is this true, Gaylord?"

He couldn't look at her. The shattered innocence on her face just then was a sight he'd never forget. "Yes," he admitted. "It's true. Matt Gardiner was too formidable a foe."

"Foe," Maria repeated in a barely controlled voice. She rose then, and looked up at Gaylord in utter disbelief. "The man was a trapper! You killed a trapper because you thought he was a threat?" Gaylord didn't say anything, just stood there, mute with guilt. Maria's fists curled at her side, her eyes clear and cold as she demanded, "Answer me."

"Yes! Yes! We developed this territory because we wanted the fur . . . Gardiner fur . . . and Matt stood in our way."

"So you killed him for the money. Is that what you're saying?"

"Yes! We killed him for profit's sake!" Gaylord cried, unable to meet the woman's rage. He cowered from her, from the eyes that accused him, blamed him, hated him.

"And the rest of the family . . . his mother and brother and sister and wife . . . they were all a threat too?"

Gaylord was too stricken to answer. One of the soldiers, another guilty party, spoke up instead. "We had to kill them. Our orders were to accomplish the murder without being seen . . . and they were all there."

"Having Sunday dinner!" Langdon's voice spat from behind the steel shield that kept him pinned to the hearth. Maria looked at him, at those hazel eyes once so friendly and now so furious. "And that's where Beau found them . . . slaughtered like cattle around the dinner table!" Maria didn't want to hear anymore but Langdon was not finished. "What do you think those nightmares were about, eh? Can you imagine what kind of dreams a man would have after living through something like that . . . coming home one night for what he thought was just another Sabbath meal . . . and finding his entire family dead?"

Maria could feel herself backing away from Langdon, from this heinous truth, from this perfect explanation of why Beau had been so desperate with grief when she first met him.

"But they missed Matthew. He was sleeping upstairs, unknown to the killers who were murdering his mother while he slept."

"Stop it. Stop . . ." she gasped.

"No! I want you to know all of it, everything this man went through . . . all the reasons why he is the way he is . . . why he had to do what he did."

"Enough Langdon!" Beau commanded. His eyes were pinned to Maria, who was staggering backward, her hands covering her ears as if she couldn't bear to hear another word. He had never seen her look so stricken. It alarmed him, made him jerk at the hands holding him. "She's heard enough! Maria, listen to me."

She couldn't hear what he was saying. She was aware of nothing but the cold-blooded crime her father had committed, of every place inside her that was filled with the blood of him. Revulsion made her stomach turn. She wanted to vomit, purge herself of this despicable man who had created her.

Everything was closing in on her. Langdon feigning friendship when he knew all along it was just a ruse. O'Keefe sneering about the death of Beau's beloved mother, the woman he had remembered so fondly just a few hours ago.

And Beau. *How could you do this to me? I loved you! Loved you all the way down to my soul!*

She saw it all now, so clearly. He had used her,

as a weapon against her own father. His affection was just a pretense to keep her satisfied while he enacted his revenge.

She could feel herself unhinging. It was all a game. Her happy life here was fictitious. She was back where she had started; alone, abused, worthless. Why did God allow her to be so heartlessly betrayed a second time? She put her hands to her head and tried to stop the terrible pain.

In a moment of sheer agony, Maria screamed aloud her hatred.

"I HATE YOU . . . HATE YOU . . . ALL OF YOU!"

She ran from the cabin and into the woods. She slammed into a tree and fell down, then regained her footing and ran even harder. Her moccasins slid over the earth in a wild, teetering dance.

She had to get away from this place of deception. *Fool! Fool! It was all a lie. Everything with Beau was a lie!*

"MARIA!"

Beau. He was coming after her.

Her heart was hammering in her temples. She could barely hear the hem of her gown tearing as she raced through the jagged foliage. She was numb. She felt nothing, only this driving need to run.

"STOP! MARIA!"

He was getting closer. How did he escape those soldiers. Why did they let him loose?

She couldn't face him. Never again. What a fool he must think she was, falling in love with him, giving up her body to him like some shameless, stupid whore, for what she thought was mutual passion. Just the thought of what she had done with him last night made her whole body cringe with shame. And all the while she had thought it was so good, so right, such a perfect medicine to heal her broken heart.

She felt crushed by this most supreme hurt. The world was pain, betrayal. It was worthless to go on living and suffering this way.

She turned toward the river. Thoughts of Matthew ran through her mind and she wept for the child. *He* hadn't betrayed her. His love was real. It was honest and good. She held a vision of him in her mind and wanted to die thinking about him, the only person in this world who had ever really loved her.

Maria plunged over the embankment and felt only the slightest flutter of fear as she sank into the icy water.

The world hushed, turned silent. She heard nothing but her own heartbeat thumping in the murky depths. All the stiffness drained out of her limbs as she fell into the arms of her own death. She wanted it, opened her mouth, sucked in a huge mouthful of water. It would be over soon. She could die here, in this tranquil river that brought her the only happiness she had ever known. Yes, this was the only way to escape, to die, to snuff the life from the veins that swelled with the blood of an infidel.

Something wrapped around her waist, ruthlessly yanking her upward until her head splashed through the surface. Beau. He had her and was furiously propeling her toward the shore. She was sliding in and out of consciousness, vaguely aware of being dragged onto the banks, upended, his hand slapping her back, the water gushing out of her lungs.

"No . . . no . . . dear God, no . . ." He was collapsing over her, covering her shivering body with his warmth. She just lay there staring up at him, unable to speak, to cry, to do anything but listen to his hoarse and broken words. "Please don't do this . . . don't make me lose you too . . . I can't lose anymore . . . no more . . . please Maria . . ."

She didn't talk, move, make even the tiniest motion. She was in a state of shock.

"Come around . . . look at me . . . listen to me. . . . It's not what you think. Can you hear me? Maria? Answer me!"

"I hate you."

"Don't say that . . . please."

"I won't live like this anymore, Beau."

Her voice was so dead, dull empty. What had he done to her?

"Let me explain."

"No. I can't live with this, Beau."

"Just listen to me!"

"I want to die . . . let me die . . ."

"Never!"

He scooped her off the ground and rushed back to the cabin. She felt limp and lifeless in his arms.

There was no fight left in her. She was completely broken, betrayed once too often.

None of the guards even attempted to stop him when he carried her inside. Except Gaylord. He reached for her but Beau flung him aside. "Get away from her, you murdering pig!"

"If you told her the truth—"

"SHUT UP!" he thundered and Gaylord shrank away. "Spend this time praying, lawyer, because I'm going to kill you and send you straight to hell!"

He climbed into the loft, hurriedly dressed Maria in dry clothes, and managed to pack a satchel for her and Matthew before the guards regained their courage and came up to watch him. He ignored them, finished what he was doing, then pushed them out of his way as he brought her downstairs. He tossed the satchel at Langdon.

"Put some toys in there for him." He looked at his boy then, sitting under the kitchen table, his eyes wide and full of tears. "Come here son . . . it's all right." Matthew immediately crawled toward his father and Maria. For a long moment, Beau held them both, his heart aching for all of them, for the peaceful life that was now shattered.

Michael, still dazed and sitting on the floor, managed to order both Beau and Langdon to be tied up. They had to struggle to get the woman away from the trapper, but the boy he refused to relinquish.

"Leave him be!" Langdon shouted as Matthew struggled to hang on to Beau's neck. The boy was kicking and wailing for his father. "You took the rest of his family without giving him a last word with them. The least you can do is let him make his peace with his son!"

Everyone watched this towering giant clutch the toddler close and huddle with him in a far corner where none could hear what he said to his child.

"Be brave for me, Matt. I must go away now . . . and if God shows me mercy, I'll come back for you. If not, let me live in your heart the way my father lives in mine. I want all your days on this earth to be as warm and safe as I would have made them for you." From some distant corner of his mind, his father's words whispered, "A man should be of few words." No. Not this time. "I love you, Matt." He sighed into the boy's downy crown. "I love you most of all."

"What is he saying?" Michael winced in pain. "Get the kid away from him."

Matthew was snatched away, and Beau's hands tied behind his back. They shoved him forward, into the sudden commotion of the cabin as they prepared to leave. Matthew was crying for him, looking at him over the guard's shoulder, reaching his little hands for him.

"Paw-Paw . . . Maffew . . ."

Pain sliced through his heart at the sight of Matthew being taken away. They'd been inseparable since it happened, together every day. Matthew had been the only light in his darkness, for such a long time, the only reason he had kept his sanity.

A soldier swung the cabin door wide, presenting a picture that brought everyone to a sudden halt.

Indigo.

He was standing perfectly framed in the doorway, a deadly delight in his dark eyes as they slowly scanned the room. His gaze settled on Beau, and he said in Savannah, "They will die the minute they walk out this door." He pointed at the stoop. "We have followed this league of jackals for many days, since the traders saw they were gone from the village."

The soldiers began looking around nervously, not really sure whom Indigo was talking to. While they wondered, Beau nodded at several of the men standing around him, made sure Indigo saw each one. "Those you can kill but these five . . . they're mine. They did the killing. You can have the rest."

He turned to Langdon, who was following this conversation with a ruthless, satisfied grin on his face. In Savannah, Beau directed, "See Matt safely home to your parents. You can join me in England later, Lang. This is more important to me . . . that he's safe."

"And you?"

To both Langdon and Indigo, he said, "My turn has come, brothers . . . my turn to kill."

"What are you telling him, trapper?" One of the soldiers rushed between them and gave Beau a rough shove backward. "Why are you letting them talk like this, Michael?"

"What?" O'Keefe asked, shook his head, then growled thickly, "Stop them, you fools! Must I do everything?" He doubled over, grabbed his broken jaw, spit a mouthful of blood on the floor.

The soldiers saw that their leader was in no

shape to command this group. One of them came forward in an attempt to take over. "Get them outside!" he ordered.

Indigo stepped aside, letting them go out onto the porch.

Beau looked around and saw no one. "How many braves have—" he began to ask but a soldier launched a fist into his mouth, effectively halting his words and sending him staggering a few steps backward.

"Say no more, trapper, if you know what's good for you!"

In English, Beau retorted through his split lip, "Now how would a dead man know what's good for me, eh?"

"Why you arrogant half-breed!" In one swift motion, the soldier launched his knee straight into Beau's groin. Pain exploded in his belly and he doubled over, dropping helplessly to the ground.

The soldiers were laughing, taunting him.

Then a new sound erupted. The bloodcurdling howls of a dozen Savannah braves who were suddenly springing out of the woods.

Through a veil of excruciating pain, Beau forced himself to focus on what was happening around him. Men were screaming, Langdon was tearing off into the woods with Matthew, Gaylord was running downriver with Maria in his arms. Then a soldier fell over him, blotting the view as he collapsed on top of him.

There was an arrow in his back, an arrow tipped in bright blue feathers.

Indigo was there, untying him, helping him to his feet, steering him around the corpse-strewn yard. He was back in the cabin now, panting over the hearth.

A black mahogany crossbow was thrust before his face. "Take it and go now, brother."

He shook himself hard, snatched the bow, slid his arm into a full quiver. Indigo handed him a hatchet, well honed and decorated with a flourish of white-and-blue feathers.

"No other hand but mine has ever wielded this weapon. But your hand is my hand today and so I give it to you . . . give it to help bring back the man who died many moons ago. You were meant to live, Beau. It was their lives that fell into the dark tunnel. Not yours. Go now. Fight for your life. Get it back."

The six of them ran until they couldn't manage the pace anymore.

"Stop here!" O'Keefe gasped. His men dropped to the ground beside the river in a panting pile. "It's obvious he's not chasing us."

Michael withdrew his kerchief and tied it around his head in a way that held the broken bones together and supported his jaw. The pain was staggering but he forced himself to do it. He had to think quickly. This mission was falling apart.

"He let us go, Michael," one of the soldiers choked, holding his aching side. "He deliberately let the five of us escape the savages."

"What are you talking about?" Gaylord said. He

still cradled the unconscious Maria in his lap. She had no idea what had just happened at the cabin. "What does he mean, Michael?"

"He's saving us for himself!" Michael snapped. "It's not just coincidence that we're all connected to the murders, you idiot."

Gaylord looked at him in sudden terror. The theory made sense. "But we have no defense against him, Michael! He could kill any one of us with his bare hands . . . and every tribe in Carolina is at his beck and call!"

"You think I don't know that?" O'Keefe yelled, pressing his hand against the stabbing pain in his chest. His ribs were broken; how many he didn't know. "Alone, that man is more lethal than all five of us!"

"What are we going to do?" one of the soldiers asked.

"Get back to Charles Towne as fast as we can."

"But Clarendon wants Gardiner!" Gaylord reminded. "He wants him as bad as he wants Maria!"

Michael scowled at Gaylord in disgust. "Use your head, barrister! Gardiner didn't go to all this trouble for nothing. He'll be back all right . . . long enough to see us all dead."

They didn't linger at the river. They set off once again, trudging through the labyrinth of timber. Hours passed, then days, an endless succession of miles. Maria gradually began to be aware of her surroundings. From the depths of her shock, she discovered a new and changed woman. A part of her had turned hard, as solid as a rock. The wound from this latest hurt would never heal into soft skin, she knew, only a rough scar.

And so she followed the men but kept her distance. They were all barbaric killers and their frightened prophecies of what Beau planned for them didn't upset her. Why should it, after what they had done to him?

They deserved to die.

"It's been three days and we haven't seen him," one of the soldiers mused aloud. "Maybe he lost his nerve and ran off."

"Don't be ridiculous," Michael sneered. His face still puffed and swollen, he scanned the forest around them. "He's out here . . . waiting . . ."

"Yeah? Well if he doesn't kill us, exhaustion will. And starvation!" another soldier complained bitterly. "Why don't we slow down a bit."

"You'll do what I command!" O'Keefe thundered.

"Why are you so angry at us?" Gaylord demanded. "If you hadn't taunted the trapper about his mother, he never would have known you did the killings!"

"He's right, Michael!" the three soldiers chimed in.

"To hell with all of you!" Michael cursed and stalked off. He made sure Maria was with him, pushing her ahead of him on the path. She was their only protection. The trapper wouldn't hurt her. Gaylord hurried after them, not wishing to be alone in the woods without her.

* * *

Beau perched high in the trees on a sturdy palmetto limb, watching the three soldiers recline around a small fire pit. They looked haggard and hungry and defeated. This was no place for broadswords, plumed hats, heeled boots, leather jerkins. The rugged terrain of the frontier demanded strength and mobility from a man's body, not clothes.

"We shouldn't be this far away from the girl," a soldier named Muller was saying to his companions, "but I swear I can't move another muscle. I need a long, long rest." He glanced around warily but he didn't see anything. Finally he shrugged and eased back to the ground.

"I've been on a dozen missions with O'Keefe and I never saw him blunder as bad as this," the youngest soldier, Dobson, said under his breath. "Ever since Gardiner thrashed him, he's been like a different man."

"Yeah," the soldier named McIlhinney agreed. "He's meaner than usual."

"Man's in pain," Muller explained. "I never saw anything like that before . . . the way the trapper came at him . . . like an animal . . . must have landed fifty fists in a matter of seconds! Phew! And every fist was dead on the mark from what I could see. After twenty years in this business, I'd say O'Keefe just met his match. And he's scared, you can bet. He knows he can't stand up to the trapper and that's knocked him off his guard!"

"He ain't the only one scared," McIlhinney said. "We all took a whack at the Gardiners and the trapper knows it. I saw him look at each one of us when he was talking to that savage."

"How many innocents did we have to kill in our day, eh?" Muller scoffed. "The Gardiner mission was routine! Who'd have thought we'd miss someone and he'd cause all this trouble?"

"None of us," Dobson said. "Maybe O'Keefe went wrong right from the beginning . . . last year . . . when he came here without the information he needed."

"That's why he hates the lawyer so much. He blames Gaylord." Muller told them as if they didn't already know. "I could have sworn I saw an empty chair at the table that night. Guess I should have spoke up about it, eh?"

"What good would it have done?" Dobson shook his head. "We couldn't linger out there, not after how that boy hollered. No telling who might have heard him, maybe someone in the woods . . . on a nearby homestead."

"That boy's hollering was your fault, Dobson," McIlhinney chimed. "You didn't kill him right away and had to come at him again."

"Aw hell! you seen how he was struggling. He didn't want to die, that's for sure."

"I had the same problem with that pretty blond woman," McIlhinney confessed, "except she was hurt enough that she couldn't scream. She didn't die right away either . . . just crawled over to the corner to hide."

Beau couldn't bear to hear anymore. These heartless descriptions of his dying brother and bride made his whole body twist in agony. Black despair swept through him and he slumped forward, weak and trembling, his cheek pressed against the scratchy bark. How could they sit there and talk about them like this? Didn't they know how much he loved and missed the people they described?

Long-suppressed memories rose in his mind, tormenting him. He remembered the feel of his mother's arms around him, the melody of her voice washing away a child's fear of the dark. He saw Michael as a toddler, could still hear him begging Beau to spare a trapped raccoon so he could keep it as a pet. Julia came to him as she had on their wedding night, wearing an ivory dress with a lace bodice that revealed her creamy white skin for the first time.

An invisible power wrapped around his neck. He could barely breathe as the pressure moved down his throat, clutched at his guts, made him feel as if his insides were about to explode.

A strange noise rifled through the treetops, the sound of a man trying to cry, straining to release some horrible pain that had been locked inside him for too long. Beau knew those sounds were coming out of his own throat. Whatever had been holding him together all these months finally snapped apart.

He reared up in the tree, threw back his head until he could see the sky, the domain of his beloved family. To them he cried aloud. Beau watched his hands lift and claw at the sky as if they belonged to someone else. Maybe they did. He didn't feel as though he was in this world anymore.

Someone else was climbing down the tree. Someone else's eyes were watching the whirling dance of brush and vine fly by as he ran toward the soldiers.

The hunted men flew off in every direction, yet he saw each place they went. A great rushing wind filled his mind until he couldn't hear anything, not the terrified soldiers or the songs of the birds flapping through the woods.

The face of McIlhinney loomed before him, precisely framed between the parallel spokes of his bow. He could see the white around the lone eye in his aim, watched the slender arrow spring through the spokes and pierce it. The blade in his moccasin whipped from its sheath and slashed across the soldier's throat.

Julia.

The sight of his bow focused on the back of Dobson's head. His weapon bobbed and swayed in a graceful, errorless dance that precisely followed the soldier's every movement. An arrow was swept into the groove of his bow and fired. The colored feathers blurred and flashed through the air. It stuck into the back of Dobson's head, vibrated a few times, then snapped still. Dobson didn't fall right away. He stood like a man suspended between two worlds, this one and the next, his eyes staring into the woods in an expression of surprise.

Michael.

Muller was crossing the creek. The wet rocks gleamed in the sun like bright yellow flares. He watched the man's foot land on a rock, then slide off. Muller reached out his arms to catch himself. Nothing but air met his grasping hands. He turned then, saw his pursuer. An arrow launched, pierced Muller's temple. He fell into the water, his head bouncing lifelessly as he tumbled a few feet downstream. Again Beau watched the blood spread into the stream, long red tendrils tumbling playfully in the current.

Mother.

A yellow-bellied woodpecker hammered at a tree somewhere overhead. The woods seemed so still now that the terrible wind was gone.

He felt numb, except for the palm of his hand. Something sharp was pricking him. He looked down at an object that brought instant comfort to the jagged pieces of his broken heart.

A tiny turkey figurine.

Maria couldn't understand what Gaylord was saying about the soldiers. He was vomiting too violently. It took several minutes for them to calm him down and ascertain that all of the soldiers had just been killed.

"But how?" Maria gasped in disbelief.

"Shot with arrows . . . their throats slit . . ."

Her blood ran cold. She watched O'Keefe slowly rise from the ground, caught his gaze above the weak and peaked Gaylord. It was like looking into the dilated gaze of a deadman. She shuddered, then looked way. "Oh, my God . . ."

Beau.

"The trapper did it, just like I said he would." Michael said to Gaylord.

"He'll kill us all!" Gaylord cried. "Dear God! he's going to kill us all!"

"No, he won't," O'Keefe said confidently. His two companions looked at him with interest. Michael turned to Maria. "You can save us," he said to her. "You're the only one who can stop him."

"What? And how would you have me do that?" Maria wanted to laugh. How dare he even suggest she help spare his life after what he had done!

"Talk to him . . . lure him out of the woods . . . ask him to spare our lives. Tell him we'll make a deal with him . . . and Clarendon . . ."

"You take me for a fool, O'Keefe," Maria said. "Why should I lure him out just so you can kill him?"

"I'm not going to kill him! Clarendon wants him alive."

"Then let him come here and get him!" she shot back. Furious, Michael reached for her. He was about to thrash her when Gaylord sprang off the ground and knocked his hand away.

"Leave her be! She has nothing to do with this! We committed the crime, now we suffer the punishment!"

Beau watched them from the woods and felt a twinge of respect for the lawyer, not just for admitting his guilt but because he jumped to Maria's defense.

"You're out of your mind if you think I'm just going to sit here and let him kill me, Simmes!"

"Maybe I am out of my mind, Michael. Maybe I'm just not strong enough to defend myself against the man. What I did was wrong! I never wanted a part in this crime, but Vandenburgh made me do it! I had no choice and—"

"Oh, stop your guilty whining!" O'Keefe looked as though he was ready to kill him.

"You could learn a lesson from Gaylord," Maria taunted Michael. "Like how to be human!"

O'Keefe glared at her but she wasn't cowed. Gaylord had told her everything last night, about the brilliant scheme Beau had used against her father, publicly exposing him, making him the laughing stock of London, driving him into Clarendon's custody. He was ruining Arthur, finally making him pay for the cold-hearted greed that had destroyed so many lives already. And Gaylord was being dragged down with him. She applauded the lawyer for secretly joining sides with Lord Ashley. It might save him. It should. After all, Simmes was just another victim of Arthur Vandenburgh's.

"Don't you think we deserve his wrath?" Gaylord asked, standing over O'Keefe as if waiting for a full confession. "You were told to kill Matt Gardiner and instead slaughtered the man's entire family, then left them lying there for him to find. What do you expect from him, Michael? Are you so damned heartless you can't feel even the slightest twinge of pity for what the trapper suffered—"

"You waste your breath on him, Gaylord," Maria interrupted. "The man has no—"

She stopped abruptly, her eyes alighting upon something behind Gaylord that stunned her.

Michael turned around, slowly looking into the woods to see what had the woman so transfixed.

The trapper. He was standing only ten feet away, casually leaning against the trunk of a magnolia. He seemed unaware of them, his head bent as he lit his pipe. Except for the dramatic blue-black color of his hair, the forest seemed to absorb him. The ruddy shade of his skin and his fawn buckskin britches blended into the foliage. Over each shoulder he sported two pelts of beaver, held in place by the crossed straps of a beaded quiver.

O'Keefe inched backward. Gardiner's head instantly snapped up, his left hand in control of a black mahogany crossbow. Michael froze.

"Stand up, lawyer," Beau said softly. Gaylord didn't move. Maria sucked in her breath and held it. "I said, get up," he repeated icily.

Gaylord rose on legs that shook so hard he teetered like a drunken man. He looked at Maria. The horror in his eyes made her feel physically sick.

"Move away from Maria," Beau said quietly, using the tip of his bow to point at a spot safely away from her. "Over there."

"Wha—what are you going to do to me?" Gaylord's voice cracked. He was going to cry. Maria put a hand to her lips. With only her eyes, she begged Beau to show him mercy. But he didn't even seem to notice her. His eyes were like two cold stones in his face, wholly focused on Gaylord.

"Are you so afraid to die, lawyer?"

"I wanted no part of it!" Gaylord cried. "You must believe me!"

"Oh, but I do believe you," Beau said. "Like I believe my family wanted no part in my father's death."

His attention shifted to O'Keefe. "Do you remember how he died?"

O'Keefe said nothing.

"This might refresh your memory." He drew a freshly honed tomahawk from his belt. Maria noticed it was decorated with bright blue feathers. Indigo's colors.

O'Keefe made a move to run.

The tomahawk whistled through the air, tumbling end over end until it thumped to a halt in the back of Michael's thigh. He screamed and fell to the ground. Beau flashed out of the woods, leapt upon his fallen prey, yanked the ax free, and flipped Michael face down in the clover. He straddled him.

Maria shrank around the other side of the tree and clenched her eyes shut, unable to watch.

"My father was a noble man. He didn't deserve to die like that . . . butchered like cattle. That's the hardest part for me, O'Keefe, the way you made them suffer."

"Damn you!" Michael cried. He tried to crawl out from under him and Beau allowed him a few inches. Then his powerful thighs cinched around his legs like a brutal iron clamp. "Coward!" Michael said. "You fight like a coward . . . allowing Indians to take my men . . . then stalking us while we're defenseless! Fight me like a man!"

Beau threw back his head, his diabolical laugh spiraling into the trees. "You neglect the simplest rule of warfare, O'Keefe. Know your enemy. In this case, your enemy is a trapper. Trap . . . render helpless . . . then kill. It's somewhat ruthless, I admit, but very appropriate on this occasion. You're helpless now, aren't you, O'Keefe?"

"Bastard!"

"And scared to die."

"Son of a bitch!"

"Go on and cry out. There's no one to hear you, no one to help you, just like it was with them. Now you know how they felt!"

Maria looked around the tree just as Beau brought the ax down toward the back of Michael's head. She shut her eyes again, heard only the sickening thump of the weapon as it struck its mark. She jumped up, tried to scream, to run. But she couldn't. Instead, she turned around and around in confusion until the sky overhead began to spin and the trees seemed to turn upside down.

Gaylord stared into Beau's frozen blue eyes. Gardiner walked toward him. Gaylord couldn't move an inch.

"Won't you fight for yourself, Simmes?" Beau goaded him.

"I can't . . . I'm guilty . . . I arranged it."

Beau wondered if the lawyer was losing his mind. "You want to die?"

"Yes! Nothing less will quiet my conscience. I can't live like this anymore . . . knowing what I did . . . the horrendous crime he made me commit!"

"You could have refused him."

"No! Not Arthur. No one refuses him and gets away with it. He'll ruin you. At the time, I thought that was important. I was wrong. But you know how evil he is. . . . Everyone knows it. . . . Lord Ashley won't be alone with him, you know. . . . He said Arthur was the devil incarnate. That was the day I started to work for Ashley."

"What are you babbling about?"

"Someone had to stop him!" Gaylord ranted. "Arthur destroyed her life and your life and my life. . . . How many others? I don't know. Probably hundreds! I let Ashley confiscate his records while Arthur was out of the country. That's how Clarendon managed to link everything together—the trouble in Charles Towne and Maria's kidnap—from the ledgers! Why do you think he took Arthur into custody? I think he knows we killed Matt! He hasn't said so yet, but I think he knows."

Beau stuffed the tomahawk back into his belt. Gaylord's frantic confession was oddly credible. Whatever madness had possessed Beau throughout these killings suddenly began to disappear. He started listening more intently.

"So he sent me here to investigate . . . with O'Keefe! Can you imagine that!" Gaylord laughed but Beau didn't understand what was so funny. "The same man I had hired to do the killings . . .

only Clarendon doesn't know that . . . probably never will now. But you see, I went along with it because O'Keefe would make it easy to lie about who killed the Gardiners, if the traders somehow knew it was us. We could sabotage the investigation, cover it up. But then we found out you were still alive, that you were the April Fool. If we turned you over to Clarendon and you had some evidence, we'd all hang in the Tower. We were going to do it anyway, figured you didn't have any evidence . . . but what does it matter now, eh?" He just looked at the trapper and shrugged. "I'm a dead man and you're free to take her to Clarendon . . . finish him off . . ."

"Who?"

"Arthur!" Gaylord exclaimed and his face became suddenly animated. "Hang him, Gardiner! Destroy him! Convict us both but let it be known that I died to clear my own sins . . . not his! I'll never die for that scheming devil! I hate him. I've always hated him! Now even more because of what he made me do—kill innocent people just to line his pockets with more money. My life has been a living hell ever since. Kill me so I can finally have peace."

"No."

"What?"

"I said no, lawyer." Gaylord looked at Beau in amazement. "Why should I kill you just because you were his lawyer, forced to do his bidding? I might as well kill Maria because she's his daughter."

"But you—"

"—can only kill when it's justified," Beau finished for him. "To eat, to make a living, to revenge an injustice. Life is revered here, in this 'barbaric' land. It's never wasted."

"But I can't stand to live like this anymore!"

"There are other ways to silence your conscience. Of all people, you could ensure Arthur's conviction. With your knowledge and my evidence, we can destroy him together, Simmes. You and me. Then deliver him to London and watch them crucify him."

"But how can you trust me?"

"I don't. I trust your hate."

"They'll throw us both in the Tower . . ."

"Maybe, but I have a deal to offer Clarendon that he just might take, if he wants the fur badly enough."

"He does."

"Then he'll set us both free and believe it was the smartest thing he ever did."

"How can you be so sure?"

"Because greed is a two-sided coin. One side is strong and the other weak. It's an easy coin to flip."

"I hope you know what you're doing, trapper."

"I've done it before, lawyer."

Beau turned away then, looked for Maria, and finally saw her sprawled on the ground in a dead faint. He ran to her, forgetting Gaylord. Gaylord's knees hit the ground hard but he didn't feel it, just knelt there grinning like a buffoon. Was he dreaming that the trapper had just spared his life? Gardiner believed him, believed he was innocent! Maybe he was. Maybe he'd been too hard on himself this last year, blaming himself for a crime he'd had little choice but to commit.

He looked around the woods then, wondering why it didn't seem so ugly anymore. The world looked different, calm and serene, the way it hadn't looked since before his nagging conscience had distorted his life. As he watched Beau carry Maria off to a nearby stream, Gaylord sank forward, put his face in his hands, and wept.

Beau knelt on the banks of a woodland stream, cupped a handful of water, and splashed it on her face. Maria jerked, then gasped awake. "It's all over now, princess."

Maria heard his voice, as soft as a dream. She stared into the concerned blue eyes that met her gaze. At first, she didn't see the Beau Gardiner who lived in her heart, saw only the man who just killed four men in cold blood. He was the same man who had betrayed her more callously than her own father.

"Leave me alone!" she cried, her hands whipping at his face, his chest.

"Stop it . . . please . . ." he groaned, holding her tightly. Her hatred slashed at his heart like a sharp edge. He couldn't bear it, even if he deserved it.

"What do you want from me?" she railed. "Haven't you done enough?"

There was no answer to her question. None that he could think of. He just held her closer, the way she always liked, with her head buried on his breast and his hand rubbing her back. He savored the feel of her in his arms again.

"I'm so sorry . . . for all of this. I never meant to deceive you, Maria, you must believe me. So many times I wanted to tell you the truth but I couldn't."

"If you cared about me, you never would have let this charade go on so long."

"Charade? You're wrong about that. Nothing between us was ever false."

She grimaced against his words, wanting them to be true as desperately as she wanted to protect herself from them. He could not be trusted, no matter what! No man could do such a thing to a woman he really loved. He would never take such a risk with her.

"But to tell you the truth would have put too many other lives at risk . . . not least of which was my son's. If they found out we were still alive, they would have killed us."

He was getting under her skin now with his logical explanations, spoken in a deep and husky voice that never failed to reach straight into her womanhood. Her resolve was weakening, as she became aware of the way he was holding her on his lap.

"I had to do it the way I did. Matthew was the only mercy God showed me . . . he was all I had left. He was the only part of me left alive after that night . . . whatever part of me lived in him. Can't you understand how much I loved them . . . what kind of black malice inspired this scheme? Have mercy on me . . . but when I realized what was happening between us it was too late. I had to chose between hurting you and forsaking my family."

"So you picked me." She sighed bitterly. "A wise choice. Why not hurt Maria? She's been hurt before! She's used to it!"

She jerked out of his arms then and started scrambling up the riverbank.

He came after her, despising the bitterness in her, the cold mockery. What had he done to his sweet Maria?

"Dammit!" he cursed, angry at both of them now. "Why don't you blame your father, eh? He's responsible for this! How can you blame me for doing what I had to do?"

From atop the bank she whirled around, her eyes sparking with a brilliant mixture of pain and rage. "It was the way you did it that hurts most, Beau! Now I know why you never once mentioned love to me . . . did nothing to find a priest to marry us! You never wanted me! You had every intention of casting me aside when you didn't need me anymore."

"That's a lie and you know it!" She knew better. He reached out a hand and ensnared her ankle. She let out a whoop of surprise and tumbled down the bank, right into his arms.

"What kind of a man do you take me for?"

"I don't know what kind of man you are!" she wailed. "Not anymore!"

"Yes, you do! You know me like I've never let a woman know me!" He clutched her close, until her face was level with his own. "I want you . . . I've always wanted you . . . since the moment I saw you standing in the hallway of your father's house. You were so delicate and beautiful and hurt . . . like an angel born of the devil himself. I couldn't get you out of my mind . . . kept seeing you there in the doorway, so lost and frightened. I talked about you all night long . . . like a babbling idiot . . . like now. Forgive me, but there's never been any sense in the way I want you, Lady Vandenburgh."

He was back, suddenly, the real Beau, the tormented, grieving man who had first come into her life on a night she would never forget. As if it was yesterday, she could still see him standing in the shadowy corridor outside the dining room. A giant of a man with the most captivating and sensitive eyes, a stranger until that last moment just before he left. He looked at her now the way he'd looked at her then, boldly, unabashedly, so intensely, she felt his touch in her deepest and most intimate places.

The anger drained away, fled from the love swelling inside her, making her wrap her arms around him and hold him tight as the first desolate sobs escaped her lips.

The agony in her heart broke free then, not her pain but his. It had never been so poignant as now, when she knew it all, every unspeakable horror he had endured. A deep and profound compassion flowed into her love for him. She wanted to caress the hardness from his face, forget how savage he had looked when he killed O'Keefe. Now he seemed so drained, as if these last murderous hours had completely exhausted him. He had suffered so much.

Without thinking, she found herself kissing him, his face, his hair, his neck, drawing him into those warm and tender places of hers that belonged to only him. As always, he responded to her slightest touch, covered her seeking lips with his own. He kissed her deeply, urgently, as if he couldn't bear to be banished by her.

It was a sorry flame of passion that grew between them now. They slumped to the ground, their bodies moving close until every inch touched. Something wet trickled down the side of her face.

She was crying.

Beau felt her wipe away the tear. He rolled with her onto his side and brushed her hair away so he could see her face. "Why are you crying?"

"Because I'll miss you, Beau, miss you until the end of my life."

"What are you talking about?" He let her go then and sat up, staring at her as if she'd just betrayed him.

She couldn't bear the sight of his disbelief. She looked at the winter-swept branches above them and suddenly noticed how bare they were. "We can never go back to the way we were. But it isn't you. It's me. I'm different now. I've just had enough."

"You'll get over this, Maria. So will I. One day, it will pass."

She looked at him then. "You don't understand. I don't want this world; it's done nothing but hurt me, betray me. My world is the convent. I want to go there. Life can't hurt me there, Beau. It's safe. I never should have left."

"I won't let you do it," he said, his gaze as level and direct as her own. Only there was anger in his eyes, an anger Maria didn't feel. She felt only peace at this moment, now that she had made up her mind.

"I suppose it doesn't matter what you do now, Beau. I'll always belong to you anyway, until I die."

"I want you with me . . . and Matthew. I'll stop you if you try to run, Maria. I won't let you run from me."

"You don't understand, my love. I'm already gone . . ."

Cape Fear, Carolina
January 10, 1675

Maria stood on the shores of Cape Fear and remembered her first landing here as if it were yesterday. She turned away from the beach, watched the cypress and palmetto sway in their never-ending forest dance. The sweet scent of magnolia still clung to the trade winds even though those blossoms were long since withered by winter.

Pain stabbed at her breast. The memories were still too vivid. Through her mind flashed visions of sun-filled summer days, when she had rested in the shade of willows with a sleepy babe curled on her lap, memories of falling asleep at night while listening to the nightingale's peaceful song. In her ears,

Matthew's sweet voice whispered, "I wuv you, Ree."

The wonders of this life would fade, she knew, becoming a distant memory. She'd never come here again.

Maria could feel herself beginning to cry. She laid a hand on her belly and wondered if, by some trick of fate, a last hope might grow there. A baby, Beau's baby, with the azure heavens of Carolina in his eyes, the black forest night in his hair, the strength of the land in his body, her Savannah dreams forever alive within him.

21

London, England
February 20, 1665

Their coach paused only briefly beside the gate of Buckingham Palace while Gaylord used his credentials to get them inside. None of them was dressed for the occasion, having come straight here from the *Savannah Wind.* Salt-stained and weary, Maria felt the tension rising in her, watched her fingers twist together in her lap.

She stole a glance at Beau. He was sitting across from her, next to Gaylord, quietly staring out the window at a dreary London morning. How could he be so calm? There was no telling what Clarendon would do to him. This coach ride could very well be like a ride to the gallows for him.

Maria wanted to say something, to take a long

look at him. They'd seen little of each other during the voyage. Any time they met face-to-face, their talk turned to the same painful topic, Maria's desire to return to the convent and Beau's desire to change her mind. Each encounter only made the wall of conflict between them loom larger.

"Why are you letting him destroy our future, Maria? Hasn't he done enough to us?" She could still remember the pain in his eyes when he'd said that, holding her close at the rails of the *Savannah Wind,* shielding her from the wind with his own cloak. "I want you more than ever now . . . now that the truth is out and I can finally be at peace with you."

How warm and good he'd felt under the mantle of his cloak, his touch as inviting as it had always been. But now she was threatened by her greatest fear; that she would trust him again and have to live with the worry that he would betray her again. "What brings you peace is what brings me torment, Beau," she'd said, beseeching him with just her eyes to understand.

Their pain was like a mirror in that moment, reflecting all the ugly ravages of Arthur Vandenburgh. His murdered family and her unwanted life. It was too terrible to look at. She tried to pull away from him, but he wouldn't let her. He slid his arms around her and held her fast the way he always did whenever she mentioned leaving him.

His caresses were sweet, tender, the way they'd been that afternoon in the backyard of their Savannah home after he'd spent the night in Cussitah. For a moment, she let herself enjoy them, savored the way his kiss made her body awaken with a warm pulse of life.

"Come home to me, Englishwoman." He'd breathed the words against her lips, coaxing her, urging her to stay. "Please come back to me."

"I can't, Beau . . . I just can't . . ."

She'd broken away then, before it was too late, spinning out of his arms and hurrying downdeck until she could disappear into the companionway.

It was the last time she had seen him until they landed this morning. She had kept to her cabin, praying mostly, taking her meals alone. Beau didn't press her. But she knew he wouldn't. He would respect her wishes, come to her only if she invited him.

But she didn't. Never again. She suddenly regretted it. There was so much distance between them now, too much, especially when she considered how short their time together might be.

He felt her attention upon him and looked away from the window into her worried face. For the briefest moment, when their eyes met, there was a flash of closeness between them. But it was gone as soon as it came.

"I'm afraid for you, Beau."

"Don't be. Think of yourself." He looked away again and said to the open window, "Remember what Indigo told you. Be brave enough to face him one last time."

"I don't want to. How can I look him in the eye now . . . knowing what he did to you?"

His attention floated back to her. This time, Maria wouldn't let it go. She reached across the coach, engulfed one of his big brown hands in her own, and held it tight.

Her touch affected him. She could feel the way he seemed to pause at the instant of her contact.

"But I'll do it, Beau, for you and Matthew. You must be set free and returned to him."

His fingers moved in hers. The silky texture of her skin, the sincerity in her frightened eyes, drew him forward. For the first time in what seemed like years, he brushed his fingers across her cheek, watched her shield of bitterness finally drop away. Her sigh was sweet, enchanted, and she was once again the tender young woman who had stolen his heart upon the majestic shores of Carolina.

"For once in your life, think of yourself, Maria. Face the truth. See him for what he is and break the evil grip he has on you. Never mind my battles. Today you must wage your own."

"But I—"

"No, you waste the worry on me, princess." The sound of his voice, whispering that affectionate title, made her lean forward to let his strong arms come around her. "They can do nothing to my body that equals the pain I've known in my spirit. If I die, I rejoin my loved ones and for them I'll give up my spirit. But you . . . you must live on, be who you are . . . someone very special. Look at you now, worrying for me when your own spirit knew the ravages of his hand."

He bent his head, let his chin graze the sable softness of her hair, his nostrils fill with her fresh feminine scent, his eyes see her pretty face. He committed it all to memory now, just as he'd done during those last few minutes with Matthew. They would live in his mind even when his eyes could no longer see them.

"From where does your goodness come, my lady? You lived your whole life without the touch of love, yet your heart is so full of it, so willing and eager to give it. You humble me."

Gaylord watched them, pitied them, saw what a broken mess Arthur had made out of these courageous young people. They didn't deserve this, to stand on the edge of death, racked with the agony of knowing they might never see each other again. It was too unfair. The way they loved each other was sacred.

The coach stopped and they slid away from each other, their fingers lingering for one last moment before the coachman opened the door and let in a shower of rain. They fled inside, Maria tucked in the shelter of Beau's arm.

She didn't look good, Gaylord noticed. The voyage had left her pale and weak. He wondered if they should have left her at the estate this morning so she could rest. But Maria had insisted on coming.

When they entered the outer chamber of Clarendon's office, the keeper of the lord's appointments looked up from his writing desk, annoyed at their interruption.

"My lord's appointments are full—" he began, then stopped short when his eyes fell upon Beau's buckskin-clad body. Indignant at his manner of dress, he threw down his quill and haughtily snapped, "Members of the court are not accessible to the lowborn . . . and certainly not to men so scantily attired."

Beau crossed his arms over his chest and said, "Your lord will receive me in whatever form I might appear. My name is Beau Gardiner but you probably know me better as the April Fool." The clerk's eyes widened. "And the lady who accompanies me is Maria Vandenburgh."

The clerk was startled out of his chair. "My lady . . ." he muttered as he jerked in and out of a bow. He gave Beau a baffled look. The combination of his barbaric dress, articulate tongue, and the fact that he claimed to be both a Gardiner *and* the April Fool left the clerk completely confused. In acute discomfort, he cleared his throat and stammered, "You'll . . . er . . . wait here." He made a rather frantic adjustment to his cravat just before disappearing behind Clarendon's ornate office doors.

A moment later, the door opened and the minister himself stood poised on the threshold. There was no expression on his fair-skinned face as he coolly assessed the three of them.

"My lord," Maria murmured, bending in a deep and elegant curtsy.

Clarendon approached them, took her hand, and graciously aided her upright.

"I daresay, no lady in London has derived such concern and endearment from the public as you have, Lady Vandenburgh. With enormous relief, I welcome you home."

She nodded pleasantly, her flawless grace and striking beauty instantly impressing the minister. But the pleasure in his eyes didn't last, not when his gaze fell upon Beau.

A subject of the Crown would have bowed just then, but Beau didn't. He had no reason to. If Clarendon was insulted, he didn't show it. He offered his arm to Maria and led her into his office.

She was given a chair to the right of the desk, Gaylord to the left of it. Beau was pointed to a place between the two, where there was no chair. Obviously, the minister meant for him to stand.

To the clerk, Clarendon said, "Get rid of my appointments."

"My lord." The man bowed out of the room.

The minister sat down and focused his attention on Gaylord. "I trust you found O'Keefe a capable man."

"Indeed, sir."

"He chose not to attend with you today?"

"He's dead sir."

"Oh." Clarendon paused. "How unfortunate."

"They're all dead. I'm the only survivor."

"What? There were nine men."

"Indians, my liege," Gaylord said. This brought a sharp glance from Beau. He was obviously going to withhold part of the truth in order to spare Beau a murder charge.

"Why don't you start at the beginning, Gaylord. I want to know exactly what happened over there."

Whatever hesitation Gaylord felt was overridden by Lord Clarendon's crisp command. He took a deep breath and, for the next twenty minutes, told Clarendon the entire truth. The minister sat back in his burgundy velvet chair and uttered not a sound.

It took enormous emotional stamina to say what Gaylord said in those twenty minutes. Gaylord stared at his knees during the entire confession. When it was all told, the room fell so silent he could hear the distinct breathing of everyone there.

Clarendon leaned across the desk, his normally stoic face becoming animated. "You are a man of the law. Surely you know how many criminal charges I can bring against you . . . more than enough to hang you."

Gaylord tried to swallow but the saliva couldn't get past the constricted muscle in the back of his throat. "If this is my fate, I accept it," he said. "From the moment Arthur told me Matt Gardiner must die, I knew it was wrong. I could have refused him . . . let my career be destroyed instead of killing those innocent people . . ."

Clarendon's shrewd eye caught a movement from the magnificent young man standing before him. He was just quick enough to catch the look crossing the trapper's face when he heard how easy it could have been to spare the lives of his family. An immense sadness seemed to radiate from him.

Clarendon was not an emotional man, yet he understood the human heart enough to perceive just how devastated this man was by the shocking and senseless death of his entire family. No wonder he'd had the courage to enact such a dangerous scheme.

Clarendon turned his attention to Maria. Careful not to upset her, he coaxed from her a full account of the events that took place from the night of her announcement ball to the present. She spoke softly, and he had to lean close at times just to hear her. At the conclusion of her statements, he found himself genuinely surprised.

"Interesting . . ." he said, allowing himself a moment of quiet reflection. "You had no idea you were kidnapped?" This affair was becoming quite an adventure. "None at all?"

"None, my Lord."

"And so you lived all these months in a cabin on the Savannah River, thinking you were his son's governess?"

"Yes, my lord."

"Not wishing you any disgrace, dear Lady, I must ask if you ever suffered any . . . er . . . personal harm at his hands?"

Her head seemed to drop an inch lower on her chest. Clarendon saw her fingers brush together in her lap as if she secretly yearned to clench them.

"My lord," she whispered at her slippers, "in my heart, I was never his captive. To have not known of my own kidnap until the moment Gaylord Simmes appeared on my doorstep is the best evidence I can render of my treatment by Beau . . . er . . . Mr. Gardiner." Her voice cracked then and Clarendon saw the trapper's eyes snap toward her, his whole body seeming to lean closer to where she sat.

"I will not pursue this line of questioning if it will distress you—" Clarendon began but Maria stopped him.

She had to make Clarendon understand the truth. It could save Beau's life.

"No, it does not distress me, my lord. You see, I was really running away from my father. I wanted to go, to get away from my rather humiliating life in father's care. In Carolina, with Mr. Gardiner and his son, I found happiness. Those were the most rewarding days of my life. You must know that no hand so kind or gentle ever touched my life as that of Beau Gardiner."

Once again, the room was still, silent. Clarendon stared at Beau and, oddly enough, didn't find the woman's testimony hard to believe. After all, he had spared the attorney who was forced to order the murders. It was apparent that this young trapper was not an evil man. On the contrary, the picture painted of him in both testimonies was a man of wisdom and strength, who possessed the kind of fortitude amid heinous circumstances that could only be attributed to greatness.

"Where were you when the family was murdered, Mr. Gardiner?"

"I was in Sampee Bay with Cowachee, a Sanchee elder."

"How did you learn your family was dead?"

"I found them."

Clarendon paused before speaking. "And you immediately suspected Arthur?"

"He was the only proprietor who had threatened

my father with death, more than once in fact," he said. He reached into his pocket and withdrew a fistful of paper. He tossed it unceremoniously in front of Clarendon. "You can read it for yourself."

"I will."

"He wanted the traders to stop marketing fur illegally, as Arthur called it."

"Then you admit it?"

"Admit what?"

"That you sell fur illegally!"

"I sell my fur to the highest bidder, whoever that might be. Where's the crime in that?"

"When it's done against Crown wishes, it's a crime!"

Beau crossed his arms over his chest, looked at Clarendon, and shook his head in complete bewilderment. "I respect who you are in this realm, Clarendon, but you're nothing to me. Your king is not mine . . . your laws mean nothing to any of the traders. In Charles Towne, you have dominion, but beyond the colony walls, you're just another buyer."

Maria wanted to faint in the face of his audacity, certain that Clarendon would have him hanged for such blatant disrespect.

Clarendon didn't say anything, just stared at the man and tried to look more severe than he felt. This was a trader all right: arrogant, hard, beyond control.

"Let me explain it another way," Beau continued dauntlessly. "In Prussia this year, twenty pounds of beaver brings a half ounce of pure gold. In England, the same quantity brings a barrel of salt-pork. Which deal tastes sweeter to you?"

Clarendon snorted a laugh. He wasn't so put out anymore. This was the kind of man-to-man dialogue he relished. "So you do it for the money, eh? Greed. Just like the rest of us."

"If I were a man of greed, I would hardly be standing here in buckskins."

Touché, the minister thought, then sat back in his chair. His fingers drummed on the desk, his gaze sharp as he stared at the trapper. "I suppose I could get rid of all the Charles Towne Traders, couldn't I? Then I'd have it all to myself."

"No, you'd have what you get now—what Charles Towne manages to mine."

"A half ton?"

"If they're lucky."

"Where does the rest of it come from?"

"Us! And the tribes of the interior. The night my family was killed, I was trading whiskey for Sanchee beaver. That's how we come by it. Trust and trade."

"We could make friends with the tribes—"

"As well as Woodward and Colleton?" Beau laughed. "To date, they've done a fine job of nearly getting themselves killed . . . incited two Westoe raids on Charles Towne by declaring the settlers responsible for my family's death."

Clarendon snapped upright in his chair. "What proof have you of that accusation?"

"You can have all the proof you want when you learn how to talk to Tomawausau."

"Who?"

"The Westoe chief. He's not a very trusting sort, but try if you like. Kill us . . . open up the territory for your complete plunder . . . risk ten tons of fur just to get another half-ton or two by the few tribesmen who might think you're worth your word."

Touché again, Clarendon thought. He was beginning to enjoy this. He was used to men who cowered, told him what they thought he wanted to hear. Not this one. He knew exactly what he was talking about.

This could be quite an opportunity for the realm, couldn't it? he wondered.

"What is it that you want then? Arthur's money?"

"No. I want to take from him what he took from me."

"Which is?"

"My most precious possessions . . . my kin. So now I take his most precious possession."

"His only daughter?"

"Come now, Clarendon, you know Vandenburgh far better than I. What do you think is more precious to him: the daughter he lifted not a finger to help? I think not. It's his money. That's his soul. And that's what I did this for—to cut out his soul in one fell swoop, leave him with nothing . . . like he did to me."

Clarendon watched him closely. He admired the man, not because he'd nearly accomplished his aim, but because he was so sure that his cause was justified.

"Of course you realize my hands are somewhat tied in regard to this affair, Gardiner, seeing as you've told all of London. Some announcement will have to be made about Arthur's crimes and his subsequent fate. I can arrange that. But, of course, I have prices of my own, Gardiner."

"Fur." Beau answered for the minister.

"Precisely."

"A compromise?"

"I'd like it all."

"I'd like my family back."

"Touché. Compromise then."

"The time has come for the proprietors and the traders to meet face-to-face and dispose of these conflicts between us. I can arrange that."

"How? Everyone thinks you're dead."

"Not any more."

"What?"

Clarendon's look of surprise turned to dismay when Beau explained. "They've been told the truth —all of it—that my son and I survived, that Vandenburgh is responsible for the killings, and that I kidnapped his daughter in order to bring it to the Crown's attention and see the man appropriately punished."

Not even Gaylord knew this fact. Maria could tell by the way he looked up at Beau just then. What a brilliant maneuver! Beau would mantle himself in the protection of Charles Towne's knowledge, making it doubly difficult for the Crown to get away with punishing him for this.

The point wasn't missed by Clarendon. "And they know you're here now . . . in England . . . facing punishment for this crime?"

"Yes. They know all of this."

Clarendon's reserve clouded. He scowled darkly, realizing the delicacy of the situation.

"Do you realize what kind of power you hold in your hands, Gardiner?"

Beau didn't bother to answer.

Maria grinned at her folded hands, beginning to feel the first twinges of victory in her heavy heart.

"And how will you use it? To threaten me? To destroy my interests in the territory?"

"You Englishmen are doing a fine job of destroying your own interests. You don't need my help."

After a long moment, Clarendon sat back and shifted in his chair. He gazed out the window behind him. "I'd like to argue that point, but at the moment I can't help but agree with it. This whole business of Charles Towne just seems to get worse by the day . . . and here you are . . . a trader in the flesh . . . making me wonder why it's taken this long for us to face each other." Clarendon shrugged at the gloomy day. "Amazing that no one ever tried."

"Amazing? It was more like a deadly mistake, wasn't it?"

Clarendon didn't say anything but his shoulders stiffened noticeably. "Yes, well . . . it can't be undone now, can it? I suggest we move on from here

. . . take some steps to prevent this kind of atrocity from happening again. Now then, about the meeting . . ." He let the sentence hang.

Beau had obviously prepared for this. He dictated the terms without a pause. "The traders and the proprietors will arrange to meet outside Charles Towne . . . in open territory. Leave your cloaks of authority at home and come prepared to talk business . . . not politics."

"When?"

"The sooner the better."

"What will it gain us?"

"Fur."

"I'm listening."

"Wager like men and I'll personally guarantee you another three tons of fur next season."

Clarendon turned around, his attention fixed on the terms of the deal. "But you mine over ten tons a season. Why only three tons?"

"Because that's as much as I think you're willing to pay for. In truth, you can have as much or as little as you want, but you have to pay the world price, like everyone else who buys from the traders. As an act of good faith, you get the first three tons cheap. With the profit you'll make on it, you'll be able to afford three more tons at the prevailing price."

The deal was sweetening. Clarendon was clearly interested.

Beau seized the opportunity and added, "That's a hell of a lot more than you're getting now."

Clarendon certainly couldn't argue with that particular point. "How cheap for those first three tons?"

"You'll make two hundred thousand pounds if you sell it right."

Clarendon's eyes brightened considerably. "Go on."

"It's your turn, Clarendon. What's your end of the compromise?"

"Your life, trapper."

Beau nodded, satisfied with the terms. The deal was done.

Maria stared at Beau, unable to hide her astonishment. He'd done it. He'd made Clarendon an offer no sane man could refuse. Beau would get exactly what he wanted and Clarendon would finally get a taste of Carolina fur.

With the cunning of a fox, Beau Gardiner had just outwitted the most powerful man in England.

She glanced at Gaylord. The man was grinning at his boots.

Clarendon rose from his chair, came around the desk, and stood before Beau in a moment of long, hard scrutiny. "I rather enjoyed that." Beau's eyebrows rose in surprise. "We've struck a brilliant trade, Gardiner. I'm quite pleased with this. Lord Ashley will be enormously relieved."

Amazing, Maria marveled. The minister would walk away from this meeting thinking he had just cut the shrewdest deal of his life.

Maybe he had.

But Maria didn't care. Nothing mattered to her but knowing that Beau's life was spared.

"Clerk! Get a note off to Ashley at once. Tell him to summon home those two idiot explorers of his—Woodward and Colleton. I want them back in this country at once. Then tell him to join me for dinner tonight."

Maria wanted to rejoice for Beau, for Matthew, but Clarendon issued a crisp command that stole all the jubilation from the moment.

"Summon Arthur at once."

Maria could feel Arthur enter the room even before she saw him. His cold gaze traveled from Gaylord to Beau, then finally settled on the back of her bent head.

"Maria!" He rushed to her side with a great show of emotion. "Thank God you're all right! I was frantic for you!"

She didn't move or speak, just sat rigid in her chair. He leaned over her, his withered face peering into hers. If she looked at him, he would see her disgust. She stared at the floor instead.

"Is this the man who accosted you?" Arthur asked, looking up at Beau.

A dangerous charge of energy shot through the

room the minute they looked at each other. Beau's eyes filled with cold loathing.

Clarendon wisely interrupted. "Have a seat, Arthur. Gaylord has something to tell you about this man, don't you, Simmes?"

Clarendon was punishing Gaylord by making him betray Arthur to his face. Maria noticed the lawyer never looked at his former employer as he spoke with an admirable outward calm.

"This is Beau Gardiner, the April Fool."

Arthur stared at him. "But you told me the Gardiner family was dead."

"They are . . . except for Beau. He wasn't present the night O'Keefe performed the murders."

"Then you know who did it?" Arthur wanted to grin in relief. Let this man O'Keefe take the blame. Maybe then he could get on with his grossly neglected business.

"We all know who killed the Gardiners," Clarendon said. There was a bit too much accusation in his voice.

"This is pointless, my lord," Gaylord blurted. Clarendon was doing this deliberately, making him suffer through a slow and painful betrayal. "Must we go on playing with him?"

"Playing with whom, Simmes?" Arthur demanded.

"With you!" Gaylord snapped, his fist slamming against the chair arm. "I told him the truth, dammit! I told him what we did to Matt Gardiner!"

"What *we* did? Are you including me in some clandestine affair of your own, Simmes?"

Through Gaylord's mind raced a memorable warning; "It's a common practice of his, to frame others for what he's done." Outrage grew inside him until it was a deep, burning anger. "Whatever involvement I had in this affair was solely at *your* direction, Arthur!"

Arthur met Gaylord's wild eyes with a menacing scowl. "So you blamed it on me, eh Simmes? That was stupid of you. Everyone knows you care for nothing but your career and the opinion of your peers. You'll do anything to prove you're as good as your father was. No doubt you arranged to kill Gardiner so my ledgers would improve and I'd give you due praise . . . thus silencing your doubting partners!"

"How dare you try to escape the blame! You ordered his death!"

"How ludicrous!" Arthur looked at Clarendon and shook his head sadly. "The man's obviously out of his mind with panic and I—"

"Why you—"

Gaylord flew at his throat, his coattails whipping across the desk, scattering paper and quills and ink everywhere as his hands closed around Arthur's neck. Clarendon lunged from behind his desk while barking an order for his guards to subdue the enraged attorney.

Maria cried out as the struggling men slammed into her chair and sent it teetering sideways.

Beau snatched her out of it, lifting her up. She slumped into his arms, and he crossed the room in three strides, laying her on a settee.

She wasn't well. Her complexion was so ghostly pale that the dark circles under her eyes looked like blue bruises. She needed to rest and regain her strength. He'd never seen her look so sickly before.

"Guard—" Beau began but a voice shot at him from across the room.

"Get your hands off my daughter!"

Vandenburgh.

Beau snapped upright and confronted the man, poised like a shield in front of Maria. With arms akimbo and legs spread, he towered above Arthur and growled down at him, "One step closer to her and you die where you stand."

Everyone halted in midmotion. The hate in him was downright chilling.

"Haven't you done enough to her?" Arthur demanded.

"The woman suffered at your hands, not mine. If this isn't true, let me hear you explain why she ran away on the night of her announcement ball."

"She didn't run away! You abducted her!"

"That's a lie!" Maria cried, springing off the settee. She stepped around Beau and looked into her father's cold gray eyes. There wasn't a sound in the room, not a blessed movement. She could feel every eye pinned to her, watching her. She was neither triumphant nor crushed, glad nor sorry. At this moment, Maria was filled with only the cruel reality of her life, the useless pain, the betrayal, the rejection, the loneliness, the hopes that were now, at long last, dead.

She had nothing left to lose.

"Twist the facts any way you want, Father, but you can't fool me. I know the truth, all of it, just as you do. I deliberately ran away on the night of my ball just to spite you, to embarrass you the way you embarrassed me all my life. You cast me aside like rubbish, then expected me to return home and be grateful for your hurried plans to be rid of me once more! How dare you . . . how dare you suggest that I'm so worthless!"

"I'm your father, young lady, and I'll—"

"You're not my father!" she screamed. "You are an *infidel!*"

Beau stared at her, awestruck. She stood there with her back stiff, her shoulders set, her chin lifted higher than he had ever seen it. This was her private vindication and she took it without flinching, like a sentinel possessed with the white rage of angels.

"I denounce you, Arthur Vandenburgh, denounce you down to the blood of you that runs in my veins. You're rid of me now, Father! You have never been so rid of me!"

Her hand slashed across his cheek with a force that sent him teetering backward. Arthur fell into a table and sent it crashing to the floor.

But she wasn't finished. She came upon him, looked straight into his stunned eyes, and whispered fiercely, "You are a disgrace . . . and a man not fit to touch my slippers!"

Her fists curled at her sides, her glare cutting and cold, a brilliant sword of righteousness sprung from the wounded heart she had kept so deeply hidden. And when it finally showed itself, it took all of her strength with it, leaving her suddenly weak. She swooned, dizzy and reeling from this explosion of long-suppressed emotion.

"Maria—" Beau caught her just as her knees gave way and she dropped backward into his arms. He carried her to the farthest corner of the room, turning her so she couldn't see Arthur. "Easy, my love. It's over now."

"Help me . . . hold me . . ."

"I have you."

There was a guard behind him, responding to Clarendon's orders that Maria be taken to a private chamber for rest.

"No!" She clung to Beau.

"Go with him," he whispered. "Your battle is done now. It has been waged and won." It pained him to turn her over to the guard, to see how broken she looked when he carried her away.

When the door shut behind her, Arthur turned to Clarendon. "Surely you won't consider the statement of an overwrought woman, will you?"

They were astonished by his indifferent dismissal of his daughter.

Beau just looked at the minister and sighed in exasperation. There was no point in continuing this. Arthur would only deny everything. He was obviously at fault and everyone knew it.

"I've heard enough," Clarendon said. "Simmes, authenticate those letters on my desk, will you?"

"What letters?" Arthur wanted to know.

"The ones you threatened Gardiner with."

"Those letters prove nothing—" Arthur began.

"Silence!" Clarendon commanded. "Unfortunately for you, Arthur, you're the only person who threatened to kill Matt Gardiner before he died. That's the best evidence I have on anyone at the moment. Notwithstanding the total confession of your lawyer.

"I hereby charge you with the murders of Matthew Gardiner and his family, of high treason against the king of England by the reckless endangerment of a court-appointed colony, deceiving a minister of the king, fraudulent business practices and gross abuse of power."

"I deserve a trial!" Arthur cried.

"And I intend to give you one, Arthur . . . with a jury of your peers . . . Lord Ashley will represent the proprietors, elected representatives of the people will be chosen and, of course, we'll include your exquisite daughter. In addition, I will issue a general decree to the people of London detailing what I heard today, and present the evidence acquired in this case. I will reveal the feelings of your daughter in regards to her captivity. Your fate will be put in the people's hands, and I will request a verdict within twenty-four hours. I think that's quite fair of me, don't you?"

The minister smiled at Arthur's ferocious expression. He turned to the rest of them and said, "Until then, you'll all spend the night in the Tower. As for the lady, she will be given quarters in the palace tonight in order to protect her from an overzealous response from the public when they learn of her return to London. Now then, I extend to you all my most sincere wishes for a pleasant evening."

Maria found little rest in the palatial chamber Clarendon had granted for her use. Upon a downy mattress she tossed and turned, her mind plagued by dreams, jumbled omens.

Beau came to her, over and over again, as he had that night in Cussitah, loving her as much as she wanted even while the public stood outside and chanted for his death.

Arthur escaped the Tower, stalked her bedside, his face bitter with lust and revenge. The schoolgirls were there, walking down the corridors of the convent, laughing and pointing at her.

At some ungodly hour, the dreams stopped and she awoke to find herself upright in bed. She was crying, her bedclothes wet with sweat. She looked out the palace window. It was black, silent, like her soul.

The Tower of London was no place to spend an extended term. Cold and damp, infested with bugs and germs and sickness, it was overcrowded with criminals, madmen, degenerates. Some were chained in private cells, others roamed small rooms in groups of six or more, urinating on rush-strewn floors, stepping over one another's vomit. The Tower invited the madness it contained through the blatant exploitation of every flaw and weakness in the human spirit.

There wasn't a clean place on the floor in the cell Beau and Gaylord had been given. They used their shoes to scrape a fresh spot of dirt where they could sit and rest against the grimy mud wall. They did little more than doze on and off, coming awake at the slightest moan from the cells around them.

"Shake it off, New World man," a gruff voice growled into his ear. Beau came awake and saw a pair of burly guards standing over him. In the dim light, he could see they were both of the same height and build as himself. "You've got a long night ahead of you."

They grabbed his arms and hoisted him off the floor.

"What are you doing?" Gaylord demanded.

"We've no business with you, lawyer. Just shut up and go back to sleep," the guard snarled.

"What do you want with him? Where are you taking him?" Gaylord scrambled off the floor and came after them, but he wasn't fast enough. The cell door slammed in his face.

Beau was shoved down the hall ahead of the guards, pushed into a stairwell that led into the basement of the Tower. The air was even more moist and chilling below ground; it seemed to penetrate his flesh and soak into his bones. The floor was dirt, mud in some places, puddled with water. They halted before a door at the far end of the passageway. The guard named Ames reached around him and punched at the spongy wood.

"We got him!"

The door opened. Two more guards were waiting inside. They looked at him with relish, like a pair of hungry dogs just presented a meaty bone.

"Come on in, trapper!" one of them said, making an exaggerated sweeping motion with his arm. "Ain't this a fine place for a private party?"

It was a small, square room, empty except for the lone torch burning on one wall and several sacks of whiskey in a pile on the floor.

Beau knew the purpose of this visit with one glance at the deadly malice on the guards' faces. He could fight his way out of this but where would he go? The Tower was completely secure. Beau could feel his pulse quicken, his blood surge into his muscles as his body instinctively prepared itself to endure. He had little choice but to submit and survive.

He was suddenly flung against the far wall, his arms and legs spread wide, then snapped into heavy iron shackles.

The biggest of the guards, the one named Ames, stood before him. "You didn't think Clarendon would let you off so easy, did you?"

Beau didn't say anything.

"Does he talk?" one of the guards asked another.

"He'll talk by the time I'm done with him," Ames retorted. "Clarendon just wants you to answer a few questions, see. If you cooperate, we'll let you go back to sleep. If not, we'll stay here till we break every bone in your body. How's that for a deal?"

Beau maintained his silence.

Ames grinned, leaned close in his face, and whispered, "Who helped you in the scheme, April Fool? You had accomplices, that's for sure. How'd you get those ransom notes over here, eh? Who brought them here?"

Beau looked into the guard's hard eyes and quietly answered, in Savannah, "The captain of the *Savannah Wind.*"

"What? What did you say?"

"I said, the captain of the *Savannah Wind,* you illiterate fool."

"Talk English!" Ames snapped as he clenched his hand around Beau's throat and brutally punched his head against the wall. "You get one more chance to answer, you half-breed, and it better be in English this time! Who brought the notes?"

"You're wasting your time," Beau told him in flawless Westoe. "I'll never implicate anyone no matter what you do to me."

Ames had a short temper and he lost it with exceptional power, sending an explosion of fists into Beau's face, chest, belly. Each blow lurched him in his chains until all he could hear was the jangling iron links.

The verdict arrived by noon. The people of London unanimously agreed that Arthur Vandenburgh was guilty and should be tried before the highest tribunal for his sins. If guilty, death should be his sentence. Simmes was to be deported and forbidden to enter the country for ten years, after which time it was agreed he would have sufficiently paid for the sinful ambitions that fueled his cooperation with Arthur.

As for the April Fool, well, one glance into the palace courtyard announced his fate for all to hear.

"Release him! Release him!"

Lord Clarendon stepped out onto the veranda, looked over the throng below, and nodded his head in compliance. He would bend to their demands and spare the trapper, which was exactly what Gardiner had planned. Not only did he use the populace of London as a gallows to hang Arthur, it was also his cloak of protection. Who could hang someone for so brilliantly avenging the wretched murder of his innocent family? The man had already paid the highest price any human could pay.

Clarendon agreed with the people, went back inside, and ordered Gardiner's release. He was satisfied with the outcome of this scandal, as anxious as Lord Ashley to have the long-awaited meeting with the trappers of Carolina.

Yes, this was a splendid day indeed!

Arthur could not accept the verdict. How dare the people allow his traitors to rise above him? The great and powerful Sir Arthur Vandenburgh would never give these simpering fools the pleasure of seeing him die penniless.

Especially not Maria. Ungrateful chit! How dare she denounce him, in front of Clarendon no less!

And Simmes, that treacherous coward, spewing

his guts for the sake of conscience instead of remaining loyal to the employer who had kept his family so well fed all these years.

Damn him! Damn them all!

While the guard in his cell read his fate aloud, Arthur sprang from the corner, snatched his sword, and plunged it straight through his own heart. His impaled body slumped to the floor. Blood gushed from his chest and with it spilled his life and his madness.

Before his eyes loomed the face of the trapper, those cold blue eyes forcing him to accept the unacceptable. That damned trader had destroyed him, had crushed his power and his fortune and left him here with nothing.

Arthur crumpled to the floor, only too happy to give up his life.

Beau felt as if he were trying to climb out of a deep black pit. He was aware of being dragged between two men who were struggling just to hold him up. From what he could see through the slits in his eyes, he was being propelled through the Tower. His head was pounding hard and fast. There was a loud ringing in his ears. His nose was filled with the same kind of pressure he felt when he drank spring water that was too cold. His stomach felt like a sack of warm jelly.

". . . easy with him . . ." Gaylord. ". . . released, Beau . . . free . . ."

What?

He tried to concentrate. Released. Free.

". . . Vandenburgh estate . . . hurry!"

They were in a coach. He was on the floor between the seats with Gaylord's muddy boots holding him in place. They thumped, rattled, banged along endlessly before he felt a rush of fresh air flowing over him.

There was a scent caught in it, fresh and sweet, a familiar voice that whispered somewhere beneath the ringing in his ears, "Oh, no . . . Beau . . . what have they done to you?" He closed his fingers around the silky folds of a woman's gown. Her hair surrounded him, brushing a luxurious comfort over his wounded face.

His head lolled in her lap, his beautiful hair now clumped with dried blood, both his eyes swollen shut, his lips split and bleeding. She cringed at the sight of him, tears of pity spilling down her cheeks.

Within the tent of her draping hair, she dabbed a kerchief on his cuts, whispered through a rush of the softest kisses she could give, "Father's dead. . . . He killed himself. . . . It's over now. Please, God, let it be over now. I can't bear another moment of your suffering."

She watched his head move, blood-caked lashes fluttering as he tried to open his eyes. Just this slight movement made him recoil in pain, her name briefly escaping his lips. "Maria . . ."

"I'm here, my love."

". . . dead . . ."

"Yes, he's dead. And the people of London demanded your release! You've won the day!"

Vandenburgh was dead.

A feeling of redemption washed over him, silencing his physical misery. Behind his closed lids, Beau fancied he saw his father's grinning face, his brown eyes sparkling with zest. Surely he was delirious, just imagining it. Lord! It had been a long time since he'd had such a fine view of that face. He could see every line, every curve, every nook and cranny in his father's ruddy skin.

"Father . . ."

"Jonathan! Summon the physician at once! Maureen! Ready my bed for him! What are you saying, Beau? I can't hear you."

"Sleep, Father . . . in peace . . ."

"Yes, Beau, we'll get you to sleep at once."

The vision faded away, little by little, until it was just a pinpoint of light in the middle of a dark night.

They were set free now, his beloved kin, cleansed of their tainted death.

"Wait for me . . ."

He was being carried again, gently this time, coming to rest on something thick and soft and perfumed with Maria's scent. It engulfed him, making him sigh with pleasure.

Sleep.

It came, then went. Voices were chattering all around him. Something was pressing on his chest, right where the bones were cracked and parted. A long ribbon of pain curled through his chest.

"Oh God . . ."

"You're hurting him." Maria.

A grave voice spoke close to his head, clamped a

cold compress over his eyes. "I need to look at the rest of him, my lady . . . your modesty."

"I've been with him—" Maria blurted without thinking, then felt her face catch fire as a blush of shame swept over it. Maureen just stared at her, momentarily appalled. Gaylord shifted his feet nervously.

"I see . . . very well, then."

His britches had to be cut off, parts of them sticking to the wounds. They had to soak away the fabric in some places, the warm water making Beau writhe and twist away. Gaylord held him steady, tried to make some sense out of his whispers.

He was speaking in Savannah. Maria recognized some of the words.

The last bits of his leggings were removed. He lay naked on her pure white sheets.

"Why don't you get the doctor more water," Maria gently urged Maureen, not wanting Beau to be made into a spectacle at such a time. Flustered, anxious, worried for his condition, Maria lent her aid throughout the tedious process of cleansing him, dressing his wounds, wrapping his chest full of broken ribs in a restraining bandage. And all the while, he did little more than moan, his teeth clenched tightly. By the time they were finished, he was bathed in sweat, trembling and dazed. Maria was crying as Gaylord and Dr. Stevens led her away.

"He'll be all right," the doctor soothed. "The muscle saved his life. A leaner man might not have withstood such a brutal beating. He's bleeding inside—" Maria gasped in alarm but the kindly old doctor put up a slender hand and continued, "but only mildly compared to the kind of hemorrhaging I've seen in others after such violent treatment. Now I want you to get some rest yourself, my dear lady. You've had a harrowing time."

"He's right, Maria," Gaylord agreed when they reached the front foyer. "This has all been very hard on you: the voyage . . . the verdict . . . and now your father's death."

Her face fell.

"There now, lass," Maureen said, taking her by the shoulders and leading her toward the stairs. "He's at peace . . . poor master . . . but Lawyer Simmes is right. You need rest."

"I want to stay near him." She sighed wearily.

"Very well. I'll fix you a fine bed right at his side, if you wish. But first, it'll be a hot bath for you! Saints be praised just to have you back with us again, after being in that ungodly land! Come along now. Let Lawyer Simmes manage things for a few days."

It was good advice. Maria needed her strength to manage the dizzying rush of events that suddenly invaded her life. She felt as if she were dancing in some bizarre masquerade, changing costumes for the role of the grieving daughter, the imminent heiress, the mistress of the mansion, and the nursemaid to a battered and beloved man. And through it all she knew none of the roles was hers. This was not her home, her place. Her only comfort was found on the settee beside Beau where she could sit and watch him sleep, remembering that wonderful summer sojourn with him and his baby son before this twisted affair had torn them apart.

Maria struggled to employ her years of grooming to mask the depths of her sorrow. She walked through her various roles with a polished facade. It only cracked once in those first few days, on the morning she watched Arthur's casket being interred next to her mother's in the family crypt.

Although she denounced and despised the man he was, she wept for him with a bitter regret. He could have been different. A brilliant businessman, he could have enriched so many lives instead of hoarding his money to himself.

And how well he had hoarded it during his fifty-two years of life! The sum of her inheritance was staggering. She thanked God for Gaylord, who was exceptionally well versed in the complicated details of Arthur's estate. The figures defied her imagination. So much money in her complete control! If not for the continued assistance of Gaylord Simmes, she would have been far too overwhelmed to make sense of it on her own.

Maria was impressed with Gaylord's aptitude and the enthusiasm with which he dissected Arthur's complicated ledgers. Clarendon gave him sixty days to settle his own affairs and leave the country, and she was amazed at how unselfishly he lent the majority of his time to her future instead of his own uncertain fate. Gaylord had not been disbarred and, surprisingly, had regained much of the respect of his partners which had been lost during those scandalous months of her captivity. Now that the whole story was revealed, no one disagreed with Gaylord's decision to forsake his employer. In fact, Gaylord's law guild enjoyed a new notoriety because they were partially responsible for ridding London of the Vandenburgh menace.

A part of her willingly shared Gaylord's renewed optimism for life, but the deepest part of her could not enjoy any hope for a brighter future. As the days wore on and Beau's recovery became apparent, her decision to return to the convent was reinforced. Eventually, the sensation she was causing in London would fade. Any other woman in her position would look forward to exciting courtships with the many high-society bachelors who now sent their cards to the Vandenburgh mansion.

But Maria could not accept them. She had willingly given herself to the only man she would ever love. Once discovered, she would be disgraced. The Vandenburgh name was tainted enough.

Few people knew of her plans to leave Dabney Street. Gaylord, Maureen, and Jonathan all fought her determination but obediently made her financial arrangements, packed and stored her belongings.

Beau had only a sketchy idea of her plans. Whenever he brought up the subject, Maria changed it or feigned some urgent business to tend. She knew he didn't want to press her because it was not his way. Beau always delighted in giving her exactly what she wanted. But this time was different. The stronger he grew, the harder he tried to change her mind, to stop her. They were beginning to argue with each other as they never had before. He was bitterly opposed to her plans and made sure she knew it.

"You were crying again last night," he commented when she laid a dinner tray across his lap. He was sitting up in bed now, bare-chested and still bruised.

It disconcerted her, how well he knew her. But it shouldn't be surprising. After all, they had lived together, like husband and wife, for a long time. "I had a bad dream, is all."

"Oh? What was it about?"

"Father."

"His death still pains you, doesn't it?"

"Of course."

"Yes," he whispered, letting one of her auburn curls brush across his chest as she aligned the plates on his tray. He snatched the tendril and fondled its silky length. "You're too good-hearted to hate, aren't you? Even a bastard like him."

"Let's not talk about him today."

"Then let's talk about something else. Matthew. He's your favorite subject. What do you suppose he's doing right now?"

Maria stiffened, then tried to draw her hair away from him but he only tightened his hold on it, until she was forced to sit on the bed beside him. She knew what he was trying to do.

"He's probably wondering where we are, eh?" His hand found her cheek, strong and sure again as it drew her near, captured her in the spell of his warm gaze. "It pains me to think he suffers without us . . . thinking we abandoned him."

"He knows better."

"About me, perhaps, but you?"

"Don't, Beau."

"Why not? He thinks you're his mother. Shall I sit idle while you discard him?"

"I'm not discarding him! I'll always love him! You know that!"

He could see the hurt in her eyes and felt a tugging in his heart at just the sight of it. "All right, lass . . . enough then."

"Would you like more tea?"

"No." He snatched her close, so that he could feel her heart thumping beneath her heavy breasts. "I want more of you," he murmured huskily, seeing the passion stir in her eyes, turning them dark and sultry with want. "Why are you doing this to us? Tell me, Maria. At least talk to me about it."

"I've tried to talk to you, Beau."

"When? You wouldn't let me near you on the voyage. Now you're too busy, always needed somewhere else. We've never been so distant with each other. Must I dribble after you like some romantic fool . . . tell you how much I need you? I'll do it if it will change your mind."

"No." She pushed away from him, nearly upsetting his tray in her haste to get beyond his power. "This is why I don't talk about it! Because you get so upset."

"Of course I get upset!" he snapped, his voice harsh with frustration. "What kind of man would I be to stand aside and let my woman walk away? I'll fight you on this, Maria. I won't hurt you nor will I force you to do anything against your will, but goddamn it, when I get out of this bed, I'm going to make you understand—"

"Understand what," she cried, whirling around to confront him from a safe distance on the other side of the room. "That you loved me despite it all? Maybe you did, but you knew me better than anyone on earth, Beau Gardiner! You knew all along how much it would hurt me but you did it anyway!" Why was she doing this, letting her voice rise, showing him the anger she kept hidden in her heart.

"Yes, I knew it! Just like I knew how happy you were . . . how much I wanted you to have real happiness for once in your life . . . without the taint of this blasted scheme of mine! How can you condemn me for that?"

"It was trickery!" she cried, throwing her hands up in the air and heading for the door before this discussion got any more heated. "I just can't live with it. I've tried. I can't."

"Don't go—" The door slammed behind her. "MARIA!"

She flew away, ran down the hall and into her chamber. She collapsed on the bed, her wretched and bitter sobs erupting into the pillow she clutched to her face. For both of them she cried, for the lonely survivor and the banished daughter, for the redemption of their love that she knew would never be enough to save them.

* * *

The following morning, Maria faced her last day in London. It was March seventh. A year ago at this time, she was packing her bags somewhere else. At the convent. On her way home to London. In her wildest dreams, she never imagined herself returning like this, so soon and still so very lost.

She took her breakfast in the dining room, alone. Maureen brought her tea but didn't look at her when she served it. The maid had been crying this morning. She didn't want Maria to go, but there was no way to stop her. Maria tried not to notice and hardened herself against her sadness. For once in her life, she would do what was best for herself.

There had been too much deception and rejection in her life to risk staying here with Beau. She could never live through another betrayal like that again. Never. A chilling memory of that awful Christmas Day rose to remind her how close she had come to ending her own life. She could almost taste the water rushing into her mouth, her lungs. She had genuinely wanted to die. If not for Beau, Maria was certain she would have died in the Savannah River.

The thought left her shaken. She picked at her eggs and biscuits, tried to tell herself a few doubts were normal at a time like this. But she mustn't let them cloud her perspective. She was a tainted woman, by both the murderous blood in her veins and the impurity of her body. No man in his right mind would marry her now. Nor did she want any other man. Despite what he'd done, Maria loved Beau the way she would never love another. With him in her heart, there was no room for anyone else. There were plenty of satisfying memories with him to last a lifetime. It was enough. It had to be enough.

"Why so glum, princess?" a voice spoke from the doorway.

It was a familiar voice.

"Langdon!" she cried, whirling around to see him standing there.

Oh! What a wonderful sight he was, clothed in his buckskins and moccasins, a breath of the frontier come to call on her.

She forgot herself and flew into his arms, hugging him with all her might. "Oh, Langdon! Thank God you're here! When did you arrive?"

"An hour ago," he said, grinning down at her as he planted her slippers back on the floor.

"And Matthew? How is he?"

"Being spoiled beyond repair by my mother. And you . . . how are you, dear Maria?"

She invited him to her table, let him be served while she told him all about the meeting in Clarendon's office, her father's death, what Beau had arranged between the proprietors and the traders. His lazy hazel eyes brightened when she told of Clarendon's promises for change in Charles Towne.

"Lord, but the changes won't come soon enough! I can't begin to describe what happened when we told the people about Beau, that he'd survived the murders and discovered who killed his family. It all started when I arrived with Matthew. Everyone wanted to know whose child he was, of course. Father and I worried that someone might notice the resemblance to Beau and his mother, Elizabeth. We went to the new governor—Governor West—told him everything and called a town meeting afterward. For as long as I live, I'll never forget the moment when Edmund Edinburgh stood in the front of the crowd and uttered four words that brought dead silence to everyone in the square. 'Beau Gardiner is alive.' "

At first, the announcement had stunned them. Marietta Mierda had dropped to the ground in a dead faint. When Edmund told them the whole truth of what had happened, the people's shock turned to jubilation. A riot of a celebration exploded in the square, everyone was dancing and drinking until the wee hours. It was as if the entire colony had heaved one gigantic and unanimous sigh of relief. Almost overnight, the mood of Charles Towne had changed from tumultuous to hopeful.

And baby Matthew became an instant celebrity.

But there was one last thread to be sewn and none would completely rest until Beau came home. Alive, unscarred, and promptly settled in his father's seat as the head of the Charles Towne Traders.

"He must return safely . . . unharmed and unscarred . . . or the colony will erupt in enough violence to see it destroyed by their own hands. I've heard men threaten it already. They'll tear the place down and leave the area, go with the traders, if the Crown dares to split one hair on his head."

Maria looked down at her plate.

"What's wrong?" Langdon stiffened in his chair, tense and tight. "Did something happen to him?"

"He's recovering, Langdon. . . . He'll be all right."

"What happened?"

She told him about the beatings, how Clarendon had tried to make Beau name his accomplices.

Langdon bolted off his chair, instantly outraged. "Why that split-tongued bastard!" he cursed the minister. "Where's Beau? I want to see him!"

Jonathan stopped them at the bedroom door, gave Langdon a distinguished bow, and didn't seem at all surprised at his manner of dress. He was getting used to these New World people.

Maria was surprised to see that Jonathan had managed to move Beau from the bed to a lounge by the window where he could look outside. His New World master spent most of his life outdoors and the fresh air seemed to make him rest easier on this morning after a difficult night. He hadn't slept well. He could hear his lady weeping from her adjacent chamber and had barely dozed until she finally fell asleep.

"It wasn't a good night for the master," Jonathan said.

"Stop calling me that," Beau grumbled from across the room. "I'm not your master."

Maria decided to remain out of his sight when Langdon presented himself.

"Lang!" Beau breathed, a spark of genuine good cheer showing in his face when he clasped the man's hand and said, "By God but it's good to see you, man! How's my boy?"

"He's fine. Mother's spoiling him daily and basking in his notoriety like a queen presenting a little prince to the adoring public!" Langdon made an effort not to show his shock at Beau's battered condition. "Who did this to you?"

"A few Tower guards out for a good time."

"Dammit!"

"It's nothing."

"Don't tell me it's nothing! I'm tired of seeing you all hurt and torn up, Beau! Just how much more do they think you can take?"

Beau didn't say anything, just sat back and looked at his friend, an irritated expression on his face.

"This is an outrage! Clarendon had no right! After all his people did to you . . . already forced you to endure the most despicable pain any man could ever feel in this world! For God's sake, Beau, you've borne enough pain in one year to last a man a lifetime!"

This struck a raw nerve in Beau. From the doorway, Maria saw the muscle in his jaw twitch for control. "Enough, Langdon."

"Enough of what," Langdon snapped, pacing the floor like a frenzied animal. "The Crown be damned if this is the way they treat you! And after you make such a generous proposition to them—a chance to meet with us and discuss our differences

—to hell with them! They'll be lucky we don't skin them alive the moment they land!"

"Stop it!"

Jonathan started across the room, alarmed at the way Beau was stiffening under his bedclothes.

"Forgive me, but I'm at my wits end with this and—"

"Then keep your shattered wits to yourself, man! I don't need to hear how tired you are, Lang. No one is more tired of it than I . . . tired of walking around in this strange place that used to be my life." He stopped, laid his head back, and grimaced at the ceiling for a moment. He was breathing too hard. Every breath brought a sharp pain to his breast. For a moment, he just lay there, waiting for the feeling to pass.

When he spoke again, his anger was gone, replaced by weariness. "You make me wonder where I found the strength to stay alive, but I don't want to wonder about it, Lang, for fear I'll lose it . . . and I've come too far."

"Of course you have, Beau." Langdon regretted his outburst, falling to one knee beside the lounge. "It's over now."

"Yes, all of it except the last—to see my family in their graves. I dread it, Lang, dread going back there, dread being the one they missed. But I have to. For Matthew's sake, I've got to get over this now . . . stop feeling so forsaken because everyone died without me."

Maria had never heard him talk like this.

Langdon's eyes filled with tears. "I told you I'd

be at your side until the end, Beau, and I will. You don't walk alone, man!"

"I know," Beau whispered, closing his eyes. "And one day I'm going to tell you how much your strength meant to me . . . but not now, Langdon. I'm so godforsaken tired. All I want to do is sleep . . . just sleep . . ."

They stood there, spellbound and silent, watching Beau slowly nod into sleep.

As they passed Maria's chamber, Langdon spied the packed cases on her bed. He stopped abruptly.

"Are those your bags?"

"Yes." She looked away.

"Where are you going?"

"To the convent."

"For how long?"

She stared at the rug, ashamed of her own intentions now. "I'm going there to live."

Langdon's fingers found her chin, lifted her face to make her look at the almost desperate plea in his eyes. "Don't do this to him, Maria. I beg you. Don't leave him now."

"Langdon, the scheme—"

"It had nothing to do with you personally! You must believe me! I know how hard he struggled to resist you in the beginning. I swear to you, no woman ever got under his skin the way you did . . . right from the start!"

"Please understand I can't convince myself of that. I've tried! Dear God I've tried! But I just can't believe . . . in Beau or any man. Only my God . . ."

"But you love Beau! How can you even think you'll be happy without him?"

She turned away, looked at the suitcases on the bed, suddenly longed to snatch them up and run away before her doubts overcame her. "My memories will keep me happy, and the convent will bring me peace . . . security . . . I won't have to risk my heart ever again!"

"His love for you is worth the risk, Maria. I know Beau Gardiner better than any man. I can tell you with absolute certainty that he has never been so in love with a woman in his lifetime . . . not even with his wife! He worships the ground you walk on! You say you love him but if your feelings were true, you wouldn't think of leaving him now!"

"Don't say that!" she cried, stung by the words. "There are things about me you just don't know, Langdon. But Beau knows. He knows why I've made this decision. My mind is made up and I beg you not to try to stop me. I don't want any more pain either!"

She whirled away from him and flew into her chamber before he could say any more. She clung to the windowsill, fighting her doubts. Like Beau, she hadn't the strength to endure any more agony, knew she had to get out of here now.

She summoned a coach, watched Jonathan see her baggage packed inside.

Maria stopped outside the door to his room, fought with herself against going inside to say goodbye. It would only hurt him more. Besides, if he touched her, kissed her, beheld her with those disarming eyes, she knew the last of her will would dissolve.

Maria ran down the stairs and out the front door.

She didn't look back. Not once.

Beau couldn't see the coach until it was halfway up the drive and had cleared the corner of the house that blocked his view. There were satchels on the roof, a lady's bags.

Alarm brought him to the edge of the lounge. He could see the slender outline of a woman's head through the rear panel.

Maria.

No.

He shoved off the lounge, stood up with the window ledge gripped in his hand.

The wrought-iron gates pushed open and the coach rambled through, sent up a splatter of mud as it turned into the street.

He wanted to bang on the window, call for her, but she was too far away. And so he just stood there and watched her go, clinging to the same window she had used a year ago, to run from this life and drop straight into his.

Then he was alone, with no one but the face reflected in the lead pane, a man with startled eyes and a grim, desperate face.

She was gone. Maria. After all these months of walking so closely beside him, there was nothing left but thin air where she used to be.

Beau let go of the window, sat on the edge of the lounge, and finally realized what sphere the dancer chose to settle in.

Her own.

The place in his heart that was now just an empty hole.

"*Where is the* convent, Jonathan?"

"I've been sworn to secrecy, sir."

"Oh? And are you also sworn to doing what's best for your mistress?"

"Of course."

"Then tell me how to get to the convent."

"Master . . . er . . . Mr. Gardiner, . . . I gave her my word."

"Where is the convent?"

"Please, sir."

Beau was determined now. He was healed, strong, ready. He sat back on the vanity bench, crossed his legs, and thought for a moment.

"What are you going to do now that the Vandenburghs are gone?"

"Me, sir? Why, I'll hire my services to another family."

"Who would hire the butler of Arthur Vandenburgh? Your employment history is tainted by his name, you know."

Jonathan looked stricken. "Surely someone will—"

"I doubt it. Of course, there's one man who might hire you."

"Who, sir?"

"Me."

"But, sir! You have no need for a valet!"

It was true. Beau never allowed Jonathan to bathe him, dress him, shave him, or do anything else required by European gentlemen. He was entirely too masculine for such frivolous habits. Jonathan was accustomed to his ways now and actually seemed to like his lighter duties, especially when Beau was talkative and amused him with tales of New World adventure. These always brought an almost childlike enthusiasm into his old eyes, as if he was hearing some amazing fairy tale.

"I wouldn't hire you as a valet, Jonathan, merely as an extra hand around the house. I've plans to build her a new home on Oyster Point, overlooking the sea, and I'll need help tending the grounds and the fields and my drying racks—"

"But I'm an old man! I'm beyond such rigorous work!"

"Perhaps, but tending the gardens along the sea-coast will be healthful for you. Carolina's climate is known to restore vigor."

Jonathan thought this over for a long moment. It was a good idea. He shrugged, sat on the edge of the bed, and told Beau exactly how to get to the convent in the English countryside.

"One day she'll thank you for this, Jonathan."

"I do hope so, but Maureen will . . . er—how do you New World men say it—skin me alive for this!"

"She'll do nothing of the kind. After all, she's in the same sorry straights you are, eh? Besides, Maria will need a maid, someone to help her look after all the children I'm going to give her."

"What if the lady refuses to go with you?"

"Then I'll abduct her again," Beau said brightly. Jonathan looked astonished at what he'd just said. Beau ignored him. "Now then, I'll need a suit of clothing but nothing too . . ." He made a flowing motion with his hand.

"Frivolous, sir?"

"Precisely."

"Then you don't want anything . . . fashionable."

"Absolutely not," Beau said. "Men dress like peacocks over here."

"Sir?"

"Never mind. Just make it plain. Well made, but plain. In a dark color. And the fabric should be tweed . . . no satin or lace or silk or whatever the hell else they use to make themselves look like women. And absolutely no wigs!"

"Yes, sir." Jonathan hid his smirk behind Beau's breakfast tray. "Will there be anything else, sir?"

"Yes. Take this note to a jeweler and give him a sizing from one of your lady's rings. The piece is to be made exactly the way I've described it. I'll settle for nothing less."

"I'll be sure he receives explicit instructions. And when will you be needing these things, sir?"

"By weeks' end. Can it be done?"

Jonathan grinned merrily. "For the April Fool? Need you ask?"

A week later, Beau stood in the lobby of the Vandenburgh mansion and stared at the man in the mirror. It didn't look like him at all. He felt awkward in all these clothes. There were too many of them. A blouse, a cravat, cuffs, vest, waistcoat, britches. Lord! How did men get on with their business after spending such a long time getting dressed?

But then he sighed, realizing it wasn't the clothes. All this romantic business made him nervous. It just wasn't suited to his nature. He hoped Langdon would be here to stoke his confidence, but the man had yet to return from a night on the town. Maureen and Jonathan stood aside and watched him pluck at his clothes as if trying to make them fit more comfortably. He could see they were struggling to hide their amusement.

"What's funny?"

"Nothing, sir," Jonathan said. "You look very fine."

"Indeed," Maureen said as she let her eyes wander over every inch of his exceptionally structured form. Heavens, but he was the most handsome man she'd ever seen. Especially when dressed so smartly.

Jonathan had served him well, having selected an expensively tailored suit in a dark blue color that only enhanced his sky-blue eyes. A long tapered waistcoat fit his narrow torso just right, lent his tall figure a look of distinguished elegance. Well-cut britches conformed to the powerful shape of his thighs, the cuffs long enough to disappear into the tops of a pair of highly polished black leather boots. Beau refused to wear stockings and slippers. It was inconceivable to him that men wore the same stockings as women, nor did he allow any lace on the flowing white cravat of his blouse. When it arrived with a thin piping of lace, Beau sat down, pulled out his blade, and carefully trimmed off every stitch. The ruffle was now plain and stark but somehow attractive when worn by such a magnificent man.

Maureen couldn't wait to get to the New World. After so many years as the mistress of Arthur Vandenburgh, it would be a thrilling change to closet herself with men as wholesome as this one.

"Are you displeased with it, sir?"

Beau shook his head quickly and said in that rough, whispery voice of his, "No, it just feels a bit . . . er . . . contrived. I'm used to more natural garb. Did you get me a hat?"

"Of course, sir!" Jonathan proudly presented a black cavalier's hat. It was very stylish and dashing.

Beau frowned at the piece. "What the devil is that?"

"A plume, sir."

It was an ostrich feather. "Bah!" he muttered under his breath as he plucked it off and handed it to Jonathan as if it were the most appalling thing he'd ever seen. Beau put the hat on, adjusted it on his head, tugged at his queued hair, then finally turned around for their final inspection.

"She won't recognize you!" Maureen beamed. "You'll steal her breath away!"

"I steal my own breath away every time I look at myself like this," he grumbled. "Women! How can they make men act so foolish, eh? The poets should keep their romantic notions to themselves. I should be home trapping beaver and here I stand trying to trap a woman."

Maureen giggled as she brushed a few specks of lint from his broad shoulders. After six weeks in his company, she and Jonathan were quite taken with him. Beau Gardiner had a rough and rugged exterior but his heart was pure gold. Of course, he was not a man to reveal much about his softer side, except where Maria was concerned. She was his weakness.

"There now, Mr. Gardiner, the Lord puts a soft spot in every heart, even a man's. I only hope you win the hand of the lady who won your heart."

"Yes, well, that is the purpose of this . . . er . . . scheme." He reached into the pocket of his coat and withdrew a small velvet box. "Do you think she'll like this?" He opened the box to reveal a jewel that made Maureen's eyes widen in wonder. It was fabulous, three round blood-red rubies surrounding an exquisite marquise diamond. The band was a rich bright gold. It was the most unusual piece, absolutely stunning.

"Indeed!" Maureen eyed it enviously.

Beau smiled and shut the box with a snap. "Very good. Let's hope she agrees to wear it. Now then, I better be off." He took up his own bags and strode through the front door, tall and straight and completely determined.

Maria's shovel dug the last hole in a row of newly planted rosebushes. She settled the tender young plant into it, patted the earth around it, and sat back with a sigh of satisfaction. This garden would look spectacular when it was grown, as pretty as the one she kept on the banks of the Savannah. But those flowers she would never see grown. Not like these roses. They would grow before her eyes, and she would see their limbs spread thick and tall and healthy with blooms. By the time they consumed the wall behind them, she'd be an old woman.

And Beau would be an old man. He'd have silver in his jet-black hair, she mused, his eyes would be tired and lined but still so radiantly blue. Especially when he looked upon his son, who would no doubt grow up to be as strong and handsome as his father.

The thought made her sad. It still stung to think about them. But it would go away, she comforted herself, in time. One day she would be able to remember them without pain, only joy.

She laid her shovels and picks back in the basket and sat up, feeling that nagging ache in her back again. If she rubbed it long enough, it would ease, but it never quite went away these days. She wondered what she had done to cause this injury, or was it a sickness? Even now her brow felt warm, almost feverish, despite the crisp temperatures of April. Maybe a nap would restore her vigor. She reached for her handkerchief, her fingers brushing across something that didn't belong in a garden.

A pair of leather boots.

She stiffened, looked at the shoes, then let her eyes wander up the entire length of powerfully muscled legs that were not quite hidden beneath a pair of impressively tailored britches.

Beau.

He stared down at her, his face expressionless, only his eyes revealing the pleasure he took in seeing her again, after all this time.

"How did you find me?" she whispered weakly.

"Jonathan."

"He gave his word."

"I offered him a fair trade for the information."

"Yes, you're good at that." The bitterness came back, made her wrench her eyes away before he stole the last of her nerve.

He looked so damned good, so dashing and handsome and virile.

"I wish you hadn't come," she said to herself more than to him. He was already disarming her just by being there. She could feel her insides begin to quiver.

He leaned down, took the basket from her hand. "Are you well?"

"I'm fine."

"You were rubbing your back just then."

"Never mind . . . it's nothing."

She tried to take her basket back but he wouldn't give it up, leading her to the bench beside the wall with a rather firm touch. "My wife used to rub her back like that when she was pregnant . . ."

This thought hadn't occurred to Maria. He could tell by the little shock that ran across her delicate face. But she hid it well, like everything else. There was barely a crack in her ladylike facade as she sat down and looked away.

"Maria, are you sure everything is . . . er . . . fine?"

She blushed and snapped, "I don't wish to discuss this or anything else with you."

"Well, I wish to speak with you," he retorted. He took up her hand and kissed it, ignoring the way she stiffened against him. Just for spite, he kept her hand and wove his fingers through hers until he knew she felt his warmth. It didn't quiet her shaking, however, and this pained him. "I have things to say to you . . . things I should have said before but you know how I am . . . a bit . . . clumsy about personal matters."

"I wish you would leave."

"That's a lie and you know it."

"Must you always be so arrogant?"

"New World men are known for their arrogance. It's a flaw in our characters. It never bothered you before."

"Well, I've changed."

"Yes, I see that."

"I don't know what you're about, Beau, but I won't fall victim to another one of your smooth-tongued wagers! I have good reasons for wanting this life for myself and—"

"Spare me a reiteration!" He said it so coldly that she turned around and looked at him in surprise. How dare he mock her?

She whipped her hand away and attempted to get off the bench. But he was too quick, like a jackrabbit. An arm wrapped around her waist and promptly rolled her backward, straight into his lap.

"How dare you!" she fumed, struggling for release. "Let go of me!"

His arms only tightened, and he leaned so close that she could feel the heat of his anger. "You're not the only person in the world who's been dealt some hurt in life, Maria! I've suffered just as much as you. I could blame you for what happened as easily as you blame me for it! After all, you *are* the daughter of the man who killed my family!"

"How dare you associate me with that criminal!" She would have slapped his face if he hadn't caught her hand in the nick of time.

"It's not very fair, is it?"

"You won't torment me."

"Any more than you torment me? Maybe I'll just leave now . . . without saying good-bye . . . as you did to me."

"Stop it!"

"I won't! That was a very cruel thing to do to me. I didn't deserve it . . . to be left broken and helpless within sight of your flight! Damn you, Maria! Damn you for the pain you made me feel . . . deserting me when I needed you the most!"

"I didn't!"

"You did! You sacrifice my happiness to run away up here and make everyone feel sorry for poor Maria . . . this fatherless daughter! What of me, eh? You never had a family and never knew what you missed. I did. I had a family and lost them all . . . every one . . . my last memory of them lying drowned in their own blood! I could have run away then too, into madness, despair, but I didn't. I faced what happened . . . still fight to overcome it. Not like you, Maria. You'll sit here and weep over your sorry lot for the rest of your life!"

"No!" she cried, leaping off his lap and sinking to the ground in tears. "Stop it . . . please . . ."

Beau tried to calm himself. He took a deep breath, got off the bench and knelt beside her. She didn't resist his arms, the way he plucked her off the ground and cradled her close. Rivers of agony spilled from her then and she clung to him, sobbing so brokenly it pained him just to hear it.

"Don't . . . I hate it when you cry . . . hate hurting you like this . . . but I see no other way to knock some sense into your stubborn head!"

"I hate you!" she choked into his chest but he wasn't convinced, could feel the way she melted when his hand smoothed her back.

"No, you don't, nor do I hate you even though we both have plenty of reasons to despise each other. But we made the choice already . . . a long time ago . . . when we chose to love instead."

She grew quiet then, listened to his first mention of that word as if it were a whisper on the winds of heaven.

"Haven't we lost enough already? Must we lose each other too?"

Her face turned up into his then, tear streaked and flushed. "You betrayed me, Beau . . . played with me . . ."

"You're wrong. I never played with you. I was never so serious as I was in your bed, Maria. You know that . . ."

Provocative memories flashed between them, inspiring the passion that had always been theirs. It leapt into life between them, made them very aware of how good it felt to touch again, to feel their bodies press close. Her trembling mouth invited him to taste her again and he let himself be lured, lightly brushed his lips against her own.

"You know it's true," he said in a hoarse whisper, seeing those memories in her eyes like the first weak sparks of a flint. "You know how I agonized over Julia . . . wanting it to be this way with her but I could never quite manage it. With you, I can't stop it . . . I lie there trembling like a trapped animal while you take anything you want from me."

His words inflamed her, the torrid desire in his eyes consuming the last of her will. Like a woman in a delirium she groped for him, taking his hungry kiss like a starved harlot. He commanded her now, his hands twisting and turning her face every which way so that no part of her lips remained untouched by the scorching power of his love. He didn't part from her until she was limp and breathless in his arms.

"Call this a game if you will . . . that this is the love of a betraying man . . . say it . . . damn you . . . explain what makes this fire grow between us."

"I don't know . . ." she groaned, reaching for him again, kissing him although she knew it was wrong to do so here in this public garden. But she didn't care. Nothing mattered but him, only him, forever him. "But I don't want it to stop . . . don't want to live like this . . . without it . . ."

"Then marry me . . . today . . . now . . . live your life with me."

She couldn't believe her ears. She stared at him as if struck by a sudden blow.

"Dear God, but I love you, Maria! You're as precious to me as my land . . . as my own life . . ." She barely heard her own voice gasping in surprise as he continued. "Be with me . . . come home with me . . . stay with me . . ." His lips scampered down her throat, scalding her soft skin with the fever of his words. The emotion he sent cascading into her heart felt like a sweet warm wine.

But then he spoke again, and these last words of his broke down the walls of doubt at last.

"You're as priceless to me as my own child . . . my beloved Matt. You live in the same place in my heart as he . . . in the very center of me."

Joy. It returned then, lifting her spirit. No one had said anything half so beautiful to her in her entire life. And he meant it. He wanted her, what they had on the Savannah, a home, a love, a life.

She thanked God for sending him here today, for giving her this one last chance to claim what she had pursued all her life.

A family.

"Say yes . . ." he whispered, pulling her face against his chest, where she could see his hand disappear into his waistcoat. A small velvet box was withdrawn; he flipped it open with a flick of his finger.

She looked inside, into the stunning flash of ruby-red light that sparkled up at her from a tiny black velvet pillow. It was the most magnificent ring she had ever seen, three rubies affixed to a glittering gold band, a lone diamond perched above them.

"Beau . . ." she breathed.

"Do you like it?"

"It's beautiful . . . I've never seen anything like it!"

"Because I had it made just for you, Englishwoman. You didn't think I'd show up here with something ordinary, did you? You and I are just too unusual."

She looked at him, her eyes shining with love. "But why did you fashion it like this?"

Beau told her about the prophecy Indigo had made for him, on the same night that he predicted Maria's victory over the grip of her father's evil hand. He told her about the three spheres of his heart and all the places within them that she leapt like a dancer. "You were the comfort in my grief, the vehicle of my revenge, my hope for the future. In time, two of the spheres would pass and I would be left with only one."

"Your future," she said.

"No." He shook his head. "That sphere contained only the hope of triumph over your father. Now the diamond . . . that's the place where the dancer settled."

"What place is that?"

"Your own," he whispered, turning her face up to where he could sample from her blissfully smiling lips. "The one I gave you in the midst of the darkest days of my life . . . where you always managed to shine the brightest."

It was a long time later when they surfaced, breathless and warm with desire. A slow smile curled across his lips when he coaxed, "You haven't said yes yet."

"Haven't I?"

"Don't be coy. Besides, Sister Eustace has already sent for the friar."

"That was most presumptuous of you, Beau!"

she teased, then realized that she was in a very compromising position beneath him on the bench. "Beau! The sisters!"

"You don't fool me with that blush anymore. Now say yes and for God's sake, be quick about it before I take you right here in the garden."

She sighed into his happy eyes, her mind skipping across the days ahead, every night she would sleep in his arms and every morning that she would wake up beside him.

The trapper had done it again, she thought, made an offer only a fool would refuse.

And she was certainly no fool.

"Yes . . . yes . . ."

Thirty minutes later, Beau was prowling the altar steps in the convent chapel, impatient for her arrival. It was ungodly to stand in this holy place in this condition. He made sure his waistcoat was completely buttoned.

"I'm quite experienced with anxious bridegrooms, young man, but this old rug is too worn for another tread of your pacing feet."

Father Dudley motioned to the front pew, told him to sit and cleanse his soul with prayer before receiving the sacrament of marriage. Beau obeyed just for something to do. He knelt, bent his head, looked around the floor until he memorized every crack in the marble.

He should pray. It was a long time since he had done that. He glanced at the cross above the altar, the wooden figure of Christ hanging there so broken and bloody, yet so exalted in its lofty position. As if death was a triumph, not a disaster.

Maybe it was. After all, Beau had once hung on his own crucifix, his soul riddled with the wounds of overwhelming loss. But his once empty and broken heart was now filled to the brim with new love, new hope, new life.

"We're ready now," Sister Eustace said from behind, and Beau turned to see Maria standing in the middle of the aisle. Her head bent bashfully when he looked at her and saw how she chose to dress for this occasion, in a way that had special meaning to only the two of them.

A plain white sheath, moccasins, a palmetto basket hanging from a jute belt. Her shining hair was plaited in a single braid that was drawn over her shoulder and left to hang alongside a crudely carved wooden pendant. Beau rose slowly, moved by the message in her choice, and wondered if she had ever looked so spectacular to him as she did at this moment.

Maria came to him a second time, only now there were no lies between them, no dark secrets to hide, no hurt to disguise. He saw her as she was then and now, a hopeful young woman so strong of heart she helped them to weather the longest and sorriest storm of their lives. He clung to her in his darkest moments and now he would claim her in his finest.

Beau brought her to the altar and bound his life to hers without a pause of hesitation in his spoken vow. Her eyes were misty when she repeated her pledge to him, her voice humble and sweet with emotion. He could feel her happiness, adored the way it lit up her face when she watched the ring slide down her finger with a dazzling spray of red and white light that was only illuminated more by the radiant pleasure in her shining eyes. When Father Dudley pronounced them man and wife, he opened his arms to her and she rushed into them, found her favorite spot on his chest, and clung to him the way she had so many times before.

But then he plucked her up, carried her off the altar, past the beaming Sister Eustace and out the chapel doors. The corridor was full of girls, their faces filled with romance and dreams as they watched him bear away the new Mrs. Gardiner.

"Good-bye Maria!" they called from the steps when he climbed into the coach. "Lucky girl!"

Maria opened the back shutter, waved to them, and listened to their jubilant chorus singing from the same steps where the lonely little girl had once stood waiting for a coach that never came.

"It's come for me at last," she said in a small choked voice as she entwined her new husband's fingers with her own.

"What's come, my love?"

"My coach," she whispered. "It's come."

"Yes, convent girl," he murmured softly, "it's come to take you home."

AVAILABLE NOW

COMING UP ROSES by Catherine Anderson

From the bestselling author of the Comanche trilogy, comes a sensual historical romance. When Zach McGovern was injured in rescuing her daughter from an abandoned well, Kate Blakely nursed him back to health. Kate feared men, but Zach was different, and only buried secrets could prevent their future from coming up roses.

HOMEBODY by Louise Titchener

Bestselling author Louise Titchener pens a romantic thriller about a young woman who must battle the demons of her past, as well as the dangers she finds in her new apartment.

BAND OF GOLD by Zita Christian

The rush for gold in turn-of-the-century Alaska was nothing compared to the rush Aurelia Breighton felt when she met the man of her dreams. But then Aurelia discovered that it was not her he was after but her missing sister.

DANCING IN THE DARK by Susan P. Teklits

A tender and touching tale of two people who were thrown together by treachery and found unexpected love. A historical romance in the tradition of Constance O'Banyon.

CHANCE McCALL by Sharon Sala

Chance McCall knows that he has no right to love Jenny Tyler, the boss's daughter. With only his monthly paycheck and checkered past, he's no good for her, even though she thinks otherwise. But when an accident leaves Chance with no memory, he has no choice but to return to his past and find out why he dare not claim the woman he loves.

SWEET REVENGE by Jean Stribling

There was nothing better than sweet revenge when ex-Union captain Adam McCormick unexpectedly captured his enemy's stepdaughter, Letitia Ramsey. But when Adam found himself falling in love with her, he had to decide if revenge was worth the sacrifice of love.

HIGHLAND LOVE SONG by Constance O'Banyon

Available in trade paperback! From the bestselling author of *Forever My Love*, a sweeping and mesmerizing story continues the DeWinter legacy begun in *Song of the Nightingale.*

YESTERDAY'S SHADOWS
by Marianne Willman

Bettany Howard was a young orphan traveling west searching for the father who left her years ago. Wolf Star was a Cheyenne brave who longed to know who abandoned him—a white child with a jeweled talisman. Fate decreed they'd meet and try to seize the passion promised. 0-06-104044-4

MIDNIGHT ROSE by Patricia Hagan

From the rolling plantations of Richmond to the underground slave movement of Philadelphia, Erin Sterling and Ryan Youngblood would pursue their wild, breathless passion and finally surrender to the promise of a bold and unexpected love. 0-06-104023-1

WINTER TAPESTRY
by Kathy Lynn Emerson

Cordell vows to revenge the murder of her father. Roger Allington is honor bound to protect his friend's daughter but has no liking for her reckless ways. Yet his heart tells him he must pursue this beauty through a maze of plots to win her love and ignite their smoldering passion. 0-06-100220-8

MAIL TO: **Harper Collins Publishers**
P. O. Box 588 Dunmore, PA 18512-0588
OR CALL: (800) 331-3761 (Visa/MasterCard)

Yes, please send me the books I have checked:

- ☐ LA BELLE AMERICAINE (0-06-100094-9) $4.50
- ☐ STOLEN LOVE (0-06-104011-8) $3.95
- ☐ PRINCESS ROYALE (0-06-104024-X) $4.95
- ☐ CANDLE IN THE WINDOW (0-06-104026-6) $3.95
- ☐ TREASURE OF THE SUN (0-06-104062-2) $4.99
- ☐ YESTERDAY'S SHADOWS (0-06-104044-4) $4.50
- ☐ MIDNIGHT ROSE (0-06-104023-1) $4.95
- ☐ WINTER TAPESTRY (0-06-100220-8) $4.50

SUBTOTAL .... $______

POSTAGE AND HANDLING .... $ 2.50*

SALES TAX (Add applicable sales tax) .... $______

TOTAL: $______

*ORDER 4 OR MORE TITLES AND POSTAGE & HANDLING IS FREE!
Orders of less than 4 books, please include $2.50 p/h. Remit in US funds, do not send cash.

Name ________________

Address ________________

City ________________

State ______ Zip ______

Allow up to 6 weeks delivery.
Prices subject to change.

(Valid only in US & Canada)

HO321